MW01143094

Special thanks:

To my family, friends & the Castro family for their support and encouragement,

To Gary for reading the horrendous first draft,

To Scott and David for listening and giving their feedback,

To Chrysti whom I love very much, thank you for putting up with my endless rambling about Silver.

THE SILVER NINJA

WILMAR LUNA

The hard, dry blood on my fingers reeked of someone else's life. I could feel the copper plasma create friction between my encased digits, scraping and chipping away the former existence of an innocent man. The emergency alarms screamed over and over like a wailing drunk begging for another whiskey. The commotion of people scrambling outside, like a panicked bee hive, filled the now-lifeless office with a cacophony of mayhem. The red lights blinking on the perimeter of the walls symbolized the chaos I have caused.

I could still smell the soft, sweet aroma of cinnamon lingering in the air. It was my victim's last meal, a small snack of cinnamon buns, lay scattered across blood-stained documents and blueprints that only a great mind could understand. When I stared at the fresh corpse of a brilliant man, I realized… my hands might be stained with innocent blood. I had never punished anyone who was undeserving, but the spoiling corpse at my feet said otherwise. I couldn't believe what I had done. The shock of my actions refused to leave my side. I stood there lost in my own mind, observing model airplanes hanging from the ceiling, a custom-built, glossy wooden desk, blueprints framed on the walls, and designs for an aircraft I recalled from the news. Was this really someone who deserved the punishment I had given him?

The guards were banging at the door like dogs restrained on a leash. At any moment, a horde of security guards was going to burst through and end me. I looked to the window and thought about jumping, but I was too high up in this towering skyscraper. The only way to escape the inevitable torrent of lethal gunfire was to break through their ranks. I briefly mulled over the idea of surrendering completely. The fantasy of allowing myself to be filled with a hot slag of lead and fragmented shells made me feel at peace with myself. Not because I sought my own destruction, but because having bullets embed themselves in my skin would swiftly end my pain, making me numb to the invisible wound that would define the rest of my life. I've become a murderer.

The door behind me became my clock; the entry burst open like an alarm striking midnight. With six pistol-armed security guards in black suits charging in like a lion to its prey, my time was up. One of the guards grabbed his shoulder radio and yelled, "She killed Joe. Get up here now!" They kept a tight bead on me with their pistols, never missing a beat.

Once they saw the corpse of dead guilt sprawled beside my feet, I closed my eyes and felt the world's tempo slow to a lethargic pace as the first wave of gunfire began to quake in the air. I should have tried to avoid the gunfire, but I didn't, I didn't want to. Moments of my life began to flash before my eyes, as I embraced the ensuing hail of gunfire. My mistake has become my coffin, burying my life into a photo album of glossy, picturesque memories. My mind became disfigured by the guilt and shame of my actions. The first bullet flew towards me in slow motion, eager to pierce my skin with lethal precision. It cratered into my body like a meteor crashing into the earth, its brass brothers towed in its wake. So is my fate. This is what I have chosen; this is what I have become.

I am...

CHAP7ER 1

THE FUTURE - ULTIMATE WEAPON

"So late!" the young woman cried, as her loyal, worn, cream-colored sneakers tried to distort reality so she could run faster than time itself. But reality yields for no one, and nothing could change the fact that the nimble, young gymnastics instructor was late for work. She weaved through the hordes of people struggling to keep within the invisible walls of the sidewalk; only the bike messengers dared to flirt with the yellow death by riding the razor's edge of the black asphalt. As she twisted and side-stepped through the cement gridlock, she saw a break between a man holding a suitcase and a girl thumbing away on her cell phone. Diving through the opening created by inattentiveness, she deftly moved past the ocean of pedestrians blocking her way to punctuality.

Even as she weaved through the crowds she warily watched the streets, alert to the yellow death that could appear before her like a phantom in a cemetery. Too many times, she witnessed tourists and commuters fall prey to the speeding machines. If she wasn't careful, the rest of her night would be spent removing embedded paint chips from the sides of her trim stomach. As she ran along the narrow sidewalk, she quickly bypassed the multiple aromas of deliciousness that lingered nearby, waiting to lure their victims with a siren song of tasty, non-nutritious treats. The scents of hot dogs, pretzels, pizzas and burgers stalked the streets, looking to break into the arteries of any poor fools trying to stay on a diet. Other odors, however, were also out on patrol like muggers stalking an empty alley. Instead of luring victims, they sought to attack the world with a pungent vengeance. The tardy woman raced towards the corner of the intersection, spotting her unassuming destination sitting idly across the street, oblivious to her urgency. Her face smiled with relief as she drew closer, but her nose smacked the goofy smile away when a repugnant odor hammered her unprepared nostrils.

She furrowed her brow in disgust as the smell of internal human excrement assaulted her senses. A hunched-over man with hands gnarled by arthritis and a face weathered with a thousand ordeals stared at the street. Crumbs from a recent meal clung onto his scraggly beard, to serve as a snack for later. He wore a heavy, worn, olive jacket, riddled with holes from his undocumented adventures, stained with beer and memories of a life another man had lived. In his hands, a chipped ceramic mug sat between his filthy fingers. It read in bright red Comic Sans font, "I love you, Daddy." He sat next to a massive, pristine, slate column supporting an opulent skyscraper towering above the city. A dingy, tainted cardboard sign stood next to this man, as if it were his only friend in the world. The cardboard sentinel stood proud, wearing the man's memo on its chest. "God sends his message through the homeless and the blind. Please donate what you can."

10

In the middle of her frenzied rush, the young woman dipped her manicured hands into the pockets of her indigo hoodie. With a skillful flick of the wrist, she threw a few silver presidents into the homeless man's mug. His hands, wrapped in fingerless gloves tattered from years of rummaging through garbage, picked through her donation. After calculating the amount of her deposit, he dipped his leathery fingers into the mug and yelled, "That's it?"

The woman immediately made an about-face and gave him such a stare that onlookers were concerned for the homeless man's safety. Tasting a hint of fear coating his tastebuds, he went back to his beggar ways and said, "Thank you, bless your heart." Her eyes squinted to see beyond the veil of lies, refusing to leave until he felt the unmistakable blanket of shame. After a momentary lapse of focus, a deafening sonic cry began to draw closer to the woman's ears. The vibration of the sound shook her like an earthquake rumbling beneath her feet. She looked over to her right, and saw the yellow death growling at her feet. It stared at her with emotionless headlights while its off-duty sign sat atop the roof like a crown. The taxi cab driver stuck his head out the car window and yelled, "Get outta the damn street!"

The woman realized she had unwittingly walked into the intersection of 84th and 2nd against the light. Her face became flushed with the color of stupidity, as she ran out of the way of the merciless cab. Finally arriving at her destination, she muttered under her breath, "God, I hate the city."

She hesitated to open the glass door that led to her daily fate. The building seemed like a gaping maw, intimidating anyone who would dare enter; at least, anyone that was running late. The stairs looked like wooden teeth, leading their victims up to their execution. She attempted to climb the stairs unnoticed, but the tired wood groaned and creaked, creating a loud ruckus. She feared every step she took was leading her towards inevitable punishment. As she reached the top of the stairs, a woman with golden hair charged towards her like an angry bull, ready to gore its matador into the walls of the arena.

The tall woman's voice boiled with rage. "Cindy!" she yelled. "Do you have any idea what time it is?"

Cindy replied, "I'm so sorry, Jadie. I was cleaning the house for the birthday party and lost track of time." Her profuse apology fell on deaf ears.

Jadie said in a condescending tone, "Let me show you how long it takes to clean your little house."

She clenched her fists and stacked them on top of one another, as if holding a long stick. Jadie thrust her imaginary mop around with two exaggerated sweeps, and then, popped her hands open, spreading her fingers outward like a paper fan.

"Done," Jadie said. "See how fast that was? It does not take that long to clean a super-sized closet."

"Umm, I live in a house. Second, your apartment reminds me of Picasso: a beautiful mess of details puked all over the floor," Cindy said with a patronizing smile creeping across her lips.

Jadie responded, "Don't try to be all pseudo-intellectual with me. Remember when you thought Sydney was the capital of Australia? I know that in reality"— Jadie pointed at Cindy with a sarcastic attitude—"you're a moron."

"In my defense, I was eight. I think we're getting a little carried away. I'm late; it happened; and, I'm throwing my husband a party later." Cindy paused for a moment and then playfully exclaimed, "So— do you forgive me or not?"

"Oh, I forgive you," she lied, "but you're still getting punished for being late."

Cindy whined, "I can't believe this. My little sister is going to punish me."

Jadie smiled mischievously. "You need to do the piked Arabian double front layout for the kids."

Cindy's eyes widened. "You're kidding me, right? I haven't practiced that routine in three years!"

"Next time, set an alarm." Jadie rattled her fingers like a snake as she said to her irritated sister, "Come on, let's go."

"You know, I used to like you," Cindy responded half-seriously. "You're the meanest sister ever."

Jadie, as if introducing her next act, bowed her head, and extended her lanky arms towards the door in a mocking fashion. Cindy rolled her eyes and walked towards the proving ground. Passing through the charcoal metal door, she immediately felt the fluorescent beams of the studio strike her body. The intermixed smells of plastic, foam and rubber saturated the room with a thick, dry musk. The sound of feet pattering on hardwood floors slapped through the air like a blubbery gel being smacked against the wall. Trampolines groaned and squeaked as they launched practicing little children into the air. Muffled footsteps in the distance turned into loud, thundering blows as young women ferociously sought to master difficult vaulting techniques.

As Cindy drew closer to her students, the tang of used gym equipment slowly morphed into a mixture of various scented perfumes, anointed with the sweat of Olympic dreams. Some of the students were learning a unique skill or prepping for cheerleading. For others, the broken ankles, blistered hands, and sore feet marked an American dream that only the elite dared to chase. For Cindy to guide these girls into becoming gymnasts—no, champions—she needed to showcase her hard-earned talents to give them the will to chase the impossible.

Cindy walked towards the blue runway at a brisk pace. The young girls mixed in with each other, blocking the views of some of their smaller friends. Their eyes remained locked on their respected instructor. She walked the gym's perimeter while tying her chestnut hair back into a ponytail. She kicked off her ivory sneakers as she passed the balance beams, her feet snapping the floor with a moist, soft sound following each step. Her bubblegum-colored toenails claimed that Cindy's experience as a gymnast was a farce, but her calloused soles spoke up in defense of their master. Her skin, although still youthful and peach in its complexion, bore brands of hard work and determination through scars left by failed stunts and injuries of the past.

The blurry uneven beams stood menacingly at a distance. While she unzipped her hoodie and threw it on the floor. Her cement-colored, long sleeve shirt proudly displayed the logo for her school: Ninja Gymnastics, a name to which Cindy's husband proudly took credit

"You're in New York, the city of niches," he had told her. "How many other gymnastics trainers have studied martial arts? How can you lose?"

Cindy knew he was right, even though she wanted to call the school Elite Gymnastics and was embarrassed by the ninja title. But the sign-ups were proof that it was a good choice, and the name Elite Gymnastics had already been taken anyway. Cindy did her best to make the school live up to its ninja name, teaching the students to vault over obstacles and leap across rooftops (not that this was encouraged by Cindy or her sister).

As Cindy approached the vinyl tarmac, her modest attire masked her body. The night-colored spandex garments, which blended in with the black mat walls, hid the conditioning of Cindy's body. When her toes touched the edge of the mat, Jadie clapped her hands and turned to the class.

"Girls, listen up," she said. "Cindy is about to demonstrate a piked Arabian double front layout." The class chattered with excitement, eager to see the master at work. Jadie grabbed their attention again and said, "You've seen this on TV, and yes, it is as hard as it looks. That's why we're letting the gold medalist do it."

Cindy shrugged. "You're just jealous that you always got silver."

"Oooooooh," the class murmured.

Jadie was quick to reply, "Try not to fall on your face and embarrass yourself."

Cindy's hazel eyes focused towards the end of the vinyl airstrip. It seemed so much longer than she remembered, but it was too late to back out now. *Thanks, Jadie,* she thought. Cindy stiffened her pose and began taking very controlled, deep breaths. She dropped her hands to her sides like knife blades, fanning her fingers outward. She slightly shuffled her feet into position, tightening her legs to prepare for the sudden burst of speed. What had once been a routine maneuver for her was now a difficult test of worth.

Cindy briefly glance at the faces of all the children and young adults staring at her, gazing with great anticipation. *Oh boy, if I fall on my face…* Cindy looked back at the end of the floor mat and took a brief second to herself. After taking a deep breath, she leaned forward like a bending tree. Suddenly, she bolted from the starting line like a runner hearing the starting pistol. She displayed perfect form as her arms blurred into arcs and her legs ran down the vinyl highway at blinding speed. Within mere moments, her body made a tiny hop into the air, shooting her arms straight up towards the ceiling. Once her left foot impacted on the firm surface, her body twisted and spiraled through the movements, wowing the audience with graceful maneuvers. In the blink of an eye, Cindy's body was already reversed, flipping towards the end of the ocean highway.

Cindy's blurred silhouette lifted off into the air, rolling like a pinwheel in high winds. The height of her jump was so great, she could have easily cleared the heads of all her students. She gracefully kept form while rolling in the air at blinding velocity, but before anyone could really process what had happened, Cindy stuck the landing with flawless execution. She stood poised at the end of the mat like an angelic statue. Once the moment was gone, Cindy shattered the statue of her past by lowering her arms and returning to her relaxed posture.

The girls erupted in a symphony of cheers and applause. Jadie walked up to her sister with a distinct lack of awe, carrying the pile of Cindy's clothes in her arms.

Jadie sighed. "I guess you still got it."

"Thanks," Cindy said as she struggled to regain her breath, "but don't ever make me do that again." Cindy snatched her attire from Jadie and stared at her sister with a deep scowl before walking away.

With Jadie's revenge satiated, the sisters returned to their normal instructional routine. Hours later, the end of the school day drew near. While Cindy was sitting legs crossed on the hardwood floor, she spotted Jadie with her gym bag slung across her shoulder, getting ready to call it a day.

Cindy shouted, "Jadie!"

"Yes, dear sister, how can I help you?" she said, while doing her best to mask her insincerity.

"Don't forget the party is tonight."

"What party?" Jadie asked with feigned ignorance.

"Be serious."

Jadie sighed, but still managed to put a smile on her face. "I didn't forget. Did you need me to do something?"

"Remind Mom and Dad that the party is at seven. I don't want them showing up at nine and possibly intruding on extracurricular birthday celebrations."

"Wow, eew, Cindy! I can't believe you just said that. I don't need graphic explanations of your love life."

"That wasn't graphic."

"Mentally, it was. Anyway, I will make sure to tell them to come at five. Ugh, I have these images now… T-M-I."

"When you have a boyfriend you'll understand—and it's not my fault you visualized it, B-T-W."

Jadie rolled her eyes. "Why is this such a big deal again?"

"It's the big 3-0 and he's been crying about getting asymmetrical grey hairs," Cindy said.

"I'm pretty sure you'll act the same way when your time comes."

Cindy gave Jadie 'the stink eye' and said in a biting tone, "Don't you have somewhere to be?"

"It's been a pleasure chatting with you, dear sister. Toodles!"

****

Meanwhile, in another part of town, a group of scientists were developing the tools of tomorrow. No one would ever come to disturb them because their existence was barely known. Not because the lab was hidden—on the contrary—anyone could walk in, but New Yorkers were simply too oblivious to notice.

Underneath the skyscrapers of midtown Manhattan, Lucent Labs had conceived and distributed some of the most ingenious technology throughout the country. This is where Cindy's husband, Jonas, spent most of his time when he wasn't at home with his wife. Although the company was not top-secret, some of the research conducted there was certainly deemed 'classified' by military standards. However, the guise of an ordinary office building—hiding out in the open—did an excellent job of discouraging snoops.

Jonas was on his way to the work area with a fresh cup of water in hand. The narrow corridors were illuminated with a bright blue hue cast by the recessed LED lights embedded in the walls. The silver walls reflected a blurry visage of his appearance, as Jonas walked past security personnel and employees who waved and smiled at the prophetic scientist. Before heading back to his main project, Jonas peeked in on the other experiments taking place in the labs. First, he checked the compact semi-truck prototype. Peering through the door, he observed the research team struggling to get the trailer carriage to fold down properly. He overheard a quick "Dammit!" as the folding trailer crushed the Styrofoam placeholders within the carriage.

Jonas smiled to himself as he continued to the next station. There, a team was working on an early warning system (EWS) for civilian vehicles. He heard the female computer voice repeat in an endless loop, "Warning pedestrian detected-Warning pedestrian detected-Warning pedestrian detected-"

"Can someone shut that thing up?" screamed a frustrated project manager. Jonas made a mental note to speak with the manager later and continued on to the main lab. After all of his lollygagging, Jonas arrived at the main test lab and casually pushed through the door. He didn't bother to take out his access card because the lock had been broken for weeks. Inside the lab, a young man wearing glasses rapidly clicked away on a keyboard as millions of lines of code scrolled past his lenses.

"That door's never going to get fixed, is it?" Jonas asked.

"Considering you're the owner of this company, I thought you would have asked someone by now," the programmer replied in a sarcastic tone.

"To get the money to fix it, I'd have to fire everyone I walked past, and anyone I've made eye contact with today."

"Don't look at me," the programmer said boldly.

"Michael, if you weren't the lead programmer, I'd fire you just for kicks,"

"How about we leave the door as is?" Michael replied with his eyes still glued to his screen.

"Done," he said. Jonas sauntered off with his cup of water to see what the rest of the team was working on. As he walked into the warehouse section of the facility, many bright, recessed LED lights towered high above within the ceiling. Metallic ribs and struts lined the perimeter, forming rectangular supports. The grey, pasty concrete floor displayed various nicks and scorch marks throughout its surface.

Jonas was tempted to harass the scientists by asking about their progress; however, he quickly changed his mind when one of the researchers fired a prototype grappling hook in his direction. It flew through the air like a sidewinder snake dancing across the desert sands. Jonas' quick reflexes pulled him back from the projectile's flight path, but failed to inform his hands as to which way he was going. His plastic cup of water spilled out of fear, splashing all over his arm and chest.

Jonas glared at the technician with the look of a focused jaguar ready to pounce. The moment of awkward silence felt like an hour to the bumbling technician. Jonas wiped his chest and shook his hands as drops of water showered the ground like a sprinkler system.

He looked at the technician and said, "So, speaking of firing…"

"Umm… sorry, really sorry." The technician's hands trembled with fear. "I was trying to fix the firing mechanism."

"…As I was saying, speaking of firing, Mr. Wright. Don't work on the firing mechanism until the safeties have been installed." Jonas turned to his staff and said, "Guys, do we not have a single working prototype?"

"Umm, Jonas?" a voice squeaked.

"Yes, Sid?"

"We do have some working prototypes over here if you would like to see them," the researcher said.

Michael immediately chimed in while briefly glancing away from his computer code. "Don't break anything that you look at, Jonas; you have a tendency to do that."

"Get back to work code monkey." He turned his attention to Sid and said, "Give me something, Dr. Carmack."

"Well—" before he could speak, a woman walked in with two gentlemen following in her wake.

"I'm sorry to interrupt you, Jonas, but you have visitors," the secretary said. The woman led the two men towards Jonas. One was adorned with the decorations of a wounded and honorable soldier on his left breast; the other wore glasses so thick that his eyes resembled tapioca pearls in bubble tea.

"Thank you, Gracie," Jonas said. The secretary walked back to her desk, while Jonas waved the men to come forward. "Gentlemen."

"Pleasure to meet you again, Mr. Ames." The man in the uniform shook Jonas' hand with a strong, vice grip.

"I see you brought a friend today, General Ord."

The man with the glasses had long, mangy, dirty-blond hair, and he seemed very enthusiastic to meet Jonas. Jonas shook his hand and was almost disgusted by a handshake that reminded him of holding a slimy, wet fish. The grip was virtually nonexistent, but the man continued to beam with excitement.

"Oh my God, it's such an honor to meet you! I'm a really huge fan of your work!" the awkward man gushed.

"K… so much for top-secret. Your name, sir?" Jonas asked with a suspicious look.

He replied with a raspy, nasally voice, "Oh, oh, I'm sorry. I guess I was just too excited, I didn't even realize I hadn't introduced myself. I'm Sean, Sean Roper from DARPA."

"Wow, Defense Advanced Research Projects Agency? I'm flattered," Jonas said with a returning smile.

"I'm the one in awe, sir, t—" the general gently pushed the excitable man aside.

"If I don't stop him now, he'll never quit yammerin'," he said with a thick southern accent.

"Why did you push me, General?"

"Because it pleases me. Anyway, Mr. Ames, we came to see the status of SIRCA."

Jonas motioned for Dr. Carmack. "You're just in time. Dr. Carmack was just about to inform me of the details. Sid, if you would please."

Sid's mouth began to betray him—his lips began to stammer and his face filled with a vibrant cherry red. He took a short breath to himself and exhaled slowly, looking towards the general and DARPA official. Suddenly, the quiet, reserved and meek Sid Carmack became infused with an incredible vigor. The short round fellow with thinning grey hair began to babble on about the incredible advances the staff had accomplished.

"I will do my best to keep it relatively short, General, but there is a lot to talk about. First, you will be interested to know that we have a working prototype of a retractable rail gun. As you know, original designs for these weapons made them the size of football fields with exorbitant energy costs. With Jonas' design specs and Dr. Wright's mechanical expertise, we now have a weapon that can fire projectiles without using any combustible material. The projectiles fly faster and are more accurate than any weapon in existence."

The general looked over to the DARPA chief and whispered, "This is going to take a while, isn't it?"

"What are you talking about? This is awesome," Sean said with a smile.

Sid resumed, "Take a look at this cloth. Looks ordinary, right? If we were to, say, flip this switch…"

Dr. Sid Carmack flipped the switch attached to a wire that connected to a rather ordinary-looking table cloth. Within an instant, the cloth disappeared from the naked eye.

"Wow!" Sean was breathless. His body almost fell backwards, amazed by the incredible technology. The general raised his eyebrow with interest but seemed to exude a small amount of skepticism.

"How did you do that, Doctor?" the general asked.

"Millions of micro cameras and LEDs, sir. I doubt I need to explain the advantages of a camouflage system. It's not immune to thermal sensors at the moment, but when all systems are done, we will consider working on upgrades.

"Over here, we have the gecko wall-gripping gloves. The design is almost directly copied off of the footpads of geckos. Combined with our other systems, your operatives will be able to scale any building in the world."

Although the general was fascinated by the technology being presented to him, his face showed signs of impatience. There was a nagging question itching at the back of his mind. He bit his tongue in the hopes that Dr. Carmack would answer it before he felt the need to scratch it.

"The muscle enh—"

"I beg your pardon, Dr. Carmack," the general interrupted. The hypnotized and loving stare of the DARPA chief was shattered as the general cut to the chase. "This is great and all, but what platform are these devices being delivered on? The rail gun has no triggers, grips, iron sights, nothing. How are they supposed to use the gecko system when there's nothing to even wrap their hands around?"

Jonas patted Sid on the shoulder, signaling that he would take over from there. Jonas walked over to a beaker filled with silver liquid and lifted it to the general's eye level.

"That is supposed to tell me what, exactly?"

"This, General, is the future…"

****

Back at the gym, Cindy was stuffing her gym clothes into a black duffel bag. With a simple change into a blouse and jeans, Cindy went from athlete to everyday woman. While walking towards the exit, she overheard quiet mumbling coming from the changing room. Cindy walked over to the door and cracked it ajar. She saw a student sitting alone in a corner, which was odd, considering the bench was clear.

Cindy listened in briefly to the student's cell phone conversation.

The student whispered, "Right now, Mom? Mhmm... mhmm... Oh my God."

Though Cindy couldn't hear what was said on the phone, the distressed look on the young girl's face was enough to make Cindy check if her student needed help. *I hope it's nothing too serious,* Cindy thought as the girl hung up her phone and stared at the blank screen.

"Priscilla, is everything okay?" Cindy asked quietly.

Priscilla lowered her head towards the tiled floor, counting the number of specks on each linoleum square.

"My father's in the hospital," she said as her voice trailed off.

"Oh, honey, I'm sorry," Cindy said, placing her hand on Priscilla's shoulder. "Do you know what's wrong?"

"My mom said that someone shot him while he was at some kind of party."

"I'm sorry, sweetie." Cindy briefly glanced at her phone to check the time. "Do you want me to walk you home or to the hospital?"

"No, that's okay. I know you have a birthday party to get to." Cindy was not convinced; she could tell that Priscilla's words lacked sincerity.

"Come on, I'll walk you over to the hospital," Cindy said, paying no attention to the birthday comment. She extended her hand towards Priscilla, knowing that she would resist. Priscilla's face was difficult for Cindy to read, but her body language expressed immense gratitude.

"Wait, I'm sorry," she said pulling away. "I have to grab my stuff first."

27

Cindy said, "Okay, but be quick like bunny, swift like fox."

Later that evening, Cindy and Priscilla arrived at the emergency room just a little after five. Cindy nervously bit her lip as she thought about Jonas' party. She knew that this trip would risk sacrificing all of her plans. Her eyes fluttered back and forth as she calculated whether she could make it back to Queens before seven. Hillside was still an hour, possibly two, by bus, and Cindy still had a ten minute walk from the bus stop to her house. Even though the party was extremely important, she couldn't bear to leave Priscilla alone in the hospital.

Even though it was still early, Cindy was starting to feel anxiety about the time. She held onto hope that maybe, just maybe this was still doable. She stood with her arms crossed in the hallway, looking up and down the corridor, wondering how the nurses and doctors could seem so calm. The cushioned chairs that lined the walls were supposed to create the illusion of comfort, but all Cindy could feel was the creepiness of the sterile white walls surrounding her. Cindy looked over to Priscilla, who was standing outside the hospital room, hesitant to go inside. Her hand gripped the handle, but an invisible forcefield prevented her from pushing open the door.

"What's wrong?" Cindy asked.

"I don't want to see him without my mom," Priscilla replied.

Cindy led Priscilla to the cushioned chairs across the hall and patted the fluffy, foam-filled seat.

"Priscilla, I don't mean to pry and please don't take offense, but... was your father involved in illegal activities?" Cindy said.

"Only if being a businessman is illegal."

"Well, there's all kinds of businesses," Cindy said.

"Mrs. Ames!" she snapped. "The only thing my father is involved with is politics. He doesn't do drugs; he doesn't deal drugs; and he's not involved with any bad people. The party was a fundraising event for multiple sclerosis." Priscilla looked away from her instructor, exasperated by the questioning. "Does that sound like someone who would be involved in illegal activities?"

"No, not at all. I'm sorry, old habits," Cindy said. She tried to hold back the brewing embarrassment that was bubbling to the surface, but her flush-colored face undermined all of her attempts. *That was so stupid of you*, Cindy thought to herself, refusing to make any further eye contact with her student.

Thankfully, their conversation was interrupted by the rapid clacking of high heels. The smell of expensive perfume wafted down the hallway as Priscilla's mother ran to her baby girl with her arms wide open. With the family reunited in a tight and tearful embrace, Cindy quietly excused herself and quickly rushed to catch the bus home, almost as if she were chasing the fleeting rays of the sun.

As she boarded the bus, Cindy was greeted with her daily "Broadway show" of random crazies jumping on and off the bus. Whether it was a homeless woman singing to herself or a young wannabe gangster rapping lyrics, random insanity

29

would accompany her home… for an hour. All she could think to herself was, *God, I hate public transportation.*

After quietly suffering the ravings of a madman for the last fifteen minutes, Cindy was finally dropped off at Hillside Ave. and Parsons Blvd. From there, she walked her way up to 85th Dr. and 152nd St. in order to make her way back to suburbia and more importantly, home.

The Queens suburb offered what Manhattan could never achieve: space and silence. However, these luxuries came at the cost of the convenience of travel. Hillside Ave. is an interesting walk, though; Korean grocers, Chinese 'Super' Laundromats, Latino restaurants, and other multi-cultural themed shops covered the avenue from end to end. The mecca of diversity seemed tarnished by the out of place car dealerships that shared the same space.

On her way northbound, Cindy let out a deep sigh of both relief and exhaustion. She was running late for the party but only by a few minutes. Spring Daylight Savings hadn't taken effect yet, so at 7 pm, the streets were already dark. But the night didn't bother Cindy; she felt safe walking through her neighborhood in Queens. As Cindy approached her block, she saw a man and a woman arguing up ahead.

She contemplated crossing the street to give the couple a wide berth, but realized she was acting much too paranoid over such trivial things. Continuing her walk towards the couple, Cindy could tell they were of Latino descent by the way they were yelling at each other in rapid-fire Spanglish. Figuring it was just a couple's spat, Cindy stepped past the pair and continued walking home, until…

She felt the vibration of a sharp crack pierce her ear canals; it was the unmistakable sound of flesh smacking flesh. Cindy stopped dead in her tracks and stood for a moment, her eyes darting around back and forth as her brain tried to process what to do next. She looked back and saw a woman holding onto her tear-saturated cheek. Cindy found herself being consumed by something white-hot emanating from within. A splash of empathy soaked her being, forcing her to mentally relive the horrible experience through her own eyes; yet, something felt wrong. Cindy didn't want to get involved. It wasn't her business to meddle in the affairs of others, and she could feel her intuition repeatedly telling her to walk away. She could end up in so much legal trouble if an altercation broke out, but she just couldn't allow this woman to be beaten anymore.

"Hey!" Cindy yelled. "Don't hit her!"

In a thick Spanish accent the man replied, "Keep walking."

"Trust me, I don't want to be here, just don't hit her anymore, please," Cindy pleaded.

The woman started yelling at the man, blaming him for attracting Cindy's attention. The man turned to his wife and started grappling with her, covering her mouth with his hand.

Without even thinking, Cindy took three steps forward. Not a single word

31

escaped her lips, but her eyes locked on to the man. Her body went into autopilot as she yelled a second time in a more threatening manner.

"Touch her again…" Cindy took one step forward and balled her fists.

The woman cried out, "No, por favor!"

"I told you to mind your business, you stupid puta!" The irritated man said, as he shoved Cindy back.

The man's wife grabbed onto his hand, begging him to stop. A murderous fury covered his face like war paint. With one quick, fearsome strike, he walloped his crying wife again, knocking her defenseless, frail figure back down to the cold ground. When the woman looked up towards Cindy, a river of blood fell from the woman's busted lip.

The next sound heard was the dull crinkle of a nylon duffel bag dropping onto the concrete sidewalk. Cindy advanced towards the man with vengeance dwelling in her hazel eyes. The man raised his right fist, aiming it squarely towards Cindy's powdery-tinted cheeks. She anticipated where his fist was going and dodged his punch while stepping towards his unguarded torso. Cindy lifted her hands and grabbed his forearm as it shot past her. She lunged her elbow into his jaw and simultaneously twisted his arm behind his back.

He screamed in pain as she slowly applied pressure to his wrist. The popping of bone and twisting of skin rumbled beneath Cindy's fingers. His tough-guy façade disappeared in an instant, rendering him down to a whimpering, "I'm sorry,

I'm sorry." Gallons upon gallons of cowardice leaked free from his eyes as Cindy increased the amount of pain shooting throughout his body.

Cindy held him down on the floor and threatened, "Don't, do that, anymo—"

Everything fell silent. Her body was frozen in place as a sudden feeling of shock coursed through her limbs.

Cindy found herself looking up towards the night sky, peering into the blackness. The eerie tangerine glow of the lonesome street light above watched the event unfold as an object was removed from her back. Her heartbeat grew louder in her head, filling her ears with the deafening gong of unsettling tone. Like a tree hacked at its base, Cindy fell forward and landed face-first onto the stone-filled sidewalk. She whimpered softly, as she felt pain in its liquid form spilling onto the ground. The concrete became stained with a deep, copper red; her blood spilling over the curb and dripping into the water drain below.

She turned her face onto its side and saw two more men standing next to her through her peripheral vision. The husband said to them, "What took you so long? She almost broke my arm!"

"We had to wait. That bitch knew what she was doing," the unknown man replied.

The wife, the supposedly helpless victim of this entire ordeal, walked up to the group and said in very clear English, "Next time, don't hit me so hard."

"Sorry, baby, she was gonna walk away." He wiped the fake blood off his wife's lip and gave her a deep kiss.

One of the unknown men said, "Grab the purse and let's get out of here."

Cindy felt scavenging fingers rummage through her pockets. Her eyes winced as an uninvited hand crept dangerously close to places it didn't belong.

An unknown voice yelled out, "What are you doing? Let's go!" The criminals grabbed Cindy's purse and fled into the darkness. The lowlifes had taken everything: her money, her house keys, her credit cards, license, cell phone and metro card—anything and everything of value including her pride. The only thing the criminals left behind was a cheap dagger wound which would forever remind her of the crime. She struggled to breathe while trying repeatedly to get to her feet, but it was no use. She fell back on her knees and scraped her skin against the sidewalk, tearing fresh holes into her jeans. Her strength was ebbing away, and she needed that dwindling energy to keep on breathing. She tried to crawl but couldn't even manage to match a snail's pace.

"Jonas…" her raspy voice uttered. It was as if she was hoping that saying his name would make him appear from thin air. But no one was coming and the short, half-block distance home seemed like it was miles away. Suddenly, she heard the sound of people chattering down by the street corner. She could feel hope filling her lungs with energy to keep on breathing, but there was not enough left over for her to speak. The group walked towards Cindy as she lay there on the floor, frozen

in place. It seemed to be a group of young teenagers who were strolling around the block looking for something fun to do for the night. The stench of marijuana followed behind them like an unwelcome shadow.

Regardless of the form, help was here. Cindy imagined the sound of an ambulance rushing to the scene, taking her to safety. To Cindy's relief, she saw one of the kids bring out his cell and begin to press numbers on his touch screen. Yet after a few moments, Cindy noticed that the teen was not talking on his cell phone. *He should be on the phone with someone by now,* Cindy thought, as sharp stings emanated from her lower back. Then the sickening sound of a digital shutter click made Cindy realize what was going to happen next.

"What are you doing?" the young girl said to her friend.

"I'm recording this," he replied with apathy.

Cindy knew that help wasn't going to come her way. Instead, she was going to fall victim to being the next viral sensation on Youtube. She prayed to God for strength but in the same instance, wanted to strangle this boy to death.

"We have to help her," the girl said to the wannabe cameraman.

The boy replied, "Dude, this is probably just another scam or a marketing thing for a movie."

"Are you for real?" the girl said in disbelief.

The teen turned to her and said, "If we call the cops, they're gonna bust us for the weed. Now come on, let's go." The accompanying friends giggled to themselves, too high to care about what was going on.

"Marc, please, at least call the ambulance," she pleaded.

The teen kept walking and yelled to the girl, "Let's go, Andrea."

Cindy watched the girl sigh and walk away. She didn't seem to have a purse or any pockets, perhaps too young to own a cell phone? Either way, Cindy couldn't believe what she had just witnessed. She was left alone; no one had come to save her after all. If only her breathing wasn't so labored, all of the adrenaline pumping through her veins would be fueling her anger.

After what felt like an eternity, the sound of rubber rolling on asphalt drew close to the sidewalk. A car door slammed shut as someone in sneakers ran towards Cindy's dying body. All she could hear before falling unconscious was a woman's trembling voice saying, "Oh my God, Cin—"

CHAP7ER 2

DOWNFALL

If General Ord's mouth were not attached to his head, his jaw would have been sitting on the floor. The general was astonished by what Jonas had just demonstrated to him. To his military eyes, there was no rhyme or reason for why Jonas' invention worked, but it did, and it hinted at a technological revolution in modern warfare. No longer would precious money be wasted on a state-of-the-art fighter jet that would never see the light of day except in training exercises. This invention would change ground combat forever.

"So let me get this straight, Mr. Ames. You're telling me that a beaker full of fluid can do all that?" the general asked.

Jonas replied, "General Ord, my team and I haven't even scratched the surface."

The sudden shrill of a giddy schoolgirl pierced the room as Sean screamed, "Dude, you are effing brilliant!"

General Ord continued to prod Jonas. "I don't understand. How do you have enough power to run these systems?"

"The only one that could explain that particular question is Charlie."

37

Jonas pointed over to the short, balding fellow who was drawing straws with other co-workers to see who would pick up today's coffee.

"Can we ask him?" Ord said.

"Umm…" Jonas hesitated.

Michael chimed in, "He took a vow of silence."

"Son, are you serious right now?" the General asked.

"Whoa, watch out, the captain means business!" Sean said sarcastically.

"It's *General*, Mr. Roper. How did you become DARPA Chief anyway? I thought you were required to be less of a fanboy."

"Bro, you don't want to mess with me." Sean adjusted his large circular glasses and stood next to the general. "I can hack your phone to send penile enlargement spam to the secretary of defense," he said with a confrontational look in his tiny eyes.

"Do you know what a rifle looks like shoved up y—"

"Guys! Seriously?" Michael said as he rolled his eyes and shook his head.

"Before World War Geek starts, the basic gist of the power source is this: the energy system is based off failed fusion reactor experiments. Think of it like electrically charged water. It's not an unlimited power supply—it does need to recharge often, but it provides enough power for its purpose," Jonas said.

"I can buy that for now," Ord said with an approving look.

Sean looked over to the general and said in a low energy, almost prepubescent voice, "Should we tell him the bad news now?"

The general looked to Jonas with a grim stare. After seeing this intimidating glance, Jonas immediately felt his chest collapse. The general seemed reluctant to speak, but continued in a dutiful tone.

"Jonas, I have to talk to you about the funding for your projects."

Before the general could continue, Michael stepped next to Jonas with a cell phone in hand.

"Excuse me, Jonas—Jadie's on the phone."

"Tell her, I'll call back," Jonas said impatiently.

"Okie dokey," he replied.

Jonas turned his attention back to General Ord as a concerned look spread across his brow. "What was it you needed to tell me, General?"

"Well, you know the economy isn't quite as strong as it used to be. We are having some problems sec—"

Michael tapped Jonas on the shoulder, causing him to turn in a flash of anger. "What?" Jonas asked through gritted teeth.

There was an odd look of concern emanating from Michael's blue eyes. He whispered to Jonas, *"You really need to take this."*

Jonas' lips mouthed the word *what,* taking the cell phone from Michael's hand. He raised his index finger towards the general and stepped away to seek a

place of privacy. His voice was unintelligible to the group of men standing by idly;
the DARPA Chief, General Ord, and Michael looked at each other, pondering what
they should be doing in Jonas' absence.

"Cindy? My Cindy? That can't be right," Jonas said in disbelief. "I'm leaving
right now. Where am I going?"

Jonas began briskly walking towards the exit as though he were evacuating a
burning building. With the phone held up to his ear, Jonas' eyes looked wild with
uncertainty. Panicked, he rushed to put on his jacket, swipe his keys, and made a
beeline to the exit.

"Where are you going?" General Ord asked.

Jonas replied in a hurried state, "I'm sorry, General, I have a family emergency.
Call or e-mail what you need to tell me, please. I'm really sorry, I have to go."

Everyone except for Michael looked completely dumbfounded that Jonas had
just walked out on them. Without Jonas around to make the company decisions,
the general and DARPA Chief shook Michael's hand and told him that they would
be in touch.

Jonas arrived at Queens Hospital Center and checked in at the front desk at
around 8 pm. Jonas rushed straight down the hallway heading to Cindy's room.
As he ran down the corridor, he immediately spotted the statuesque Jadie leaning
up against the wall with her arms crossed. Directly across from her, Cindy and
Jonas' parents sat quietly chattering amongst themselves. Although it seemed

normal from the outside, the hushed whispers of distraught parents revealed the great cloud of anxiety looming over their heads.

Cindy's father kept saying, "People are such scum these days. Why would they hurt my little girl?"

Her mother repeated, "I knew something terrible was going to happen tonight, I just knew it."

Jonas' father spotted his son and called out his name, prompting everyone to greet him with a morose but reassuring hug. For Jonas it was comforting, if not surprising, to see everyone at the hospital waiting to see Cindy.

"When did you guys get in town?" Jonas asked.

His mother said, "Cindy invited us to a surprise party for you."

"What, really?" He covered his forehead with his palm, becoming more upset with the situation unraveling before him. "What happened to her?"

Cindy's father looked at Jonas with a deep-seated sadness buried beneath his crystal blue eyes. "Jadie was picking up the cake and driving back to the house. When she turned the corner, she saw Cindy..." His voice began to crack as thoughts of his bloodied daughter flooded his mind. "She was lying in a pool of her own blood"—he began to sob into his hands, hands that contained the marks of a man that once lived the life of a soldier. The small scar that traveled down his right jaw did not befit the man with glassy eyes. Cindy's mother gently rubbed his back and rested her head on his shoulder.

Jadie's eyes looked up from the tiled floor. Her face was full of sorrow but her composure remained steadfast. She said to Jonas, "You should go in and see her—she's been waiting for you."

His eyes lit up with a renewed purpose. He walked past his waiting family, straight into the patient care room. He was struck by the sight of an IV line snaking its way into Cindy's forearm delivering a kiss of life. The bandage sitting on top of Cindy's head seemed to gaze at him, like a ghost trapped in the mirror, wondering… judging why hadn't he been there to protect her? The image washed waves of guilt over Jonas' body, causing his gait to slow as though he were trudging through muddy quicksand. He could not believe what he was witnessing: Cindy's beautiful chestnut-colored hair was completely disheveled, with rogue patches of hair flying in every direction. Her once-vivacious hazel eyes, which usually glowed brightly in the rays of the morning sun, were shut tight and dimmed, discolored by the trauma of the night.

The closer Jonas came to Cindy, the more he wanted to turn back to avoid his tears. He picked up her hand in the gentlest manner, just like the day he proposed to her. Her once-soft, moisturized hands had become rough in texture. Stained by the embedded dirt and dried blood wedged between the crevices of her rosy skin. He lowered his lips to her hand, placing a gentle kiss upon her knuckle. He looked back up to her face, softly rubbing her hands with his manicured thumbs. His eyes were moist, as he whispered remorse to his wonderful wife, *"I'm so sorry."*

Her index finger twitched with a small pulse of energy, limply reaching for Jonas' hand in a weakened state. Though her eyes remained closed, Cindy said to Jonas in a drowsy, crackling voice, "Don't apologize."

"I can't help it," he said, tightly grasping her hand.

She turned her head towards Jonas and forced her heavy eyes to open. The fluorescent light shimmered on her irises like distant moons. She smiled towards her husband and said, "It's not your fault. I'm just happy you're here."

"How did this happen?" he said softly.

She took in a deep breath before her morose lips began to weave her tale. "I tried to do the right thing."

"What do you mean?"

"One of my students got a phone call… her father had been shot. I felt bad just leaving her at the gym, so I decided to walk her to the hospital. After that, I got off at my usual bus stop."

"So you were almost home?" Jonas asked.

"If I were any closer, they could have walked into our house."

"Jesus," he said while running his hand through hair.

"A couple was arguing on the sidewalk. Next thing I knew, the husband was smacking his wife around like a ragdoll. I wanted to ignore it, I really did, but I couldn't leave it alone.

"I walked up to the guy and told him to stop, but he told me to get lost. He even called me a bitch in Spanish."

Jonas chuckled and said, "He's not the first person to assume you didn't speak Spanish."

"I wish it ended as harmlessly as that."

Jonas' expression returned to a grimace. The fleeting moment of humor had already passed; Cindy was clearly in no mood for jokes.

"When I realized he wasn't going to stop hitting her, I put him in one of my grips and threatened to break his arm. That's when his scumbag friends showed up and stabbed me in the back."

"No, I can't believe this; you know how to defend yourself," Jonas replied.

"It's been a while since those days, and they caught me off guard. I wasn't exactly expecting to get knifed in the back during a domestic dispute," she said.

Jonas gave a reassuring nod. "You would have been able to take them if you saw it coming."

Cindy briefly chuckled to herself, feeling a bit smug about her husband's confidence in her abilities. Unfortunately, the reality was much different than the fantasy.

"I'm not so sure about that, I'm a little rusty, sweetie," she said.

Jonas replied, "Well, you're still dangerous in my eyes."

"Umm, thanks?" she said with a look of confusion.

"What happened after?"

Her mood changed as she thought back to what felt like seconds ago. The incident may have left wounds deeper than superficial cuts and bruises. Her expression reflected the pain she felt recalling what happened after the mugging. "Umm." Her voice lowered, wavering in response to Jonas' question.

Jonas' expression reflected Cindy's mood as buckets of empathy poured over his crinkled brow.

"When I was lying on the floor, some kids came up…" she stopped, as her voice began to scratch at her throat.

Cindy was starting to relive the moment in her mind, like a war hero remembering his time over enemy lines. Although she thought she was maintaining a strong façade, the cracks in her voice began to reveal a deep weakness and vulnerability that Jonas hadn't seen in a long time.

"I thought those kids were going to help me and all they did was take pictures of me bleeding!" her voice uttered in complete frustration. "They just took a picture and walked, walked aw—"

Her mask of strength shattered, as her chest jerked several times to pump out fountains of sadness from her shimmering eyes. Jonas leaned in towards her and embraced his wounded wife tightly, hoping to stem back the flood of tears smearing her mascara. Her quiet sobs became muffled, as she tucked her face in Jonas' shoulder; his shirt stained with Cindy's moist disbelief that she was left to die.

"If it wasn't for Jadie—"

"Shh, shh, I know, I know."

Jonas was always the comforting shoulder to cry on; anything he did would make Cindy feel rejuvenated with joy. This time—this time was different. This time—Cindy was feeling a different kind of pain that no simple shoulder could fix, a hurt so deep that a warm, loving touch would not be enough to alleviate her sorrow.

"I'm sorry to interrupt," echoed through the room as a doctor quietly entered the room. "I'm Dr. Kyung. Are you the husband?"

Jonas turned his eyes towards the Korean doctor and nodded in acknowledgement, but he made sure not to let go of Cindy's hand.

"Has the pain subsided at all?"

"Yes, Doctor," Cindy said.

"You know… normally, when people come in with stab wounds, they're involved with some sort of gang. Are you in a gang, Mrs. Ames?" the doctor said with a wry smile.

"I'm in a gang of ninjas," she said in a dry tone.

"She's not kidding," Jonas said.

The doctor cocked his head in a skeptical manner and said, "All jokes aside, I recommend you go in for a CAT scan to check for a concussion. Once that's clear, we'll stitch you up; let you talk to the police; and set you free."

"Cindy, what do you think?" Jonas asked.

"The sooner we get this done, the sooner we can go home."

"You're going to have to wait with your family while we take your wife back for testing, Mr. Ames."

Jonas nodded his head and walked over to the waiting room as Cindy was carted off to a different ward of the hospital. Everyone seemed on edge after what had happened—after all, Cindy had walked home on that route millions of times before and nothing like this had ever happened. Jonas explained to everyone what Cindy had told him, and they simply couldn't believe it.

Jadie and Cindy's parents kept repeating that it was impossible for Cindy to have been attacked like this. They talked about all of the martial arts trophies she collected over the years. But Jonas reminded them the trophies dated back at least ten years or more. Inadvertently, subtle waves of guilt began floating in the air when Cindy's parents mentioned that this happened in preparation for Jonas' birthday party.

The look on his face when those comments began polluting the air... Jonas felt responsible since his birthday party played a part in sealing Cindy's fate. Tension in the group rose, as her parents sought a place to lay blame. Jadie, noticing Jonas' pain, shot up in his defense. Nipping any argument in the bud, she distracted her parents by telling them a random but funny story about one of the girls at the gym. He silently mouthed the words, *"thank you."* Then, unexpectedly, his phone began to vibrate. He stood up and walked over to a quiet hallway to take the call in private.

"Hello, General," he said in a disingenuous way.

"Is this a bad time, Jonas? I really need to discuss something very important," General Ord said with urgency.

"My wife was stabbed tonight, sir," Jonas replied.

"Is she all right?"

"She'll be fine, thank you," Jonas said.

"Listen, I know you are in a bad position right now, but time is of the essence here, Mr. Ames."

"All right, General, if it's that important..."

"That thing you showed me this afternoon? It was incredible. If I could buy it right now even in its unfinished state, I would. Unfortunately, the economy has hit the entire nation pretty hard. Stocks are falling; the reserve is trying to bail out banks; and countries in Europe are close to reaching their own recessions."

With an impatient color to his voice, Jonas said, "I've kept up with the news, General."

"Our defense budget has been cut in half, and R&D is highest on the chopping block."

Jonas' face wrinkled with concern. "What? I fall under that umbrella. Are you guys shutting me down? This is supposed to be a joint venture. I have other

48

private investors, you know."

"Jonas, some of those investors were from companies that are now starting to go under. The government's been pinching DARPA to come up with new, ready-to-manufacture solutions."

"If I can get this system out the door, I can keep my job?"

"Correct, but it has to happen soon. You know that whole government shutdown issue we just barely avoided last month? Two weeks from now, they'll cut all funds to R&D until the economy gets stabilized."

"Two weeks! That is insane. How am I supposed to get it ready by then?" Jonas paced back and forth, as he ran his fingers through his raven hair.

The general tried to reassure Jonas. "I know that's not much time, but I don't need a working, fully functional system. All you need to show them is a functional prototype without any additional features. It'll be like a magic show, where you create the illusion that the system is finished."

"I can't believe I'm hearing this," Jonas said. His despondent tone resonated with the general, but Ord could not offer any additional solutions.

Before hanging up, the General said, "It's all I could do for you, Jonas. I want you to succeed."

Jonas dropped his phone to his side and slumped into a hallway chair. His uncalloused, olive hands covered his face, blocking the outside world from his fragile mindset. The sounds of the hospital began to drown out as if he were submerged underwater. The world crashing down around Jonas began to dissipate, allowing him a moment of peace.

****

After she was released from the hospital later that night, Cindy awoke to the sound of car doors slamming shut outside of her home. She looked over to her alarm clock, but became confused when she was unable to make out any of the numbers. She turned to her new cell phone and read the time: 2:00 am glowed from the screen. She looked over to her side only to find that Jonas was missing. Cindy sat up in bed and walked over to the window, but her injuries made her movements lethargic. She pulled down the venetian blinds and looked up towards the sky. The air was covered in a thick, ominous, orange cloud as if a building were on fire.

The entire street was covered in an amber hue, and as she looked towards the city street from her 2nd story window, three men wearing dark clothing and nylon masks headed towards her front door. Cindy could feel her heart pounding inside her chest, like it was trying to rip itself out of her own body. Her wounds began to ache with a pulsing pain that matched the beat of her increasing heart rate. She ran to the living room and could hear the rattling of equipment scraping on her front door. She desperately tried to turn on the lights, flicking each switch back and forth repeatedly, but there seemed to be no power going through the house.

She whispered out, "Jonas," but he was nowhere to be seen. The wood on the door began to splinter and moan in agony, as the crowbar wedged itself between the hinges. Cindy ran towards the kitchen in fear and grabbed the sharpest steak knife she could find. Her body had become consumed by fear; every inch of her skin was shaking violently, waiting for the men to break in. With knife in hand, she readied herself by the failing door. Cindy was petrified with terror but refused to become a victim—again.

The door burst open with a heavy boot leading the charge. A man stood next to the broken entrance with a red crowbar in hand. His slow, migrating stare around the room finally locked onto Cindy. She was mortified by the man's size, but that fear was only exacerbated by the two equally large men entering behind him. The first man with the crowbar rushed towards Cindy. As she let out a blood-curdling scream, she stuck the blade forward and charged towards him like a suicidal samurai.

"Cindy!" Jonas' voice yelled as she snapped forward, shrieking in terror. Her body was quaking uncontrollably as the adrenaline began to thin out of her system. Jonas sat up and wrapped his warm arms around Cindy's shoulder.

"Sweetie, are you okay? It was just a dream," Jonas said, attempting to console his wife.

She couldn't respond to him, not now. She covered her face with her hands, trying to hide the tears and uncertainty she was feeling.

"It's okay. It's okay, were you having a nightmare?" he asked.

Cindy nodded but refused to look at him. Her mind was still disoriented from the nightmare, and she was waiting for a sign that she was back into reality. Jonas pulled Cindy towards his body and rested her head on his chest. She immediately felt the warmth of peace begin to blanket her shivering soul.

"I'm sorry I yelled at you earlier," Jonas said as he caressed her cheek, "but you kicked me pretty hard on the leg."

"What?" she asked, bewildered. She looked up at Jonas, her eyes conveying her innocence and confusion at her husband's comment.

"Yeah, you started kicking me with your tree trunk legs when you were freaking out."

"I'm sorry; I didn't even realize I did that."

"Were you dreaming that you were in a fighting game?" Jonas asked in a lighthearted tone.

"Umm, no, that's your dream," she said. "I was having this awful dream that I woke up in the middle of the night. The power was out, and you weren't in bed."

"Not to interrupt you, but the power did go out." He pointed towards the flashing 12:00 on the alarm clock.

"When did that happen?" Cindy asked.

"I'm not sure. I found out when I went to take a sh—"

"Eww. Really?"

"Sorry, please continue, my love," he said with a faux British accent.

"Anyway, I thought thieves were breaking into the house, so I grabbed a knife and stabbed them."

"Umm, wow," Jonas said as he stared blankly at his wife.

Cindy slapped him on the shoulder. "Don't look at me like I'm crazy."

"I'm not. I'm not. I just think you might be a little shaken." Jonas shrugged his shoulders, trying to mask the severity of his concern.

"Ya think? This has never happened to me before, Jonas!" Cindy said with a flash of anger.

"Hey, hey, take it easy. I'm not trying to make fun of you," he said while softly rubbing her shoulder.

She dropped her hands between her crossed legs and looked at Jonas with a shameful pout.

"Go back to bed, okay? It was just a bad dream."

"Okay." Cindy laid her head on a pillow and closed her eyes..

She tried go to sleep, but her mind was racing with millions of thoughts, and her heart was beating with a cacophony of emotions. Shame, guilt and fear all haunted Cindy's slumber. Although her pride was greatly wounded, it did not compare to the utter disgust she felt when she thought about the people who had refused to help her. She always believed good people existed in the world, but as she continued to dwell on her incident, she couldn't help but wonder if, perhaps, she had bought into a fairytale.

As the early morning sun peered through the ivory blinds, Cindy's alarm clock blared its usual, irritating anthem. Normally it would take her five presses of the sleep button before she was ready to wake up, but today, only one pass of her clock's tonal tirade was necessary. The burning of her eyes screamed that she should have slept last night, but the creeping feeling of paranoia had whispered in her ears.

Jonas stirred awake beside her, pulling the sheets from his legs as he slowly sat up. Cindy smiled as she watched her husband's back stretch out with a yawn. He looked back towards her, greeting her with a smile.

"Good morning, cutie," he whispered.

"Did you sleep well?"

"You tell me. You didn't sleep at all, did you?"

"How do you know?" Cindy asked.

"Your eyes are as red as mine when I've been sitting in front of the computer screen all day."

She let out a deep yawn. "Are they really that red? That's gross."

Jonas took a moment to himself to admire his wife. The light pouring from the windows caressed the nape of her neck with a luminous amber glow from the morning sun.

"You're still beautiful, sweetie, even with your demon eyes," he said with a sincere smile.

Cindy smiled and cocked her head without breaking her gaze. Jonas leaned in, brushing aside a few strands of her disheveled morning hair and gave her a light good morning kiss.

"Can you please take me to work today?" she pleaded.

"Sure, if you make breakfast." He jerked away suddenly, as if trying to avoid something.

"What are you doing?"

"Oh," he paused, his eyes darting like a busy highway. "I thought you were going to hit me."

Cindy yawned and looked at him with her eyebrows raised. "I think you should make me breakfast for trying to goad me to hit you," she said playfully.

"Fine," he said, defeated.

As Jonas rose from the bed to cook breakfast, Cindy dragged herself into the bathroom. She placed her hands on the edges of the sink and stared into the black void that was the drain. Her toothbrush rested in the cup; her cosmetics hid in the drawer; and her dignity and pride lay lost on an empty sidewalk.

With a reluctant, tentative motion, Cindy looked up at the mirror before her, afraid of what she would find. She saw a woman every bit as broken as she had feared. She thought to herself, *What will I tell the girls when I come in? They'll think I'm an idiot for not minding my own business. I'll just tell them I fell; hopefully Jadie won't tell them the truth. Maybe I should text her? Nah, I'm just being paranoid.*

After breakfast, Jonas had a mischievous grin and walked with an unusual pep to his step as they headed out of the house. It seemed as though he was eager to drop Cindy off at work, which roused her suspicions. "What are you so excited about?"

"You'll see."

When they entered the double garage, Cindy pouted like a small child. "We're taking the nerdmobile? Why can't we take the other car?" The maroon-colored Mitsubishi MiEV sat in the garage with all the qualities of a nerd vehicle. With four doors, tiny wheels, an electric engine, an enormous windshield and oblong headlights, the Mitsubishi MiEV screamed "Enterprise." Jonas glanced at his modest vehicle and then responded to Cindy with his usual, logical argument, "Sweetie, I can go 112 miles without recharging on this car, and it's electric. I'm not taking the other car into the city. That's insane."

"You never drive the other car," she said, her bottom lip protruded from her mouth.

"Honey, it's New York City. The other car needs to go a little faster than ten miles an hour."

As they sat down in the nerdmobile, Jonas pushed the button to activate the ignition; a sudden voice startled Cindy as the robotic female said, "Good morning, Jonas. The time is now 7:30 am. Would you like to set your destination?"

"What the heck is that?" Cindy asked.

"Set destination for Cindy's workplace." He looked over to Cindy and winked at her. "It's a prototype."

The windshield propagated with light blue numbers indicating the speed of the vehicle and a small map showing its current location. The street became covered in a semitransparent purple sheet, covering the road in a giant magenta carpet. Small little icons on the side indicated that pedestrian and vehicle detection had been enabled.

"Umm, okay, this looks cool. When did you install this?" she asked as her curiosity and interest began to pique.

"Oh, you haven't seen anything yet," he said as his eyes lit up with a cocky enthusiasm.

As they began to drive, the car informed Jonas of an upcoming turn in 1.2 miles. A small mileage counter in the corner of the windshield began to tick downwards, letting him know exactly when the turn was coming up. Not only was the computer vocally identifying the route, but also visually guiding him by highlighting the street in purple.

This was far more advanced than an ordinary GPS. It informed Jonas of obscure stop signs, left turn only, yield, do not enter and the most easy-to-miss of them all: the one-way street sign. Upon entering Manhattan, the traffic became thicker and more aggressive. This was the perfect opportunity to test the prototype.

The computer said to Jonas, "Warning, brake immediately to avoid a collision. A vehicle is pulling out from in front of the delivery truck. Slow down to avoid a collision." Sure enough, the driver of a small Porsche pulled out from an obscured parking spot, oblivious to the fact that Jonas was even approaching.

"Jonas, this is amazing. Why isn't this out yet?" Cindy asked.

At that same moment, a flood of people began crossing the street in front of the car. The system began to warn Jonas of every—single—person walking in front of him. "Warning-Warning-Warning-Warning-Pedestrian-Pedestrian-Detected-Pedestrian-Detected—" Jonas muted the machine before it caused a massive audio feedback loop.

"It's still a little buggy," he said while keeping his eyes on the road.

Cindy smiled and caressed the back of Jonas' neck with her index finger and thumb. "I think you've done an excellent job so far," she said, giving his invention her stamp of approval.

His eyes illuminated as a humble, but sincere smile crept between his lips; a compliment from his wife meant more to him than any other accolade he had received in his lifetime.

"Thank you for dropping me off," Cindy said. "Please be careful when you go to work, okay? I love you."

After she kissed him goodbye, Jonas steered his car back into the onslaught of non-stop traffic like a sea captain, at the helm, during a vicious storm.

Cindy walked up the stairs and heard a light commotion muffled behind the studio doors. When she opened the coffee-grain-colored door, the room let out a quiet gasp before falling to complete silence. Cindy paused before stepping into the room, almost as if an invisible wind were hindering her movement. Her gaze rapidly jumped to each young face that stood before her and then to Jadie, standing in the middle of them all.

"Oh my God, Mrs. Ames, are you okay? Ms. Brynfire told us what happened," Priscilla said.

"Did she now?" Her eyes narrowed as a deep frustration was focused with pinpoint precision towards her sister. "I'm okay, girls. It wasn't that serious."

"She told us you kicked their ass bef—"

"Brittany!" Jadie interrupted. "Please don't talk like that," she said in a very stern voice.

From the corner of her eye, Cindy noticed that Priscilla was shaking her head. The girl refused to look Cindy in the eye and had so many wrinkles between the bridge of her nose that she could have passed for an old woman.

"What's the matter, Priscilla?" Cindy asked, stepping into the room with a commanding presence: a necessary façade to convince the girls—and herself—that she was, indeed, OK.

"It's my fault, isn't it?" She looked up at Cindy as wavering white flags flapped inside her eyes.

"What are you talking about, honey?" Cindy said in a motherly tone.

"I never should have asked you to walk me home." Priscilla's voice was crumbling. "It's my fault you got hurt."

Her face shattered as diamonds sprinkled from her young eyes. The embarrassment and shame pushed Priscilla out of the studio to wallow in her guilt privately. Jadie nodded her head as the unspoken words of 'watch the kids' radiated from Cindy's eyes.

Cindy went out to the locker room, spotting Priscilla huddled in the all-too-familiar corner. Priscilla balled herself up into the fetal position; her crossed arms rested atop her knees and her head lay hidden beneath her limbs. Cindy crossed her legs and sat beside Priscilla on the cold tiles. She hung her head low, like a crane, to try to look at Priscilla's face. The inconsolable young girl turned so quickly to face the brick wall that a tear flicked outward towards Cindy. With a reassuring and compassionate touch, Cindy rested her arm around Priscilla's back.

"Hey," she whispered.

Priscilla sniffled but remained silent.

"Don't blame yourself for what happened."

Priscilla refused to speak.

"It was my decision to walk you to the hospital. And even if I didn't, this still could have happened to me. There was no way to know and you shouldn't feel bad for something you're not responsible for."

Priscilla looked up at Cindy."It's not fair. You were only trying to help." Priscilla's voice began to crack and undulate in pitch. "I'm so sorry. I'm really, really sorry." Priscilla leaned in towards Cindy with her arms stretched outward. Cindy hugged Priscilla tightly, as a mother would, signaling to the girl that everything was OK.

Calming Priscilla's frayed nerves was no easy task, but after a few peaceful moments, Priscilla regained control of her breathing and wiped away the tears from her eyes.

"How's your father doing?" Cindy asked.

"He's okay, I guess, but they wanna keep him there for a couple of weeks."

"Why?"

"The bullet pierced his lung. The doctors managed to save him, but he's going to be in recovery for a while."

"I'm sorry," Cindy said.

Priscilla demeanor became impatient. "Don't worry about it, Mrs. Ames. Can we just go back to class to take my mind off of it?"

"Okay."

When they walked back into the classroom, Cindy waved her hand towards Jadie as Priscilla rejoined her classmates. "Gather up the girls, and do some dynamic and static stretch routines with them, K?" Jadie instructed a senior student before walking over to Cindy.

"Why," Cindy growled, "why did you tell the girls what happened to me?"

Cindy took one menacing step forward as Jadie flinched backward into the wall.

"Whoa, back off, psycho." Jadie shoved Cindy back. "Why are you getting upset over this? You didn't tell me to not tell anyone," she said, taking a defensive stance.

"Did you not just see what just happened here? What did you tell them?"

"I told them you were brave; that you did something that no one else ever would have done."

"Yeah, and look what happened to me!"

"I didn't mention that part. I just told them that you kicked their ass and got hurt in the process. They think you're a heroine, Cindy. They really look up to you," Jadie said.

"I'm not!" she snapped. "You're the one who was in the Coast Guard pulling people out of the ocean. You're technically the hero."

"I spent most of my time rescuing drunk people who fell off of cruise ships. Does that sound very heroic to you?"

"Listen, Jadie." Her hands were restless as she continued to speak. "I'm just a woman who made a stupid decision and almost got killed for it. I don't want these girls to follow in my footsteps and get hurt."

Jadie shook her head in annoyance and turned towards the studio. Before leaving, Jadie said to her "It may not have been a smart decision, Cindy, but it was the right decision regardless of the consequences. You, of all people, should know that."

"That was a long time ag—"

Jadie slammed the door shut, sending a thundering sound wave throughout the locker room. Cindy exhaled and rolled her eyes.

Hours later after the usual class routine was finished, Cindy stepped out of the studio to call Jonas. One by one, her students would walk past her and wave goodbye, as a ringback tone buzzed in her ear.

"Pick up," she muttered to herself while faking a smile and waving goodbye to another student walking out the door.

"Good night, Mrs. Ames," Priscilla said as she walked past Cindy.

Cindy looked up at Priscilla. "Are you going to be okay going home?"

"Yeah, I'll be fine, Mrs. Ames. Thank you for everything," she said sweetly.

"Take care, hun," she said while returning her attention to the cell phone. Finally her phone call got through but just to the answering machine.

Cindy let out a disappointed sigh as she hung up the cell before the 'beep' went off. She looked over to Jadie, who was busy stuffing her things into her duffel bag, getting ready to call it a night. Cindy's pride was preventing her from speaking, especially after their earlier quibble, but she knew there wasn't much choice. She walked over to Jadie but hesitated in her approach.

"Hey," Cindy said.

"What do you want?" she snarled. Jadie's attitude implied she already knew Cindy was going to ask for something.

Cindy sighed. "I'm…" she paused.

Jadie's eyebrows arched with an uncaring demeanor. "You are, what?"

"Don't rush me!" Cindy snapped.

"Come on, Cindy. I don't have all day. I have things to do: laundry, groceries…"

"Jonas isn't picking up, and I need a ride home," she said with a wince.

Jadie paused and looked up at Cindy with a menacing glare.

"Okay, number one: you should have told me earlier before I had things to do. Number two: what a surprise, I have things to do."

"Jadie, I know you're still upset with me for earl—"

Jadie interrupted, "No, I've gotten over that. Today is the most inconvenient day to ask me for this. Why don't you take the bus home like you always do?"

"What do you want to hear? That I'm terrified?" Cindy responded in frustration. "That I'm scared to death to go home alone at night? Are you happy now?"

Jadie drew back as shivers washed down her spine. In that instant, she began to regret everything she had said. The guilt of having told her injured sister that she was too busy to take her home consumed her conscience. Her chest felt as though she were a piece of wood clenched between a vice, unable to shake off the shame.

"I'm sorry," Jadie said.

"Just forget it." Cindy turned away, waving her hand. "I'll wait for Jonas to call me back."

Jadie grabbed her apple-colored duffel bag and wrapped her arms around her sister. Cindy was not pleased, however, and stood there looking out of the corner of her eye, shaking her head.

"I didn't mean to make you mad. I spoke without thinking."

"Can we please just leave before it gets too late," Cindy said as if ignoring Jadie's apology.

"Sure," Jadie said in a hushed tone.

Later that night, Cindy's home was dimly lit with just the living room light on. The entire space was covered in a warm amber hue that ironically felt more lonesome than welcoming. Cindy had tried for the past four hours to reach Jonas, but he hadn't even called back, which was very unusual for him. A million malicious thoughts began to glide through her imagination as whispers and lies of Jonas being hurt or in danger swarmed inside her mind.

Her once-inviting living space, mixed with modern and antique furnishings, had transformed into a prison of deep shadows. Floor lamps and plants created ominous figures that stood along the walls. Old antique frames, knickknacks and furniture became symbols of an Amityville horror. She huddled into the corner of the couch and tucked her knees and arms in towards her chest. Any sounds she heard of men talking in low, audible whispers made her heart race. The beating in her chest would strike with such strength that she feared her heart would explode from all the stress. Still there was no sign of Jonas, and the longer he was away from home, the more her anxiety would build.

As she sat there counting the seconds, she heard the sound of a car door slam and people walking past her house. She jolted off the couch and ran towards the window, peering into the darkness to see if intruders were heading her way. She exhaled a sigh of relief as she recognized that it was just her neighbors coming back from a night out on the town.

The refreshing feeling of calm that had washed over her body was replaced with the stinging frustration of realizing that her husband had not yet appeared. *It's 8 pm and he still hasn't called!* she thought to herself. Cindy turned on the TV to pass the time. Multitudes of mind-numbing reality shows droned by as the hours ticked away. Before long, Cindy had dozed off on the couch, oblivious to the inane chattering of the TV.

Cindy enjoyed a brief moment of peace, where nothing could disturb her but the ruminations of random dreams. When Cindy awoke, she didn't even realize that the TV had been shut off and that the lights in the kitchen had come on. As she lie reclined, her teeth peeking from behind the lips of her agape mouth, a warm smooth sensation pressed against her cheek. A soft blanket covered her body and the subtle scent of aftershave and cologne stimulated her olfactory senses.

Her glazed-over eyes opened with a lazy grace, as she looked over and saw Jonas hanging over her shoulder, smiling, always smiling with elated wrinkles in his eyes.

"Hey you," he said quietly.

Cindy gradually stirred to life but was incoherent as she mumbled, "Jonas, wha… mm… when…?"

Jonas maintained the gentlest nature in his voice as he spoke to Cindy, "I'm sorry I didn't call you. Work was hectic today."

Cindy's groggy demeanor soon turned into a menacing frown. As her eyes awakened, so did the creature of aggravation.

"Why didn't you call me?" she snapped.

Jonas leaned back, slightly peeved at Cindy's response. "I told you that work was crazy."

"That's no excuse. You should have called me when you got out," she said. Her attitude was rushing to the surface like hot springs from an angry geyser.

"I came home as soon as I was done," he said as he pulled away. "Why are you getting so upset?" he continued as he walked over to the kitchen.

"I had to beg Jadie to take me home today. I thought you were going to pick me up."

He took a sip of water and then looked over to Cindy with an arched eyebrow. "You never said you needed me to pick you up."

"Jonas, let me ask you this. Would you want me to walk home by myself, at night, after what happened yesterday?" Cindy said. She cocked her head to the side, confident in her sound logic.

"Of course not," he replied. The sound of his voice began to hint at his dissolving patience, but he refused to allow himself to get angry with his wife.

"Do you know I actually had to beg Jadie to take me home? She had to go an hour out of her way just to drop me off."

"Cindy!" he shouted in frustration. "I said I was sorry and that work was insane. Did I want you to walk home by yourself? No, of course not. I didn't have a choice—if I could have brought you home, I would have," his irritation now seeping out of his voice.

"You still should have called regardless," she said with an unrelenting persistence.

"Cindy," Jonas pulled back his voice in hopes of ending her complaints. "This isn't the first time I haven't been able to call you. What are you really upset about?"

She tilted her head down and looked up at Jonas with a melancholy pout hanging from her lip. She needed to put aside her hubris, something that Cindy had always struggled with. "I was afraid of being in the house by myself," she said. "I just wanted you here so I could feel safe."

Jonas shook his head and said with a smile, "Sweetie, I'm not trying to poke fun. But you do realize that you're the one that kicks ass in this household. If someone comes bursting through that door, I'm… probably gonna get beat up."

Cindy placed her hand over her head and let out a brief chortle. "I know, but I'm not in a good place right now. I'm sorry if I'm being needy… I know I shouldn't be dependent on you for everything. I'm just not used to feeling so defenseless."

"I have to be honest—I am not used to seeing you like this," Jonas said.

"What's that supposed to mean?"

He walked over to the couch with his glass of water in hand and sat down next to his wife, who curled up like a scared armadillo.

"Well…" He offered her a sip of water, but Cindy declined with a soft hand wave. He took a big gulp and let out a refreshed, "Ahhh…It just means I'm not used to seeing my strong, independent wife afraid of the world."

"If the world wasn't full of selfish pricks willing to kill people for the stupidest things… maybe I wouldn't be afraid."

"Whoa," Jonas was taken aback. "Easy there, I didn't mean to get you riled up." He reached his arm towards Cindy and pulled her head in towards his chest while setting down his glass of water on the coffee table. He gave her a loving kiss unto her scalp and asked, "Are you OK?"

"I'll be fine." She sighed deeply. "I just need to… I don't know, get over it, I guess."

"I love you," he reminded her, "and I will always be here for you."

"I know you will," she said with a smile. "But! You still didn't call me."

"Holy crap, Cindy," he said exasperated. "Are you serio—"

"I'm just teasing," she said, tapping his chin.

"Oh," he uttered. His anger evaporated as quickly as it had arrived. "All right, you really want to know what's going on at my job, why I didn't call?"

"If you don't want to tell me, I respect your privacy," Cindy said with fake sincerity.

"No, no, I'll tell you." Her husband's mood soured as he looked off into an ordinary corner of the room. Cindy's eyes perked up as she read his body language, realizing that things were more serious than she was aware.

"What happened? Does it have something to do with one of those projects you never want to talk about?" Cindy asked.

"I can't elaborate too much on this, okay? I'm just going to tell you the bare bones, and you need to promise me you won't ask any further questions."

"Or you can tell me about your top-secret project," she said.

"No," Jonas replied. "Promise me you won't ask anymore questions about that."

"Okay, I promise."

"I may lose funding on all of my projects if I don't have a prototype ready, like, now." His eyes glazed over into some invisible part of the living room, his attention not focused on anything. His lips moved but it was almost as if the words refused to escape.

"Hey... hey you." Cindy sat up and pulled Jonas in for a hug. "I'm still here."

"I don't know what I'm going to do."

"I'll tell you what you're going to do. You know how you keep saying you believe in me and that I can do anything I set my mind to? Well, I believe that you can get that prototype done," Cindy said, reassuring Jonas with support and love.

"How? This is the most complicated project I've ever done. There's still so much programming and building to be done. How will I ev—"

"Shh, don't think; just do. Isn't that what I've always told you?"

"Yeah," Jonas replied, but his conviction was left wanting.

Cindy tried one last time to inquire about Jonas' project. "So you're still not going to tell me what this project is that you've been working on?"

"I would love to tell you, but I'm not allowed—and you promised not to ask!" he replied.

"Who am I going to tell? Jadie?

"And then Jadie will tell your mom, and your mom will tell everyone else's mom, and then suddenly, all the women in the world know. And the men will be clueless because women don't like to tell men about important things."

"I think you got it backwards, drama queen. It's the men who don't like to tell the women anything. We talk all the time," she said, correcting Jonas.

"See, sweetie? That's why I can't tell you what I'm working on," he said, grinning.

"Oh you—that was a dirty trick! I'm going to bed."

"You sleepy?" he said with a childish cadence to his voice.

"Yeah, some of us have to work. Ooh, burn!" she taunted.

"Technically, I haven't lost my job yet."

"Oh, too soon then?"

"Go to bed. I'm sick of you," he joked.

"I'm sorry. That was mean," Cindy said playfully. "Well, while I was waiting for you, I packed you a lunch in my boredom, so don't forget to take it tomorrow."

"Speaking of which, do you need a ride tomorrow?" he asked with trepidation.

"Umm," she was hesitant to answer.

"I'll give you a ride. I just need to know now, but I won't be able to pick you up."

"Okay, then just take me to work. I'll figure out the rest."

As she walked towards the bedroom alone, she wondered if Jonas had any idea how terrified she was about tomorrow. Her heart was beating like an angry animal trying to escape from its cage. Never in her life had Cindy experienced this type of fear. Jonas noticing that she hasn't been her strong, confident self only exacerbated her paranoia.

During the night, Cindy kept awakening not by fear of criminals trying to break into her house, but by anger and frustration that no one had caught the perpetrators who had ruined her. She had spoken to a robbery detective that night—he explained that they didn't have any leads, but were on the case. Cindy saw right through the detective's smoke screen. He didn't mention the lack of surveillance footage, no witnesses with relevant information, and no weapons from which to draw prints. He was just going to canvass the neighborhood one more time and never come back. It angered her to know this, but there was nothing she could do.

The more she imagined herself walking down that same street, the more she dreamt of different outcomes for that night. It was no coincidence that each of these daydreams resulted in her subduing or killing the criminals. Cindy was becoming possessed with thoughts of revenge. Her mind kept flooding back to the heartless teens who walked past and took photos of her dying, not lifting a finger to call an ambulance or even ask if she was OK.

Cindy realized that she was over-thinking everything; she shook her head and sighed the anger away. She couldn't understand why she was unable to overcome this, especially considering that she had been in much worse situations. She forced herself to go to sleep, hoping the suffering would be recede by tomorrow.

CHAPTER 3

AWAKENING

Two weeks later, Jonas informed Cindy that today he was revealing his prototype to investors. Cindy rubbed his shoulders and offered words of encouragement like a coach preparing a fighter about to get into the ring. "You're going to do great, kid. Just remember… Cindy loves ya," she said in a deep, grumbling voice, mimicking her best Rocky impression. A smirk drew across Jonas' face as his wife's humor diffused his nervousness. Cindy got so caught up in wishing Jonas the best that she lost track of the time.

Jonas and Cindy got caught in rush-hour traffic, which made Cindy deathly afraid of what Jadie would say when she arrived at the gymnasium. After waving her husband goodbye, Cindy walked through the door, ready for her fate.

"You know you're late again, right?" Jadie said with arms folded.

"Yes, I know. We got stuck in traffic as usual," Cindy replied

"You're in luck. Everyone else is running late too. Two girls have showed up so far, and I got them started on some floor exercises."

"Thanks, I appreciate it," Cindy said. But Jadie seemed keenly aware of Cindy's melancholy demeanor on this beautiful morning.

"So what's going on? You're usually chipper during this spring weather," she asked.

"Jonas came home late last night," Cindy looked down towards the ground, her bangs falling in front of her somber eyes.

"He told me he might be losing his job."

Jadie stepped forward and sympathetically placed her arm on Cindy's shoulder.

Cindy continued, "He just kind of dropped it all on me last night; we almost got into a huge fight over it."

"You want to take the day off? I can take your class," Jadie said.

"No, that won't be necessary. It's Jonas I'm worried about."

"Okay, if you ins—" Jadie was cut off mid-sentence as Cindy stood abruptly and looked into the studio like a deer catching the sound of a hunter's boots in the brush.

Jadie tried to ask Cindy what was going on, but Cindy waved her off and remained focused on the room. Without uttering a whisper, Cindy charged into the gym at an electric pace. Something in the air felt wrong. Jadie looked on, flabbergasted and unsure of what to do. There was uneasiness to Cindy's movements; something that just hinted of an impending doom.

In an instant, Cindy's coral sweatpants became a blur of streaks. Jadie rushed in behind her and looked up to see that the roof was salivating like a hungry animal;

yet when she looked towards the window, there was nary a cloud in the sky.

"Girls, move!" Cindy yelled, as the children looked at her with bewilderment.

The room began to rumble, causing one of the girls to stumble backwards. The girl looked up and spotted the dripping roof bulging and creaking like an alien life form, imploring her to move away. The other student, who was stretching out her legs, was oblivious to what was going on. The music in her earbuds blasted so loudly that she had no idea of the panic that was billowing inside the room.

The student screamed, "Hey!" as Cindy shoved her away from the collapsing overhead ceiling. A rusty water pipe roared out from the blackened cave above and dropped down over Cindy's head like a log going to a sawmill. "Cindy!" Jadie screamed as the avalanche of water came crashing down over Cindy with the regurgitating pipe in tow. Cindy raised her arms and braced herself against the decrepit monster. The force and weight of the pipe was immense, but Cindy sustained her ground and managed to push back against the rusted cylinder. She twisted her torso just enough to deflect the leviathan to the side of the gym, where it clanged to the ground, continuing to spew endless amounts of water.

Cindy's drenched hair looked almost charcoal. The water had washed away all of the volume and color from her usually well-maintained locks. She pushed the tendrils away from her eyes and saw Jadie talking to someone on her cell phone while protecting the child like a lioness would guard her cub. Cindy dusted the rust off her hands and looked over to the pipe as the water died down from its gaping maw.

"Are you okay, Brittany?" Cindy asked.

"That was awesome," the child said with a look of amazement.

"I asked if you were okay," Cindy reiterated with frustration.

"Yeah, I'm fine, sorry."

Jadie hung up her cell phone and looked at her sister in disbelief. "Cindy, are you okay?"

"I'm fine. Who were you talking to?" she asked.

"I called the facilities manager, so I could get the water shut—" Jadie stifled a chuckle.

Cindy's eyes squinted with suspicion. "Something funny?"

"Good thing you didn't wear white today. You look like an angry, wet dog. I would use the other word, but there's kids around," Jadie said. Despite the grim situation, Jadie had managed to pierce the tension in the room with a ray of light-heartedness.

Cindy glanced down and saw all of her soaked clothing discolored into a darker hue. She took one step off the sopping wet mat and was greeted with a loud squish emanating from her pasty sneakers. Her cold socks tickled her toes as water spilled from every pore. Everyone—except for Cindy—couldn't help but laugh at the absurdity of the situation, and Cindy's moistened anger only served to add fuel to the fire.

"You think this is funny, huh?" Cindy said in an unamused tone.

Cindy cocked her head back and flung her hair towards Jadie and Brittany, splashing them with a wide spray of water. Brittany squealed while Jadie yelled, "All right, all right. I get the point."

The studio door clacked open as a Chinese man walked in with toolbox in hand. He stood on the gym floor in complete shock and asked in a very thick accent, "What da hell happen here?"

"That is a very good question," Cindy responded.

"That's a very big hole. You gonna have to fix it," he said.

"Are you serious, Mr. Cheng?" Jadie asked, alarmed.

He laughed and said, "Of course not! I'm gonna look at the problem and see what happen. I be back."

The sisters breathed a sigh of relief as Mr. Cheng walked out of the room. Jadie stood up and walked over to Cindy, who was wringing out her clothes over a nearby cleaning bucket.

"So…" she said to Cindy with a smug look on her face.

"Yes?" Cindy responded as she squeezed the water out of her zippered hoodie.

"I don't want you to get used to this buuuuuut, I have to admit that I may have been a tiny bit impressed by your heroics today. This is the one time I can see why you lift weights," she admitted.

"Does that mean you'll stop calling me derogatory names?" Cindy asked.

"What derogatory names?" Jadie replied innocently.

"Let's see, Arnold Schwarzenegger."

"Nope, never did that."

"Hulk, She-Hulk."

"Never."

"Muscle brain."

"That was only one time!"

"And let's not forget my favorite, roid rage."

"Oh, come on, that one's funny when you're mad."

"Are you going to stop or what?" Cindy asked.

"I will… tone it down," Jadie replied.

"Funny you mention that, because I'm pretty sure you need to tone it up." Cindy pinched a tiny portion of fat on Jadie's tummy. "Fatty."

Jadie smacked Cindy's hand away. "Don't try to play the victim. You're the queen of insults." Cindy smirked at Jadie's comment, acknowledging it to be true. "But regardless, good job, sis," Jadie said.

Cindy didn't say anything, but in the back of her mind, she was awed that Jadie, again, had applauded Cindy for something. Twenty years of competitive rivalry, and it only took one rusty pipe and a mugging to get a compliment from her sister.

While Jadie and Cindy were distracted, the rest of the class had finally arrived. When they saw the mess, the girls let out a collective, "Holy crap!" At the same time, Mr. Cheng came in with a ladder hoisted between his arms. "Excuse me, girls," he said, maneuvering through the students.

Cindy and Jadie walked over to the students and explained the situation, informing them that class would be cancelled until the repairs were finished. The girls were disappointed, but they were still very proud of their instructor. In the eyes of her students, Cindy was a true heroine, whether she chose to accept the title or not.

She tried to ignore the praise, but she could not deny the thrill she felt during the rescue. The feeling of satisfaction and the relief of being able to respond to an emergency situation was empowering for Cindy. She would never say this aloud, but Cindy secretly enjoyed all of the attention. Running off the dizzying but fading adrenaline, Cindy decided that today would be a good day to surprise her husband at the lab. An offer to take him out on a dinner date would be the perfect remedy for his stress. Of course, she had to take care of some things at the studio first—and get changed.

****

Inside of Lucent Labs, Jonas, Michael and the other researchers were now preparing their prototype presentation. DARPA and a variety of companies were all present for the SIRCA unveiling. While some of the companies were mainly interested in a military platform, even investors from medical companies had arrived to view this mysterious new product and evaluate its medicinal applications.

With applications ranging from treating muscular dystrophy to stopping bullets and reducing exposure to hazardous materials, this system had the potential to be among the most profitable inventions of all time. But companies only care about the bottom line. They want it fast; they want it cheap; and they want it now. There was a very real pressure pushing Jonas up against the wall. The R&D expenditures alone had his company teetering on the edge of bankruptcy. Unless he could impress these investors, Jonas could lose his company and maybe even his home. All of his resources were allocated to completing SIRCA. There was no plan B.

Jonas downed a cup of coffee and said, "We're not ready, Michael."

"I know that," Michael whispered as his hand braced Jonas' shoulder. "But we have a prototype that 'looks' like it's working. All we need to do is convince them that we're finished and use the 'bug fixing' time to complete the project."

"What if the system breaks down in the middle of my presentation? How will that look?"

"Aren't you supposed to be Mr. Think Positive? We can still do a complete remote access if the computer bugs out. All you have to focus on is persuading them," Michael said.

"Right, just do," Jonas said as he took in a deep breath and put on his best game face.

Jonas stepped into the steel-reinforced chamber as the black silhouettes of audience members scattered into their seats, their intentions masked by shadows. In the center of the chamber, a small beaker sat on a table in the test chamber like the Holy Grail. Its contents appeared metallic in texture but fluid like water, as if someone melted down thousands of quarters into a small glass cup. Jonas walked out in front of the panel, wracked with fear. This moment would either make or break his company, and the pressure to perform could not have been greater. It was time to make history.

"Since the dawn of time, mankind has constantly sought new and ingenious weaponry. Defensive technology has similarly advanced from shields and plates of armor to ironclad warships. Defense has been just as important as offense.

"We here at Lucent Labs have developed a suit that gives an ordinary infantry soldier the strength of a bulldozer, the firepower of a platoon, and the armor of a tank all in one elegant package. My colleagues and I are proud to present to you the Stealth, Infiltration, Combat and Reconnaissance Armor: SIRCA."

With those fateful words, the liquid inside of the beaker bubbled to life. It climbed out from its glass enclosure and slithered its way down to the concrete floor. The liquid began to grow in shape, rising up from the floor, taking on the form of an androgynous human being. It stood idle with no expression or emotion, no face and no features. It was a mold of a human that reflected its environment within its silver, metallic surface. Jonas took a few steps forward and pointed at the machine.

"This, friends, is the future. Imagine this!" he said with unbridled exuberance.

He stepped into an explosion-resistant case as the silver humanoid walked onto a bullseye painted on the floor. Once the robot was in position, an invisible panel within the floor slid open and the sounds of whirring and servos echoed from within the black mouth, filling the room with smells of steel and gun powder.

A metal monstrosity rose from the floor, a turret equipped with so many illegal weapons that Jonas and his team could be thrown in jail for two lifetimes. The muzzle of the turret stood a mere ten feet away from the humanoid robot, as high-pitched beeps indicated weapon-ready status.

"An armor capable of withstanding ballistics ranging from small arms to high caliber rifles." He covered his ears and braced himself for the oncoming demonstration.

The turret whirred to life as it began to unleash a volley of hollow point and armor piercing rounds into SIRCA. Bullets designed to destroy humans and armor alike bounced off the SIRCA or shattered upon hitting the surface of the armor. Small nicks and scratches appeared where the bullets struck, leaving light colored marks on its metal skin, but neither type of ammunition penetrated the armor.

"The armor offers complete full body protection unlike anything the world has ever seen. Not a single skin cell is exposed to any danger when the armor is active. No longer would a soldier be vulnerable to explosives or shrapnel, rendering suicide bombers obsolete. Users can also avoid contamination from traversing irradiated or chemically-poisoned terrain," Jonas stated.

The humanoid robot stretched its mechanical arms in front of its body. Metal spikes jutted out from its forearms, morphing into gun platforms.

"Just to clarify, these are not machine guns, but rather miniaturized rail guns," Jonas said proudly.

Three targets popped out of the sidewalls while the robot took aim. Without missing a beat, the machine aimed its arms at each target; one by one it hit the dead center of each bullseye. The room filled with skin shaking shockwaves from each blast. The machine's weapons did not scream like a typical gunpowder weapon, but the energized blasts were still deafening. The blue muzzle flash erupting from the chamber seemed out of this world. The audience murmured with excitement as the presentation continued.

"All of the system's weapons have built-in targeting systems, which automatically adjust the user's aim to hit targets regardless of distance," he said while stepping out of his safety enclosure.

"What if a civilian or soldier were trapped under building debris, or maybe even a tank?"

The SIRCA humanoid walked over to a row of preset pipes, rebar and a steel girder. The strength demonstration commenced with the machine bending each construction material into a 'U' shape with complete ease. The demo was so effortless that Jonas needed to pick up the rebar and show that he could not bend it back. Jonas walked over to the steel girder, glanced at it, turned to the audience with his eyebrows raised, and walked away.

"You may be asking yourself, 'Jonas, we've seen the combat part of the armor, we've even seen the armor part of it. What about the rest?' You've only seen the tip of the iceberg."

Jonas turned his attention back to the SIRCA as it walked towards the wall.

"Using gecko-inspired technology and optical camouflage, we have created the ultimate surveillance and infiltration system."

SIRCA began climbing the wall like a spider. It moved about with ease and grace, almost as if crawling on walls were second nature to it. When it reached the top of the ceiling, the SIRCA froze in place and disappeared. The audience clamored up to their feet as they walked towards the glass window to see where the machine had gone. Realizing that the machine had made itself completely invisible, the audience erupted in roaring applause. Never had these veteran investors seen such an amazing display of futuristic technology.

Jonas smiled and sighed, relieved that he had managed to survive one of his most grueling ordeals. He looked over to Michael and gave him a thumbs up. Michael returned the gesture and then turned towards the other scientists in the control room, shaking each of their hands. As Jonas was walking out of the testing chamber, a strange electrical sound began crackling in the room. The stench of burning rubber wafted into everyone's noses as an immediate panic draped over the attendees.

Michael walked out of the control room and looked around the chamber, trying to track down the smell. As he walked up to Jonas, they followed the sound and smell of burning electrical wire. When they looked up to where they had left the SIRCA, they saw that the machine was seizing violently. The cloaking device flickered in and out, as sparks burst from the metallic human.

Like a dying insect, the SIRCA dropped from the ceiling and splattered all over the floor. Everyone in attendance looked on with disbelief as Jonas and Michael ran to the now-lifeless puddle. Jonas screamed in panic as he cried out, "Turn it back on! Turn it back on!"

The team in the control room scrambled around like chickens with their heads cut off in a desperate attempt to reactivate the system before it was too late. Their attempts were futile—the system refused to respond to any commands. The audience stood by watching, displeased and wrought with a feeling of deception. The collapse of the system revealed to the investors that this prototype wasn't even that—it was snake oil being sold by a con artist. The DARPA chief tried to convince them that SIRCA was worth their money, but his pleas fell on deaf ears.

Jonas watched helpless, as his financial future walked out the door. There was nothing he could say or do to bring them back. How could they believe him after what had just transpired? Both General Ord and the DARPA chief walked up to Jonas and expressed their sincerest apologies as they broke the news that the funding for SIRCA and Lucent Labs would be cut. Sean said to Jonas before leaving, "I'll find a way to get your funding back. I know you guys tried your best. I'll give some people I know a call, maybe they can get you a job."

As the General and DARPA Chief walked out, Jonas stood there in silence. The rest of the team appeared behind him with their heads held low, ashamed and disappointed of their failure. They patted each other on the back trying to reassure one another that it would be all right, but nothing could cure their sense of defeat. Some team members took it harder than others, breaking down in tears upon realizing that they were unemployed. These brilliant men may have been capable of designing groundbreaking technology, but even geniuses cannot surmount the obstacles of a struggling economy. Finding employment would be difficult for everyone, and there weren't enough funds left to finish developing any of the other projects. Lucent Labs would have to be shut down for good.

"Sorry, man," Michael said. Jonas was unresponsive, staring at the floor. "We did our best. I'm not sure what happened."

Jonas looked up at Michael. "The camouflage overheated."

"But we installed the heat resistant materials," Michael countered.

Jonas shook his head, "Yes, we did, but Sid was still finishing the code regulating the temperature and evening out power distribution. He couldn't finish it in time. I'm sure if he had just a minute or two, he would have been done."

Michael turned away and pushed his hands through his oily, black hair, exasperated that they had been seconds away from success.

"This company is done for," Jonas said.

"I'm sorry I let you down," Michael replied.

"Damn..." Jonas muttered while shaking his head.

"What?" Michael asked.

Jonas turned his head away in shame. "I have to tell Cindy what happened."

Michael grabbed Jonas' shoulder and pulled him away from the lab. "Let's take the guys out for drinks or something. We need to get outta here."

"Yeah, let's do that, I'll go get the boys," Jonas replied.

The team followed Jonas and Michael out of the demonstration area, defeated, shamed and depressed. The greatest insult was not that the system failed. It was the fact that, for a moment, they had almost gotten away with it. The test lab became a silent ghost town, occupied only by the lonesome buzzing of fluorescent lights.

****

When Cindy arrived at the lab that evening, she discovered that the workplace was abandoned. She put away her visitor ID card after realizing that the security guards and receptionist were gone. It was all very strange and surreal. Cindy, not sure what to think, walked deeper into the complex, confused as to what was happening. Her steps were gradual and paced, but every once in a while, a shiver would go down her spine whenever she thought she had heard someone behind her.

As she made her way down the corridor that Jonas frequented on a daily basis, Cindy realized this might be her best opportunity to satiate her curiosity. For years, Jonas had refused to tell Cindy what top-secret projects he had been working on, and it peeved her to no end. She respected his privacy, but she found herself unable to resist the temptation of discovering what he's really been up to. She walked down to the end of the corridor and spotted a sign that read, "Test Lab—AUTHORIZED PERSONNEL ONLY."

The door was closed and had a black access card pad attached to it. Cindy exhaled deeply through her nose, recognizing that this would be a dead end for her. Not wanting to give up just yet, she whipped out her visitor ID card and waved it in front of the pad. It beeped as Cindy's eyes gaped open in excitement. But just as quickly, they closed in disappointment; the access pad retained its red light, and mocked her relentlessly.

Having surrendered, Cindy made a last-ditch attempt to open the door by giving it a soft push. To her surprise, the door began to open and continued to open like a treasure chest revealing its gold stores. She was in utter shock as the excitement began to kick into overdrive. She stepped inside the test lab and gazed in awe at the sophisticated equipment surrounding her. The control room was full of advanced computers, with another door that led into a server room. Beside it, a huge test lab was filled with various gizmos and alien-looking devices.

She spotted the robotic turret and began walking towards it, avoiding the charred black ash on the floor. Knowing that this was a weapon, she made sure to stay away from the front of the device and looked at the menacing robotic creature from a safe distance. *Is this what he's been building?* Cindy wondered as she turned her attention towards the location where the attendees had been sitting. The small room was full of empty maroon seats with the occasional magazine left behind on one of the cushions. Cindy did an about-face and saw targets scored with an unknown bullet type, and various bent pipes sitting scattered on a table.

"I guess he was working on this gun, then," she muttered to herself. Although she had only partially sated her curiosity, she had seen enough to start heading home. As she began dejectedly walking towards the exit, her footsteps echoing in the chamber, a small glimmer of light caught the corner of Cindy's eye. The glint was so small it would have been undetectable had it not been for the fluorescent lights above.

She followed the sheen to the puddle where Jonas' experiment had failed. She noticed its unusual texture and color; it was definitely not transparent enough to be water. She saw her reflection blur on the surface of the pool and wondered if perhaps it was liquid metal. She double-checked the environment to make sure she wouldn't trigger any alarms as she drew near, but the coast seemed clear. Cindy bent down to get a better view of the chrome liquid and marveled at its beauty.

She reached down towards the liquid and instantly pulled back. Jonas was working on top-secret projects. There was no telling what that innocuous-looking puddle could be—acidic, toxic, gruesomely lethal? Cindy glanced back towards the nearby pipes and debris; she just couldn't help but wonder. She walked over to the table and grabbed the bent pipe, dipping the tip of the bent tube into the pool.

With a fine sample collected, Cindy pulled the pipe to her eyes for a closer inspection. She was wowed by its innocent beauty. It shimmered like a teardrop encased in silver, reminding her of a beautiful piece of jewelry. Cindy held her index finger near the metal drop, waiting to touch it. She listened for sounds of burning and waited to see if the pipe would melt her hands. *Could I touch it?* she wondered. It seemed harmless, but would she be able to wash it off afterward? Would her index finger be forever branded with a silver blotch?

Cindy's finger hovered mere centimeters from the silver jewel, but she had decided not to touch it. As she pulled her finger away, the silver splotch jumped from the pipe and latched onto her finger! The cold temperature was startling and the stickiness annoyed Cindy, but all of those sensations were put aside as one unsettling feeling rose above the others. The reflective liquid was still moving...

Cindy tried to rub the metal off of her finger, without any effect, almost as if her finger was soaked in permanent ink. Cindy remained calm and searched for any faucets to rinse off her hand. The puddle suddenly sprouted hideous tendrils that latched onto Cindy's clothing.

"Holy crap!" she yelped, as the metal wrapped itself around Cindy's arm, twisting like yeast, consuming her turtleneck in the process.

"Oh no, no, no! Get off, get off!" she repeated, while attempting to shake the metal off her clothing. Despite her best efforts, the silver continued to crawl up her arm like a man-eating worm. She did, however, start to notice that the chrome creature was only sticking to her clothing and not her skin—besides her finger—so Cindy did the only thing she could think of.

Cindy pulled her blue sweater off and kicked her dignity to the curb, praying that no one would walk in on her in this vulnerable state. Her philosophy—dating back to at least one horrible date in college—was that it was better to lose one's dignity than to be eaten alive by a possibly-sentient metallic monster. Throwing her sweater to the ground, Cindy's body tattled on her little secret. Her stomach tightened, revealing developed abdominal muscles with each breath; the paired six muscles ran up along her torso with obliques attached on opposite sides. Her back had various dimples and shapes spread across the length of her body, representing years of grueling gymnastics training. Her biceps were full and her shoulders were strong, feminine but powerful. Her conservative attire had masked the strength that Cindy harbored within.

Yet despite all the strength exuding from her body, muscle mass did nothing to prevent being consumed alive. The fear of being eaten by a blob-like creature pushed Cindy up against the glass observation window. She watched the living puddle eat away at her crumpled sweater like a starving moth. She trembled with fear as her skin squealed as she slid across the glass pane. Her hands gripped onto the lip of the glass ledge so tightly that the tips of her fingers became milky white.

Suddenly, Cindy felt a strange hand grab at her sculpted leg. She looked down near her high-heeled leather boots and saw that the liquid had broken off into segments and followed Cindy to the wall. It was wrapping around her khaki pants like stretched bubblegum, except this time it hardened with each successful inch it stole from Cindy. The sticky syrup began transforming into a hardened shell that was fusing with her body.

She thrust herself away from the observational window, leaving behind an impression of her back muscles and natural skin oils pressed upon the glass pane. She looked up towards the ceiling with her eyes closed, her hair falling over her nose, and whispered, "Please, God." She clawed at the metal and tried to wedge her thumb between the goo and her skin so she could pull it off. It was no use, trying to remove the metal was like trying to tear off her own skin.

She grabbed onto her hardening leg and tried to scratch off the silver slime with her rose-colored fingernails, anything to get the robotic monster off of her body. It, unfortunately, had the opposite effect; the metal began to stick to her cuticles and began accelerating up her body. She ran back to her discarded sweater and saw that there were still remnants of the puddle clinging to the remains of her shirt. She threw caution to the wind and picked up the blouse to try wiping off the metal slime. Her muscles worked in unison as she attempted to remove the reflective mercury, but it was only a temporary success.

The resolve of the SIRCA was too great. It adapted to Cindy and began to harden the instant it made contact with more of her body. It stiffened near the joints in her knees and forced Cindy down into a crawling position. Her arms shook as her hands slammed the ground with a wet slap. She whimpered in frustration. The liquid continued to travel throughout her body, making Cindy's worst fear a reality. The metallic puddle was now attached to her skin and went between every line separating her muscles.

It continued to eat everything in its path, from the threads of her clothing to the buttons and zipper on her waist. The machine tightened around Cindy's torso, pushing inward, crunching her body like a car compactor. Cindy's breaths became strained and raspy, almost as if she were suffering an asthma attack. The chrome slime had now eaten away Cindy's bra, encasing her chest in a thick, hard shell. Her entire form was now enveloped like a chocolate banana dipped in metal.

The time for the sealing process to complete had arrived. Tendrils on Cindy's neck slowly crept upward, oozing from her jaw up to her cheeks. Cindy had become muted, paralyzed in place, quaking in terror as she lost all control of the

95

situation. The silver threads shot outward like a spider wrapping its victim in a cocoon. Cindy's vision was blinded when her entire head vanished into the silver helmet. Within the darkness, she felt the warm air of carbon dioxide stagnate in front of her. No new oxygen was coming in and the air was pooling inside the helmet.

The metal skin squeezed even tighter around her chest. Little bulges of bone popped out of place near her ribs, causing excruciating pain. She tried to hold back her screams, but the agony was unbearable. Cindy bellowed a deafening shriek, muffled by her eggshell helmet. The remaining oxygen disappeared from the helmet, locking Cindy in with whatever air she had left in her lungs.

Tears blurred her vision as the feeling of being blindfolded, suffocated, and crushed overwhelmed her senses. The reflective steel began to reshape her body in ways that were not intended like someone pulling her arms out of their sockets. It was an excruciating experience. Her body deformed into a twisted visage of a human like a stretched-out scarecrow. The lack of oxygen and the encroaching liquid silver brought Cindy crashing down and rendered her prostrate. There was no help in sight; Cindy's curiosity would be her swan song. Her breathing slowed with the pace of her heart; Jonas' invention was going to kill her. Fleeting thoughts of her life whizzed through her mind like orange lights in a tunnel.

Suddenly, a hiss similar to the firing of a hydraulic piston began to fill Cindy's helmet. The excess carbon dioxide began absorbing into the suit's skin, where it was converted into usable oxygen. A cool breeze blew past Cindy's bangs as an ice-blue, illuminating light pierced the blackness in her helmet. A screen appeared in front of her eyes with the word "loading" encompassing her vision. Various displays, menus, and icons began to pop into existence. The darkness faded away as the image of a concrete floor appeared beneath her. The tightness squeezing Cindy's body released its grip like a plastic jug unfolding itself after being crushed.

While her body regained its shape, two black parallelograms formed in place of her eyes. They flashed to life in a brilliant cyan, glowing like a lighted pool at night. Digital readouts and numbers appeared in front of her eyes like a holographic display. She waved her hand in front of her eyes to check her sanity but stopped abruptly when she noticed her appendages were encased in silver. She freaked out for a few seconds and placed her hand back down onto the floor, nice and slow, she still couldn't believe what she was witnessing.

Her breathing sounded mechanical, almost like she were a scuba diver using a breathing apparatus. The foul odor of burnt electrical equipment still lingered in the vicinity, wafting through her helmet's air filters. Without realizing what she was doing, Cindy raised her hand to her head and took a deep whiff. The smell reminded her of a silver necklace left to tarnish jewelry store.

"Umm, what are you doing?" a male voice interrupted.

Startled by the man's entrance, Cindy yelled, "Oh my God!" As she fell onto her bottom and scurried backwards. "Michael! How long have you been there?"

"Long enough to save your life. Who are you, and what are you doing here?" Michael replied with a stern tone.

"What?" Cindy was confused by Michael's question. It was then that it hit her, "Oh!" she yelped. "It's me, Cindy."

Michael's eyes widened in disbelief. "Cindy? Jonas' Cindy?" he said, placing his hands on his waist, unsure if what he was seeing was real.

Cindy nodded. She sat up on her knees and said, "I was just coming to visit Jonas, I swear."

"How did this happen?" Michael asked, as he placed his hand on his forehead in disbelief.

"Well you see, what had happened was…" Cindy paused in mid-sentence as the words "scanning" hovered next to Michael like an ethereal ghost, "Uh, Michael?"

"Yes?"

"There's… number thingies appearing next to you and"—the sound of a camera click rang in Cindy's ears—"apparently I have taken a snapshot of you."

Michael's eyes squinted in confusion. "What?"

"Your driver's license was revoked in Greece because you were deemed improperly dressed while driving?" Cindy asked, befuddled by the report.

Michael's mouth gaped open. "How do you know that? I was studying abroad. I was only nineteen."

"They can do that in Greece?"

"Yeah, or if you are considered unbathed, not joking. Are you scanning me right now?" he asked.

"Yes?" Cindy said unsure, "but not because I want to."

"What else is it telling you?" he asked with building interest.

"You wear glasses because you're near-sighted."

Michael pushed his glasses back towards the bridge of his nose. "So it does work after all," he said, pleased. "Are you seeing anything else?"

"You're 29 years old, graduated top of your class from MIT, have black hair—duh, I could see that—love long walks on the beach, and are looking for a girl who is outgoing and into virtual sexual encounters."

"Interes—wait, what? Is that really in there? That has to be a bug. That's gotta be a bug," he said in a panic.

"J-K, I couldn't resist teasing you," she said while smiling beneath the cover of her mask.

"You really shouldn't joke about that. Jonas and I worked really hard on that suit," he said with a tinge of anger,

"Relax, it's just a joke," she said, appeasing Michael. Cindy suddenly looked down at her reflective, metallic body as a shimmer of light caught her attention. She tapped her breasts with both hands, causing the metal to clang like two steel bowls banging into each other.

"What are you doing now?" Michael asked, clearly flummoxed by her actions.

"Testing to see if this is real metal," she replied nonchalantly.

"Okay... do you have to smack your boobs to do that?"

"Get your mind out of the gutter," she said, as she rotated her arm admiring the light's reflection off different angles of the suit.

"All right, hang on, let's rewind. Why are you wearing our three hundred billion dollar project?"

"Three hundred billion and you couldn't afford better security?" she replied.

"Well all the money went into research. No one was even supposed to know this place existed. Security was fine till you showed up," Michael said annoyed.

Cindy stared at Michael for a few moments, gathering her thoughts. After much introspection she said, "Three hundred billion doesn't sound very cost effect—"

"Cindy!" he yelled.

She sighed and said, "Wow, you have no social skills. Okay... so I was coming down to the lab to surprise Jonas. But no one was here and I've always wondered what the heck that top-secret project was. So, when I saw that the entire building was empty, I decided to take a teeny tiny peek."

"Let me guess. The lab door wasn't locked," he said in a condescending tone.

"Yeah, the door felt a little loose. Is it broken?" she asked.

"Forget I mentioned it. Please continue."

"When I walked into the lab, I saw a silver puddle on the floor and I thought to myself, 'that's weird.' So I walked over to the puddle—I didn't touch it! I poked it with a pipe, and then, it jumped onto my finger."

"It jumped onto your finger?" Michael looked befuddled.

"Yes, it jumped onto my finger, and I tried to get it off, but then, the rest of it latched onto me and here I am," Cindy said.

"Are you sure you didn't touch it?" His words wrought with suspicion. "That's very weird for it to jump onto your finger."

"I promise you; I did not touch it."

"You know, you're lucky I came when I did. If I didn't have to come back for my phone…" he shook his head, thinking about what could have been.

"Thank you for saving me, even though I don't quite understand how you did it," she replied.

"It was simple. I just had to finish writing Sid's code and adjust some values to allow for proper airflow and 'oxygenization' into the helmet. I also had to factor in body mass and skeletal structure," he rambled.

"Translation: you fixed it so I could breathe and not get crushed. Oh, and I am pretty sure that 'oxygenization' is not a word," Cindy said.

Michael looked surprised and asked, "You speak geek?"

"Do you think my husband would have married me if I didn't?"

"Point taken. He does act like an elitist sometimes."

Cindy quickly defended her husband. "No, except maybe when he's in a terrible mood."

"That's, like, all the time," he said.

"Not with me, he isn't," she replied.

Cindy stood up from the floor and did some very basic stretching moves to test out the flexibility of her armored shell. It moved like a second skin and even managed to make Cindy utter a quiet "wow" when she was able to perform a full split without any issues. She strutted over to Michael as her statuesque body reflected images of the lab around her.

"So... am I naked?" she asked Michael.

Michael was made uncomfortable by the question. "Technically, yes, underneath the suit your clothes are gone."

"Okay, then where are my..." She pointed towards her breasts and then her groin.

Michael paused before answering, "Oh, that." He looked down to the floor, realizing he was ogling his friend's wife. "We designed the suit so that it would create extra padding for the sensitive areas. No one wants to walk around with their junk hanging out. Think of it like an invisible layer of underwear that masks all your unmentionables."

Cindy tapped her metal finger on her helmet where her chin would be. "Interesting."

Michael said with exasperated impatience, "So, you want me to take this thing off you, or what?"

"Umm, sure. I don't see why not."

Michael walked over to the control room and woke the computer from standby. Cindy trotted over to where the pipe was lazily lounging about. She lifted it off the floor and placing both hands on each end, began unbending it as if the pipe were a balloon animal. She chuckled as she uttered, "Wow, that's cool." She set the pipe back down on the table in its newly-straightened form.

Cindy glanced over to the control room and saw frustration emanating from Michael's face. The digital code in the terminal scrolled through his lenses as he slammed his fist on the table. He muttered unintelligible, technical jargon to himself, prompting Cindy to walk over and investigate.

"Is there a problem?" she asked while leaning over his shoulder.

"We didn't write any programming to make the suit detach itself from a host. You can turn it off, but you can't remove it." He seemed ashamed by such a basic oversight.

Cindy became alarmed and said, "You're saying I'm stuck like this?"

"Did you not listen to what I said? I said you can turn it off, but until we finish the code, I can't remove the suit from your body."

Cindy paced back and forth. "This is terrible news. Jonas is going to kill me. Can't you just finish the code while we're here?"

"I may be the lead programmer, but I had, like, 10 other very intelligent guys working on the code with me. This is all Charlie's territory. I don't know anything about chemistry or biology," he said.

"Michael, I can't walk around like this," she said vehemently.

He shook his head, rejecting the blame. "Well, I can't fix that right now. I would need help or Charlie's notes. It could take months."

"Fine!" She threw up her hands in frustration. "How do I turn it off, then?"

"You have to 'think' that it's off," he said with a smug grin.

"It can't be that simple. How can it read my thoughts?" she contested.

Michael smiled, reveling in explaining his labor of love. "The skin of the suit is transmitting data from the brain, kind of like electrodes. When SIRCA receives a command from the brain, the suit decrypts the message and executes the command."

"So just visualize myself without the suit, that's it? There's no zipper or anything?"

Michael nodded his head, "Yep."

Cindy raised her head towards the ceiling and closed her eyes. The subtle beeping and buzzing in her helmet tried to break her concentration, but her focus remained steady. She continued to visualize herself without the suit, causing the beeping to stop, and the ventilation inside her helmet to die down. She could feel the suit melting off of her skin, like ice dissolving in hot weather. She sensed a cool kiss of air stroke her back and kept her concentration until Michael suddenly interrupted.

"Umm, Cindy," Michael said.

Her concentration shattered as the beeps and ventilation reactivated.

"What, what?" she said, looking around wildly.

"Were you planning on walking out of here nude? Aren't you feeling a little cold?" He pointed to the splotches of exposed skin spread throughout her body.

Cindy glanced down to see that portions of her breast and back were exposed. She was mortified by what was happening and felt the cold air nipping at her feet. Cindy placed her foot forward and saw her painted toes blink in the light. She looked at her arms, expecting to see metal, but instead, saw the peach skin wrapped around her biceps.

"I thought you said just to visualize myself without the suit?" she complained.

"Yes, but you need to visualize yourself with the clothes you wore today," Michael retorted.

Cindy replied, "Well, you didn't specify that."

Cindy stepped back and tried again, imagining herself with the suit on. Her splotches of skin were enveloped with stainless steel. The armored suit began warming her body, signaling that its activation was complete. Again, Cindy imagined herself with the suit off, but this time, she remembered her blue long sleeve turtleneck sweater, beige khaki pants, and even her underwear.

Little sparkles of light dazzled around her as the suit began to absorb into her skin. In its place, threads of clothing were being rebuilt, almost as if the suit were manufacturing the clothing from scratch. Her leather boots reformed over her feet as the familiar feeling of fabric replaced the sensation of nudity.

Cindy stood there with her eyes held tight, while Michael amused himself by not telling Cindy that she was fully clothed. When she opened her right eye, her gaze darted around the room, searching for assurance that she was not naked.

She opened both of her eyes, looked at her body, and breathed a sigh of relief. Cindy turned her attention back to Michael and said, "Thank God."

"You're not in the clear yet. It's still inside of you."

"I don't care, I'm just glad to be normal."

"Ya sure about that?" he said.

Cindy glared at Michael. "Of course I am, why?"

Michael had an inquisitive look on his face, and pushed his glasses up the bridge of his nose. "Scientifically speaking," he paused for a moment before blurting out, "you're freaking ripped! There, I said it. Did the suit make you that way?"

Cindy cocked her head and smiled. In a very sweet, low voice, she said, "I'm a gymnast. What were you expecting?" She secretly took pleasure in his reaction.

Michael sighed as a look of disappointment draped his demeanor, "So the suit didn't do anything to physically augment you?"

He turned away and muttered to himself, "Man…"

Cindy felt a strange pang of guilt from Michael's disappointment and said, "Hey, hey… don't be like that. I felt a little augmented or whatever."

Michael turned to her with a skeptical look and said, "You're just saying that."

"No, really, I was able to bend that pipe over there…" She stopped herself as a hint of cockiness spilled out into her last sentence, "…but that's not saying much."

Although Michael seemed pleased by Cindy's words, he suddenly became very suspicious and said, "Hang on, hang on, I'm confused."

"How so?" she asked.

Michael's analytical mind fluttered to life. "Well, you said the suit enhanced your strength, but then you said 'that's not saying much.' So, then, you're proud of your body, correct?"

Michael's questions perturbed Cindy as they delved into creeper territory. She played it off like a champ and said, "I have sacrificed many delicious, sugary treats to achieve this. So, yes, I am quite proud."

"Okay, then, why do you cover yourself up? I mean, logically, people who have great bodies tend to show them off."

Cindy looked disgusted with Michael and said, "What? Is this a real question; are you objectifying me?"

Michael stammered, "What? No! Well I mean… ego you know? Like, if you train that hard, obviously you want to show it off. Was that the wrong thing to say?"

107

Cindy laughed realizing Michael was just a socially awkward nerd. "Michael, your questions intrigue me," Cindy teased.

Cindy's statement worried Michael. "This does not fill me with confidence."

Cindy said, "Let me ask you a question and then I'll answer yours." She leaned onto a nearby desk with an entertained grin on her face. "Do you have any sisters?"

"No."

"Have you dated anyone recently?"

"No."

"Have you ever had a girlfriend?"

"What's the point of all this?" he whined.

"Have you?"

"In third grade," he mumbled.

"So that's a no."

"What are you trying to accomplish here?" Michael demanded.

Cindy replied, "Well, your question was so chauvinistic. I had to figure out if you were a jerk, or a harmless nerd with no social skills."

"I fell under the jerk category, didn't I?" His sigh was full of disappointment. "I knew it."

Cindy was confused. "What? No, you're definitely just a nerd. Actually, I think my sister would find you a little endearing, but she's…"

Cindy found herself at a loss for words.

"Can we please stop talking about this?" he begged.

"Yeah, sorry. To answer your question, you don't need to show skin to be sexy," she said with a smile.

Michael grinned as he grabbed onto his chin with his fingers. "Hmm, I like it."

Cindy looked at the computer clock and began to fidget around, almost afraid to ask Michael a very important question. "Can I leave now?"

Michael replied, "Absolutely not. The SIRCA is still attached to you."

"The what now? Circa? What is that?" she asked.

"The suit!" Michael yelled in frustration. "Haven't you been paying attention? Stealth, Infiltration, Reconnaissance, Com—"

"I get it!" Cindy interrupted. "What am I supposed to do? You said you couldn't finish the code without the others."

"Well, maybe I exaggerated a little bit to get you to keep the suit on longer."

"Excuse me?"

"Well, y'see, you're the first person to wear it. I was curious to know if it really worked."

Cindy crossed her arms and grimaced. "You could have just asked."

"Sorry."

"Can we get on with this?" Her leather boot tapped on the floor with aggravated impatience.

"Okay, come over here then."

Michael directed Cindy to sit down on the black swivel chair and went off to grab some tools to unlatch the suit from Cindy's body. While he gathered materials, Cindy spun around in the chair a few times like a bored child. When Michael returned, he caught Cindy spinning in her chair, prompting an awkward moment of silence.

Michael shook his head and pulled up Cindy's sleeves. He attached one electrode between her bicep and her forearm and two more onto Cindy's temples. The plastic wheels of his swivel chair rumbled on the floor as Michael glided over to the computer desk. He awoke the computer from standby and accessed the SIRCA control system.

"Okay, I'm getting readings from the suit and your biometrics. I should be able to figure this out. It's rather simple, in theory."

Cindy snatched her arm away, dragging the wires beside it. "What do you mean, 'in theory?' is it going to work or not?" she asked.

Michael pushed his glasses up the bridge of his nose.

"I've never done this before."

She shot him a doubtful glare as she hesitated to relax her arm. Michael seemed insulted by Cindy's reaction, prompting her to reluctantly return her arm to the programmer.

"Okay, I'm going to manually turn on your suit now." Michael began clacking away at the keys, each stroke streamed letters and code across the width of the screen, reflecting on his glasses.

The terminal came to a screeching halt as warning text popped onto the screen, "ERROR: This program cannot be activated due to foreign presence." Michael tapped his chin. The crease between his eyebrows began to form as he exhaled deeply through his nose. Cindy looked over to him, wondering what was happening but was too nervous to ask. Without a word of warning, Michael turned to Cindy and ripped the electrodes off her body. The instantaneous transformation caught Cindy by surprise. Ninety percent of her body became enveloped by the metal hard-suit leaving only her face unmasked.

Michael victoriously exclaimed, "Hah!" as he reattached the electrodes to Cindy's shielded body.

Cindy couldn't help but ask, "What were the electrodes for anyway? Can't you monitor the suit remotely?"

There was a long, uncomfortable pause. Michael's stare was so blank that any thought he tried to form instantly seeped out of his ears. The only thing Michael could muster was, "Valid."

"I have to be honest," she said. "I am slightly concerned about having you responsible for my wellbeing."

Her bluntness stung Michael, causing him to growl as he removed each electrode. He resumed clacking away at the keys, causing the suit to shift and slither across her skin like a living jelly. The suit began to twist and tighten around her arm like a braided rope. It felt as painful as it looked, causing Cindy's legs to squirm under the increasing pressure.

"Ow, OW, OW, stop! That hurts!" she begged.

Michael looked at Cindy, confused. "What? What did I do? What did you feel?"

Michael Ctrl-Z'd his way back through the program to revert the changes made to the suit. The metal skin began to unwrap itself from Cindy's arm like an un-crumpling piece of aluminum foil.

Cindy rubbed her wrist as the lingering aches faded away. "Did you not hear my bones cracking?" she said in anger.

Michael brushed off her complaint, shaking his head. "Don't exaggerate."

"I'm not!" Cindy countered.

"Do you want to know what happened or not?" Before Cindy could respond, he said, "Too bad, I'm telling you anyway. I accidentally changed the suit setting to someone who was smaller than you."

Cindy's eyes narrowed, "You say 'accidentally,' but I'm not convinced you're telling the truth."

"Okay, fine!" His guilt spilled from his words as he said, "I needed to see if the suit would stop itself from ripping your arm off."

"I think you still have some work to do... creep," she whispered with contempt.

"I'll get on it," he grumbled. Brushing aside Cindy's comment, he refocused his attention back to the terminal. "Anyway, let's see if this disables it." He clicked on a few prompts with his mouse and waited patiently for a few minutes.

"I don't think that's working," Cindy responded.

"Why?" he asked with scientific curiosity.

"It's giving me a headache. I don't know, it feels like I'm getting really agitated," she said.

"What are you talking about?"

Cindy's face contorted into a scowl as annoyance lifted her lips and bared her teeth. Like a flash of lightning, Cindy smacked Michael on the cheek, causing his glasses to fly across the desk. Before he could even realize what was happening, Cindy cocked her hand back and struck him once more. His face became red and swollen like a child left out in the snow for too long.

"Stop hitting me!" he cried.

"I'm so sorry!" She covered her mouth as her gaping eyes refused to believe what happened.

Michael went searching for his glasses. "What the hell did you do that for?"

"I... I... I don't know," she stammered. "I couldn't control myself."

"Whatever that was, I am deleting it for good. I might even add a line. Don't... hit... Michael... ever."

"I'm really sorry. I promise I didn't do it on purpose," she said.

"If this suit can modify electrical impulses in the brain, hmm, I don't know. I'm going to have to review this later."

Cindy seemed reluctant to speak to Michael while he typed away at his keyboard, but a nagging issue kept blazing a path to the forefront of her mind.

"Michael…"

"What?" he replied without taking his eyes off the monitor for even one millisecond.

"You're not going to be able to finish the code tonight, are you?"

The sounds of clacking keys came to a complete halt as he rested his hands onto the sterile, ivory-colored desk. His look of displeasure sent chills down Cindy's spine. "What makes you say that?"

"Well…" she said, stumbling over her words like a minion challenging a totalitarian office manager. "It just seems to me that you'll need more than just a few minutes to finish writing the code."

Michael rolled back in his chair and swiveled towards Cindy's direction. He crossed his arms and legs, taking the posture of a curmudgeon-like turtle. The office chair creaked as it reclined into a lazy boy position.

"I didn't realize you were an expert at writing code," he said with distinct snarkiness.

"I'm not trying to offend you, and I didn't claim to be an expert. I've heard Jonas complain millions of times about how long these projects take."

"Do you want to leave? Because you can't," he said irritated.

Cindy said in a most diplomatic fashion, "I'm not saying that, Michael. It's been a very long day for me."

Michael released his arms and legs from their shielded position and allowed himself a moment to relax.

"You're probably right, but I don't feel comfortable letting you walk out of here with that suit."

"My husband is the designer. If anything were to go wrong, I'm pretty sure he can help fix it," she replied.

Michael's survival instinct kicked in and he said, "Absolutely not. Promise me you won't tell him you have that suit, Cindy."

Cindy was perplexed. "Why not? He's my husband and it's his project. He should be allowed to know."

"Well, ya see… all of us signed a contract that made us responsible for the security of the suit. The fact that some civilian snuck into our lab, activated the suit, and walked out with it…" He paused almost as if he was going to puke. "Oh God, we would all go to jail. I don't want to be Diablo's bitch. No one else should know you have the suit, period. We need to contain the problem so Jonas doesn't go ballistic."

"Okay! I promise I won't tell him. But I can't stay here. It's getting late and Jonas will come looking for me."

"You're seriously going to do this to me, Cindy?" Michael shook his head in disbelief, almost angry at entertaining the thought of letting her go home with the suit.

Cindy let out a deep sigh. "I'm not trying to cause trouble. I just… I had a very traumatic experience recently, and I don't want to take the bus home late at night. Okay?"

"What happened, if you don't mind me asking?"

Cindy looked down at the cold floor, praying to get lost between the grout wedged between the tiles. "I'd rather not talk about it," she replied.

Michael relented. "Fine, I understand." He sighed deeply as he looked away towards the door. "I'll let you go home. Just let me set up some precautions first."

CHAP7ER 4

CORRUPTION

The twilight of the evening descended upon the suburbs of Queens. The noise and bustle of the city quieted, replaced with the mellow sounds of crickets chirping in the breeze. The sweet smells of fresh, evening air filled the neighborhood with nostalgic memories of beautiful spring nights. Children played outside until the street lamps ignited, telling them it was time to go home.

Cindy approached her home, nestled deep within the suburban jungle. Her heart began to race as paranoia flooded her thoughts with hallucinations of attackers lurking in the bushes. The well-lit street felt more like a tangerine tunnel with no escape or safe haven in sight. Cindy noticed that a group of teenagers were shambling down the street towards her house. Some of them were wearing hoodies while others wore sideways caps with their pants always struggling to stay atop their waist. The dark street was making it hard to see who these kids were, and in her mistrustful, poisoned mind, she assumed that these were delinquents on the prowl.

Cindy shifted into panic mode as she scurried to find the keys in her purse. She kept digging through the bag, pushing aside her makeup, toiletries, cell phone,

117

pens, notebooks, wallet... No keys were in sight and the youths were drawing closer. Their chatter grew louder as their obnoxious cackling bounced off the brick buildings of the empty street. Cindy shook her purse. She heard the jingling of the keys but was still puzzled as to where they could be. Then, as if the devil was finished playing pranks on her, Cindy found her keys tucked away in a side pocket.

She seized her keys, like a frog catching a fly, but in her haste, dropped the brass teeth on the floor. The keys jingled loudly, catching the attention of the young boys who were, at the time, minding their own business. Cindy's breathing accelerated, matching the beating of her heart. She grabbed the keys off the floor and struggled to put them into the keyhole. Her free hand balled up into a fist as each knuckle cracked in preparation for the ensuing conflict. She cursed at herself realizing that she tried to force the wrong key into the lock. Her mistake allowed the punks to come within mere feet of the walkway to her house.

A dull thud hit her front lawn followed by two distinct footsteps. Cindy began placing each key between her fingers, creating a homemade claw of jagged brass that she hid from their sight. As Cindy turned around, she saw one of the teens had walked onto her lawn. Her arm tensed as she prepared to lunge herself into conflict, only to realize that the boy was picking up an orange and blue foam football. The young man looked up at Cindy and paused for a moment. Both looked like deer caught in headlights. The teen said, "Sorry, Ma'am," and walked back towards the group while spinning the football in the air.

When the teens walked away, Cindy noticed that some of them were wearing blue t-shirts that read "Boys & Girls Club of America" on the front and "Volunteer" on the back. Cindy stood there, speechless at what had just occurred, but her emotions were still rising to a boil. Cindy, ashamed of her stupidity, screamed at the top of her lungs. She slammed her palm into the front of the door. Crack! Cindy pulled her hand back unveiling a portion of the door now splintered inward. The unpainted wood revealed itself in a brilliant orange. The pristine, white door however, was now scarred with the impact of her might.

She looked at her hand and watched the chips of paint and wood flake off and fall to the ground like snow. *"Oh my God,"* she whispered, wiping her hands clean of the damage. While removing evidence of vandalism from her palms, Cindy was startled by Jonas' sudden appearance as he swung the door open with a furious pull. "What the f—huh?" Jonas was surprised to see his wife looking up at him with innocent puppy-dog eyes, fragments of wood and paint scattered on the porch next to the tips of Cindy's leather boots.

As he inspected the damage on the door, he couldn't help but ask, "Umm, what the hell just happened?"

Cindy looked down at the concrete doorstep as she twisted the ball of her foot into the floor. "I… broke the door."

"You did this? I thought someone got slammed into the door." He further analyzed the damage and said, "Jesus, Cindy—sorry, Lord. Maybe you shouldn't

119

be hitting the weights anymore."

Cindy heaved a sigh and pushed Jonas out of the way, barging into the security of her home. But Jonas kept his gaze locked onto his wife, observing all of her body language. He followed her around the house like a lost puppy.

"Are you okay?" Jonas asked.

"I just smashed our door in. I'm great!"

"Would you like me to look at your hand?"

"I'm fine. Don't worry about it," she replied, brushing him off.

Cindy walked towards the counter with a slow but poignant gait. Jonas snuck up behind her and grabbed Cindy by the waist, pulling her strong body into his arms. Despite being a miniature powerhouse, Cindy allowed herself to fall back into his loving embrace. He wrapped his soft hands across her navel and placed the softest kiss upon her neck. He hugged her tightly and whispered into her ear, "What's wrong?"

She closed her eyes and rested her head against the crescent moon shape of his neck. Her mighty figure shriveled inside of him as her defenses gave way to a calming sense of security.

"I'm just tired of being afraid," she confessed.

"Afraid of what?"

Cindy replied, "Of being a victim again."

Jonas rubbed her arms with reassurance. "That was just a fluke."

"Like me breaking the door?" she said lightheartedly.

"Yeah, about that, what did you do?"

"I thought a bunch of kids were gonna jump me. Turned out they were just tossing around a football. I was so mad at myself that I hit the door and it ended up splitting by accident."

Jonas grinned and said, "You're lucky Jadie wasn't there to witness it. She probably would have called you roid—"

"Don't, even, say it."

"I never make fun of you, sweetie," he said smiling.

Cindy locked her eyes on his and tilted her head with a playful scowl that hung from her eyes.

"Okay, maybe, sometimes," he relented.

She lowered her head even further, her grimace becoming more severe. Her eyes almost scraped the bottom of her eyebrows like the blades on an ice skate.

"Fine, I do it all the time but only because you're so adorable," he said.

Cindy looked at him with a stoic face and responded, "Uh huh."

Jonas adjusted his gentle hold into a full vice grip as he lifted Cindy up into the air. She squealed and giggled with glee as Jonas threw her onto the couch.

"Stop it," she said, with a playful smile spread across her delicate face.

"So," he paused while taking his seat next to her, "why are you late?"

"Late? What are you talking about?" Her body language betrayed her lies.

Jonas glared towards his wife and said, "Cindy…"

She replied, "I was going to surprise you with dinner today and went to your job. Obviously, things didn't quite go according to plan."

"I'm starting to think you should stop trying to surprise me," he said.

"You might be on to something."

Jonas changed the subject back to his original question and said, "Well, regardless, I still got here before you."

"My train was delayed," she replied.

"Oh, that's right, I saw that text message earlier."

"Yeah," she agreed, even though her expression was in complete shock that her lie was, in fact, truth.

"I'm sorry, I didn't mean to grill you. I just worry about you, is all."

"Well, thank you for looking out for me. You always take good care of me," she said with a sweet smile.

Jonas delighted in his ego being stroked. He stretched his arms in a cocky manner and said, "Well, ehh, a man's gotta do what a man's gotta do. Speaking of which, umm…" His facial expression quickly became despondent.

Cindy already knew of the impending doom and asked, "What happened?" in a disapproving tone.

"I got… fired today." He lowered his head in shame.

"Oh, no, what happened?" Her condemnation quickly changed to concern.

"The prototype malfunctioned during the demo and my funding was cut after."

"I'm so sorry." She rubbed her hand across his back. "What are we going to do now?"

"Well," he said, scratching his head. "I'm not gonna lie, money's going to be tight. No one else wants to pick up the project because of the cost. I tried to get other investors, but they thought it was sci-fi mumbo jumbo."

"Are you going to find a job at another company?" she asked.

"I'm going to look at other options I have first. But, I might need to borrow some of your money from the gym to keep us afloat. We have enough in savings to get us by for now."

"Okay," she whispered.

"Anyway, I need to use the bathroom."

Jonas stood up and made his way towards his porcelain throne, replete with dainty, refreshing scents.

He said to Cindy while walking away, "I shall return, my love."

"Oh, God." She rolled her eyes and said, "What was I thinking when I said 'I do'?"

"That's not nice!" Jonas yelled before closing the bathroom door.

Cindy, now left to her own devices, spotted the TV remote resting on the table nearby. She debated whether to fill her mind with the muck of reality TV shows or go to bed earlier than usual. Filth it was. Cindy reached for the remote and was about to push the power button when a strange tone filled her ear. It was not an unfamiliar tone; the sound was very reminiscent of having been struck in the ear. The tone was piercing and loud enough to cut through anything blocking its path. Whether Cindy tried to bury her head in a pillow or cover her ears with her hands, the sound was relentless. Cindy feared the worst—could she have gotten tinnitus?

Just as she was about to consider going to the hospital, the ringing faded away replaced by the garbled sounds of demons chattering in her ear. The distortion in the speech began to clear up over time and what were once demons morphed into ordinary men speaking through a cell phone with a corrupted signal.

[Look— *static* — we have your sister— *static* —colm — work with us and she wi— be harmed— *static* —. We have — of work a—d *static* I —ed everyone's full cooperation— *static* —.]

A morbid terror gripped Cindy's chest, its icy cold fingers digging into her ribs. Every beat of her heart sent this tingling chill throughout her breast, making it difficult to breathe. She couldn't grasp how she was hearing this signal. She looked at the TV and saw nothing but a grey canvas. She checked around the couch to see if her cell phone was on speaker, but there was nothing: no TV, no laptop, no mobile, just her sitting alone in an empty room.

[—*static* — remember where to meet right? *static* the galvanizing plant in Jersey City, the one you can see from Secaucus. Come down so — discuss *static*.]

Cindy looked over to the time set on the cable box, 9:17 pm. She squirmed on the couch as the leather creaked and moaned to her movements. Her hands were unsure of what to do as they flailed about with nowhere to go. She couldn't shake the feeling that although the unknown message did not seem intended for her, if she was wrong, then Jadie would be in great danger. How could she live with herself if something were to happen to her sister?

Her intuition told her to stay but her mind kept goading her to grab the car keys. After all, at this time of night Cindy might be able to avoid heavy traffic on the highway. She didn't know what to do. Although it was only a few minutes of pondering, it felt like hours' worth of wasted time to Cindy. What was she to do? It was already 9:20 and time was ticking away at a slow, consistent pace.

Then, Cindy was hit, like a freight train, by a sudden realization. It crashed through her brick wall of ambivalence and dropped off the silver passenger. The suit, she remembered. Her feelings of uncertainty were replaced with an intense curiosity. Michael had forbidden her from ever activating the suit, at least in front of Jonas, he never said she couldn't use it to save someone's life.

If Cindy was wrong, she could activate the SIRCA to protect herself from danger. If she was right, she could use the suit to save her sister. Once this idea of invulnerability boarded her train of thought, Cindy couldn't help but grin to herself about the endless possibilities. She walked over to the keychain rack and saw two sets of keys hanging like bats asleep in their cave.

One key was for Jonas' smart car and the other...

If there was anything that was never to be touched or disturbed, it was the second key. If Cindy were to grab that item, she could make it to Jersey City in record time, but run the risk of Jonas' lashing fury. The excitement of taking the car out for a spin to pull off a daring rescue was just too much for Cindy to resist. She snatched the keys off the rack as they jingled in protest. Disregarding all consequences, Cindy opened the door to the garage and ran in.

With the flick of the switch, the fluorescent lights flickered awake from their slumber. In front of Cindy sat the maroon MiEV waiting patiently, eager to serve its owner, but right beside it, a wild, silver stallion was untamed and ready to roar to life. The Saleen S7 was Jonas' pride and joy, the one vehicle he promised to get himself if he ever really made it. Of course, working in the city had made it impossible for him to drive the car around, so it sat in the stables waiting for the day to be set loose.

Cindy popped open the gull wing doors and sat on the luxurious leather. Although the car had aged in the past couple of years, the new car smell still lingered within, almost as if it had rolled straight off the factory floor. Its pristine, glossy skin was in perfect condition, reflecting the lights and lawn equipment surrounding it. She gripped the steering wheel and gave it a nice rev. The leather rumbled between the palms of her hands, almost as if it were being held for the first time. Cindy pressed the button to the garage door curling the industrial wall into the ceiling above. The pitch-black darkness revealed itself in front of Cindy, waiting for her to plunge into its depths.

Cindy jumped in shock as she turned on the ignition, caught off-guard by the vehicle's powerful engine flaunting its untapped supremacy.

Cindy whispered to herself, "Thank God you don't know how to drive stick, sweetie."

She shifted the car into drive and turned on the headlights. The dashboard cast off a soft light blue. The spaceship-like interior only fueled Cindy's desire to slam her foot on the accelerator, but instead, she gave it a gentle tap. The car screamed out of the driveway, causing Cindy to slam the brakes. This monster was wilder than she thought. Once she regained her composure, she set her foot back on the accelerator and screeched her way out into the quiet suburban street.

Jonas ran out following the sound of commotion, screaming, "Cindy!" She glanced at the rear-view mirror just in time to see Jonas' arms dropping down to his sides, his eyes staring helplessly as his prized possession sped away. Cindy focused her attention back on the road. "Sorry, sweetie," she said to herself. As she smiled and gunned the accelerator to the floor, Jonas went inside and called Cindy's mobile. He yelled in frustration when he heard Cindy's phone ringing inside her purse. He threw his phone onto the couch and stormed off into the bedroom.

Fifty minutes later, Cindy found herself pulling up to the entrance of a massive industrial facility. "Raymond Galvanizing" was printed on the rusted sign swinging from the chain-link fence. As she pulled into the parking lot, she could see orange lights decorating the steel girders like bland Christmas bulbs. The towering, smoke-spewing chimneys were dotted with little red lights, warding away aircraft that drew too near.

The factory resembled an intimidating prison for dangerous chemicals and toxic fumes. The red girders that created the basic exterior skeleton made it seem as though anyone could be hiding anywhere, waiting to take a shot. As she walked through the parking lot, she could see that it was mostly vacant except for a handful of vehicles, a black and hardened SUV, a white van, a limo and empty delivery trucks. Under normal circumstances, Cindy would find herself petrified to take even one step towards the factory, but now with the security blanket of an armored suit, Cindy was eager to find trouble.

As she walked inside the factory, the strong odor of iron, steel and zinc punched Cindy with a pungent stench. *This factory is definitely not abandoned,* she thought. The equipment looked as if it had been used during the day; lubrication spewed from the joints of the mechanisms on the machines. The facility was very clean and well-maintained. Pools of molten zinc sent heat waves dancing from the tops of their vats. The catwalks overhead reflected the ominous lava glowing from the vats, casting wavering shadows of the grid floor flickering on the ceiling above. She saw stacks of steel and iron sitting next to each other, including a stack that looked as though it came fresh out of production. The steel was enveloped in zinc, preventing the metal from succumbing to rust damage.

Cindy stepped into a wide-open area located in the middle of the factory platform. The sound of someone picking up a microphone clunked over the intercom followed by a frightening voice.

"What are you doing here?" the voice asked in a threatening manner.

Cindy, unsure of where to look in her response, settled for looking up at the ceiling. "I'm looking for my sister."

A silence befell the factory for an almost eternal period of time. Cindy's eyes were shifting at a rapid pace, alert and cognizant of her surroundings, looking into each empty catwalk and shadow for signs of trouble. She was scared to death but also weirdly excited to be in such an unusual situation.

The voice responded. "She's not here. That message was not intended for you."

The sound of a door slamming open reverberated throughout the factory's hollow expanse, followed by dozens of footsteps clanging on steel catwalks. The sounds of movement abated, followed by a parade of guards disabling their safeties. They loaded up their empty chambers with bullets, quivering to rip into Cindy's flesh. She froze in place, like a criminal facing a firing squad, and made a desperate attempt to plead for her release.

"I… I'm sorry, I'll just leave then."

"No," the voice said with complete apathy.

She backed away slowly, "You don't need to kill me; I promise I won't tell anyone."

"Dead people tell no tales," the voice replied.

Fear manifested itself as a sharp, stinging pain pulsing in the back of Cindy's neck. She could feel the terror begin to rush in as the fight-or-flight response kicked into gear. She knew her life was in danger, and she didn't have much time to act. Cindy summoned her knowledge of gymnastics and ran towards the stack of steel girders. The bullets began to rain from the catwalks like hail from a deadly hurricane crashing upon the shore. Cindy performed an aerial over the steel beams, precisely locking her legs in the air and easily clearing her head past the obstacle. After she landed, Cindy ducked behind cover as the pings and pangs of bullets struck the barricade behind her, ricocheting with each impact.

She was at a dangerous disadvantage. The steel girders would not keep her safe for long; one inch in the wrong direction could have fatal consequences. Yet Cindy, the woman who had been afraid of punk kids attacking her, didn't care. She relished the excitement of being under attack and felt her inner warrior erupt to the surface. She focused on imagining herself enveloped by the armor. Pools of liquid metal formed atop her skin and hardened into flexible steel.

Various numbers, meters and boxes fluttered into existence before Cindy's eyes. The sound of the cavernous industrial complex became muted as if submerged under water, and then transformed into crisp, clear audio. The stench of molten metal and fresh steel was reduced to a mere whiff, as a stream of oxygen hissed into Cindy's helmet. The suit came alive and transitioned into combat mode. While scanning the area, it detected five hostiles armed with weapons. It continued to power up, feeding Cindy a constant flow of information, alerting her to the combat readiness of the suit. When the words "Deflection Armor Active" appeared in front of her eyes, Cindy felt a smile creep across her lips.

She was ready to move. She cracked her metallic knuckles and slinked away from the girders without the guards even noticing. The bullets continued to pelt the shadows until one of guards got wise and yelled, "She's not there!" They looked around the vicinity, unaware that Cindy was crawling underneath the catwalks. The shadows of the grated flooring washed over her body with every movement she made like the shadows of leaves when walking through a forest. She could see the soles of their dirt-encrusted tactical boots standing in place, oblivious to her presence below.

Cindy jumped up and grasped onto the steel grates above her head, making sure not to make a single sound with her movements. Cindy used her incredible athletic strength, to pull herself underneath the catwalk; crawling upside down her muscles flexed through her armored skin as she clung to the flooring with ease. To her surprise, she discovered that she could stick to the catwalk without having to wedge her fingers between the grates. The suit was sticking to the walkway like a magnet, allowing her to stay aloft without tiring her muscles.

She crawled into position like a gecko clinging to a wall. She found the ease of her movement surprising, and was impressed by the suit's capabilities. With the guard right above her, Cindy was ready to make her move. Just like her days practicing on the uneven bars, Cindy pulled herself to the side of the catwalk and allowed her body to hang off the ledge. Her back muscles tensed as she waited for her prey to pass, anticipating the right moment to strike. As soon as the guards peered over the railing to look down below, Cindy struck like a cobra and tore into the guard. She grabbed his collar with her left hand and pulled him straight into the iron railing. His head made a loud clang upon impacting the metal bar, causing blood to gush from his forehead.

The blow pushed his body backward, causing the guard to stumble away from the edge. Cindy grabbed onto him a second time and pulled his staggering body over the barrier. He screamed as he plummeted down onto the rock-hard cement floor below. His body and gear made a loud thud as he writhed in pain for a few seconds before succumbing to unconsciousness. Cindy turned back to the railing and yanked herself over the rusty guard rail. Her feet clanked onto the catwalk as her glowing-blue eyes set its sights on the next target. A little red triangle appeared on Cindy's radar, notifying her that his buddy was coming over investigate. Not wanting to be spotted by the suspicious guard, Cindy looked towards the ceiling and spotted a pipe stretching across the length of the factory.

She leapt onto the pipe and wrapped herself around the cylinder like a snake.

She closed her eyes and prayed that she would be invisible to the patrolling guard. The suit contextually identified Cindy's intentions and asked, "Do you wish to enable stealth mode?" Cindy mentally selected yes causing her metallic skin to change in hue and color like a chameleon. High-pitched, digital sounds filled her helmet as her silver membrane turned into a glass, transparent surface. During the transition, the suit began to flicker and had difficulty maintaining its invisibility. Even so, it granted Cindy just enough time to remain undetected by the second guard who had just walked beneath her.

The suit error'ed out just before shutting off the cloaking system, but it didn't matter, Cindy was ready for her next maneuver. She adjusted her position in the quietest way possible and tightened her legs around the pipe, unaware that she was crumpling it inward with her thighs. She lowered her upper body with her hands extending towards the clueless mercenary like a cave centipede catching a flying bat. Cindy snatched him into her arms and dangled him off the floor, cutting off the flow of oxygen to his brain. His muffled screams of panic were too quiet to pierce through the booming industrial sounds. The man tried to claw his fingers into her slate forearms to no avail. With no way to free himself from Cindy's vice grip, the guard surrendered, falling unconscious in her powerful arms.

Cindy scanned the immediate area and detected the remaining three guards switching formation to widen their search. Two guards were now travelling as a pair while one lone guard kept an eye on his compatriots. Cindy quietly dropped

133

the body onto the prison-like walkway and crept along the pipe to get into a better ambush position against the remaining mercenary guards. While crawling over a vat of molten zinc, Cindy slipped and lost her grip on the pipe. She screamed as she fell into the glowing lava, plopping into the burning liquid like a stone thrown into a pool. The guards heard her cries and ran over to the vat. They watched as her metal hand sunk into the inferno, flames shooting from her skin. The guards radioed the man in the factory control room and said, "Target down, she fell into the vat."

The men turned away, believing that their target was eliminated; no one could survive a fall into that cauldron of fire. Suddenly, Cindy leapt out of the vat like a demon flying out of the gates of hell, flames roaring from her body. The guards shrieked in absolute terror and unloaded all of their ammunition onto her glowing, lava-colored body. Sparks erupted from each bullet that struck her skin as she drew closer to the horrified mercenaries. Cindy, drunk from the sensation of invincibility, grabbed the guards by their faces and slammed their heads into each other. Cindy's strike may have been mere seconds, but the guards' second-degree burns and scorched complexions were grossly apparent.

The last mercenary, who was keeping watch nearby, dropped down onto his back, petrified by fear. The fruitless rapid fire clicking of his empty gun only served to carve out his terror. Cindy approached him with deliberate, slow steps. The bright orange glow faded back into silver as the lights nearby created a glossy sheen off of Cindy's suit. The dancing light accentuated her sculpted abdominals and biceps. The muscles on her legs tremored with each step forward. Her ice cold eyes stared into the soul of the whimpering guard as her compassion slowly whittled away.

She relished the feeling of power the suit was giving her; the ability to make these men tremble in fear was intoxicating for Cindy. She knew she was in command of the entire situation, and they had no choice but to bow down before her will. As she stood before the last guard, Cindy placed her foot upon his chest and forced him to lay down flat. He whimpered, but his pleas fell on the deaf ears of an apathetic woman. Then Cindy moved her foot onto his neck, gradually applying pressure. The whimpering guard began to gurgle and choke while trying to speak through his strained breathing, "Please… have mercy on me."

Her response was as cold as the icy-cyan glow of her artificial eyes, "That's funny. You didn't show me any mercy when I begged you to let me go."

The guard replied, "That wasn't my call!" He shook his head rapidly as he felt his own pulse stinging throughout his neck. "I was just… uhnn… doing my job."

He groaned in pain as she applied more pressure onto his fragile throat.

"Enough, let him go," the voice boomed over the P.A.

Cindy released her grip over the man's neck and delivered a swift kick across his jaw, rendering him out of commission.

135

Cindy turned to the control room, which overlooked the factory. "Are you volunteering to go next? I know where you're hiding."

The voice paused as the gravity of his situation kicked in. "No, I... apologize... for what has transpired."

"You could have just let me go, but instead you decided to play it the hard way," she replied, her victory swelling her head like a bookworm who beat up a bully.

The voice said, "You're absolutely right, and I'm sorry. I have a proposition for you that I hope you will find more agreeable."

"Speak," she commanded.

"Where did you get that suit?" the voice asked.

"None of your business. You're one question away from me crashing through that window and killing you."

The voice stammered, "Forget I ever said anything... Are you for hire?"

"What?" the sound of stretching could be heard as she balled her fist. "Could you repeat that? I don't think I heard you right."

"I asked, if you were for hire?" the male voice said with distinct fear.

"After all you put me through, you want to offer me a job?" Cindy replied.

"Yes."

Cindy was simultaneously flabbergasted but intrigued. Her curiosity prompted her to ask, "Doing what?"

"I want to hire you for freelance contracts to take out political targets."

Cindy, amazed by the audacity of whomever she was speaking to, said, "You must be out of your mind if you think I would assassinate the President of the United States."

"Not the President. I'm talking about legislators who allow corporations to rape the working American." His speech became impassioned with vigor. "Officials who support building oil pipelines not because it will help our country become self-sufficient, but because it would stain their pockets with black gold. I'm talking about the people who support Super PACs and lobbyists, to serve their own interests over the needs of the taxpayers who put them into office. Those are the people I want you to punish. You would be serving the greater good."

Although it sounded like the ravings of a madman to Cindy, she couldn't deny that there was some truth to his passionate words. A glint of light reflecting off her suit reminded Cindy of how Jonas was fired from his project due to "lack of funds." These were the very same legislators whose gross misunderstanding of finances caused the government to shut down more than once. These inept politicians had the nerve to demand Jonas build a project that they had no intention of paying for. The offer was too tempting to pass up.

Cindy relaxed her fist and asked, "How much?"

The man was taken aback but delighted by the response. "Fifty thousand for your first kill and up to one million for… trickier ones. Does this tantalize you?"

Everything but her mind was telling Cindy not to agree to this proposal. Her heart was set against it and pushed along the walls of her psyche, but her brain argued its case with lies of impending poverty. The more she pondered the offer, the more she fell in love with it. Finally, the brain convinced her of the one thing that she found impossible to resist—revenge for her husband. With the man hitting all the right chords, he had manipulated Cindy into forgetting about the very reason she came to the factory in the first place.

"All right, I'll do it. How will this work?" she said.

"Does your fancy little suit read PDF files?"

She didn't know the answer. "Umm… sure."

"Good, we'll figure out the rest on our end. I'll contact you when I'm ready. Have a nice night."

The lights in the control room shut off as the man disappeared into the shadows. Cindy began making her way back to the parking lot with plenty of thoughts racing through her mind. She thought about what had transpired tonight… the secret meetings, mercenaries, being fired upon, and the unexpected transformation into a superhuman. It was a thrilling experience. Not many people could stare down the barrel of a gun and keep walking forward with complete disregard for safety. What could match jumping out of a molten vat of bubbling magma and taking down well-trained soldiers without even batting an eyelash? Cindy couldn't help but feel powerful beyond all descriptions of the word. As she sat back down into her husband's stolen car, she magically transformed back into her normal self. Her slender, athletic muscles were now hidden beneath her modest clothing, allowing Cindy to blend in with the populace. As she turned the key to the ignition, she smiled to herself and thought, *I could get used to this.*

An hour later, Cindy found herself back in Queens. She steered the car into the garage and left it just as she had found it, except for the fact that it had more miles and dust than before. When she opened the door to the house, she was startled to see Jonas standing there with his arms crossed. The scowl on his face sent chills down her spine. She walked passed Jonas and tried to ignore him while putting the car keys back on the rack.

"Hey!" he yelled. "Don't you have something to say to me?"

Cindy tapped his chest softly. "Shh, calm down. I know you're angry, but just please, calm down."

"Calm down?" His eyes beamed with fury. "You left the house without your cell phone, without your license. You're not insured to drive any cars, and you stole the one car I told you I worked all my life to get. The one that I only drive for special occasions, and you took it God knows where. How did you *think* I was going to feel?"

"I'm sorry," she said.

"Just explain yourself so I can think about forgiving you."

"I had to go help Jadie with something."

Jonas stared at Cindy with a blank expression. His silence put her on edge, as she bit her lower lip in anticipation.

Jonas stepped closer to Cindy. "Are you kidding me?" Cindy flinched in response. "Do you think I'm a moron? If I call Jadie right now, she's going to tell me that you were at her apartment helping her out?"

"No, wait," she stammered. "Don't call her."

"You know what?" Jonas grabbed his phone and began dialing Jadie's number. "Let's call her right now and wake her up."

Cindy tried to grab the phone from Jonas' hands but he turned away, holding the phone up to his ear. Cindy continued to reach for the phone as he blocked her. She didn't have the heart to use her full strength to easily overpower him.

"Hello, Jadie? It's Jonas," he said.

Jadie responded in a groggy stupor, "Mmm... what time is it?"

"It's pretty freaking late. Listen, I have to ask you a question and it's very urgent," he said.

"About what?" she said in a dry, crackly voice.

"Did Cindy go to your apartment a few hours ago to help you with something?"

"What are you—hang on." Jadie fell silent on the other end, while Jonas tapped his foot and looked around the house.

"Yeah, she came over earlier."

"What?" he said, shocked.

Jadie replied, "Well, it was late and I didn't want to take the subway."

"Right, so you call a c—"

"Yes, of course I called a cab," she interrupted. "And that cab got into a horrible accident that I barely got out of alive."

"Wow, sorry to hear that."

"I asked Cindy to pick me up and take me home. There was no way I was taking any public transportation after that."

Jonas felt his foot kick him in the mouth. "I understand."

"Is that all you wanted to know?" she asked.

"Yeah, sorry to bother you, Jadie," Jonas replied.

"I'm gonna go back to bed now. Please don't call."

"Sorry."

Jonas hung up the phone and looked over to Cindy. "I guess you were telling the truth."

There was a gentle innocence lingering about her, but the subtle aura of deceit rested upon her skin like a thin layer of film. Jonas sighed and shook his head, walking away towards the bedroom without saying another word. As soon as he was gone, Cindy pulled her smart phone out from between the couch cushions. She had a text message from Jadie: "cm l8r."

The next morning Jonas made sure to get up especially early, around 4 am. The sky was still dark with a deep azure blue that encompassed the suburb. While moths fluttered around buzzing streetlights in the distance. Cindy lay asleep in her pink night gown while Jonas was traipsing about in the living room. His hair shot off in different directions, messy from his night of unrest. He tried to hunt for Cindy's cell phone with blurry eyes obscuring his vision. After turning on the tungsten lights, he spotted the black phone, in its hot-pink rubber guard, sitting on the coffee table. The screen displayed a huge lock icon with a password barring entry to Cindy's private conversations.

He scratched his cheek and stared into the digital display. In just three attempts, Jonas figured out her password and accessed her private archive. Jonas browsed the call history to see if Jadie contacted Cindy last night. The only phone call he was able to find was the one he made to Cindy as she was driving away in his prized possession. He could feel the dagger of betrayal stab him in the chest, twisting and wrenching out his bleeding trust. He pushed onward and checked Cindy's text messages, dreading what he might find. To his dismay, he discovered the conversation that went on between his wife and Jadie.

Cindy: "Tell Jonas that I was with you tonight. Please!!!!"
Jadie: "cm l8r."

Jonas hit his boiling point and charged into the bedroom, rousing Cindy from her slumber.

142

"Cindy, what the hell? You lied to me and got Jadie involved," he screamed.

Cindy, having just awakened, felt disoriented and confused. "What time is"—blinking away the sleep from her eyes, she saw her pink cell phone in Jonas' hand and said, "Were you going through my cell?"

"Yeah, did you really think I would believe that bull crap story you told me last night?"

Cindy immediately sat up and said to Jonas. "How dare you."

"How dare me? How dare you not tell me the truth. Why did you leave the house last night?" He demanded an answer and wasn't going to leave without one.

"I can't tell you, Jonas!" Her volume matching his own.

"Why the hell not?" he responded as a screaming match erupted between the two.

"Because I just can't!"

"Cindy." He tried to lower his voice to appear calmer. But his tone was still laced with volatile intentions, fooling no one. "We're a married couple. We don't keep secrets from each other. If you tell me what you did last night, I promise I'll calm down."

The word "secrets" triggered such a violent response from Cindy that she jumped out of bed and stood right in front of Jonas. Her bare feet couldn't make her tall enough to look him in the eye, but despite her shorter stature, she was still able to make Jonas flinch.

"You've got a lot of nerve telling me that we don't keep secrets from each other, when you haven't even told me what projects you work on."

"That's different, Cindy," his voice escalating again. "I was working on something that dealt with national security. Do you think CIA agents tell their families what they do?"

"Then pretend I'm in the CIA and don't ask me about what happened last night," she said, frustrated.

"Cindy, I normally leave you alone when you're pissed off, but I can't do it this time. Tell me what you did last night, and don't lie to me."

"Goddammit, Jonas, leave me"—Cindy snapped and thrust her hand straight across his face—"alone!"

The sharp crack of skin being slapped brought the screaming match to a halt. The room fell silent as Jonas' turned cheek carried a deep red imprint of Cindy's fingers. Her hand was held frozen in the air while they both stood motionless. Instead of being angry, a haunting look of regret befell her like drops of rain. Jonas blinked several times as he rubbed his cheek in an attempt to massage out the hurt. Cindy continued to look at him in disbelief about what had happened.

Covering her mouth with both hands, she whispered, "I'm so sorry. I didn't mean to…"

Jonas dropped his hands down to his sides and walked towards the bedroom dresser. He grabbed mismatched clothes from out of the drawer and began dressing himself as quickly as he could. Cindy tried to stop him from putting on his clothes, but he yanked anything she held out of her grip. She continually called his name, but her profuse apologies had no effect. He grabbed his wallet and phone, snatched his keys off the rack, and stormed out the door without once looking back at his wife.

She stood in the doorway begging him to come back; tears welled in her eyes as her husband drove out of her life. Cindy went back inside and shut the door tight, locking out the world with every bolt. The stinging of Cindy's tear-stained face mimicked the pain she inflicted upon her husband. Cindy lay atop her bed with her moistened eyes buried deep within the pillow. She didn't hide under any sheets or bother closing any doors. She merely sank into the bed. Her happiness drowned in a sea of cotton and polyester, the aroma of his cologne disappearing into the past.

Around 8 o'clock, Cindy was stirred awake by the lyrics of her favorite band blaring away in ringtone form off in the living room. Cindy's eyes practically rolled into the back of her head as she got up, irritated that she had left the phone out of arm's reach. Her annoyance multiplied when she realized it was Jadie calling.

"Yeah, Jadie?" she said with a distinct lack of patience.

"Are you coming to work?"

Cindy walked back to the bedroom with her cell phone on her ear. "I don't think so. I had a rough night."

"I meant to ask you about that. Is everything OK?" Jadie asked.

Cindy rubbed her forehead. The pain from earlier was still fresh in her memory. "I got into a huge fight with Jonas."

"He didn't believe my story, huh?" Jadie said.

Cindy shook her head. "And he found the text that I sent to you."

"Ouch," Jadie said.

"Yeah, you could say that again."

"Ouch," Jadie repeated.

"I didn't actually mean that," Cindy said annoyed.

"Well…" Jadie paused, hesitant that her next question would bury her in sister's wrath. "What *did* you do last night?"

Cindy wasn't quite sure how to respond. "I…" —she rapped her fingers on the dresser— "I trust you, Jadie, but I can't tell you."

"Is that what you told Jonas? I could see why he got pissed," Jadie said, tapping into her inner smart aleck.

"That's not funny," Cindy's voice boomed.

Jadie whined like a child, "Cindy, just tell me."

"You wouldn't believe me anyway."

"Just so I'm clear, you'll tell me about the incident that made you leave the police force. But you won't tell me why you snuck out last night? Did you do something worse than what had happened when you were a cop?"

"This is way different and a lot m—" Cindy's thought was interrupted by a beep on the other line. "I have to call you back."

"Umm, don't forget I'm responsible for your punkass kids when you're out," Jadie said. "So the sooner you come back to work, the better it is for me. Kay?"

"I'll be in tomorrow. I'll call you back."

Cindy switched over to the call waiting and was greeted by an unusually excited Michael. "Cindy! You have to come down to the lab."

"Did you figure out how to remove the suit?" she asked.

"Better, I have a new firmware update for the suit and a new build to install."

"How is that better? I thought we were going to remove this thing?"

"I'm working on it. Just come down,"

Not even allowing Cindy to respond, the line fell silent. Cindy let out a deep sigh; her motivation to do anything was sapped to nothing. While getting dressed, she spotted a photo of her and Jonas atop the Great Wall of China. She pulled the photo into her hands and rubbed his cheek with her thumb. With her blouse still undone, she placed the photo on the bed and buried her head into her hands. She didn't weep or sob, despite the tears banging on the walls of her tortured eyes, demanding to be let free. Cindy let out a sigh. She gathered her resolve and buttoned up her blouse before heading to Lucent Labs.

An hour later, Cindy arrived at the lab and greeted Michael, who was buried in programming code as usual. She said hello to Michael, but her voice was quiet and somber. Not that it mattered to him, he was too busy being excited on updating the firmware to his baby.

"Cindy, glad you could make it," he said with excitement.

She said nothing as her eyes glazed over the lab, uninterested in anything happening in this place. Her distracted demeanor and emotionless grimace only further revealed her lack of enthusiasm. Michael tapped the chair beside him as Cindy took lethargic steps over to the seat. She plopped down into the black swivel chair, collapsing like a rag doll. Her normally proud shoulders slouched inward like a shrunken old woman.

"Couldn't you just make the suit download this update you're talking about?" Disinterest dripped from Cindy's every word.

"Not yet. Remember that a lot of this suit is incomplete. You're lucky you were even able to survive a night with this thing. There's no telling what it's capable of."

As Michael prepped the update for installation, Cindy couldn't help but wonder how Michael would respond to last night's incident. The need to tell someone of her amazing super heroics was gnawing at her, poking and prodding, doing everything it could to make her lips pop.

Her fingers rapped on the desk while Michael stared at the progress bar on the screen. The temptation was growing by the second. Her eyes were darting back and forth almost as if her body were trying to distract her from blurting out something she would regret.

"So, Cindy," Michael said, as he rested his chin on top of his interlaced fingers. "Jonas has told me a lot about you over the years."

Thanks to Michael's interruption, the nagging feeling of wanting to spill her secrets dissipated. Now the urges only cruised beneath the surface like a submarine in the depths of the ocean.

"Good things, I hope," she replied.

"Well, he said you were on your way to becoming a detective. But he asked you to quit the police force because he was afraid you were going to get hurt."

Cindy laughed. "Is that what he told you? That's very sweet, but it's not true."

"Which part, you being a former cop?"

"No, I was going to be a detective, but things didn't quite work out."

"So what really happened?"

Cindy sighed as she thought back to that fateful day. Her eyes dropped down to the floor in a lost gaze as she stepped back through time.

"I was with my partner Josh O'Hara. He was the most stereotypical Irish cop I had ever met. Bright red hair that was kept tight and short, blue eyes, fair skin, freckles, and a really big chin that seemed to push his mouth up to his nose. There were some days when I thought I was partnered with Conan O'Brien. Actually, he looked more like Damien Lewis, now that I think about it." Cindy tapped her chin and thought back for a moment. "Josh was a pretty good looking man, I must admit."

Michael interjected, "I don't know who any of those people are."

Cindy's eyes popped open in shock as she leaned in and said, "Are you serious?"

"I don't watch TV," Michael said. "But I do listen to technology podcasts. The Woz is my role model."

"Who's The Woz?" she asked.

Michael took his glasses off and also leaned in, mimicking Cindy. "You don't know who the Woz is? The real brains behind Apple computers?"

"I guess that makes us even," Cindy said with a smile.

Michael gave her a sideways glance and said, "You disgust me. Anyway, please continue with your story."

"I was with Josh trying to track down leads on a narcotics case. We had found a stash of drugs in an abandoned car with no license plate. Millions of dollars' worth of cocaine."

Michael whistled in awe.

"Yeah, tell me about it. We're standing by the car and I'm getting ready to call in the detectives. After all, we were just beat cops with no business meddling in narcotics affairs. But Josh had this bright idea that we should be the ones to nab the guys picking up the drugs. If we called in the detectives, they'd set up a crime scene, and the traffickers would know that we found their stash.

"I explained to him that we weren't detectives and that it wasn't our job. He didn't care. He kept telling me that if we cracked the case, we would get promoted.

Two of our veteran detectives had retired, so it wasn't like his logic was flawed or anything."

Michael chimed in, "So you two had the perfect opportunity to become hotshots."

"Exactly, so Josh convinced me to hold off on calling division headquarters and we waited. It didn't help that we were in a patrol car, so we had to park out of sight and use binoculars. We must have waited maybe... 45 minutes? I don't remember. I just know it wasn't too long before the suspects rolled up in an SUV. Josh was ready to go in guns blazing, but I convinced him that we should follow them and see if they could lead us to a bigger fish.

"I mean, think about it, if you had that much cocaine, there's no way you could sell it all without distributing it to your dealers first. We watched them transfer all the bags into the SUV and took pictures of the whole thing. When they finished loading up the car, we followed them to the distribution center, which wasn't easy because of the car. Eventually, they led us all the way up to Hunts Point in the Bronx, straight into the projects."

"Were you scared?" Michael interrupted.

"Of course, you don't want to be in Hunts Point late at night. I knew without a doubt in my mind that these guys were carrying guns... We should have called for backup..." Cindy trailed off as her memories crashed to the forefront. "We should have called for backup."

She regained her focus and looked at Michael with a regretful look in her eyes, reluctant to continue the story. Michael remained silent and waited with bated breath to hear the rest of the tale.

"We recognized one of the guys coming out to greet the 'mailmen.' Caifas Maròn, an immigrant from El Salvador who got involved with the Mexican Drug Cartel. We had arrested him so many times, but somehow we never had enough evidence to lock him down for good. Josh was just itchin' to get out and bust him—we had all the evidence we needed. All that was left was to collar him and call it a night.

"Josh reached for the horn—I mean the radio—and called for backup. You would think calling for backup would make me feel better, but it actually mortified me. It meant we were going in so no one could escape. I begged him not to get out of the car but he just said to me, 'Cindy, this is our chance. We have to take it.' He flashed the lights and got out of the car screaming, 'Police, put your hands up!'

"At that point, I had no choice. I had to go with him. I got out of the car, grabbed my gun and yelled, 'Don't move, don't move!' So what did they do? They ran. O'Hara chased after Caifas into the projects while I chased after the deliverymen with the drugs. I was lucky. They only had knives. When I caught up to them and drew my gun, they immediately surrendered. I cuffed them both and ran back to the projects.

"When I went inside—ugh, I could smell the stench of urine all over the walls—I could hear struggling nearby. I went upstairs and turned down the hallway to see a pistol in Caifas' hand and Josh trying to keep it at bay. I pointed my weapon at the two of them and said, 'Drop the gun now.' It did nothing, like I wasn't even in the same room. Caifas must have been a lot stronger than he looked, because O'Hara was a pretty tough guy and should have put him down already. Josh kept yelling, 'Shoot him!'

"When a cop tells you to shoot while he's interlocked with a suspect, that's a sign of desperation. I tried to aim my gun, but my hands couldn't stop shaking. Caifas and Josh were too close together. I couldn't get a good bead on him—I was too afraid I would shoot my partner. But Josh just kept yelling, 'Shoot him, Cindy!' He wrestled Caifas towards my direction, which gave me the only opportunity to take the shot. I steadied my hands as best I could, but you cannot understand how hard it is to keep calm when you risk shooting your friend.

"I took a deep breath and fired my weapon... a second too late. Caifas had turned Josh around just in time for my bullet to embed itself in my partner's back. When I realized what had happened, it felt like I had been stabbed in the chest. The back of my neck ached and I wanted to drop my gun to the floor. That scrawny prick Caifas was just standing there, looking as surprised as I was. His gross, shaggy hair and thick, scraggly beard disgusted me, but what set me off was his delighted expression: grinning from ear to ear. I became livid. I put my gun in my holster and charged at him, blind to the fact that he still had a gun in his hand. It was stupid, very stupid to do what I did... but I was so angry.

"He aimed his gun at me, but I kept on running towards him. I used my Krav Maga training to get control of the weapon. I hit his forearm and forced the gun to point down towards the floor. I stepped in, twisted the gun out of his hands, and rendered him completely defenseless. I could have arrested him, but instead I threw the gun down the stairs and beat the living daylights out of him. I slammed his head into the wall, stomped on his groin... ugh, it was awful. I had become some kind of a monster, completely out of control. When I was finished, all I could see were the whites in his eyes as his pupils rolled into the back of his head."

"You killed him?" Michael asked in disbelief.

Her sorrow rendered her unable to speak as she mouthed the word... *"Yes."*

"What happened after? Did your partner die?" Michael asked.

Regaining her composure, Cindy shook her head. "No, thank God, he was wearing a vest. He still needed to go to the hospital, but he survived without being paralyzed. A miracle. After the incident, I was charged with police brutality and voluntary manslaughter."

"Holy crap," Michael said.

"Yeah, thankfully, the jury was on my side, especially after Josh's testimony. But I couldn't bear to look at myself in the mirror while wearing a uniform. Even though Josh survived unscathed and apologized for dragging me into that situation, I just... I couldn't do it anymore."

Michael replied, "I understand, sorry I brought it up. I had no idea—"

As if decreed by fate, the computer chimed, indicating that the installation of the new build was complete. Michael rubbed his hands together with glee, eager to test the results of his bug fixes.

"Why don't you go ahead and pop the suit on for me."

"Sure."

As the suit poured over her skin, like molten lava oozing down a mountainside, Michael had to stop himself from staring at her body. He gave himself a little tap on the cheek and shook his head as if trying to banish any impure thoughts from his mind. When the suit came online, he discussed some of the fixes he had made to Cindy.

"So I found this weird bug where your suit could intercept cell phone signals and radios at the same time. Basically, it would make the signals cut each other out and give you static or phone calls that you could hear in the background. You probably didn't notice, but it's fixed regardless."

Cindy looked away, pretending not to know what he was talking about.

"Right."

"Let's run some tests and see what we've got here."

To Cindy's disappointment, Michael's tests verged on the tedious. He would throw a cup of pens in the air and ask Cindy to track each and every one of them. Little blinking red squares would appear in front of her eyes accompanied by a little chime confirming lock-on. She could see the estimated trajectory of the pens, where they were going to hit the floor, and how fast they were falling.

Although interesting to see, it wasn't the most exciting thing Cindy thought she would be doing. For the next test, Michael made Cindy run through some basic calisthenics and placed her on a treadmill. While she jogged, Michael found himself unable to keep his eyes off of her. He tried his hardest not to stare, but his curious eyes scanned every portion of her fit body. He kept trying to turn away, looking at the drab monitor. But his peripheral vision kept luring him back to the image of this goddess, flooding his mind with lustful thoughts. He asked himself if he thought she was sexy, wondering if maybe he was confusing loneliness with real attraction. As she ran on the treadmill, Michael caught himself staring at her ample breasts and tried to snap himself out of his infatuation.

"How are you feeling?" he asked.

"At this pace, I could run from here to New Jersey and not break a sweat," she replied enthusiastically.

"Really?" he said impressed. "You're running at a pretty good clip there."

Cindy shrugged her shoulders while running and said, "I feel all right."

"So is your sister single by any chance?" he blurted out without even realizing what he was saying. "Umm, forget I said that, actually."

Cindy laughed as she continued her jog. "Are you single and looking?"

"Well," he paused, "you know, I firmly believe that there is a hidden balance in life. The smarter you are, the less likely you are to get la—I mean, have relations."

"You won't get a girl with that kind of language, young man. But yes, Jadie is single."

"Is she hot?" Michael asked.

"Michael!" Cindy stepped off the treadmill and flicked him in the head. "No wonder you're single. You can't talk about girls—wait, no, women—like sex objects."

"I'm sorry. I'm really bad at this."

"I don't know what websites you've been reading, but if you act like a typical gross male, you're going to find yourself alone, like you are now. If you're going to ask me what my sister looks like, ask, 'do you think I would find her attractive?' Not 'do you think she's hot?'" she said with her best dumb jock impersonation.

Michael cleared his throat. "Dearest madam, do you believe I would find your sibling attractive?"

"Okay, that's weird, but an improvement. Yes, my sister is very pretty, but don't ever tell her I said that."

"Is she... single and looking?"

"You're asking for trouble if you date my sister. She's not exactly an innocent little angel."

"That's a very mean thing to say about your sister."

"Sibling rivalry, Michael. I must always be the prettiest one when compared to my sister."

Michael smiled and shook his head. He quietly uttered to himself, "I don't think you have to worry about that."

Cindy looked at Michael, hiding a smirk behind her mask. "If you really want to meet my sister, I can put in a good word for you."

Michael's eyes looked hopeful. "I would like that very much."

He went back to his computer terminal and saw something that drastically altered his facial expression. He glanced at Cindy, who was looking away stretching her arms, and turned back to his monitor. He made a few simple key strokes and sighed as he turned his attention back to Cindy.

"I think that's all for today, Cindy."

"Well, that was boring."

"Yeah, bug fixing always is. I'll try to have something more interesting next time," he said with a distinct lack of energy.

Cindy deactivated the suit. "Will you be able to remove the suit in your next build?"

"Eventually it will get removed. Whether it's the next build or not, I'm not sure."

"Okay," she sighed and bit her lip. "I would like to stop lying to Jonas."

"I understand. I will do what I can to get the suit removed. I'll be in touch."

Cindy waved Michael goodbye and left the lonely lab. Walking down the city street, thoughts of her husband leaving without saying a word still weighed heavily upon her conscience. She would see couples strolling hand in hand down the avenue to the annoyance of the always-rushed New Yorkers. She kept mentally kicking herself for having smacked Jonas and knew she needed to make it up to him. She brought out her cell phone and gave his mobile a ring, but it went straight to voice mail.

When she heard the robotic answering machine, it felt like a balloon had popped inside of her and expunged any happiness she had been holding onto. She leaned up against the wall of a nearby business building when a sudden, pleasant chirp oscillated within her ear. She looked around to see if someone's cell phone was going off, but no one checked their pockets or reached for a phone. When the chirp ceased, a familiar voice overcame the boisterous sounds of the city.

"Testing, 1, 2, 3. Can you hear me?" the voice said.

Cindy looked confused. She pressed her fingers up against her ear and said, "Yes, I can hear you."

"Good," the voice replied, followed by a very low dialogue in the background.

"Tell him the connection worked," she barely heard him say.

"Who are you?" Cindy asked.

"Did you forget I was going to call?"

"You're the man from the factory?"

159

"Correct. You may call me Samuel Adams, or Sam for short."

"You know, I get the feeling the name is not a reference to the beer. Are you tired of paying your taxes, Sam?"

"If ye love wealth greater than liberty, the tranquility of servitude greater than the animating contest for freedom, go home from us in peace. We seek not your counsel, nor your arms. Crouch down and lick the hand that feeds you; may your chains set lightly upon you, and may posterity forget that ye were our countrymen."

"—Samuel Adams. I don't think anyone remembers those words," Cindy said.

"I'm impressed you knew who the quote was from."

"Deductive reasoning, Sam."

"Hmph, not bad. So, what do I call you?"

She thought for a moment. "This may seem a bit contrived, but I feel that Silver Ninja best describes what I'm capable of."

"An assassin armored in silver, infiltrating the most secure places in the world? Very well, Silver Ninja it is. Are you ready for your first assignment?"

"Give me one second," Cindy replied.

Cindy looked around, trying to find someplace hidden to duck into, but she only saw overpopulated city streets. People from all walks of life flooded the saturated sidewalk with their mindless meandering, preventing Cindy from activating the suit discreetly. Then she spotted a fire escape dangling in an alley nearby. Cindy made her way to the ladder but stopped short, realizing that there was no dumpster nearby. But that wouldn't stop Cindy.

She took a hefty running start and dashed for the ladder. Cindy hopped into the air and kicked off the brick building in front of her, twisting her body just enough to grab the rusty, bottom rung of the ladder. With her hands firmly in place, Cindy pulled herself up with incredible ease, as if she were as light as a feather. When she reached the top of the roof, Cindy found a nearby water tower and hid within the shadowy struts supporting the bucket. Even people watching from their windows would have had a hard time seeing her. After a few moments, the brightly glowing blue eyes emerged from the shadows. Cindy stood before the city with her fists clenched tight, defiant to the fear that would cause others to cower.

"I'm back," she said to Sam.

"I'm uploading the mission now. Do you see it?"

Text read across the top of Cindy's eyes stating that it was retrieving files from a remote location. While the files were downloading, Cindy could see dossiers and information popping into her line of sight, augmenting her reality. A Googled image of Samuel Adams appeared in the upper-left corner, identifying whom Cindy was talking to, and another image scrolled up from the bottom with a picture of the target.

Cindy asked, "Why does the target look so familiar? Oh, and nice profile pic. Did you Google that yourself?"

"Haha, you're so clever," Sam said sarcastically. "Anyway, you should recognize the target because your state voted for him. That's James Albright, a notoriously corrupt senator. All of the issues he voted for have served his own interests: companies being allowed to abuse their workers to meet profit estimates; kickbacks from oil companies; kickbacks from solar farm operators; a ban on street protests. You'll be doing this nation a favor."

"Wait," Cindy said, realizing something was amiss. "This is really high profile. Your surveillance shows he has bodyguards in his house 24-7. And the media will be all over this."

"Which is exactly why I recruited you. You can get in and out without leaving a trace. If you didn't have that super suit, I wouldn't have asked."

"Old Westbury. Long Island, huh? Guy's got money."

"Of course he has money. It's how he keeps buying elections. Payment for this contract will be fifty thousand."

"A little cheap for a senator, but all right, I'll head over there now,"

"I'll be in touch. Good luck, Silver."

The little picture of Samuel Adams disappeared into nothingness as the communication line closed down. *Now how am I going to get over there?* Cindy thought to herself. It would be counterproductive for her to turn off the suit, take the subway, then take the bus back to Queens. Instead, Cindy explored the depths of the suit, searching for systems that would allow her to overcome the NYC obstacle course.

A menu appeared on the left side of her Heads Up Display (HUD). It was located right above a curious little outline of Cindy's body filled in with a cool aqua color. Cindy deduced that it was probably an indicator to monitor the status of the suit. She scrolled through the menu and saw text for various features that Michael had not told her about. With a blink of the eye, Cindy could give herself access to the most futuristic weaponry in the world. She ignored all those features, however, and went straight to the travel menu. The button became a vibrant, deep red and blinked a few times before opening a sub menu that read, FLV-X-00 Motorcycle. Trying to activate the cycle did nothing except cause an error to appear with a placeholder graphic of an ordinary motorcycle.

"Okay..." she said aloud while closing the menu. Cindy moved to the next section of the travel menu which listed a grappling hook. Upon activating the selection, she felt a strange heaviness weighing down her arms. She looked down to her wrists and witnessed a massive blob forming atop her forearms. The formless mass morphed into a housing unit for a grappling hook with giant spear-headed hooks nestled within their shells, waiting to be fired. *Whoa,* she thought to herself. Within moments, multitudes of green boxes appeared on buildings throughout the city. She pointed her arm to one of the nearby high rise apartments, which prompted the computer to ask, "Do you wish to proceed?"

Cindy was afraid to select yes. After all, there was no telling what would happen if she did. Yet the chance at an exhilarating ride through the city compelled

163

her to take the plunge into the unknown. Against her better judgment, her impulse kicked in, triggering Cindy to say yes to the prompt. Her arm shot out in front of her in complete rebellion to her will. She nodded her head in a panic as she tried to pull her arm back down, but it seemed locked in place. The hook blasted from the cannon as a silver coil spiraled out in front of her. The grapple wedged itself into the ledge of a nearby rooftop, causing the tether to snap straight like a power line. The synthetic rope began pulling Cindy off the edge of the roof as she cried out, "No, no, no, no, no." Her feet skidded along the rooftop causing amber and ivory rocks to fly up into the air like a water spray, until finally she was pulled off the roof and into the city street below.

Cindy began to glide through the air, kicking her legs in a futile attempt to touch land. She dangled across the looming skyline, prisoner to the cybernetic machine trapping her helpless arm. As the towering building barreled towards her, she had no hope of avoiding a head-on collision. Cindy braced herself for impact but was suddenly caught off-guard when her left arm shot a separate hook to an adjacent building. The first hook detached itself from the approaching tower, allowing Cindy's vector to change course and avoid impact with the monolithic glass mirror. The wind rushed through her helmet like a motorcycle speeding down the highway. She screamed in exhilaration as the thrill of flying through the city corridor shocked her senses with weightless excitement. Cindy noticed that if she aimed her arms at the green boxes, the hooks would lock on and fire at each target automatically. Each successive swing pulled on her arms so tightly that they would shake from the extraordinary G-forces.

As the colorful dusk sky continued its slow transition to shadowy nightfall, she began pushing herself to climb higher and higher into the heavens. The purples mixed with oranges and an encroaching dark blue, as if the earth were putting on mascara and eye shadow. At these altitudes, Cindy felt as though she could almost see the universe. The horns and traffic from the streets below were barely audible at Cindy's height. All that could be heard around her was the serenity of freedom and the wind peacefully blowing past. That tranquility was shattered, however, when the topic of landing crashed into her head. Swinging through midtown suddenly didn't seem so calming when Cindy realized she would have figure out a way to land in one piece.

She spotted a rooftop with a wide berth off in the distance. With the landing zone approaching, Cindy had only seconds to figure out how she was going to slow down her velocity. Before she knew it, the rooftop was already rolling under her legs while she was still moving at top speed. Cindy lifted her knees up to her chest and smacked down onto the surface with her bottom. Sparks flew out from under her legs like a welder fusing metal in a workshop. The hook released itself and retracted back into Cindy's arm as she tumbled and crashed into the protruding rooftop exit.

Cindy laid there with her legs held up in the air, resting upon the walls of the rooftop egress route. Her vision was blocked by a prompt that asked, "Do you wish to enable automatic grappling?" Cindy growled to herself and said aloud, "I think I'm going to take a cab." She deactivated the suit and shamefully made her way downstairs. Recognizing her grappling techniques needed fine-tuning, she hailed a cab and headed back to Queens, to once again steal Jonas' car.

Around 11 pm, Cindy found herself rolling into Old Westbury, taunted by opulent mansions, backyard tennis courts, and luxury vehicles hidden within the guarded walls of each home. Lush forests protected the old money living there, hiding golf courses and country clubs within a maze of winding streets and dense forest. Jonas had originally wanted to move there but decided against it because their commute would be even worse than it already was.

She wondered how a senator could afford a rich neighborhood like this and thought about what Sam had told her. Unless he was a surgeon or a CEO of a booming industry, there was no way the Senator could afford living here without some kind of kickback. It was difficult to find parking for the Saleen as most of the homes in Westbury were secluded and isolated from the riffraff that could wander into their protected village. Cindy had no choice but to park on the dirt shoulder and walk the rest of the way to Albright's mansion.

Walking through the woodland forest under the cover of night, leaves rustled and twigs snapped. Her attempts at passing through gingerly were failing miserably, but thankfully, there was no one in range to make a fuss about it. After a few minutes of creeping through dense woods, Cindy saw a dimly lit clearing and several well-dressed guards patrolling the perimeter of the mansion. Their yawning and card-playing revealed their lack of professionalism, thus exposing their weakness. *These weren't hardened mercenaries,* Cindy thought to herself, just well-trained security guards who probably didn't take their jobs too seriously. Cindy felt an impulsive urge to charge in and massacre the hapless brutes. She stepped back and snapped herself out of her bloodlust, frightened by the strange feeling that had overcome her. She shook it off as a fluke, a random thought that could invade anyone's mind when presented with new superhuman capabilities.

Cindy scanned the mansion with a binocular feature that allowed her to tag targets and identify weapons. There also seemed to be an ability to do an area scan of the perimeter of the mansion, detailing how many guards were on patrol. Once everyone was tagged, Cindy planned her course of action. She found a branch that extended just far enough into a balcony on the 2nd floor of the estate. It wasn't quite close enough that she could just drop in, but she was confident in her ability to make the leap.

Cindy climbed the maple tree, like a squirrel, and utilized her balance beam training to tiptoe her way to the end of the branch. The tree limb bent downward under Cindy's weight, shaking the leaves with each movement she made to stabilize herself. It wasn't until she approached the end of the branch that Cindy realized that it was more like a tight rope than a thick stable beam. After steadying herself,

167

Cindy leapt across the gap onto the balcony. Her landing made a dull, muffled thud, surprisingly soft given that her body was encapsulated in heavy metal. She stood up and leaned against the wall, checking the soles of her feet to see if she could figure out how she landed so quietly. Cindy noticed the bottoms of her feet were coated in a light rubber which absorbed all the sonic vibration.

The soles reminded Cindy of her free-running days as a youth, when she tried to outdo Jadie in dangerous stunts. For a moment Cindy questioned how she had come to this point: an assassin about to murder a man she had never met. She shook her head and put aside her feelings of doubt. She had a job to do. Cindy opened an unlocked French door and entered an empty guest room. There were two king-sized beds properly made in uniform fashion, a dim lamp sitting atop a very lavish wooden end table, green walls and dark green carpeting. The room had sort of an outdoor sportsman feel. The tangerine glow from the lamp made the room feel cozy and inviting. Cindy's silver-encased body glowed like polished gold, seeming out of place in this welcoming abode.

She thought to herself, *I wish I could see through w—hat the heck?* Right on cue, the thermal imaging activated itself and drenched Cindy's vision with a rainbow of green, blue, yellow, orange, and red. She could see the door before her turn into a transparent blue while a row of yellow orbs dotted the wall on the other side. As the suit continued scanning, Cindy spotted a massive orange and yellow blob walking up to the door. The nebulous figure stretched out its glowing hand

and grabbed the doorknob, which let out a quiet click as it began to turn. Cindy flattened herself up against the wall, standing near the hinges, as the door creaked open.

The lazy guard gently shut the door behind him. Dragging his feet, he made his way towards the fluffy bed, trying to sneak in a few winks without anyone noticing. But just before he laid down, the guard spotted the open balcony door and ran towards it in a frightened state. He clutched his radio and attempted to report an intrusion when Cindy's leg appeared over his head. The back of her knee wrapped around the man's neck, preventing even one syllable from being uttered. Using her incredible balance and strength, Cindy gently lowered the guard to the floor as he lost consciousness. Cindy guided him down and released his neck upon reaching the floor. As he slept in peace on the plush carpet, Cindy stood up and ventured into the ambiguous hallway.

The hallways' décor befitted an Old Westbury manor: French-style lighting fixtures protruding from the drywall, expensive vases set atop coffee-colored stands with meticulous floral prints painted upon them, and an intricate oriental carpet with complex designs and shapes woven from end to end. The scent of freshly-vacuumed floors still lingered in the air, warning Cindy to be cautious of any cleaning maids still going about their business. From the looks of it, the mansion was massive, and she needed to know exactly where she was going. Before she could take one more step, Cindy's comm link beeped with an incoming transmission.

"I have some additional intelligence for you. The master bedroom is on the second floor of the north section of the mansion. Going up the stairs in the main foyer and through the center hallway should take you straight to him. Mr. Albright tends to stay up watching late-night TV shows. I'll leave it to your discretion on how to proceed from that point, but don't get caught."

"Got it," she replied. Armed with new intelligence, Cindy crouched down and crept her way towards the main foyer. The two elegant stairways snuggled the edges of the wall, greeting her with royal courtesy. *Pretentious much?* she thought, while tiptoeing up the gold-trimmed stair case. Looking over the railing, she saw a gorgeous chandelier filling the negative space with glittering diamonds that sparkled in the light. Further down near the main entrance, Cindy spotted two guards who seemed bored out of their minds with slouched postures and deep, moaning yawns. Had she not glanced back to admire the chandeliers' spectacle she might have noticed the third guard patrolling on the opposite end of the room sooner.

With no time to think, Cindy dropped down onto the stairs into a prone position and prayed that the stealth camouflage would work. As the third guard looked in her direction, her body became translucent. She breathed a sigh of relief until her skin began to flicker like a badly damaged TV signal. The guard took notice of the flickering light and started walking towards her location. Cindy didn't

170

know what to do. She didn't have anything to throw and the stealth camouflage was splattering error messages all over her HUD. If she didn't do something fast, her protective invisibility would shut off and leave her as stealthy as a glowing disco ball.

Cindy spotted a painting of some stuffy old bastard hanging above her head. Out of sheer desperation, Cindy stood up and pulled the painting off the wall. The guard felt his courage evacuate from his body as the phantom painting lifted itself from the wall and went flying towards the chandelier. The masterpiece lighting fixture lurched slowly to one side before slipping off its harness and plummeting to the floor below.

"Andre, what the hell did you do?" a guard yelled from below.

"Did you see that?" the second floor guard yelled in response.

While the guards were distracted, Cindy ran into the hallway as fast as she could. Her body blinked back into existence as the stealth camouflage failed once again. As she jogged down the hallway, she could hear someone saying, "What the hell was that?" off in the distance. She ducked into a nearby closet and hid within the dark's tar blanket. Peering through a crack in the door, she saw a guard and the senator walk past, then she could hear infuriated yelling. Cindy waited out the torrential scolding the Senator was unleashing on the guards. When the room fell quiet, Cindy waited for the senator to walk back to his master bedroom.

It was time to make her move. A quick thermal scan of the area let her know that the coast was clear. She darted over to the bedroom and pressed down on the brass handle in front of her. She gave the chestnut door a gentle lift and managed to open it without even a creak. She was surprised to find that this room was not the master bedroom but rather a portioned hallway to additional rooms. Although there were multiple doors in the darkened corridor, one door stood out from the others. A glowing, shifting blue light danced beneath the crack of the door as muted laughter followed lame jokes delivered by a television host. She closed the door behind her and sat down next to the bedroom entrance.

Mere moments later, it was time. The TV clicked off and the blue lights emanating from beneath the door disappeared in an instant. She heard the sound of someone rolling over in their bed and then... silence. She pulled herself off the floor and stood in front of the door with her hand hovering near the knob. Cindy took a deep breath in order to calm her racing heart, but the fear and anxiety overwhelmed her at every pass. Her metallic hand wrapped around the doorknob, opening it with a ginger touch. The entrance cracked open and the sound of deep snoring could be heard echoing within the bedroom chamber. There he was, Senator James Albright, fast asleep in his bed without a care in the world.

She stepped into the quiet bedroom, one patient step at a time, refusing to allow any opportunity for sound to escape from the floor. Cindy didn't know how she was going to finish the job. There are millions of ways to kill a human being and she couldn't even come up with one. Doubt bloomed into her mind as reservations about this mission began to deteriorate her confidence. Upon seeing his middle-aged face, she wondered if this man had a family, a child, someone he mattered to. Cindy shook her head and banished any thoughts that might generate sympathy. She needed to remember the objective. She needed to finish the mission, even though everything, except for her mind, told her not to.

Cindy stood before the defenseless old man like a church gargoyle, motionless but ever-present. His body reflected upon her hardened shell, smeared by the texture of her silver skin. The poisonous cocktail of fear and excitement churned inside of Cindy, breeding a hideous creature of wanton destruction. Rationalism faded into the background. The psychological id burst through the surface, commanding Cindy to follow its beckoning. She grabbed a pillow laying next to him, gripping its sateen texture between her fingertips. She sucked in as much air as she could, puffing out her chest, warding off all the theoretical consequences that attacked her mind like banshees.

With one motion, she thrust the pillow upon his fragile skull. Senator Albright awoke in an instant and struggled to fight off Cindy's assault. Flecks of red pigment splattered over the pillow case as he scratched his fingernails across Cindy's reinforced skin. His muffled screams were unintelligible, but the meaning behind them was clear: save me. Cindy shut off all emotion as the corded muscles in her arms locked in place. Ice-cold blood coursed through her veins as her humanity left the scene in disgrace. After what seemed like an endless struggle with his attacker, the stripes of the senator's pajamas stopped writhing with his body. His flailing arms and legs stopped resisting, and the squirming of his life ceased.

She didn't need the suit to tell her if he was still alive. The lack of movement beneath her stone-cold hands was telling enough. Cindy looked at the wrinkled pillow clenched between her fingers and debated whether or not she wanted to pull it off to see the damage. A sudden horrible feeling of nausea overwhelmed her, convincing her she did not want to see her own handiwork. She left the pillow where it was and turned to the nearest exit.

She opened the window in the master bedroom and saw the steep drop before her. There were no trees nearby, just a garden and a patio below. Normally, a jump like this would have broken her legs, but these were no longer normal circumstances. She dove out of the window and vanished into the black forest without a trace.

"Silver..." the comm link beeped. "Well done. My spies confirm the elimination of James Albright. I have wired a sum of fifty thousand dollars into your account. The first shot towards freedom has been fired. I will contact you at a later time for another contract assignment."

CHAP7ER 5

ANTI-HERO

"With us now is Raymond Levreux, President and CEO of 1st Continental Technologies. Good morning, Mr. Levreux." The TV droned on in the background as Cindy prepared her morning breakfast, alone. The camera cut to a well-coiffed man in his early fifties, sporting a dapper suit and a clean-shaven face.

"Good morning, Sally," he responded to the anchor with a charming smile.

Sally addressed Raymond in a very matter-of-fact fashion, "Mr. Levreux, as you may have heard already, Senator Albright was found murdered in his Westbury mansion."

"Yes, absolutely horrible news."

"The question on everyone's mind is 'will you be running for office?' With the vacancy in the Senate, it seems you're a prime candidate to fill the seat; however, you have stated in the past that you disagreed with many of Albright's policies. Do you plan to repeal his policies if you fill the seat?"

"That's two questions, Sally," he said with a smirk. "Yes, I have been debating whether to run for the Senate, but haven't made any formal announcements as of yet. As for reversing his decisions, my policies would be in the interest of the

American people, not the corporations."

"And how would you respond to critics that are concerned about your criminal record?"

Raymond's pleasant demeanor shifted into a much more serious disposition. "I thought I'd have at least three more questions before you pulled out the big guns. Let's set the record straight before continuing any further discussion. I was arrested for protesting corporations that abuse honest, hard-working Americans. I did not get arrested for murder, drugs or theft. I cannot apologize for exercising my freedom of speech."

Sally was quick to backpedal. "My apologies, Mr. Levreux. Regardless, you yourself lead one of the world's largest tech firms. How can you say your policies will be any different when you are in bed with the so-called enemy?"

"If I may loosely quote Bill Cosby: 'If you're going to beat the man at chess, you need to learn the rules of the game.'"

"So occupying Wall Street didn't work out for you?" she said with a light smile.

He replied with impassioned fervor. "It may not have accomplished much, but it did educate me about how our country works. You can't be an average-joe punk trying to change the world. You need to be somebody in order for your influence to carry weight. Being the CEO of a highly successful company has allowed me the opportunity to make a difference."

"Raymond, thank you for joining us today."

"It was my pleasure."

Sally turned towards the camera and said, "Coming up next, will the late Senator Albright's anti-demonstration policy still go into effect without his support? We'll be right back…"

Cindy shut off the TV while finishing the last of her cereal and turned to her silent phone. She stared into the black void encased in plastic and wondered if Jonas ever called. The screen came to life at the touch of her fingers. She rushed through the different screens eager to check her missed calls; nothing. No one had called. There was only an ever-present emptiness. Cindy's body sank into her chair, deflating along with her inner self. Suddenly, the black void in her phone blinked to life, vibrating on the table. Cindy snatched the phone with excitement, only to be disappointed by who was on the other line.

"Hey, Jadie," Cindy said in a morose manner.

"You comin' to work?" Jadie asked.

With a distinct lack of energy, Cindy said, "Yeah, I'm on my way now."

"Are you all right?" Jadie asked, concerned.

"I'm fine. I'll see you soon."

As she rose from her chair, Cindy's slouched posture and slow gait told tales of her misbegotten adventure. Her usual morning vigor was drained out of her body. Instead, she was filled with an immense burden of sadness. She made another futile attempt to call Jonas, but only a robotic answering machine answered. She needed to deal with this angst before it took her to the dark place she had once escaped. Lifting weights and kicking the crap out of punching bags were her therapy, but she needed more than therapy for the misery that plagued her.

She got dressed and walked over to the mirror to apply her makeup. The mirror, once an ally of beauty, disgusted her. She would look into the reflection and see the image of a psychopath, a murderer. What she had done weighed heavily on her conscience. Nausea would grip her throat and trick her into thinking that she needed to expulse the bile within her, but there was nothing to expunge. Even the cereal she had eaten revolted her. The excessively sugary food was meant to be a treat, but she felt miserable after consuming the sweet cereal. Tired of wallowing in her own self-pity, Cindy left her home and made an attempted to return to her normal routine.

Along the way, Cindy found herself struggling with a most uncommon conflict. She had to be persistent in resisting the urge to shirk work and put on the suit. Despite being disgusted with herself and having told Jadie she was coming in, Cindy felt compelled to suit up. It goaded her to put on the suit, not for long of course, just a few exhilarating minutes. The power would pull her into its arms, like a long lost lover, seducing Cindy to succumb to its world. *Just for a few seconds,* she thought to herself. Even though she knew it was neither the time nor the place.

She began to daydream and hallucinate while riding the subway. Images of metal ribbons tying up her arms and wrapping her body haunted her psyche. She would struggle to free herself from the tentacles; her hands balled up in a fist as her arms quaked from trying to break free of the glue-like tendrils. Even her strong muscles were no match for this metallic creature, which was doing everything in its lifeless power to consume her whole. Her name repeated over and over as the silver monstrosity choked the life out of her, "Cindy, Cindy, Cindy."

"Cindy!" Jadie yelled.

Lost and confused as to how she got to the gymnasium, Cindy's eyes blinked rapidly as her gaze darted around like a hockey puck.

"Class is over. It's time to leave," Jadie said while masking her unease.

"Class? I thought I was riding the sub—"

"What's the matter with you?" Jadie interrupted. "You've been acting like a zombie all day. You almost let a student break her neck in a somersault."

Cindy's confusion became even more apparent. "Really?" she said with a lost look in her eyes.

Jadie's worry for her sister grew. "It's like you weren't even there. Did you get any sleep last night?"

"No, I guess not," Cindy replied. *Did I sleepwalk?* she wondered to herself.

"I really don't want to be responsible for your kids, Cindy. You need to pay attention to what you're doing. Someone could have gotten hurt today," Jadie said in a scolding manner.

"I'm sorry. I don't know what's with me today."

"Did you talk to Jonas at all?"

Cindy looked down with a melancholy expression. "No, he's not answering his phone."

Jadie sighed, unable to prevent the sympathy from seeping into her heart. "You should just go home."

Cindy nodded her head and walked out the door with her head held low. Jadie watched her pathetic wretch of a sister as she shambled her way towards the door and thought, *Oh, Cindy.*

Cindy felt as though she were living in perpetual darkness, even though the sun had not yet relinquished the evening light to the moon. As she walked down the street, she continued to dial Jonas' phone, but still he refused to answer, and her heart sank even further. She stood before the subway entrance, looking down into the urban ratway. She was only a few steps away from boarding the train to take her back home—but not her home.

All she could think of was images of an empty house—no Jonas to pop out and scare her, no five o'clock shadow to scratch her cheek, no scent of his cologne, no warm hugs to embrace her. All that was left was a cold, empty space. It was then that Cindy was randomly reminded that she was in New York City.

She decided to throw her diet out the window and went to the nearest fast food joint. She binged on forbidden foods that once plagued the diet of the now healthy gymnast. Burgers, ice cream, hot dogs… no processed food was safe from her gluttony. Cindy followed her impulses at each junk-filled restaurant with reckless abandon. The one treat she wanted the most was the one food that she had not even allowed herself to look at. She craved a good, old-fashioned cheesecake.

She popped into the nearest bakery and ordered the fattiest cheesecake she could possibly eat. While her muscles endured unhealthy amounts of fat and cholesterol, her taste buds rejoiced at the reunion with savory foods that haven't visited them in years. Bits of cream cheese and chocolate splattered across her mouth as she licked her fingers clean. But in that same moment, she felt herself falling apart. Cindy detested herself. Though the food was supposed to bring joy, all it did was make her self-hatred grow even more.

As the sun receded below the Hudson River, Cindy accepted the fact that she needed to go home. While walking back towards the train station, she spotted two men entering a grocery store and a third man standing outside who appeared very fidgety, nervously looking around. She could sense her gut telling her something's not right. Her previous indulgence of chocolate and cheesecake had caused Cindy to feel sick to her stomach. She wanted to go home, but her conscience wouldn't let her leave unless she knew everything was OK. Cindy hid in the shadows of a building across the street and watched the men like a hawk.

There was still a little bit of daylight left, so she wasn't quite certain if her intuition was correct. It would be a very stupid move for these guys to try to rob a store while there were still plenty of people walking the streets, but she stayed just a little longer just in case. Over time, the man standing outside would swivel his head with increasing frequency. He tapped his foot and couldn't seem to keep his hands in one spot. Something was going to go down—she could feel it rattling her bones. Instead of waiting for someone to get shot, Cindy sprung into action. She ducked into a darkened alleyway and transformed herself into the Silver Ninja.

When the transformation was complete, she used her binoculars to zoom into the grocery store. She observed the two men pulling out weapons in front of the store clerk. There wasn't much time for Cindy to react; someone was about to get hurt. Cindy ducked back into the alleyway and leapt from wall to wall, like a reversed Pachinko machine. When she reached the roof, Cindy activated her grappling hook and vaulted across the busy street to the grocery store rooftop. She turned herself upside down and rappelled down the line like a spider. Her head dropped down behind the unassuming suspect as he continued to watch each corner of the city street.

She hung behind the unassuming lowlife for several seconds until he took a step backward and banged his cranium onto Cindy's helmet. He gasped in fright and turned around, only to gaze deep into Cindy's glowing blue eyes. "Hello," she said while snatching him into a headlock. She retracted her grappling hook and pulled the thug up towards the top of the building. She muffled his screams until he blacked out in her arms. Once at the top, she tied the grapple line around his ankles and dropped him over the side of the building. His limp body swung back and forth as Cindy dropped down and entered the grocery store. Passersby gawked at the dangling body but stayed away from the comatose perpetrator as if he had a contagious disease. Eventually, one of the onlookers pulled out a cell phone and finally called the police.

Cindy stepped inside the grocery store and stood in front of the door in a bold, intimidating stance. The two suspects turned in her direction and fell in awe to the metal behemoth that blocked the path before them. Although she was short in height, the suit enhanced her physique to give her a dominating presence that no mere mortal would dare stand against. Without saying a word, she stared at them like a stone-cold sentinel, frozen in place, but ready to spring a trap. Her visor scanned their weapons identifying both pistols as Raven Arms MP-25. Cindy rolled her eyes as she was reminded as to how cheap and unreliable the dinky little pistols were.

The first suspect yelled at Cindy through his nylon mask, "Who the hell are you?"

The second suspect, somehow, stayed focused on the task at hand. He flailed his gun about, pointing it at the clerk. "I didn't tell you to stop filling the bag!"

Cindy took one step forward, spooking the thieves to make rash decisions.

"Take one more step and I'll shoot!" he screamed while pointing his low quality pistol at Cindy.

She stared at them, her silver mask void of any emotion and took another three steps forward. The fluorescent store lights glided across the surface of her

183

suit as the reflections of the suspects warped into view.

"I said, don't move!" His pistol trembled as doubts clouded the criminal's mind.

Cindy cracked her neck and rolled her shoulders. "Go ahead."

"What?" he asked, flabbergasted. His accomplice, meanwhile, was still bullying the clerk to finish filling the bag.

The second suspect looked to his accomplice. "Dom, we've got the money. Let's go."

"She's in the way," the first suspect snapped.

Realizing that the only way to freedom was through Cindy, the thieves fired all their rounds at her armored skin. The gun shots filled the grocery store with deafening booms of gunfire, amplified by the acoustics within the building. The bullets flew through the air and bounced off her armor like pieces of hail hitting a windshield. It made an oscillating clang like a pebble striking a stainless steel pot. Cindy looked down towards her untouched physique and then back up to the two delinquents. The mortified look on their faces filled Cindy with restrained glee.

She cocked her head to the side and said, "I hope you two had a plan B."

Her armored suit emanated an aura of oppression, giving the thieves pause, they crossed their legs as if preventing their bowels from evacuating. The thief holding the money bags became so terrified that he bolted for the door.

Cindy stepped to the side as if she were letting the culprit leave with all the goods. But when he reached the door, Cindy spun around with her leg lifted high in the air. In one thunderous sweep, her leg crashed into the criminal's chin like a semi-truck through a barricade. His body hovered in the air for a split second before landing flat on his back like a pancake. The lowlife was unconscious before he even hit the ground. Her body shifted back into its original position, ready for the last man standing.

The perp dropped down to his knees and slid his pistol across the floor towards her feet. Cindy picked the gun up off the floor crushing it in the palm of her hand, before throwing the mangled metal debris back to the felon.

"I think you can imagine what else I can crush with my hands."

"Please don't. I'm so sorry."

"Sorry?" she scoffed. "Is that what you would have said if you killed me? Probably not."

He shook his head while waving his hands in surrender. "I didn't want to shoot you. You didn't leave me a choice."

Cindy had a flashback to her mugging and felt a familiar, uncontrollable anger boiling to the surface. She did her best to hold back her furious whip, but the challenge was proving immense. She walked over to the thief and picked him up off the floor, slamming him into a shelf of bread. The trays collapsed behind his powerless body as loaves of bread rained down onto the floor.

"You always... have a choice," she threatened. "My choice would be to kill you. It's only fair..."

She squeezed his neck as she pressed him up against the wall. "Isn't it?"

"Oh, God." Tears spilled from his eyes as urine soiled his grungy khakis.

"Lucky for you, you're worthless to me. There's no reward for killing you. You're a gutless coward who hurts innocent people because you couldn't teach yourself to have a better life." Cindy's radar chimed as it began detecting radio band frequencies from police chatter. The sirens began closing in from the distance, forcing Cindy to finish her business with the wretches. "I'll let the police deal with you."

She dragged him over to the floor in front of the cashier's counter and found the second perpetrator's gun in his pocket.

Cindy gave the empty gun to the cashier and told him, "Make sure you turn these guns in as evidence when the police get here."

The cashier replied, "Thank you so much. Take whatever you want."

"Got anything for an upset stomach?"

The clerk smiled. "Aisle 4, grab what you want."

"Thank you."

It wasn't long before the wail of sirens was parked out in front of the entrance to the store, but Cindy was already long gone. As she traversed the Brooklyn Bridge, grappling through each of the arches, she still felt the lingering anger simmering inside of her. She found it repulsive how far a person would go to steal money: taking an innocent life for the pettiest things. Had she not arrived when she did, would they have shot the clerk?

When Cindy arrived in the Queens suburbs, she found herself wandering down an all-too-familiar path. The desire for vengeance fueled her courage to walk down the street which had wounded her. If she wasn't going to have Jonas back, then the only other thing she wanted was to hunt down the people who had hurt her. She scanned the area with her suit, using the thermal scanner to see if they were hiding in bushes or ducking in a neighbor's backyard. A garbage can fell over in the distance. She turned in the direction of the sound, combat stance at the ready. She looked around, ready to bury her fist into their always-grinning faces. But there was no one there except for the neighbor's cat Sparkles. "Sparkles, what are you doing, kitty?" she said while making kissing sounds.

She bent down and did a come-hither motion to Sparkles, who purred as he rubbed his cheek against her calves. Cindy petted the black cat and took one final look around the area. She let out a frustrated sigh, knowing that vengeance would elude her tonight. Cindy refused to come to terms with the fact she might never see those people again. In a sheer bit of irony, she thought about how much she would hate it if they were arrested. Cindy hid from plain sight, deactivated the suit, and walked into her lonesome house, feeling just a little bit defeated. She made a beeline to the fridge and retrieved a quart of ice cream.

With spoon in one hand and cookie dough in the other, Cindy turned on the TV and drowned her sorrows with food. As the TV droned on, a breaking news segment interrupted her reality TV brain drain.

"Breaking news: A grocery store clerk working the evening shift at an Upper East Side grocery store claims to have been saved by a 'superhero.' He claims that the heroine entered the store and incapacitated two suspects, both wielding pistols. Watch this unbelievable footage."

The TV cut to a shot of the security footage from within the grocery store. Even though the footage was grainy and choppy, you could see Cindy, clear as day, armored up in her silver suit. The almost frame by frame footage showed Cindy first deflecting their bullets and then thwarting them with martial prowess. The video ended with Cindy walking out of the store with a bottle of Pepto-Bismol.

"Incredible footage, simply incredible, but I have to ask. What was the deal with the bottle? Was she feeling sick or something?"

Cindy smiled and changed the channel as she shoveled another scoop of fatty ice cream into her mouth. At that same moment, her ringtone began blaring from inside her purse. She set down her ice cream and began frantically rummaging through the contents of her pocketbook for what seemed like an eternity to Cindy.

"Hello?" she said, hoping the caller hadn't hung up.

A quiet voice greeted her from the other end, "Hey, baby."

"Hey..." Cindy wanted to tell him that she missed him and she loved him, but the rapid tapping of her fingers on the cell phone hinted at her trepidation of what Jonas might say.

"I miss you," he said. A brief pause took place between the two before Jonas sighed and told his wife, "I was really upset by what happened. I thought maybe that I had become a bad husband."

"No, you didn't," she replied in a syrupy sweet tone. Her nervousness was fading away as his attempt to reconcile became apparent.

"Either way, I've been pretty miserable these past few days. How have you been holding up?"

Cindy rubbed her lip, afraid to answer the question. "Well…"

He recognized the guilty inflection in her voice and cut straight to the chase, "Just tell me." He braced himself for the worst.

She reluctantly admitted, "I started eating again." She winced upon uttering those words.

Jonas deciphered her cryptic message and unveiled its hidden meaning. "You mean binging?"

"Yes, it was bad. You don't understand, Jonas. I've been depressed; I'm going through a really hard time," she confessed.

Jonas asked a flurry of questions: "Are you going to be okay? You're not throwing up, are you? Do you need to go back to Overeaters Anonymous?"

"No, no I definitely haven't been doing that. I'll be fine; I just binged is all. I didn't do anything else, I promise," she said, trying to reassure him.

"Please take care of yourself, Cindy. I don't know what I would do if I lost you. I think about you every day."

Hearing her husband reaffirm his love for her brought a smile to Cindy that stretched from cheek to cheek. "I'll be fine. Are you going to come home now?"

Jonas hesitated to respond. "I… can't."

"Why not?" Cindy snapped. "I thought we were going to work things out?"

"We are… it's just that I found a new job and they're working us to the bone. The pay is incredible, but it means that I won't be able to come home for a few more weeks. Just pretend I'm away on business, okay?"

Cindy questioned her husband's reasoning. "Okay, you can't sleep at work. Are you doing something illegal? Why are you not coming home?"

"I promise I'm not doing anything illegal. I have a place to sleep and they made me sign a contract not to discuss what I'm doing with anyone. I had to hack a few systems just to be able to call you," he whispered.

Cindy stood up as if getting ready to pounce into action. "You're not in trouble, are you? I will come get you right now if you are."

"It's okay; I'm fine; I'm safe. This company is, like, hardcore classified. All I can say is that I promise I'll be back—you don't have to come in tearing everything up," he said, followed by a chuckle.

Cindy replied, "Okay, I love you."

"I love you too. I'll talk to you later, sweetie."

The phone clicked, but Cindy refused to put it down. She looked at their wedding photo resting on the mantle and sighed. Cindy spotted the quart of ice cream sitting on the couch laughing at her. She walked over to the taunting snack and chucked it straight into the garbage. It would suffer a slow, melting death at the bottom of a plastic bag and haunt Cindy's conscience no more.

That night, Cindy began having intense, vivid dreams, reliving that fateful night. Even in her dream, she had no control over herself or her actions, despite her intuition telling her not to go down that sidewalk again. Her mind continued down that dark path once more, stepping deeper into the unknown. She looked down at her hands and watched as the silver crept across her limbs and armored her body for the inevitable conflict.

Just like it was on that cool night, Cindy found herself walking into the middle of the domestic dispute. Except this time, she was shielded by her astonishing techno suit. She threw the attacker down on the floor causing blood to splatter from his body like a gory horror movie; yet, he was still moving around and acting as if nothing had happened. Cindy became angry at the fact that the man had not died, despite all the blood spilling onto floor. Nothing was making any sense! At long last, the inevitable muggers had arrived, knife in hand.

They approached Cindy and plunged the blade into her back. She screamed in agony as the dagger cut through the armor as if it were a sheet of plastic. She cried out, "Please stop," as the sting of the blade caused her back to ache. Her mind couldn't comprehend why the knife was still able to cut through the impenetrable suit. She thought she was invincible. How could something so small cut so deep?

When Cindy awoke from her nightmare, she found herself clinging to the side of a building somewhere in Brooklyn. The afternoon daylight blinded Cindy's vision as bright glints from nearby windows shone in her eyes. The suit adjusted the ambient brightness of the environment and toned down the brilliant sunlight. When Cindy was able to read the HUD indicators again, she saw that the clock read 12 pm. *How the hell did I get to Brooklyn?* she wondered. Cindy worried the suit might be turning her into a sleep walker; maybe she was even being mind controlled. While clinging to the building, Cindy heard the piercing screams of a woman coming from down below. She peered over her shoulder and looked down to see a girl with pink hair being attacked by two young males.

Cindy sensed a recurring theme of women being assaulted and wondered if she was being haunted by what had happened that horrible night. She felt taunted in the sense that she would never find the resolution she so desperately wanted. As Cindy began crawling down the wall to save the poor woman, the suit began to flash a bright red error message with a bunch of gibberish code that only a programmer could read. The grip on Cindy's fingers and knees shut off without warning. She slipped off the building wall, plunging straight to the ground. When Cindy made impact with the unforgiving concrete below, her suit made the sound of a metal bowl being dropped on the kitchen floor.

The HUD elements in her helmet began to warp and distort as the red error message blinked on and off. This was the worst possible time for the suit to malfunction, but she still had to face those creeps in order to help the girl. The thugs looked bewildered as Cindy rose from the ground. They drew their knives keeping their eyes locked on the silver meteorite. Cindy gave the two criminals a quick scan and noticed that they were wearing clothing of the same color. Red bandanas with white-flourished details hung out from their pockets in a very deliberate way.

Cindy shrugged off her embarrassing fall and said, "You may want to reconsider this gang initiation."

One of the thugs said to the other, "That's the chick from the news."

As Cindy attempted to take her first step, a sharp, piercing screech tore into her helmet. She clutched the sides of her head and stumbled around the alleyway, knocking stacks of cardboard boxes over.

"Yo, something's wrong with her. We should get the hell out of here!" the one criminal shouted.

"No, we gotta finish this. If we leave now, they'll kill us when we get back."

The duo of gang neophytes turned their attention back to the woman while Cindy struggled to regain control of her degrading suit. Despite the screeching still blasting in her ear, Cindy ran up behind the first criminal and threw him to the ground. The knife flew out of his hand, clinking as it tumbled onto the street. Cindy gave the assailant's right leg a merciless twist.

The bones made a sickening snap like, dried branches succumbing to a storm,

193

as he cried out in pain. His accomplice panicked at the sounds of the teen's agonal screams. A quick strike knocked out Cindy's first target, but his terrified friend had taken the screaming woman hostage. He poked the blade into the side of her neck, forming a black dimple around the knife. Although no blood had been drawn, if something were to jar the cowardly delinquent, the woman's life would drain, all over the grungy alley floor.

The situation was becoming grave, and Cindy was still struggling with her suit. The digital humanoid outline representing the status of her systems began to grey out. The right arm in the outline of the HUD status indicator began to change color, which was something Cindy had not seen before. She watched as the color changed from its normal cyan to a dull slate, causing her arm to feel numb. The weight of her suit became heavier and heavier, slowing her graceful movements to that of a lumbering oaf.

"Don't move. I'll cut her right now!" the youth yelled.

The girl wailed as tears streamed down her face, her deep, panicked breaths blowing on her locks of dyed pink hair. Cindy's predicament had become more dangerous. The suit was shutting down on her, and now a gang initiation had escalated into a hostage situation. Without the suit at full efficiency, Cindy would not be fast enough to stop the thug and save the girl. In a desperate panic, she scrolled through the menus of the suit and discovered the weapons systems' submenu. With her other arm beginning to shake, she discovered the 'rail gun' weapons and hoped that they would activate.

Long tubes began to form on the tops of Cindy's forearms, morphing and stretching into weapons she had never seen before. The guns, with blue rings wrapped around the muzzle, looked more like plasma cannons ready to fire. Cindy pointed the rail gun towards the desperate criminal.

"You have two options: If you don't release the woman, I'm going to fire this gun and kill you. If you let her go, I promise not to chase you down."

"You'll let me go, just like that?" the punk kid asked with skepticism.

"Yes, but you have to let her go. Trust me, I won't miss," she bluffed. Her HUD error message continued to tell Cindy that the gun would not fire, period.

He stood there thinking for a few moments, trembling with fear. Cindy realized this was not a hardened criminal. It was just a stupid kid who had made some dumb decisions with his life. After much internal deliberation, the kid let the woman go. He took little cautious steps towards the streets as Cindy lowered her weapon and let him walk away. The criminal newbie stashed his knife in his pocket and made a dash for freedom. The girl who had been held hostage collapsed down to her knees and wept into her hands.

Cindy struggled to pull her own weight as she lumbered over to the distraught girl. She could feel her body waning as more systems in the suit began shutting down. Ignoring all of that, Cindy asked, "Are you all right?" The girl still had tears coming down from her eyes, but nodded her head yes. Cindy turned away, exerting great effort just to move one leg in front of the other. All of her strength was being sapped as though she were wading through piles of mud. She just couldn't seem to go further; she leaned up against the corner of the building, panting with exhaustion.

The young girl ran up to Cindy and placed her hand against Cindy's weary shoulder. "Are you okay?" she asked. Cindy's eyes began to fade in and out. She shook her head, prompting the girl to run out into the street and hail a taxi. As the cab pulled up to the curb, the young woman attempted to drag Cindy over to the vehicle. After witnessing the Silver Ninja's flexible, lightning-fast maneuvers, the girl was surprised to find Cindy was much heavier than she looked, and she was unable to budge the heroic woman. Realizing what the girl was trying to do, Cindy clomped her way over to the cab. Her legs shuddered from the waves of vibration caused by the weight of each foot meeting the ground.

The cabbie looked over at Cindy and the girl taking their sweet old time to get into the car. He impatiently tapped his fingers on the steering wheel and anxiously looked back and forth between Cindy and the street. Just as Cindy and the girl were about to step off the sidewalk, the cabbie sped off down the street. The girl left Cindy's side and ran into the street. "Hey!" she screamed, waving her arms frantically. Cindy stepped onto the street and aimed her arm towards the rear of the cab. The girl stepped back and watched as Cindy fired the grappling hook through the trunk of the car. The hook broke through the aluminum shell and deployed upon piercing the black leather upholstery.

Cindy grabbed onto the cable and began pulling the car backwards as smoke billowed from the squealing tires. The girl watched Cindy's muscles pull the car back in perfect rhythm. "Holy crap," she muttered in astonishment. Cindy leaned back, leveraging herself as she pulled on the synthetic rope in a one-sided tug of war match. The cab driver looked at the two in complete shock. The two women stepped into the backseat of the car and noticed the puffy, gaping hole protruding from the seat cushion. Cindy turned to the cabbie and said, "You forgot us."

"Sorry, I had to go to the bathroom," he said with a thick Indian accent.

"Do you still need to go?" Cindy asked.

"No, I'll be fine."

"I'm paying for the ride. Do you want to go to the hospital?" the girl asked Cindy.

"No, take me to the Latini building."

The cab driver complied and began driving towards Upper Manhattan. While en route to Lucent Labs, the girl exchanged idle chitchat with Cindy.

In a nervous and shaky voice, the girl said, "Umm… thank you so much for saving me."

Cindy took a deep breath and acknowledged her statement. "You're welcome." She turned to the girl and asked, "What's your name?"

"Carissa," she replied with a smile.

"Carissa," Cindy said, "thank you for getting me out of there."

"It's the least I could do after you saved my life."

After a brief pause, Cindy said, "I like your hair; it's cute."

Carissa smiled. "Thanks."

"Excuse me one second," Cindy said as she made an emergency phone call to Michael. The phone rang once before Michael answered.

"Cindy, where the heck have you been? I need you to come by the lab now."

Her breathing was heavy through the receiver. "I'm... on my way now." She continued to pant through the comm link, unable to conceal her suffering.

"You don't sound well, Cindy. Are you all right?"

"I'll be there, in a couple, of minutes," she said before hanging up.

Several minutes later, the cab arrived at the Latini building, which had served as headquarters for Lucent Labs. Cindy's system was going into complete failure. The video link feeding the visual information to Cindy was garbled with static and gibberish code. The oxygen within her helmet was no longer circulating, forcing Cindy to breathe in her own carbon dioxide. Her arms had become paralyzed and her legs buckled under her own weight. As she exited the cab, Cindy thanked Carissa and logged the taxi's information to anonymously pay for the damages later.

When Michael rushed out to greet her, Cindy collapsed onto the floor. Her helmet shielded her fragile skull from the head-splitting impact. The lack of oxygen and utter exhaustion had caused Cindy to faint. The blue lights of her eyes dimmed into a stark black, blinding Cindy to the world around her. She stared into the darkness for what felt like only seconds before the HUD went through a boot-up sequence. The SIRCA began to power up as a gust of oxygen began to flow into the helmet. Cindy stared at the ceiling above her and looked around to find Michael leaning in next to her with a big grin on his face.

"Well, looks like I fixed it," he said in a cocky manner.

"How long was I out?" Cindy asked.

"Oh, about ten minutes," Michael said. "But don't worry, I had the oxygen feeding into your suit in under a minute."

"Sure didn't feel like ten minutes."

Michael ran his fingers through his hair as his elation at his suit repair turned to anger at Cindy's escapade. "What the hell were you doing running around with the suit on? Oh, and don't try to move— I left you paralyzed so you would cooperate."

"Michael!" she yelled, but it was true. She couldn't move her arms and legs.

"Talk," he demanded.

"Okay," she relented, "I've been using the suit to fight crimes."

Michael replied as if his suspicions were confirmed, "So you're the one everyone's been talking about in the podcasts."

"Yes, I was on TV, too."

His disposition soured further. "You got caught on camera? What part of 'don't tell anyone' did you not understand?"

"Look, I just happened to be at the wrong place at the wrong time. Should I have let those people get hurt?"

"I should leave you paralyzed. I told you not to wear the suit in public," Michael said in a threatening tone.

"Are you trying to take advantage of me in my vulnerable position?" she flirted.

Michael was taken aback by her comment. "Umm, you're married. I wouldn't do that to Jonas. And even if you weren't, I really wouldn't want to tell the doctor why I had to get a tetanus shot."

Cindy became embarrassed. "I have no idea why I said that. Forget I said anything."

"Deal." Michael scratched the back of his head. "Anyway, I'm going to install some updates for you. Don't go anywhere."

"Ha, ha," she said with sarcasm.

Michael stepped away from Cindy's limp body and began running the install program for the new firmware update. Cindy regained feeling in her fingers and toes, but she didn't seem comfortable with the fact that the suit could cripple her. Once she felt confident that everything was back to normal, Cindy deactivated the suit and sat up on the examination table.

When Michael came back into the test lab, Cindy asked,

"So what have you been doing these past few days?"

Michael looked confused. "What do you mean?"

"Well, you seem to be the only one showing up here to the lab. Shouldn't you be with the rest of the crew working on some other project?"

"Umm," Michael seemed caught off-guard by the innocent question, "I am working with them, actually. I only come to the lab because we still have all the data hosted here. Until we do a server migration, I have to fix your suit here."

Cindy pressed harder with her questions. "But are you still getting paid to work on the suit? It just seems weird to me that you're the only one working on the project."

Michael's expression was blank as he responded in an almost robotic way. "No, I'm not getting paid to work on the suit. This is just my own personal project."

Cindy scrunched her eyebrows in disbelief. "Are you working with my husband?"

Frustrated, Michael said to Cindy, "Why are we playing twenty questions?"

"Well, wouldn't you be a little suspicious if the only person fixing your suit was one programmer?"

"I already explained what was going on," he said with obvious impatience.

"Okay! No need to get testy." She took a quick breath and placed her index finger on her lip. She looked at Michael as if trying to hold back her words.

Michael noticed Cindy seemed to have more to say. "Out with it already."

"Can you tell me about the suit?" she asked with childish excitement.

Michael sighed and slapped his forehead. "Like what, how it works or something?"

"Anything, I don't care. From what I've been able to do while wearing it, it's pretty freaking awesome, just sayin'."

Cindy's excitement was contagious. He had never had a woman express interest in one of his geeky projects before. He turned to Cindy with a huge smile on his face and said, "All right, I guess I could show you something."

He sat Cindy down on the same, old rolling office chair and hummed a merry tune as he pushed her into the lab with the SIRCA control terminal. Setting her next to the terminal, he cracked his knuckles and prepared to demonstrate his baby. The first thing he did was activate a portion of the suit onto Cindy's left arm. She looked surprised that it didn't envelop her whole body.

"Did you test out the super strength yet?" he said with glee.

Cindy's smirked. "I did pull a cab back while it was still accelerating."

"You could do more than that," he said, shaking his head.

"Like what, lift cars over my head?"

"You're thinking too small." Michael dragged the mouse over a plus icon and clicked to increase the numbers on the screen.

Cindy had an almost disgusted look on her face as she looked down at her arm. "What... the... hell?" she uttered as the muscles in her arms became swollen.

"Relax, it's not real," Michael said.

"What do you mean? Look at my arm! How is that not real?" she said, pointing to her enlarged biceps.

"What I mean to say is that these are all synthetic muscle strands. The suit weaves metal strands of silk that add onto your natural bundle of muscle fibers. It's not unlimited, though. If I jack it up too high, it'll just become a deformed blob—want to see?"

"No! Put my arm back to normal right now," she cried.

"I'm just teasing. Anyway, you should be able to lift five-hundred times your body weight."

"Holy crap!" Cindy said, amazed.

"Don't get too excited," Michael warned, "you can still hurt yourself if you lift too much."

"Lame."

Cindy's arms deflated back to normal size as Michael changed the settings to default values. Then, he clicked over to a different menu which had a collection of surface textures and picture thumbnails. With the thumbnail window open, he switched over to a 3-D model of Cindy's body.

"Is that me?" she asked.

Michael grinned and said, "You like that, huh?"

"Is that data from the suit?"

"Yep. So now, I can twirl you around in 3-D space." He rolled the mouse across the screen, spinning Cindy's 3-D model around. "Whee, whee, w—."

"I get it," Cindy said in a flat tone. "Actually, now that I think about it, I'm a little uncomfortable that you can see that much detail."

"Don't worry. I can't undress you," he lied. "Anyway, if I click on your arm and then click on this basketball surface texture, watch what happens."

A light chirp went off, followed by the sound of something being fastened by rope, but nothing seemed to happen. Upon closer examination however, Cindy could see that the texture of her metal skin had become bumpy just like a basketball. As Michael clicked through the different textures, the skin continued to morph between smooth and rough surfaces.

Watching the suit change texture gave Cindy a revelation. "Aha. That's why I don't slip when I walk."

"Correct. That's the magic of friction," he responded with pride.

"Clever," she said impressed.

Michael's eyes beamed, overwhelmed with joy. "You can control the friction just like you control the suit. So, if you want to slide on a surface without stopping…"

"I gotcha."

"Before I forget," Michael said, turning to Cindy. "There are still some flaws we couldn't fix that you need to be aware of."

"You mean the flaw where it constantly tries to kill me?"

"I fixed that!" he said defending his baby. "Don't get electrocuted, and don't run low on power."

"I can guess what will happen if I get electrocuted, but what's this about power?" Cindy asked.

"The energy supply isn't very stable. If you drain it too much, the power will thin out until everything shuts down. To put it simply, you won't be bulletproof anymore."

"Am I going to need to plug into an outlet?" she asked with a wry smile.

"No, smartass, it'll recharge while you're idle or the suit is off. You just have to watch your energy budget is all."

"Okay, last question and I will leave you alone."

"Go ahead, I love talking about the suit."

She lifted her hands as if pretending to hold him back. "Are you ready for this? It's the million-dollar question."

"Stop being so dramatic and tell me."

"What is this suit made of? This technology sounds way too advanced to be manmade."

Michael swallowed hard and stared at Cindy. "That's top-secret."

Cindy gave Michael a cold stare. "Really? I've been wearing the suit for a few days now, and you're going to play that card?"

Michael's response chilled Cindy to her bones. "The reason I haven't been able to remove the suit from your body is... well, it's not completely cybernetic."

Cindy was speechless. There was a distinct grip of terror running through her mind, wondering what the secret ingredient was lurking within her body. "You need to tell me right now what this thing is."

"I can't. I promise it won't hurt you," he said.

Before Cindy could say another word, she felt a gentle vibration in her ear; she could hear a familiar voice within the soft oscillations.

"Silver, it's Sam. I have another job for you."

Cindy turned to Michael. "We'll have to continue this conversation another time."

"Why? Are you going somewhere?" Michael asked.

"Yes, but don't think this is over," she warned.

Michael lowered his head and muttered, "All right."

Cindy stepped out into the twilight settling on the city streets and resumed her conversation with Sam.

"Hey, I'm here," she said.

"I'm uploading a new dossier for you. The target is Joseph Van Eisler. He is the world's leading developer in space aeronautics at Starlight Enterprises."

Cindy furrowed her brow. "That doesn't sound like a political target, Sam."

"Let me finish. In addition to supporting bailouts for huge banks and mass deportations of immigrants, Van Eisler has been selling classified technology to countries like Iran. Did you ever wonder how Iran was able to hack a U.S. drone and bring it down? Joseph is planning to use all his finances to fill the Senate seat with someone that will push those policies."

"A traitor to his country?"

"A regular Benedict Arnold. Ci—lver, you must realize that bailing out big banks only perpetuates the greed."

Cindy grumbled to herself. "Well, I'm sure there's more to it than just that."

"What about selling technological secrets to Iran? What if he gives them the capability to develop nuclear weapons?"

"I'll do the job for you," Cindy said, half-heartedly.

"Good. I'll send my agents to set up a perimeter around his office building. The payment will be one-hundred thousand. I've also taken the liberty of uploading the building's blueprints to your suit. Good luck."

When the comm link shut down, Cindy felt revulsion twisting inside of her. Something just didn't feel right, and for some odd reason, she couldn't summon the willpower to tell Sam no. It was as if her backbone and conscience had never existed. Although reluctant to do the mission, Cindy found a hidden place to power up and grappled her way over to the financial district in downtown Manhattan. While en route, Cindy couldn't help but think about the events of the past few days.

She had noticed the changes happening to her. It was as if she had a distinct lack of impulse control like buying the candy grocery store's so conveniently place at the register; even though, she wasn't hungry or craving it. The worst part for Cindy was knowing that she was doing something wrong, but felt powerless to stop it.

At 8:30 that evening, Starlight Enterprises came into view. Cindy landed on a rooftop a few buildings away from the skyscraper. She noticed a broken mirror resting up against the wall and stepped towards the shattered looking glass. The reflection staring back at her was dirty and stained. It was as if some evil creature were living within an alternate reality. Her eyes looked menacing, and her body appeared ripe with filth strewn across her plated skin. The mirror made her seem as though she were disassembled with the various broken pieces offsetting her streamlined silhouette.

The cracked mirror only magnified Cindy's self-loathing as the image of this hideous creature multiplied over shards of broken glass. Would Jonas still love the woman in the mirror? The question repeated itself like a stuttering loop in her deteriorating psyche. The taste of power was intoxicating—one lick and boldness filled the body with an unstoppable vigor. How could she fight back the temptation to rule the world when she knew she was invincible? Cindy repeated in her mind, *don't do this, turn around and find Sam to put an end to this.*

Her mind served as an invisible force, trying to push her away from the skyscraper that housed her next target; but her body was moving on its own accord.

Cindy had to put aside her denial and accept that maybe… maybe she did possess the heart of a killer. The ghost of her conscience vanished as she walked through her imaginary forcefield. She looked up at the top of the Starlight Enterprises building; its bright white logo illuminating the night sky with its all-encompassing aura. The feeling of excitement returned, spurring Cindy forward.

The moon reflected off of Cindy's armor as the pale fluorescent and tungsten lights glittered off her body like a sequined cocktail dress. Stepping to the edge of the building, the grapple targeting reticules flickered into position. Using the new World Trade Center as cover, Cindy grappled onto the WTC tower and swung in an arc around the side of the building. The sound of car horns honking down below was almost inaudible as she flew through the open sky; the pristine tower almost seemed to scoot over to its side, allowing Cindy passage.

Using momentum from the swing combined with trajectory auto-correction, Cindy was able to propel herself into the underground garage of Starlight Enterprises. She flew through the ceiling without even a glimpse from the security guard. When the time came to land, Cindy twisted and contorted her body into such perfect form that she landed with the silent grace of a light feather. The blueprints Sam uploaded triggered a contextual radar map to appear in the upper right corner of her HUD.

A little white dot, representing her location appeared on the map. Additional green and red lines represented walls and doors while other markers and dotted lines represented security guards and their estimated lines of sight. The digital map surprised and impressed Cindy; but the ability to rotate and switch the map from 2-D to 3-D mode on a whim put her in awe. Cindy scanned through the map and saw tons of open space at her location. Without delay, Cindy infiltrated her way into the building before her reflective suit caught someone's attention.

All elevators, even service elevators, were out of the question for a stealth mission. Most modern elevators contained security cameras, so there was no way she could take one up without getting caught. Further scanning revealed several entrances and exits from the garage. The one main staircase that would lead to the top was locked from the inside. She could have just broke the door open. Although abusing her limitless power was tempting, she feared that a busted door would alert Joseph, prompting him to escape.

According to the map, however, there was an alternate set of stairs that led up to rooms connecting to the main stairwell. They wouldn't take her to Joseph's office but offered an avenue for reaching her target. Using the cars as cover, Cindy snuck her way into the stairwell and discovered a door locked with an RF card access reader.

Finding it hard to believe that this high-tech suit would be foiled by a simple keyless lock, she placed her hand on top of the receiver and tried to think of opening the door. The suit began scrolling numbers across her HUD, freezing numbers in place when the correct one had been found. As the last number locked in place, the red light on the receiver turned green, causing the metallic click from the unlocking door to echo in the stairwell. With a gentle push, Cindy was able to open the lumbering metal door without even a squeak.

Cindy snuck into the unknown room, unaware of what she would find. Surrounded by darkness she found herself knocking over a stack of cardboard boxes and multiple mops. The cascading mops made a dissonant symphony of loud cracks while the boxes uttered hollow thuds as they tumbled to the ground. Cindy fought back frustrated curses as she tried to set the boxes and mops in place. She couldn't seem to find either in the black room. Just then, the sound of a wheeled bucket rolling down the hallway approached the nearby door.

Cindy looked around the room in a panic and wished for the capability to peer through the blackness. When the night vision mode activated within her HUD, she cursed herself for not having thought of it sooner. Through the green haze, Cindy could see slime-colored boxes scattered all over the floor including the several mops she had knocked over. Upon further inspection, she realized that she was in a very vulnerable storage closet. The rumbling of the wheels would interrupt itself with a loud click as it rolled over the grout between the linoleum tiles. The metal handle twisted open, forcing Cindy to lean against the wall.

Cindy held her breath as the sound of loud classical music, blaring from earphones, filled the little closet. A young, swarthy male entered the storage bay and immediately said, "What the hell?" The scattering of cardboard boxes and mops caused him to click his tongue in protest. The janitor's irritation was evident.

Cindy, who was still lurking behind the door, had him in her sights. The suit placed a red targeting reticule around his body, indicating that red meant enemy, and enemies should be killed. She found herself, once again, struggling to fight the impulse to murder. It pained her to resist reaching out and ending his life like walking away from an item you want but don't need. Her body quivered as she continued to fight back her murderous urges, trying to figure out in vain why this desire was gnawing at her.

The janitor began to organize the cardboard mess, and Cindy's temptation to kill grew sharper and sharper. The more time he spent stacking the boxes, the more his body would turn towards Cindy. She became flushed with adrenaline as her mind raced with a million scenarios about how to neutralize the innocent janitor. She hoped for his sake that he wouldn't take much longer because her strength to resist this urge was ebbing away. Her hand reached out towards the back of the oblivious man's neck, ready to grip him like a hawk's talon.

His cell phone rang. He looked down as he pulled his mobile out of his pocket. "Hello," he answered, unaware of the danger behind him. The sudden phone call snapped Cindy out of her trance, pulling her out of the sticky tar pit of unwanted desire. Cindy bolted out of the door and ran towards the main foyer. The thoughts of killing momentarily vacated her mind. Cindy thought to herself, *what's happening to me?* She hid behind a leather couch and buried her head between her hands. She dropped down into a crouch and gripped her helmet in frustration. She was struggling with her personal identity, and the fear that she was becoming part of a group that she had arrested all those years ago.

She shook off her feelings of angst and tried to focus on the mission. Cindy slapped her knees and rose back up, convincing her mind not to feel guilty about something that didn't happen. She took a few paces away from the couch and was awestruck at the grand atrium above the lobby. Its immense height looked like it towered above the building itself. The entire area was swarming with a hive of security forces that seemed much better trained than the last batch Cindy dealt with. The challenge for her now was getting to Van Eisler's office. She tried, once again, to utilize stealth mode.

Cindy activated her stealth camouflage, but the transparent image kept flickering like a broken fluorescent light bulb. She shut the stealth system down while letting out an irritated growl. *How am I going to get past these guards?* Cindy asked herself. She knew she could take these men out one by one, but after having that internal conflict a few moments ago, she was paranoid about being unable to hold back. She could feel the push to kill growing stronger. It terrified her so much that her hands shook at the impure thoughts invading her mind. She used all of her willpower to suppress the primal urge, unaware of the dangers from bottling up this craving.

She spotted a nearby ventilation duct and wondered if that would be a possible

213

way in. As she stood in front of the narrow opening and looked at her own massive body, she realized that crawling through ducts was just a movie myth. Not even a toddler could fit into the duct. Cindy was becoming aggravated; she couldn't climb the lobby wall because she would be spotted a mile away. She couldn't shut down the cameras because security would notice that the cameras were offline. She turned to her map and searched through the blueprints in the hopes of finding something she could use. She browsed through the different levels of the building, and found a power generator room located deep within the belly of the beast.

A nearby entrance displayed a prominent DANGER sticker on the wall. It was obvious to Cindy that this was her next destination. Sneaking her way into the generator room, Cindy saw various signs warning of an electrical hazard. If she shut down the power, the office might assume it was just a blackout. The first thing she did before accessing the power generator was to disconnect the line powering the camera backup systems, so that when the backup generator kicked in, the cameras wouldn't remain online. With that business out of the way, Cindy broke the lock off of the fenced in enclosure and was greeted by an LCD control panel. *How am I going to turn this thing off?* she wondered.

Hack the terminal and turn it off? No, that would be too easy. Security would just come down and turn it back on before I could even reach the stairs. Cindy paced back and forth as she tried to figure out the best way to shut this generator down. Suddenly, Cindy was struck with an epiphany—she could use the rail guns to blow up the terminal. A quick selection through the weapons menu and Cindy was faced with an error message, flashing across the screen: "Error! RGDriver. dll MISSING please reinstall." It seemed as though nothing was going right for Cindy.

Seeing no other option, she decided the only thing she could do to shut this terminal down was to punch it: American-style. She balled up her hand into a fist and practiced a few fake strikes to make sure she didn't miss the target. She took a moment to focus as the HUD targeted the console and locked on. The innocent high tech creature sat there staring at Cindy, wondering what she was doing as her fist cocked back like a gun hammer. She released the trigger and punched through the console. The LED console shattered before her might, but Cindy had forgotten that breaking through the console meant being shocked with 30,000 watts of electricity.

She screamed at the top of her lungs as electrical bolts of lightning spewed forth from the maniacal machine, laughing at her stupidity. Violent spasms shook her body as electricity coursed through her metallic armor. The suit read out an error log to Cindy's HUD:

*****SYSTEM ERROR***** Electrical damage! ERROR CODE 00000x0000000 1Ac0001000xxxx0000 ****CRITICAL SYSTEMS FAILURE IMMINENT!****

A garbled transmission from Sam pierced Cindy's auditory senses, *"*STATIC*WhAt HAppenEdE!?#$? -@ndy! *STATIC* @Re U 0K?$ Cin— *STATIC*."*

****COMM LINK OFFLINE****

Cindy was blasted backwards into the air and slid across the ground. Her HUD became a mangled mess of error codes and scrolling video as the emergency alarms screamed in her ears. Her natural skin throbbed with a pulsating pain like a migraine that travelled to every limb. Just like a bullet impacting a Kevlar vest, the armor absorbed the brunt of the electricity. Though Cindy was protected from the worst, she could still feel its electrifying bite. Her blurred vision came back into focus, but the damaged HUD was preventing her from seeing anything.

She wobbled back up to her feet as the lights and cameras shut off. The red emergency backup lights came online as the entire building fell silent. It hurt to walk, but Cindy needed to get out of there before security showed up. As she stumbled her way to the exit, Cindy noticed that splotches of her French manicured cuticles were beginning to appear at the fingertips of her suit. She pushed herself to move forward, even though every step sent painful, pulsing aches throughout her body. Her vision kept blurring in and out of focus and her head was pounding, but she was too deep into the mission to turn back now.

Cindy couldn't even keep her balance stable and continued to trip over her own feet, but her tenacity edged her onward. Upon exiting the generator room, Cindy arrived back at the main stairwell and collapsed to the floor. When all hope seemed lost, the SIRCA prompted Cindy to activate the emergency repair. The system warned her that not all systems would be in full working order, but Cindy paid no mind, commanding the repair system to continue. A little screen popped up with images of motherboard circuitry scrolling through the window. Various red circles would shrink in size as the suit activated each system to engage repairs.

With the repairs underway, Cindy could see her vision beginning to stabilize. As the medical features came back online, the SIRCA was able to administer a minor dose of analgesic. It didn't take away the pain completely, but it did reduce the severity enough that Cindy could finish the mission. Once repairs were completed, Cindy looked down and watched as her confidence, arrogance and power evaporated before her very eyes. Splotches of her skin were now becoming visible throughout her body. Her metallic shell was gradually becoming about as protective as aluminum foil. As long as she didn't drain any further energy, the remainder of the suit would still protect her from gunfire even if the suit was not operating at peak capacity.

Cindy walked over to the main stairwell and began her arduous climb to Joseph's office. The stairwell smelled of old paint with washed out walls branded with tattoos of numbers for each floor. Forty floors later, Cindy's legs felt like they were about to burst. Her calves burned as if dipped in scalding hot water, and her lungs cried out for oxygen. When she reached Joseph's floor, the door was locked; a simple keypad with thumbprint scanner blocked the way in. Cindy cried out, "No, no, no, no!" With most of the suit's functions offline, including the hacking and augmented strength, there would be no way for Cindy to hack or burst through the door.

Before turning around in defeat, she placed her hand on the door knob and gave it a firm tug. To her surprise, the door pulled open towards her. She wanted to squeal in glee, but instead settled for a sigh of relief. Cindy entered the dark office through its kitchen area and passed the refrigerator into a long hallway filled with cubicles. In the distance, she could see frosted glass doors masking the entrance to Joseph's office.

Clusters of employees were loitering about the space. Some had set up little communes of office chairs as they chatted with each other, while others stood outside office doors with a cup of coffee in their hand. Despite the huge amount of people, Cindy was able to creep around the office using the carpeted flooring to muffle her footsteps. She used the cubicle walls as cover and snuck past the unassuming employees. Upon reaching the opaque doors to Joseph's office, Cindy entered his room undetected. The employees continued to chat about the power outage, never even suspecting Cindy's presence. As she entered Joseph's suite, Cindy saw a lavishly decorated room filled to the brim with knickknacks symbolizing his career. Model airplanes, from old World War II fighters to modern day stealth aircraft, hung from the ceiling. Photos of satellite images across the earth and historical space shuttle photos gave a telling tale to his fascination with aeronautics. However, the one thing that caught Cindy's eye was a model aircraft that she had never seen before, a strange prototype, which looked like a spaceship.

Sitting before her in the black leather chair, Joseph was chatting on his office phone, eating a sugary diabetes-inducing snack of cinnamon buns. Cindy was not surprised to see that Joseph was a rather large black man with gold circular glasses and a tight, well-coiffed haircut. His wedding band gleamed through the darkness as he laughed and chatted with his wife.

"Yeah, the power's been out for twelve minutes. I don't know what's going on down there. The guys are telling me that the panel to the generator got all busted up. Yeah, I asked them, 'how the hell did that happen?' 'I don't know,' they told me, could you believe that?"

His wife asked, "Does that mean you'll be coming home early?"

"Yes, darling. If they can't fix the power, I'll be on my way home to see y—" The phone call was interrupted with a sickening crack, followed by multiple brutalizing thuds. His wife screamed into the phone, "What was that noise, Joseph? Joseph?"

Cindy hung up the phone to silence the guilty pangs throbbing in her conscience. Pulsating aches travelled up the back of her neck, inflicting sharp pressure to the backs of her eyes like an electrical current looking to ground. She held the man in her arms as his bloodied, beaten, lifeless face etched itself into her memory. *If I'm doing the right thing, why does it feel so wrong?* Cindy thought to herself. Her self-hatred had reached its apex. She had justified the killings before, except now she not only questioned her motives, but who she really was. She realized she was not the hero but the villain. Her heart wept for this man that she did not know. *I'm so sorry.* She looked to her hands and reflected on what she had done…

CHAPTER 6

Breaking Point

The hard, dry blood on my fingers reeked of someone else's life. I could feel the copper plasma create friction between my encased digits, scraping and chipping away the former existence of an innocent man. The emergency alarms screamed over and over like a wailing drunk begging for another whiskey. The commotion of people scrambling outside, like a panicked bee hive, filled the now-lifeless office with a cacophony of mayhem. The red lights blinking on the perimeter of the walls symbolized the chaos I have caused.

I could still smell the soft, sweet aroma of cinnamon lingering in the air. It was my victim's last meal, a small snack of cinnamon buns, lay scattered across blood-stained documents and blueprints that only a great mind could understand. When I stared at the fresh corpse of a brilliant man, I realized… my hands might be stained with innocent blood. I had never punished anyone who was undeserving, but the spoiling corpse at my feet said otherwise. I couldn't believe what I had done. The shock of my actions refused to leave my side. I stood there lost in my own mind, observing model airplanes hanging from the ceiling, a custom-built, glossy wooden desk, blueprints framed on the walls, and designs for an aircraft I

221

recalled from the news. Was this really someone who deserved the punishment I had given him?

The guards were banging at the door like dogs restrained on a leash. At any moment, a horde of security guards was going to burst through and end me. I looked to the window and thought about jumping, but I was too high up in this towering skyscraper. The only way to escape the inevitable torrent of lethal gunfire was to break through their ranks. I briefly mulled over the idea of surrendering completely. The fantasy of allowing myself to be filled with a hot slag of lead and fragmented shells made me feel at peace with myself. Not because I sought my own destruction, but because having bullets embed themselves in my skin would swiftly end my pain, making me numb to the invisible wound that would define the rest of my life. I've become a murderer.

The door behind me became my clock; the entry burst open like an alarm striking midnight. With six pistol-armed security guards in black suits charging in like a lion to its prey, my time was up. One of the guards grabbed his shoulder radio and yelled, "She killed Joe. Get up here now!" They kept a tight bead on me with their pistols, never missing a beat.

Once they saw the corpse of dead guilt sprawled beside my feet, I closed my eyes and felt the world's tempo slow to a lethargic pace as the first wave of gunfire began to quake in the air. I should have tried to avoid the gunfire, but I didn't, I didn't want to. Moments of my life began to flash before my eyes, as I embraced the ensuing hail of gunfire. My mistake has become my coffin, burying my life into a photo album of glossy, picturesque memories. My mind became disfigured by the guilt and shame of my actions. The first bullet flew towards me in slow motion, eager to pierce my skin with lethal precision. It cratered into my body like a meteor crashing into the earth, its brass brothers towed in its wake. So is my fate. This is what I have chosen; this is what I have become...

****

...A murderous bullet impacted Cindy's armored body and bounced off harmlessly into thousands of little pieces. She pushed her way towards the stairwell with a herd of guards hot on her heels. Cindy ran into the cubicles and leapt over the copier. She knocked over the mammoth machine and attempted to block the guards' route; however, that brief moment she took to create a makeshift roadblock gave one of the guards the opportunity to blast a heated slug towards a fleshy, unprotected portion of Cindy's body. It missed—and ricocheted off of her metal dermis, but each deflected shot weakened the suit further. With the stairs in sight, Cindy gave herself a burst of speed to outrun the guards.

As she entered the infinite stairwell, Cindy slammed the door shut and pushed her back up against its iron surface. With the guards hot on her heels, Cindy was taken aback by the sudden brute force that crashed into the door behind her. Her

223

little frame bounced forward with each impact, but she dug her heels into the floor and pushed back against the strength of several men. She struggled to keep the door closed as the suit continued to systematically shut down, taking her super strength with it.

Her teeth gritted against the incredible force coming from the iron slab, each second that passed caused more sweat droplets to fall from her brow. Their arms were pouring from the opening like zombies trying to burst through a boarded window. Cindy twisted herself around and pressed back against the physical onslaught, grunting loudly as her tired arms shook, struggling to push against their combined efforts. She tried to heave all of her body weight into the door, but her small frame stood little chance against five huge men.

Cindy couldn't even *think* through all the exhaustion. Her limbs burned while her feet slid across the floor, like sneakers on a basketball court. She was losing ground in this life-threatening tug of war, but Cindy refused to surrender. She said to herself through gritted teeth, "Come on, come on, come on." She braced her body as the muscles in her back and arms flexed into position. With one final push, Cindy yelled at the top of her lungs and rammed into the door. The barrel hinges snapped off, turning the door into a rectangular wrecking ball. The guards fell backwards as Cindy pushed the metal slab on top of them.

Cindy froze in her tracks and stepped back to look at the collapsed guards. Dizziness swirled in her head caused by her rapid panting. *I gotta get out of here,* she thought to herself. She ran down one flight of stairs and almost tripped down the steps as the 39th floor entrance exploded open. Guards poured out of the entryway and fired their guns at Cindy, as additional reinforcements charged in from down below. Cindy grabbed one of the guards who came through the 39th exit and threw him over the railing. The guard screamed as he fell on top of the approaching swarm. Cindy was caught unaware, as another guard came from behind and tried to put her in a headlock. Cindy elbowed the attacker in the stomach and shoved the back of his head into the wall. His head let out a sick crack as the concrete exploded. Cindy spotted the horde of guards approaching and pushed through them in order to pass the closing stairwell door. Cindy entered a corridor full of offline elevator doors, the screaming guards clamoring behind her. She ran up to the closest elevator door and wedged her fingers between the narrow opening, in an attempt to pry the entrance open.

Her muscles were fed up with all the abuse they've suffered and burned themselves in protest. Cindy pulled on the doors so hard that she almost passed out from exhaustion. But her efforts were not in vain, the doors slowly rolled open as the guards burst through the 39th floor entrance. Cindy fell into the elevator shaft and grabbed onto the elevator cables, sliding her way down the industrial gullet. As her descent began to accelerate, sparks flew out from her hands and legs, showering the shaft below. The friction from the metal on metal caused the temperature to increase with each passing moment. Her silver hands began to glow

225

a molten orange, burning Cindy's skin. The pain was so excruciating that it felt like she placed her hand on top of a hot stove and couldn't let go.

She began switching out hands in a futile attempt to reduce temperature, but she was moving too fast and needed both hands to control her speed. The worst part was yet to come—the floor was approaching below and it was time to start slowing down. There were no brakes for Cindy to press; there was only one way she could slow down and it wasn't going to be pleasant. Cindy whimpered in anticipation of what was to come.

She clenched her hands tightly around the cables, jolting her body to a complete stop. Her flesh sizzled under the extraordinary heat. She shrieked as the smell of burnt metal and flesh polluted the air around her. Tears fell from her eyes as the startling sting of burnt flesh almost put her body into shock. Cindy popped open the lower level elevator doors and crawled into the now vacant parking garage. Cindy walked over to the guard post and saw the attendant asleep in his chair, oblivious to the happenings around the facility. Her body had been pushed harder than ever, and just thinking about walking up the exit ramp of the garage caused Cindy to die a little inside.

She trudged up the gentle slope towards the sidewalk. Her body had checked out long ago, but somehow, she still managed to move forward. Cindy crossed the street and entered a vacant alleyway. Cindy collapsed next to the dumpster bin as her body surrendered to exhaustion. Passerby's could have mistaken her for a bum. As Cindy lay broken, splotches of skin began to appear through the suit with various bruises covering her body. Her hands looked as though they were put through a meat grinder, hinting at a need for skin grafts. She had overestimated her capabilities—even SIRCA had a limit.

When Cindy awoke, she found herself blinded by the medical lights hanging over an examination table. The bite of her injuries was dull but still present. Her body was much too sore to even consider sitting up. The lights above her became obscured by a shadowy silhouette of a man with glasses. The man said to her, "What were you doing?"

Her eyes darted about inside her eyelids, as they tried to relay to her brain that she was still alive. As Cindy looked up at the man, the silhouette revealed itself to be Michael.

"Am I in the lab?" Cindy asked.

"Yep, drove you here myself," he replied.

"How did—"

"How did I find you?" Michael interrupted. "GPS. I set the suit to alert me if you suffered a critical systems failure. I had no idea I would find you like this."

Cindy looked away, as the dirt clinging to her neck undulated with her skin.

"What the heck happened to you, Cindy?" Michael sounded more concerned than annoyed.

"I got electrocuted," she said in a quiet whisper.

Michael waited for a moment, anticipating a more detailed version of the story. But when Cindy didn't say anything, he said, "That's it? You're not going to tell me *why* you got electrocuted? Or why your hands are burnt? Or why the suit is fubar'ed?"

Cindy refused to answer. Her eyes blinked in silence. Michael shook his head and stepped away to retrieve a hypodermic needle. "What are you doing?" Cindy asked.

"Charlie finished the formula to the cloning system. It was one of the features we didn't get to install into the suit. In theory, you should be able to regenerate all that damaged tissue, but as usual—"

"You haven't tested it," she said perturbed. "That's just great."

"Have we ever? Right now, it's your only shot," Michael replied.

Cindy sighed reluctantly. "Okay."

Michael injected the solution into Cindy's arm, which caused her to squirm as little warning flags popped up in her mind. "If this is supposed to be installed in the suit, why are you injecting me?" she asked.

Without looking at Cindy, Michael said, "Because it's for the organic part of the suit, not the nanos."

As Michael pulled out the hypodermic needle from her arm, Cindy snatched his neck like a cobra, threatening he spill information about the suit or suffer the consequences.

"Michael, tell me what's in this suit right now or I'm going to hurt you!"

The ripped and flappy texture of her skin disgusted the mad scientist. He struggled to breathe as Cindy's vice grip squeezed tighter around his Adam's apple. "OK! I'll tell you!" he screamed.

She released him from her hold as he clutched his throat and gasped for air. Before saying another word, Michael stepped away from her reach.

"Something is seriously wrong with you. Why are you acting like this?" he said.

"Answer me, Michael!" she demanded. Cindy shuffled around as she tried to sit up by using her elbows, but her body shook as weakness consumed her.

"Just lay back down. I'll tell you."

Cindy rested her head back on the table without taking her apathetic eyes off of him.

"It's an alien bacterium."

"What, like from another country?"

"Mars," he replied.

Her eyes spread wide like saucers. "You're not serious. Are you telling me I'm sharing my body with an alien parasite?"

"It's a bacteria not a parasite. It's more of an alien symbiote. Do you see why this is top-secret? If the world knew we had a primitive alien life form here on Earth, in the form of something commonly associated with disease and infection nonetheless. How do you think the public would react? Look at how freaked out you're getting now."

"Screw the public! It's my body this thing is sharing." Her anger seethed with every word. "What does the bacteria do, Michael?"

Michael replied, "It's the factory that produces all of the unusual elements in your suit. It stores the hydro fusion in its cells, interacts with your internal organs to protect them from damage, produces the silk armor, and establishes the connection between you and the machine."

"Then what the hell are the nano machines for?" she yelled.

"The nano machines instruct the bacteria as to where they should produce materials for your armor. The nanos guide the silk into position on and around your skin, form the guns, generate your HUD, control the oxygen supply, and direct the flow of hydro fusion throughout the suit. They are the construction workers and the bacteria serve as the building materials and storage."

"I can't believe this."

"This is exactly why we weren't allowed to tell anyone."

Cindy chewed on her lip for a few moments and calmed herself down. She asked Michael, "Can the bacteria heal my wounds?"

Michael replied, "In theory yes, that's what Charlie's formula is for. I just need to put the instructions into SIRCA."

"Okay."

Michael disappeared into the control room suite to access the SIRCA terminal. He installed the new cloning system into the armor and hoped for the best. As Michael initialized the protocol, Cindy could hear the sound of chittering tingling over her wounds. She looked at her hands and observed a peculiar pink foam bubbling over her palms and bruises like fizz from an Alka-Seltzer pill.

As the foam continued to work its magic over her wounds, Cindy started to feel a bit more rejuvenated. The lactic acid that had formed in her muscles began to dissipate along with the cuts and bruises she had accrued in combat. Cindy wiped away the foam, which instantly dissolved to nothingness. When she looked at her hand, it seemed as though she had just stepped out of the shower. Her skin was pure and clean—there were no burn marks, no blood and no bruises. It was as if nothing had ever happened.

Cindy looked at her former injuries. "That's incredible."

"Are you feeling better now?" Michael asked as he walked back into the lab.

"Michael, you guys need to be selling this stuff. Can you imagine how much money you could make from the pharmaceutical sector?" she said excited.

"Doesn't work without the suit. Trust me, we've considered it."

"That's a real shame."

Cindy swiftly sat up on the examination table as if she had just received a massage. Michael however, carried a detestable scowl across his face. Cindy glanced towards him and asked, "What?"

Michael crossed his arms and said, "Are you going to tell me what you've been doing?"

Cindy sighed as she looked down. She knew this question was going to come up again. "You have to promise not to get upset."

"A little too late for that. Out with it."

Cindy played with her fingers, refusing to look Michael directly in the eyes. She whispered unintelligibly, "*I've been killing people.*"

"Excuse me, what was that?"

"Oh God," her breath quivered as the nervousness settled in her chest. "I've been killing people, Michael." She grabbed onto her forehead and turned away in shame.

Michael did not seem surprised by her response. "I know... I just needed you to confirm my suspicions."

She pulled her head away from her hand and looked at him in shock. "What?"

"I've been monitoring the data since day one. I just didn't quite understand what it was telling me. Now it makes more sense than I care to know."

"I promise I didn't agree to kill any innocent people. I would never do that."

Michael sat down next to Cindy and wrapped his arm around her. She leaned in and rested her head on his shoulder, placing her hand gently on his chest.

"I believe you."

Cindy furrowed her eyebrow, distrustful of Michael's response. Something didn't feel right, he was a little too quick to be so understanding. Despite the doubt, she was relieved that he wasn't badgering her with any more questions.

"These past couple of days have been so hard, Michael," she said, defeated and exhausted. "Do you know what it's like to go home to an empty house every day?"

Michael replied, "Yes."

Cindy looked up at Michael, his somber expression told of many isolated nights without a companion. For Michael, even touching Cindy's shoulder was the closest he's been to a woman's embrace. Having lived in a life of computer code and tech news, he never had time to devote to another human being, let alone a woman.

Cindy felt a quiver in Michael's hand and asked him, "Are you nervous, Michael?"

Michael replied, "Umm, yes, I haven't really been close to girls before."

"There's no girls here," she said in a sultry tone.

"Okay... women."

As if spotting a ripe apple ready for plucking, Cindy found herself enticed by Michael's lack of *experience*. His nervousness was all Cindy needed to confirm that she could exert complete control over him. The temptation to toy with Michael triggered her impulses, making her act without thinking of the consequences to her actions.

"Michael," she purred, "have you really never been with a woman?"

"Umm…" He fidgeted. "No, why, did you finally tell your sister about me?"

"Forget my sister," she smiled and stared deep into his blue eyes. Cindy didn't seem herself, it was as if another woman had suddenly inhabited her body.

Michael jumped from the table and jogged towards the exit, keeping his distance from Cindy.

"What's gotten into you? Are you nuts?" he said in a panic.

Cindy hopped off the table and gently shoved Michael into the wall. The ravenous look in her eyes hinted that Cindy might not be in control of herself.

"You've never been kissed before, have you?" she asked.

Michael squirmed in front of her. "I don't want to talk about this anymore."

"You're attracted to me, aren't you?" she said with a smile. Michael's shirt sounded like static noise as her metal bosom pressed against his chest.

"What's gotten into you?" he whimpered.

"Just answer the question."

"You're a very beautiful woman. Now can we please just stop this?" he pleaded.

Cindy shook her head no and leaned in to give Michael a deep kiss. She used his inexperience to exert control over him. His lips quivered as he embraced her kiss, unwillingly taking pleasure in the moment. She placed Michael's hand on her chest, causing him to utter her name. He found it difficult to protest. His mind kept telling him to stop but he was becoming addicted to kissing her.

"Cindy?" a voice called out from behind.

Cindy's eyes burst open as she pushed herself away from Michael. She felt her rational thoughts flood back into her mind as if snapped out of a hypnotic trance. She turned towards the doorway and saw...

"Jonas?" Michael said.

Cindy turned away from her husband, hiding her face shamefully between her hands. Jonas rolled his tongue inside his cheek, not knowing what to do with this volcanic emotion fuming within.

"I don't even know what to say right now." He tried to mask his anger, but the cracking of his voice hinted at an unpredictable fury. Jonas' fingers danced around the tube of a nearby beaker. His hands clenched and released the tube as if saying, "Yes? No." Debating whether to turn the beaker into a projectile or not. His hand gripped *yes*. Jonas threw the beaker in their direction, not caring where it went, only that it hit something. Michael and Cindy ducked out of the way as the beaker exploded on the wall and fell like rain on a glass pane.

Cindy ran up to Jonas and placed her hands on his chest saying, "Jonas, it's not what you think."

"Get away from me!" he howled, as he shoved Cindy into the wall.

Michael cried out, "Jonas, stop, you're going to hurt her!"

Jonas pointed at Cindy and said to Michael, "Really? She's wearing the suit!"

Jonas realized what he had just said and felt his blood pressure skyrocket to such a point that he almost fell faint. "Oh my God, you're wearing the suit." Jonas rubbed his face, not wanting to believe what was happening to him. Cindy leaned over the table facing away from Jonas and broke down in tears. Michael was speechless and Jonas was waiting for an answer from either of them.

Jonas looked over to Cindy and said, "Did I really deserve this? You're the one that slapped me and made me leave in the first place. Then you went and did this even after I called you to tell you everything was okay? I guess that just wasn't good enough for you, was it? *And* you even hid the fact that you were wearing my suit. That's why you stole the car isn't it? You've been sneaking behind my back all this time."

"Jonas, I don't know what's gotten into me." The *real* Cindy appeared back on the surface. "I swear I didn't do this to hurt you," she said with tears streaming from her eyes.

"How am I supposed to believe that?" He turned to Michael and said, "And you—you of all people! You did this to me?"

"I didn't want to, Jonas, I swear! Cindy's the one that started all of this."

Cindy glared at Michael with such venom that she almost lunged at him.

"Is that true, Cindy?" Jonas asked.

She turned back to Jonas with mascara running down her cheek. Her back shook as she confessed her sins. "It's true… I don't know what's wrong with me, Jonas. Please believe me."

Jonas' voice cracked as he said, "You've hurt me more than I can bear. We're done—I never want to see you again."

Jonas walked over to the SIRCA terminal and disconnected the external hard drive that was attached to it. With the hard drive snuggled between his arms, Jonas walked out of the lab and out of her life. Cindy didn't bother to chase after him. She knew it was futile and her guilt prevented her from trying to persuade him. Cindy broke down on her knees and burst into tears, paralyzed with dishonor.

As she wailed for the loss her husband, Michael walked over to the SIRCA terminal and noted that Jonas had taken all of the data and research files from the suit. However, Jonas had only taken the back up. Michael still had the latest build and code to work from.

Michael looked over to Cindy and whispered, "You should go home. I'll clean up here."

Cindy looked at him suddenly, mascara dripping all over her cheeks. Her voice boomed, "What home, Michael? I don't have one anymore!"

Michael walked over to Cindy and lifted her up off the ground, tears still spilling from her eyes like a mournful waterfall. He draped a lab coat over Cindy and walked her outside of the building. Michael hailed a cab and paid the cabbie to take Cindy home.

With Cindy on her way, Michael walked back into the lab and spent the rest of the night poring through all of the computer code, fixing every serious error he found. If there was a chance the suit was the cause for Cindy's odd behavior, he would find it. The regret weighing on his heart motivated Michael to save their marriage, staying up all-night if he had to.

****

The cabbie was just a few blocks away from boarding the Long Island Expressway. Cindy's head craned back onto the leather cushion, her eyes were closed in an attempt to hide in the solace of darkness, but her body was restless. While wallowing in her despair, Cindy felt the comm link vibrating in her ear.

She was about to answer the call when she realized that she didn't have a cell phone on her; the cabbie would think she was crazy. Instead, Cindy retracted the metal on her hands and pretended to hold a blue tooth receiver to her ear. It wasn't like the cabbie noticed, anyway. He was too busy talking on his cell phone in a foreign language.

"Silver, are you all right? I lost contact with you after the Van Eisler job."

Cindy replied, "Yes, I'm fine. I had some technical difficulties." She wiped the mascara off of her face, almost as if she felt pressured to look presentable.

"Well, I'm glad to hear you're OK," Sam said with genuine concern. He took a moment to gather his nerve and proceeded to tell Cindy, "I know it's a little early, but I have another job lined up for you tonight."

"Sam, it's eleven at night and I nearly botched the contract. I'm exhausted and I just want to go home."

"I'm aware of that, but the window of opportunity to strike the target is closing quickly. If you wait any longer, you'll have to deal with a government security force. You've been dealing with mercenaries and professionals so far. Do you really want to risk this going up to a federal level?"

"Stop the cab," Cindy said to the cabbie.

"You're not going to Queens?" he said through a thick Middle Eastern accent.

"No, just drop me off here," she commanded.

The cabbie dropped Cindy off somewhere in Tudor City. As he drove off, Cindy snuck into a hidden crevice near one of the office buildings and fully reactivated her suit. She took off the lab coat and used the nano machines to absorb the fabric, removing all evidence of her passing. With her suit powered up, her artificial blue eyes flared up as all systems reactivated. She leapt up the side of the building and climbed to another generic rooftop.

"Cindy, are you there?" Sam beckoned.

She responded in a very short manner. "Yeah, I'm here."

"Are you going to do the job?" Sam asked.

"Yes, just upload it," she said with an attitude.

Sam briefed Cindy on the mission. "The last target for the night is a naturalized citizen named Alvaro Montez. He's running for a congressional seat."

239

Cindy became impatient and said, "Just tell me why you want him killed."

"He's becoming a serious political contender. He will work his way up from the House to the Senate. Maybe even the Presidency."

"I didn't ask for his life story. Just tell me the why," she demanded.

"Testy tonight, are we? If Mr. Montez takes a position of power, he will try to push legislation outsourcing jobs to illegal immigrants coming into the United States. He'll weaken security around the Mexican border and make it easier for illegal immigrants to become citizens."

Cindy replied, "Wasn't America built by illegal immigrants? And didn't you just ask me to get rid of Van Eisler because he supported deporting immigrants? You're contradicting yourself, Sam, and I don't like it."

"It's complicated…"

"It sounds to me like these assassinations have nothing to do with the target's political platform. Is this about their political power and influence, Sam?"

"Enough. Are you going to deal with Montez or do I need to resort to Plan B?"

Cindy took a deep breath, conflicted with the choice presented to her. "No, I don't want to do this anymore."

"Cindy, if you don't do this many innocent people will die. Do you want this on your conscience if I enact Plan B?"

"Damn you, Sam!" she yelled as her voice wavered from guilt. She paced back and forth trying to hold back the tears. She thought about all the horrible events that had happened, events that were caused by her own hands. The tears were not a reaction from Sam's words, but from the realization that she had destroyed everyone's life by taking the suit. She shook her head and said, "I'll head over to the hospital now."

"Good, try to stay in touch this time."

As the comm link shut down, Cindy found herself questioning everything. She broke Jonas' heart, and murdered men who may not have been guilty of what Sam stated. Should she really go and kill this Alvaro Montez? Cindy looked at her hands and stared at the reflection. She just wanted the nightmare to stop, but it just kept going and going. She was obligated to carry out this contract in order to prevent more lives from being lost, and it tore her up inside like razor blades on whips. Cindy looked out towards the skyline and grappled her way over to the hospital.

As she drew close to the hospital, Cindy was beset with sounds of wailing ambulances screeching out of the drop off area to rescue another hapless victim. She landed on the side of the hospital wall and crawled her way down to the open window where Montez was presumably located. She passed through the curtain like a ghost visiting the living. The soft fabric moved over her slate skin like a grazing set of fingers.

The beep of the heart monitor guarded the room as IV fluid dripped into

Montez's arm. Cindy looked around the hospital room and could smell the aromatic scent of flowers blanketing the sterile room. He wasn't sharing his space with any other patients and his spot was decorated with various get-well-soon cards, flowers and balloons. While approaching Montez, the walls reflected the glow of her eyes like a diffused spectral aura. Cindy dropped into a killing stance, approaching Montez with emotionless stealth. But stopped short, spotting a picture frame next to his bed.

Cindy took the frame between her ironclad fingers and caressed its reflective white border. She zoomed in to see Montez's arm embracing two women of varying ages. One looked to be his wife, while the other seemed to be…

"Priscilla?" Cindy whispered to herself. She swallowed hard and investigated the rest of the well-wishes near him.

Priscilla's name was plastered all over the room. She was in the cards embedded in his flowers, pictures, letters and balloons. Cindy stepped back from the sleeping Alvaro and shook her head. She refused to believe this was her student's father. Cindy retreated towards the window and reestablished communications with Sam.

"Sam, Sam. Are you there?" she whispered.

"What's the problem, Silver?"

Cindy replied, "I can't kill this man."

"We discussed this already."

242

Cindy pleaded, "This is my st—it's someone I know. Just cancel the contract."

"It doesn't work that way. If he doesn't die, the cycle of corruption will never be stopped. What you're doing is going to greatly benefit the health of this country. There are too many lives that are going to be affected by what you do. I cannot cancel the contract," he said in a very cold demeanor.

"I understand."

Cindy stood by the window, staring into the stark hospital room, unsure of what to do next. These were men with families, human beings. Even if the nation considered politicians incompetent and a blight upon the society, Cindy thought to herself, why should she fight the battles for a man she doesn't even know? Presidents have been assassinated in the past and for what? The politics and policies never seemed to change. It only transferred the power to someone else's greedy hands. For all Cindy knew, she was doing the dirty work for another slimy politician.

Cindy hesitated as she approached Alvaro. Her hand was reluctant to reach out and disengage his life support. Cindy had once upon a time, felt the impulse to kill as many people as possible. But now faced with the life of someone she cared about, the thought sickened her, as it always should have. Her finger hovered over the switch, the consequences of going through with this would be disastrous. If Cindy couldn't look herself in the mirror now, how would she feel looking at

Priscilla in the eye?

She clenched her fist and pulled away from the machine.

"I'm not doing this, Sam."

"I didn't give you an option to back out," Sam replied.

Cindy stood up straight and looked at the sleeping man. She said to Sam with defiance in her voice, "Call your Plan B. I'll kill anyone who enters this room."

"Fine, then you leave me no choice." The line fell silent.

Cindy stood there for a few seconds, it seemed as though nothing was happening. After a minute or so of silence, Cindy suddenly heard the sound of screaming thundering from the downstairs lobby. Bursts of gunfire from submachine guns silenced their cries, but more blood-curdling screams would follow shortly after. She could hear the radio communications of elite soldiers echoing throughout the hallway.

Cindy yelled into her comm link, "Sam, what are you doing? Sam? Sam!"

There was no response.

Suddenly, Cindy turned to the window as a pair of combat boots flew through the opening and pelted her with machine gun fire. The bullets pinged like firecrackers upon her armor as she rushed towards the window and ripped the soldier off of his rappelling line. She grabbed him by the edges of his Kevlar vest and threw the soldier back out the window. His horrified scream reverberated throughout the city block—until silenced by a loud thud.

She turned around as two more soldiers with night vision goggles and black balaclavas burst into the room. They instantly lined their sights on a sedated Alvaro. Cindy ran up to one of the merc's and ripped the machine gun out of his hands. She crushed the weapon between her palms and used the ball of tempered steel to whack the soldiers face. His helmet flew off as he fell flat on his back, but the second soldier was already in firing position. Cindy grabbed the opportunistic grunt from behind and slammed him into the ground. She smashed her fist straight through his night vision goggles, splitting the equipment in two.

Cindy could still hear the rattling of gunfire booming down below as men and women ran for their lives in terror. She wanted to save them, but she couldn't be in two places at once. It pained her to hear everyone's suffering. She had no idea that Plan B would entail this… this massacre. Cindy ran up to Alvaro's bed side and looked for a way to move him to another location, but he needed the machinery to survive the wounds suffered from his previous shooting. That's when it dawned on her—Sam had ordered that initial assassination.

As she watched Alvaro sleep, Cindy's radar detected more movement behind her. She clenched her fist and turned around just in time to see and hear—a bullet blast from the chamber. Cindy's targeting computer instantly locked on to the traveling projectile as time slowed to a crawl. The bullet flew through the air, rotating like a clock counting down to someone's demise. Cindy fanned out her hand and let the SIRCA guide her movements, pivoting her arm like a windmill to intercept the incoming killer. The bullet deflected off her forearm and flew into the background making a subdued pop. The soldier holstered his weapon and retreated from Cindy.

"We're Oscar Mike. Recover the bodies," he said into his radio before vanishing.

Cindy stood triumphant over the soldiers as they began to withdraw from the hospital. She turned her attention back to Alvaro and froze in horror. A stain of dark red liquid began to expand from Alvaro's chest. The heart monitor belted out a steady, cutting tone that reverberated in Cindy's head. Despite her best efforts, she was unable to save Priscilla's father. Cindy couldn't look at the body. She turned away, trying to cover her mouth even though the helmet was blocking her hands.

She braved going into the corridor and discovered dozens of dead bodies scattered all over the floor. It was a bloodbath. The staff lay brutally murdered as streaks of blood smeared the walls and pools of life gradually dried into death. *All this senseless killing*, Cindy thought to herself. *None of this had to happen.* A fleet of police and ambulance sirens began approaching the hospital at full speed. Cindy went back into Alvaro's room and saw the poor man resting peacefully. How was Priscilla going to react to this? Cindy jumped out of the window and grappled her

246

way back to Queens, utterly destroyed by what had happened.

At around 2:30 am, Cindy was back in the suburbs with tears filling the inside of her helmet. Through her blurry eyes, Cindy spotted something peculiar on her street. She saw a man and a woman chatting and counting money with two other men standing next to them. She zoomed in using her suit's optics and felt her blood boil inside of her veins. Cindy dropped down into her neighbors' driveway and deactivated her suit. Without thinking about the danger or consequences, Cindy wiped her tears and stormed her way over to the group lollygagging on her street.

There was a bloodlust burning inside of her eyes. All of the events that had happened to her pushed Cindy to the edge of a nervous breakdown. Her life was crumbling all around her as she transformed into a shell of her former self. Cindy had been bottling up all these violent feelings of revenge for what felt like ages and now, now she couldn't stop herself from opening the vial of rage. She recognized the couple as the con artists who lured Cindy into their trap. Right beside them was the disgusting man whose hand crept up her thigh, his buddy standing right beside him. She walked up to the husband who was in the middle of talking to his wife and tapped him on the shoulder saying, "Remember me?" Before the man could speak, Cindy's fist barreled through his face. Her punch was so strong that her wedding band branded itself into his cheek. As he fell down to the ground, Cindy grabbed his leg and snapped his knee in half. He screamed while banging his fist on the concrete sidewalk, overwhelmed with excruciating pain. Cindy was on the warpath and nothing was going to stop her. She kicked the tortured man across the cheek and rendered him unconscious.

"What are you doing?" the woman screamed, while charging towards Cindy. Cindy without even looking behind thrust her elbow into the woman's chest and smacked her face with her wrist. She turned to the injured woman bearing her teeth with a wolf-like snarl. Cindy kicked the woman in the stomach and thrust her hand onto the woman's neck. The woman gasped for oxygen as Cindy lifted her into the air with one arm and choke-slammed her to the ground. *Only two left*, she thought while turning her attention to the remaining thugs.

She said to the one felon with a menacing smile, "You're the one that stabbed me, aren't you?" There was a wild, uncontrollable fury, flickering in Cindy's eyes. The sweet, loving wife was gone, replaced by this avatar of destruction.

"I don't even—oh... you're the one that fought back." He brought out his switch blade. "Mmm, you had a fine ass on you girl," he said with a sadistic grin.

"Are you insane? Did you not just see what she just did to Jose and Monica?" the friend yelled to the suicidal knife-wielder.

Cindy exhaled with a deep hiss that seethed with rage. This lowlife had the nerve to brag about what he had done. After all the suffering Cindy had gone through this cursed day—she was going to make the world feel her pain. She was going to cut the grin right out of that scumbag's face. Cindy had reached her breaking point. All the anger that she had been storing up spewed out of her like Mt. Vesuvius destroying Pompeii. Cindy bounded towards her attacker and jammed her foot up his groin. He wasn't fast enough to defend himself and took the full brunt of the impact. She grabbed his wrist before he could drop the knife and pulled him into a headlock. Cindy leaned into his ear and whispered, "Now you're going to get a taste of your own medicine."

Cindy wrapped her manicured fingers around his hand and pulled the knife up to his neck. Despite being shorter than him, the loathsome thug couldn't free himself from her vice grip. His arm shook violently as he tried to resist Cindy's great strength. His friend tried to jump in and save him, but Cindy pulled the assailant's arm towards his comrade and stabbed him repeatedly in the stomach. She bellowed a chilling war cry as her emotions exploded out of her. Her face distorted with her cries, upset that she was going this far for revenge. The friend clutched his stomach and fell to the ground as blood spilled from his belly. The headlocked thug screamed, "You killed him! Why did you kill him?"

She whispered like a demon into his ear, "Now you're alone with me."

"You weren't supposed to fight back," he said, as his cowardice revealed itself.

"That's your excuse?" she growled into his ear. "You ruined my life and now you're gonna feel my pain. The pain I didn't deserve!"

Cindy kicked out the back of his leg and brought his knees crashing down onto the sidewalk. She didn't let him fall however. No, she grabbed a handful of his hair and pulled his head back, exposing the man's soft neck. She pulled the rusty switchblade up to the surface of his skin. Nothing was going to stop Cindy now, her conscience left weeks ago, and her suffering urged her to continue. She forced the lowlife to hold his own weapon to his throat. There was no joy in her actions, no masochism. It was pure, poisonous revenge. It flowed like black venom through her veins.

There were no witnesses in sight, no police on patrol—no one to disrupt what was about to take place.

Cindy held the blade near her tormentor's neck and asked him, "Any last words?"

"I'm—"

"You don't get any."

Cindy slid the knife across his throat, spilling crimson liquid from his jugular. He gasped for breath as the oxygen escaped his lungs but never returned. Cindy held onto his head and made sure that he perished within her guilty hands. She threw his head down and watched the blood pour onto the sidewalk. Cindy was so wrought with adrenaline that her body trembled uncontrollably. Her breathing was erratic and her heart was racing, but her revenge was, at long last, satiated.

All the pent-up anger, all the trauma, all the sorrow was released from Cindy's body like a cathartic release. Her body shook violently as her emotions tried to calm her down. Yet even with her assailant dead by her own hands and his associates equally punished, Cindy only felt a small portion of peace. She had thought that getting revenge against those who had wronged her would make the world align itself and make her feel normal again.

It just wasn't enough. Yes, she found peace in bringing the criminals to justice, but what about all those people who died at the hospital tonight? She freed herself from one prison only to be transferred to maximum security. Her breath quivered as the last of the virulent energy dissipated out into the atmosphere. Despite her victories, Cindy still felt defeated. She walked home to her empty abode and thought to herself, *I can't take this anymore.*

CHAP7ER 7

SELF-DESTRUCTION

The next morning, Michael arrived at Cindy's home and found the front door suspiciously unlocked. With a laptop bag slung over his shoulder, Michael walked into the home with caution. He was repulsed to find hundreds of wrappers and empty containers littering the floor. As he took one step into the house, he squashed an empty ice cream container with his sneaker. Half-eaten cupcakes, an open bag of Oreos, and an empty cheesecake box were just a sampling of the revolting pig pen that surrounded him.

"Cindy?" he called out. Walking deeper into the living room, Michael overheard the sound of coughing and gagging coming from behind him. He turned around and found Cindy lurched over the porcelain bowl. Nauseating, retching sounds emanated from the small bathroom, followed by stomach-churning plops splashing inside of the toilet. The vomiting continued for several minutes until finally the repulsive horror show was drowned away by a simple toilet flush. Cindy rested her head on the ceramic tile floor while still keeping her hands wrapped around the base of the commode.

Cindy looked up at Michael revealing glassy, red eyes. They weren't red from just exhaustion; these were eyes that had been weeping throughout the night. Michael's heart broke as he watched this once proud woman crumble into a poor wretch.

Cindy said quietly, "Don't look at me…"

"I need to talk to you," he whispered.

"Go away," she said with deep sadness, turning towards the wall.

"It's important."

Cindy sighed and strained to lift herself off the ground, still sore from last night's events. It was as if she had aged fifty years, plodding out of the bathroom at a snail's pace. Michael stood by awkwardly, as Cindy walked out of the door, wiping her mouth with her sleeve.

"What are you doing here?" she asked, displeased with his presence.

"I… I think I've found out what's been going on with you. Are you okay? Your eyes are bloodshot. Did you get any sleep?"

Cindy scoffed and walked past Michael, paying no attention to him. She sat down on the couch and began stuffing herself with cookies; yet the sugary treats did nothing to abate the hurt she felt inside.

"Should you be eating those?" he asked.

She responded with a light cadence, "No."

"I should call Jonas and tell him what's going on with you."

"He's not going to care," she said while laughing in delirium. Her despondent tone lingered with every word. "Why would he talk to you after what happened?"

"Valid point, but listen. I really think I found the problem to—"

"I don't care, Michael. I hate myself, and I don't want anything to do with this stupid suit anymore." She began to confess her sins as if hoping it would bring redemption. "I've… killed people; my husband left me because I kissed you like an idiot; and I'm responsible for innocent people getting massacred. I took for granted and abused everything that had been given to me." She looked at Michael with sadness in her weary eyes and said, "Just let me eat until I get fat, puke it all up, and do it all over again."

Before she could stuff another cookie down her throat, Michael slapped the poison out of her hand. "Cindy! You're going to let yourself be killed by an eating disorder? You're better than that."

"Hey! Knock it off." She raised her fist and threatened Michael to back off. He flinched, and jumped away from her. Cindy quickly realized she was reverting back to that dark place and put her hand down. She paused for a moment and turned away while crossing her arms. "Just leave me alone," she said shamefully.

Michael lifted his index finger and said, "Look, I want to show you something, okay? Don't eat any more junk. Just look over here at my laptop."

With her arms still crossed, Cindy looked away while he unpacked his computer. Michael placed the mobile PC on Cindy's lap. The SIRCA app was open and thousands of lines of code stared at Cindy all at once.

"I don't know what any of this means."

"Just hang on a second, Cindy." Michael scrolled down to the cognitive section of the SIRCA and pointed out to Cindy a very peculiar line of code.

===============================

Cognitive Commands

===============================

;Apply fight or flight response to prefrontal cortex?; ;Yes

"Isn't that supposed to go to the hypothalamus?" she asked.

"Okay, I thought I was going to explain that part. Yes, it is supposed to affect the hypothalamus, but the code was wrong. I rewrote the entire thing from scratch and got rid of anything that would influence brain function. Cindy, the suit is what's been making you destructively impulsive." He paused for a moment and looked into her unbelieving eyes, which were staring at the screen. "It's not you," he said reassuringly.

"Even the sleepwalking?" she asked.

Michael looked surprised. "When did you start doing that?"

"There were a few instances when I woke up and didn't know how I had gotten somewhere."

"All of that should be fixed now. Nothing from the suit will interfere with your brain function anymore."

Michael clicked on a few different menus while Cindy leaned back into the couch covering her forehead. Cindy was unsure what to feel. On the one hand she should be relieved that the horrible things she did were not entirely her fault; yet her life had been ruined by one line of code. *Was that possible?* she thought.

"I have more news," Michael said.

"Michael." Cindy lifted her head from the couch and looked at him. "I've had all I can take."

"I figured out how to remove the suit," he said.

Cindy sat up from the couch, now fully attentive. She pondered if this was going to be it; if she would be free of this curse that had turned her life into a spiraling nightmare.

"What do I have to do?" she asked.

"Nothing. I just need to install the updates. This is going to be a huge patch Cindy. After this, the suit is going to be fixed of all bugs. I also fixed that stupid stealth system from shutting down. That damn thing ruined everything. Anyway, if you let me install the patch, I will be able to remove the suit afterward."

"Okay." Cindy clasped her hands and nodded her head.

As Michael commenced the upload to Cindy's suit, she waited in excited anticipation for the changes to take effect.

"So, about last night," he said.

"It was the worst day of my life," Cindy said while looking out the window.

"I shouldn't have let you kiss me. I'm sorry."

Cindy scoffed as brilliant rays of sunlight illuminated her hazel eyes. They couldn't hide the embarrassment and shame behind their beauty.

"You're a good person. I know you are. Don't kill yourself over this. It wasn't your fault."

"And what am I going to tell Jonas?" she snapped. "That 'evil' Cindy was in control, that the woman he saw kiss his best friend was just some kind of diabolical clone? I've killed people. Should I not take the blame for that either? I never should have gotten involved with Sam."

"That's another thing I've been meaning to tell you. I've known about—"

Cindy interrupted him. "Hang on, Sam's calling me right now."

Michael sat on the couch and monitored the chat conversation on his computer.

Cindy lifted her index finger towards Michael and said, "Don't say anything—hello?"

"You know, Cindy, I had really enjoyed working with you."

Cindy's eyes opened in shock. "You know who I am?"

Sam laughed in response to Cindy's naïve question. "I thought that such a smart woman would have figured as much. After all, how does one *collect* money for contract assassinations?"

"My bank account, but I didn't give you—"

"No, you didn't, yet you still received the money. Let's ignore that for now. I want you to come in and surrender the suit. I'll give you an hour or so. If you don't give up the suit, your sister and Jonas will end up like those people in the hospital."

Michael rubbed his mouth and said, "Oh sh—"

Cindy jumped up. "You don't need to hurt them! I'll give you the suit. I don't even want it anymore. Okay? I don't want anything to do with this."

"I'm glad we could come to an agreement. I am really sorry it came to this."

As the comm link shut down, Cindy turned to Michael. "Did you get all of that?"

"Yeah, what are you going to do?"

"I'll tell you what I'm not going to do. I'm not giving that lunatic the suit," she said with determined boldness.

"But what abou—"

Cindy interrupted him. "I'm not going to let him hurt them either. I'm going to call Jadie right now and tell her to get out of town. Could you pass me my cell phone, please?"

Michael looked around like a lost child and found the cell phone buried under a pile of candy wrappers. As he handed the phone to Cindy, Michael immediately wiped his hands on the couch in disgust. Cindy attempted to reach Jadie but was greeted by an automated voicemail.

"Damn," she stomped her foot on the ground. "Her phone is off."

"What are you going to do?" Michael asked.

"What can I do?"

"You know what I think?"

Michael typed away at the keyboard as the new build for the SIRCA system completed its installation. He looked up at Cindy and said, "You're gonna have to suit up." He turned to the laptop and clicked on a few windows. "I'm unlocking the suit and giving you access to all the weapon systems."

Cindy yawned as little glimmering tears inched out of her drowsy eyes.

"You really haven't slept at all, have you?"

"No, I haven't," she said.

Michael began having doubts. "Maybe this isn't such a good idea."

"Michael! This is my family we're talking about," she said with urgency. "I'm going with or without the suit."

"Fine. Before you power up though, I have to tell you about the energy weapons you have now—don't turn them on yet! You'll destroy your house. You have a sword and a knife that can be deployed from your suit. The sword will extend like a whip if swung hard and the knife will come out from your wrist for emergency self-defense."

"Okay, is that it?" she asked.

"And super speed. I'm not sure what your top speed will be, but you can probably outrun a car. Don't use it for too long or you'll burn yourself out."

"Got it. Thanks, Michael."

260

"Be careful."

With those final words, the liquid metal began to surface on Cindy's skin. The liquid hardened into flexible steel as silk strands shot out from her neck like streamers at a fireworks show. The strands formed the cocoon around her head and pushed her hair inside the forming helmet. Her clothing dissolved away as the nanomachines wrapped her body in unbreakable quicksilver, enhancing her muscle structure.

This time Michael turned away from the transformation and never looked at Cindy even once. As the shell forming on Cindy's head hardened and morphed into her helmet, her eyes became infused with unstable glowing blue energy. Her HUD booted up—and for the first time, there were no errors. The Silver Ninja was ready to go unto the breach once more, but Cindy was doubtful about this being the best decision.

"Are you sure about this, Michael?" Her words shook with uncertainty. "I don't want to go down that path again."

"I promise you; you're in control," he said.

Cindy nodded and prayed that he was right. She left on her journey to save her family, hoping to put an end to the nightmare once and for all; however, the lack of sleep was taking a toll on Cindy's constitution. Even though grappling through the city was exhilarating, she couldn't stop herself from yawning. It felt as though heavy weights had been stapled to the tops of her eyelids.

Staring at the HUD, various video feeds burned her retinas like scalding water. If it weren't for her extraordinary determination and the high stakes, the exhaustion would have crushed any other human. Cindy was approaching the HUD's banana-colored waypoint that was prominently displayed on her radar. It was directing her to the 1st Continental building. She had heard about the multibillion-dollar technology company in the news and wondered if the suit was malfunctioning. *Had Michael truly fixed the bugs in the suit?* she wondered.

She double-checked the address Sam uploaded to her suit and, sure enough, the drop-off point was on the fiftieth floor of the 1st Continental building. The wind rushed through her ears as she continued to flip and roll through the air like a paper in the wind. Cindy activated the stealth camouflage and began to fade into the skyline. Her metallic skin flickered on and off until she vanished out of sight.

Cindy released the grapple line and flung herself onto a window on the fiftieth floor. She landed with a strong —thunk!— like a bird crashing into a windshield. Cindy's body flickered for a second, revealing just a brief glimpse of her in the super suit crawling along the glass. She glanced down and saw the street below. At her elevation, it seemed almost as wide as a very thin line. She shrugged off the daunting height and searched for a way to enter the office building.

She scrolled through the menu selections in her suit and found some new menus. She opened the brand new infiltration menu and accessed the claws feature. She turned off the stealth camouflage and watched as her fingers extended into razor sharp nails. She formed her hand into a circle and clinked her fingers onto the tempered glass. Turning her hand as if she were holding onto a radio dial, she cut a perfect circle into the glass. But just before she could pull out the circular disc, the window crinkled; its cracks spreading into a giant spider web. Cindy growled and pushed her foot into the window causing the glass to concave around her leg. She placed her heel into the office and took her first steps onto the blue-carpeted floor of the 1st Continental building.

Upon entering the building, the HUD reported that a jamming signal was preventing outside communication. Cindy spotted a lone security guard patrolling the corridor. She slipped back into stealth mode as he took notice of the broken glass window and made his way over to investigate. While raising the radio to his lips, Cindy blinked into existence right beside him. His eyes were as wide as saucers as Cindy lifted her knee up in the air and aimed in his direction. She held her balance like an elegant crane and snapped her foot into the guard's mandible. His skin undulated backwards as the shockwave traveled through his face, turning his jaw into an accordion. Cindy hit him so hard that he instantly lost consciousness.

Cindy walked down the hallway and spotted a glass room filled with men in white lab coats. Upon further analysis, the room seemed to be chock full of robotics, computers and engine blocks. *What is a lab doing up on the fiftieth floor?* Cindy thought. Just then, she spotted Jonas walking around, directing the team of scientists. *Was this the crew from Lucent Labs?* Pieces were starting to fall into

263

place, but the puzzle was still baffling. *If the Lucent Labs crew was working here at 1st Continental, was Michael working here as well?*

She continued to peer inside the lab and saw a strange cadaver wrapped in a shiny red cellophane-like material lying on a table. She couldn't tell if it was a robot or a human and didn't care enough to give it a scan. Right now, all she cared about was getting Jonas to safety. Cindy leaned against the drywall and took several steps towards the glass. With two distinct taps, Cindy made sure to grab everyone's attention. Cindy took a gamble and hoped that with Jonas being the lead designer, he would be the one to check out the disturbance. She waved her hand in front of the glass until she heard, "What the hell is that?" come from within the lab.

Cindy stepped away from the wall and ducked into a nearby hallway, using her radar to monitor anyone who came out of the lab. One red triangle began making its way towards her location, with its line of sight staring straight ahead. The muffled footsteps on the carpet drew closer, as Cindy carefully planned out in her mind how she was going to get Jonas out of there.

After a few moments, Cindy noticed that she no longer heard footsteps. When she looked up towards the ceiling she saw that Jonas had poked his head around the corner instead of walking into the trap. *Smart boy,* she thought. Cindy snatched him into the hallway before he could even respond.

"Jonas, we have to get out of here," she said in a hurry.

Jonas was visibly upset. "What are you talking about, why are you here?"

"You're not safe here. Someone from this company is trying to kill you."

Confusion was written across Jonas' face, unsure of what Cindy was talking about. "That doesn't make any sense. I work here now."

"Please, you just have to tr—"

Cindy felt her head jerk back abruptly as her arm flung through the air and impacted something hard. Gravity pulled her down to the floor, allowing Cindy to see the ceiling tiles roll across her eyes like a scrolling movie background. As she lay on the floor confused, Cindy looked over to where Jonas was and saw a huge welt across his head. He was out cold and his skin was swollen and purple. Cindy must have accidentally hit him with her hand when she fell back. While staring at Jonas, a red leg dropped down in front of Cindy. She tried to get up, but the leg placed its foot atop Cindy's helmet and pushed her back down to the floor.

Cindy couldn't believe her eyes. Standing before her was a blood-red statue in the form of a woman. It stood tall and slender with subtly-toned musculature spread throughout its body. Cindy looked at her reflection in its scarlet-colored skin and then proceeded to look up to the woman's eyes. It was the same exact helmet that she was wearing, just in a different color. It was like staring at a Valentine's Day mirror from hell.

The crimson figure gripped Cindy by the neck and lifted her straight off the ground. Cindy choked as her feet dangled in the air. One flick from the woman's wrist sent Cindy flying across the hallway and through the drywall of one of the offices. Cindy's ears rang like the church bells of Notre Dame. She shook off her daze and leapt to her feet before the crimson woman could launch another assault. The scientists, upon hearing the commotion, scattered from the labs and evacuated to a different floor.

Cindy spotted a nearby computer monitor and pulled it free from its wires. In a desperate attempt to save herself, she threw the monitor at the crimson woman. The woman slapped the monitor away, but not before Cindy could charge in and pummel her with a flurry of blows. Yet the red woman was too fast. Each blow Cindy attempted to land felt empty and hollow. There was no resistance, no impact, only negative empty space. Cindy's endurance drained from each missed strike she attempted.

The woman was fast, and Cindy's strikes were sloppy, slow and predictable. The crimson woman struck her with precision and force. The red reflection delivered targeted blows against Cindy's torso through every opening Cindy failed to protect. The health overlay in Cindy's suit began to change in color. The bright blue overlay began to morph into a bright yellow, warning Cindy to get out of danger.

Her stubbornness refused to let her to leave. She knew deep down that this metallic woman shouldn't be able to stand a chance against her. Yet several kicks to the head suggested otherwise. Cindy's hubris was blinding her to the reality that

266

she was too exhausted to fight back. All Cindy could see before her were flashes of red moving so fast that it was all just a blur to her. Cindy couldn't dodge, couldn't block, and couldn't avoid the merciless pounding.

Cindy tried her best to ignore the blows and managed to catch the red woman by surprise when she delivered a swift, forceful kick to the woman's stomach and knocked her back. While the woman clutched her abdomen, Cindy capitalized on the opportunity and delivered another explosive kick to the woman's head, knocking her flat on her back. Cindy stomped towards the woman not wanting to lose her momentum but was stopped short when the crimson woman knocked the legs out from under Cindy with a sudden leg sweep.

Cindy slapped her hands on the floor, growling in complete frustration. She was being bested in everything, and she questioned whether she could beat this Ruby Ninja. As Cindy spotted the woman getting ready to pounce on her, she leapt to her feet and threw a cross punch towards the ninja's helmet. The dissatisfying sensation of punching air returned to taunt Cindy, causing her to lower her guard. The woman fell forward into a handstand and wrapped her legs around Cindy's neck with perfect gymnastic form. Cindy gripped the woman's calves as she felt her entire body get lifted off the ground.

Cindy was thrown so quickly and so elegantly that Cindy didn't know she was on the floor until her whole body shook from the impact. Before Cindy could even get her bearings, the Ruby Ninja picked her up off the floor and rammed her into a wall. She unleashed a rapid fire barrage of kicks and punches that dented Cindy's armor. Warning signs blared in Cindy's HUD as the structural integrity of her suit began to fail. Her exhaustion was taking over. She knew she wasn't at the top of her game and this woman, robot, whatever, was going to exploit that weakness to its fullest. Even seeing Jonas unconscious on the floor couldn't give Cindy enough energy to fight back.

Cindy's spirit refused to surrender, but her body had given up the fight a long time ago. She was hurting. Her once-powerful arms had gone limp; her shins and calves trembled as they verged on collapse; and her courage began to falter. The woman released Cindy from the wall and watched her struggle to land a single hit. The Ruby Ninja pushed Cindy's head back, which caused her to stumble backward towards the window opening. She toyed with Cindy; taunting and hitting her with quick strikes as Cindy wobbled around like Jell-O.

Her spirit continued to fight, but it was like continuing a car race without an engine. Her dented and scratched armor lost its beautiful sheen, and the HUD flashed red warning signs of Cindy's pending doom. The visual feed in her helmet scrolled and distorted, making it impossible to see the woman in red. All Cindy could view through the mess of warped video was a zippered blue light streaming from the woman's hand. It wasn't clear if she was holding an item or if it was actually coming out of her hand—the suit was too damaged to make sense of what was going on. She watched the woman charge at her like a screaming samurai.

268

The light sliced in front of her eyes followed by a horrible, burning explosion of electricity erupting from her chest.

Cindy screamed in pain as the suit began rapidly beeping, notifying her that it was entering system failure. Her skin split open as the suit began to dissolve off her body. Each step she took backward continued to feel heavier than the last. The sizzle of her flesh overpowered her senses as unfathomable torment ravaged her chest straight down to her stomach. The Ruby Ninja was too powerful. She had given the Silver Ninja her first taste of defeat. Cindy began to feel weightless as the shock from her laceration began to dwindle.

A pop up appeared in HUD: "Activating Emergency Quick Start Reboot." Her vision went dark, but the weightlessness she felt was comforting and relaxing. A new prompt called, "Safe Mode" appeared before her eyes advising Cindy that the neural network was shutting down. A final pop up appeared shortly after that said, "Emergency life support activated."

Cindy watched as white specks of sparkling glitter twinkled before her like angels far off in the distance. She looked over to her hand and watched as the metal armor softened into a thick viscous liquid. The armor dissolved into her skin and revealed her soft, delicate hands.

It was then that Cindy realized why she was feeling so weightless. She looked forward and watched her beautiful long hair unfurl before her very eyes flapping like a flag in the breeze. She watched as the 1st Continental building shrank in the distance. The specks of light were pieces of glass from the broken window Ruby had pushed Cindy out of. The wind rushed through her ears causing her clothes to flap in the wind. The protective, indestructible suit left her when she needed it the most. Her body continued to plummet the fifty stories as hundreds of windows flew past like a flip book animation.

Cindy released an ear-splitting scream that echoed throughout the cityscape as she fell towards her death. In just a few seconds, her screams fell silent as a revolting smack echoed throughout the busy streets below.

CHAPTER 8

REVOLUTIONARY ROAD

"Raymond, are you going to eat your dinner?" a woman asked in a gentle voice.

"In a minute, honey," he said while furrowing his brow. The weight of the world rested upon this man's shoulders. He watched the news broadcast with focused intent, waiting with anticipation to hear whom the governor would select for the interim Senate seat.

The haunting glow from the television illuminated Raymond's weary eyes. Behind the creased wrinkles, earned for every year of life he had survived, was an epic plan devised by a great thinker, a visionary. The governor appeared and then stood behind the podium to address the press. The governor cleared his throat, sending a boom throughout all the speakers within the press conference room. "Speakers work," he said as a light laughter rolled across the room.

He paused for a moment as he looked around the room, immune to the blinding flashes of hundreds of cameras.

"I have to be honest with you. I was not expecting to ever be in this position. I mean, who could really anticipate having to fill a vacant Senate seat? Filling the seat of a great man is a heart-breaking task. So imagine my horror when my second

271

candidate Joseph Van Eisler was murdered and my third candidate..." His voice began to crack as he continued reading his speech.

"My third candidate, a good friend of mine, Alvaro Montez narrowly survived a pair of assassination attempts. Thankfully, he's one tough son of a b—gun. My last candidate up for selection was Raymond Levreux, the CEO of 1st Continental. As I sat in my office, preparing my speech for Raymond's nomination, I received a phone call from Alvaro begging me to take a different path.

"When I asked him why, he told me that he felt someone was making a power play to take the Senate seat. Too many political leaders have died in such a short time. He didn't trust Raymond Levreux, especially considering his involvement with the Occupy Wall Street protests and lack of political experience. Alvaro's solution was for me to hold a special election. With that being said, the public election will be sched—"

"God... dammit!" Raymond flipped his dinner plate and threw the remote control at the LCD screen, destroying his television set. His wife ran up to him and clasped onto his shoulders as he covered his forehead with his hand. "I can't believe Alvaro survived twice. Those public elections are just a scam."

"How do you know, Raymond?" his wife asked.

Raymond replied, "When has a vote ever mattered, Barbara? It's going to be like always. Two of his preferred candidates will run and no one will vote. He might as well have named the replacement."

"What are you going to do now? Are you going to call Alexis?"

"No, I don't want to get her involved in this. She's done enough for this country. I have no choice but to go to plan B. You should get out of town."

Barbara shook her head. "Raymond, no. You can't be serious."

"Sometimes people need a good smack to the face before they listen. Take the private jet and go to our spot, all right?"

"I don't want you to do this, Raymond. Please, reconsider," she pleaded.

"This is my last chance to try to fix a broken system. The ends justify the means."

Barbara sighed and turned to the bedroom to pack her things. Before leaving, Raymond said to her, "If you talk to Alexis, don't tell her what happened. It'll upset her too much, and I don't want her to be ashamed of me."

Barbara nodded her head in reluctant agreement and walked away. A week later, the unsuspecting New York populace endured a barrage of attacks by a high-tech army. The anti-terrorism unit was useless against Raymond's sophisticated mercenary forces. Even though NYC boasted a private army, they were no match for the futuristic weaponry of the 1st Continental army. The news reports from across the world latched on to the events as they unfolded and repeated them ad nauseum for all to see.

Well-armed mercenaries with bright green laser sights burst into the homes of numerous political figures, snatching them from their warm beds and transporting them over to cold, empty cells within the 1st Continental building. Tanks rolled through Times Square, crushing cars beneath their treads as thousands of mercenaries secured a foothold in the landmark location.

People ran screaming in terror as various eruptions of violence took place between the mercenaries and the U.S. armed forces. Air Force bombers would fly through the city corridors dropping bombs, but 1st Continental shot down numerous aircraft with futuristic weaponry. The Marines and Army led simultaneous strikes against the 1st Continental forces, but their monstrous four-legged walkers and powerful tanks outclassed anything the military had to offer.

Raymond's military forces locked down all of the boroughs surrounding Midtown Manhattan and prevented the military from breaching the perimeter every step of the way. No one could stop the 1st Continental army, and the forces remained entrenched for months to come. Raymond was attempting an old-fashioned coup d'état, and it was working. During the violent overthrow of the NYC government, Raymond captured a TV station from a major news network and sent out a chilling broadcast throughout the nation.

"Good evening. My name is Raymond Levreux. A lot of you must have a lot of questions, wondering what possessed me to take on the business capital of the world. Maybe you even think I'm crazy and harbor anger towards me for the lives that have been lost. It was a necessary price to pay. This conflict marks the first step towards taking back our freedom from corporations too big to fail. My intention was never to harm or kill the citizens of this city. I have a wife, two daughters and a son, all of whom I love very much. But I could no longer idly stand by as your governor spread lies about being able to vote for your next senator.

"How many of you sat awake in your beds wondering how you were going to pay your next bill? Working yourselves to the bone only to never be offered a pay raise by your employer? I have been in your shoes; I've had those nightmares; and I lived through the poverty of supporting a family when I barely had money to fill my tank just to get to work. America's broke; yet we have enough money to build mega malls, stadiums and launch attacks on third world countries. We elect politicians to serve our best interests and instead, they suck the teat of their rich masters.

"You're led to believe by the media, that you're voting democrat or republican without realizing that both parties are one in the same. We, as a country, have lost our voice and have let corporations make decisions for us. Ninety-nine percent, I'm talking to you. We're going to take back this nation, one city at a time. Blood will be shed, but that was the way we won our independence from Great Britain. If you do not want to be oppressed by your government and its corporate masters, join me in the fight."

At the end of Raymond's broadcast, the battles continued to rage on within the city. There was no hope for the U.S. forces in uprooting the mercenaries from their foothold, and there were no resistance fighters to fight back. Yet deep within the bowels of Manhattan, life stirred within the ruined walls of a bombed-out hospital. A man sat next to a woman lying in a hospital bed, waiting for her to awaken. The woman shuffled beneath the covers as life returned to her fragile body.

"Whoa, whoa, easy now," the man said.

The woman opened her eyes as if waking from an eternal slumber. The glassy highlights in her eyes shifted from side to side as her pupils contracted in reaction to the soft light. She noticed the gentle presence of an oxygen mask strapped around her mouth and nose. As her energy began to return, she looked down towards her body and saw her blouse torn open from her stomach to her chest. Her embroidered bra was filthy and stained with weeks of neglect. She turned toward the African-American man sitting in front of her and watched as he put away shock paddles into a rolling cart. He turned to her and grinned with his goatee following the form of his lips.

The woman spoke, "Who are you?"

The man replied, "I'm the guy who brought you back to life."

The woman tried to sit up, but the glancing pangs of pain shooting through her nerves made it difficult to do so. The man placed his hand on her shoulder and gently pushed her back to the bed.

"You shouldn't move yet, Cindy," he said. The fact that this stranger knew her name worried her.

Cindy looked at him with suspicion. "How do you know my name? Who are you?"

"Malcolm Douglas at your service, former Tier 1 operator," he said with a smile. "Before you ask, just think of Tier 1 as Navy Seals or Delta Force."

"You ripped my shirt," she said, annoyed.

"Sorry, ma'am. Your heart stopped. The shock paddles didn't seem to work, so I resuscitated you manually."

"You didn't—"

Malcolm cut her off, "No ma'am, I did not give you mouth-to-mouth. I actually wasn't sure if you were going to make it. You've been comatose for a few months. Here, let me take that oxygen mask off of you."

When the mask was removed, Cindy looked around, confused. "Months, how is that possible? I just passed out for a few seconds."

"That's not how it went down. You fell from the 1st Continental building and went…" he dropped his hand into the other making a loud slapping sound. "Everyone thought you were dead, but somehow you were still breathing. An ambulance picked you up and rushed you over to the hospital."

"And that's where we are now?" she asked.

"Yes, ma'am."

"I've never met you before, and you're not a paramedic. Why were you trying to revive me?" Cindy asked.

"Do you remember that night you came to the galvanizing facility? Someone told you that your sister was going to be harmed if you didn't show up?" he asked.

"You mean the night I should have minded my own business?"

"That message was intended for me, Mrs. Ames. I saw everything go down."

Cindy's expression turned to a scowl. "You just sat there and let me get shot at?"

"Hold up, I'm no superhero. Charging in there would have been suicidal. I was waiting for the right opportunity to pick them off, but you powered up and took them down like they were pre-schoolers."

"That's a terrible simile."

"Well, either way, you kicked some serious ass."

"That still doesn't get us to now, Malcolm," she said.

Malcolm sighed. "If you must know, I started following you around. Even though the situation at the plant was resolved, my sister was still missing. I had hoped you would lead me to her."

Cindy became impatient and asked, "Who is she?"

"Kendra Douglas. She was running for office as an independent," he said.

Cindy rolled her eyes. "I'm getting sick and tired of being followed around by politics. Does it run in your family or something, Malcolm?"

Malcolm replied, "Both my parents were in the military, Mrs. Ames. Service runs in our blood."

"My father was in the military," Cindy said. "But he was already out by the time my sister and I were born, so there wasn't any moving around."

Malcolm raised his eyebrows in interest. "Oh, so your daddy taught you to fight?"

"Well, he taught me Pencak Silat back from when he was stationed in Indonesia. I didn't start Krav Maga until I went to the Police Academy. I won a few fighting tournaments when I was a kid, you know."

He chuckled. "You're a trained killer."

With that innocent little comment, Cindy's face warped into a grim expression. She whispered to herself, "Yeah, I guess," while looking off into a covered window.

"Listen, I know you've been having a rough couple of months, but we need to get out of here and take the fight to 1st Continental. I tried to find a way into that building, but it's locked down tighter than a skeeter's ass in a nosedive."

Cindy shook her head and slowly blinked her eyes. "…what?"

"It's well-guarded," he replied.

"Oh." Cindy clenched her teeth as her jaw jutted in and out of her cheek. "So you only revived me to help you bail out your sister, huh?"

"That suit of yours is what revived you. All I did was make sure you survived."

Cindy replied, "Well, I'm sorry to disappoint you but I'm done with the suit. Once I'm feeling better, I'm going straight home and forgetting I ever put this damn thing on."

"Really, you're going home? Just like that," he said.

"Yes, I am."

Malcolm grabbed Cindy's hand and helped her up to her feet. "Come on, get up. I wanna show you something," he said while pulling her towards the window. As Cindy limped her way over to the windowpane, she noticed bullet holes had riddled the walls and ceiling tiles were missing. Pieces of plaster and exposed insulation revealed the ribs of the hospital like an emaciated, beaten cadaver.

Malcolm lifted the blinds. They flapped, like a million bats in a cave, while making way for the miserable sight beyond. Cindy's discolored fingers covered her mouth as the ominous glow of embers glimmered in her eyes. The once-busy city streets were now filled with lines of captured soldiers, marching with their hands atop their heads.

Huge mechanical walkers and tanks lumbered through the avenues, shaking the earth to its core. No dissidents would dare attempt to free the POWs. Mercenary soldiers in advanced armor watched each captured U.S. soldier through glistening black visors. Strange hover bikes flew through the air, like a swarm of mosquitoes, chasing after military jets while blasting the sides of buildings with weapons that echoed throughout the corridors of the city block.

Cindy said with an empty voice, "What happened?"

"1st Continental attacked the city while you were out." Malcolm pointed towards the ruined skyline and said, "That right there is why I can't save my sister. You don't have a home to go back to, not right now, at least."

"My family is out there," she whispered.

Malcolm turned towards Cindy. "Well, now we've both got a reason to fight."

Cindy looked Malcolm directly in the eyes and said, "All right, but I'm in no condition to fight."

"Let me handle that."

Malcolm had convinced Cindy to join the fight and found himself rebuilding the broken woman from scratch. Her weakened body had atrophied from months of neglect, and her injuries were so severe that she couldn't carry her own body weight. Her knees would give out from under her, bringing her crashing down onto the dirty tile floor. Malcolm, however, was standing right there, picking her back up when she faltered.

He put her through the training he learned back in the military, pushing Cindy to her limit. To his surprise, Cindy pushed herself beyond anything he could have ever anticipated. Within a few days, she was able to walk normally, defying all conventions of rehabilitation. Whenever she struggled to grab onto the silver pull up bar, Malcolm would come up from behind and lift Cindy from the waist. As she wrapped her fingers around the metal bar, Cindy would handle the rest on her own, wasting almost all of her energy on just one chin up.

But she never stopped at one. Just when Malcolm thought he would have to catch her fall, she would pull herself up for another and then another, rebuilding what had been lost. When Cindy was finally able to move under her own power, Malcolm began to refresh Cindy's combat techniques. Years of neglect made many of her movements slow, predictable and sloppy. Her combat skills needed to be updated. Under Malcolm's tutelage, Cindy was able to turn rusted, cobwebbed knowledge into a pristine, stainless steel weapon. Her movements became fluid like water; her strikes landed with precision; and she became faster and stronger each day. Her self-

281

esteem, once a broken marble statue built on a foundation of guilt and failure, was reconstructed under Malcolm's training; her imaginary statue now took a stance of defiance and victory. After weeks of grueling training, Malcolm had finally given Cindy the nod of approval, meaning Cindy was ready to fight once more.

Malcolm made a makeshift battle plan using scraps he found from around the hospital. The ketchup bottle served as the headquarters for 1st Continental, while the IV lines were laid out to simulate the Queensboro and Brooklyn bridges. Nuts, bolts and screws were used to simulate the troop movements, while the IV bags formed the outline of the Manhattan Island. Finally, a little cardboard box signified the location of the hospital.

"Which one am I?" Cindy asked.

Malcolm gave a dry response, "You're the box."

"Which one are you?"

"I'm the box too." He waved his hand over the map. "We are the box; the box is the hospital; this is our location."

"What if I wanted to be the screw?" she asked.

"Are you being fresh with me right now?"

Cindy looked surprised and said, "What? No, I'm trying to be funny."

"How's that working out for you?"

Cindy glared at Malcolm as he continued to explain his plan to Cindy.

"So we're here at Roosevelt Hospital on 58th street. 1st Continental is over here on 53rd street. A big chunk of his forces are clustered near Wall Street, and he's got reinforcements coming in from the Queensboro Bridge. Over here at Times Square, U.S. forces are fighting a losing battle. To infiltrate the 1st Continental building, you'll need their help," he said while pointing to the nuts and bolts.

"So rescue the soldiers first and then make my way to 1st Continental. What are you going to be doing?" she asked.

"I'm going to use my stash of C4 and disable the Queensboro Bridge.

"You're not going to blow up the whole bridge, are you?"

"Just enough that they won't be able to make it to headquarters in time. The damage will be easily repaired afterwards. Once that's done, I'll meet up with you in Times Square."

With the plan established, it was time to set it in motion. Cindy's breath shuddered as she closed her eyes and once again imagined being enveloped in the glistening, stainless armor that had tarnished her rather peaceful life. The familiar tightness of the suit wrapping around her skin, compressing around her arms, like an overgrown blood-pressure cuff, brought back the nostalgic feeling of power that she now hated. Malcolm stood back with his arms crossed and nodded, impressed by the piece of technology Cindy wielded. As her blue eyes flared up, she looked at Malcolm, who was already making his way towards the door. "Good luck," she said to him, but Malcolm continued walking away. He waved without ever once looking back.

Cindy made her way up to the rooftop of the hospital. She gazed beyond the horizon and was saddened by what she saw. What was once a streamlined view of monolithic pillars of human industry was now a ragged edge of bombed-out buildings teetering on the brink of collapse. In front of her, dust swirled in the air as sorrowful clouds loomed overhead. She looked down towards the city streets as units of mercenaries marched onwards like an army of evil. Cindy zoomed in and began scanning each of the individual soldiers, adding their data to the computer library.

The first unit she analyzed was the standard infantry. Her suit would generate a revolving model of the soldier, whose slender body armor with blue accents represented his grunt status. When she scanned the next batch of soldiers, she found infantry with much heavier armor decorated with red accents, signifying troops equipped with heavy ordinance such as rockets, grenade launchers and heavy machine guns.

When the sorting was complete, Cindy stepped up to the edge and found herself struck with a bout of vertigo. Her arms flapped like wings as she kept herself from falling over the edge. It was then that she realized that fear was clasping onto her ankles, refusing to let her move. She looked down towards the street and felt the altitude increase along with her anxiety. Acrophobia hugged her body like a clingy child never learning independence. It made her body tremble with terror as flashbacks of falling fifty floors played back in her mind.

Doubt clouded her confidence like the forming storm clouds above. *If I can't handle grappling through the city, how will I have the courage to fight an army?* Cindy thought to herself. She found it difficult to focus. Her vision blurred as the fear pushed her back away from the ledge, telling her that she was going to fall and die all over again. Cindy closed her eyes and took several deep breaths in attempt to calm herself down. She thought back to her days as a young gymnast when the eyes of students, friends and family were all on her, waiting for that spectacular routine.

Unlike most people, Cindy enjoyed the attention of performing. A stadium swarmed with flashing lights felt like a second home to her. Cindy bent over and placed her metal-clad hands on the edge of the building. She pretended that she was holding onto an uneven bar. She imagined the crowd falling silent as the cameras flashed in a burst of glittering stars, waiting with bated breath.

With a light grunt, Cindy lifted her body with perfect form into a flawless ninety-degree handstand. Her arms shook under her still-recuperating strength, but she was able to hold on strongly. Ever so subtly, Cindy's body began to tilt forward like the Leaning Tower of Pisa. She could feel the emptiness in front of her; there was no wall to stop her from tipping over. Only the bleak chasm of a war-torn city lay before her.

She imagined that everyone was waiting to be amazed. Cindy allowed gravity to pull her forward while maintaining her perfect form. She whispered to herself, "Courage is not the absence of fear; it is the conquest of it." Cindy tipped forward, her arms sustaining her body, which peered over the edge like a curious construction crane. Cindy swallowed her hesitation and allowed herself to finally let… go.

She tipped over and broke through the invisible barrier blocking her road to redemption. The guilt and shame that haunted her for all these months did their best to follow her. But they cowered in fear as she dropped to the street below. She opened her eyes as the targeting computer locked onto the highest building and fired the grappling hook. Cindy flew through the air as the wind whooshed past her like a roller coaster.

She danced through the motionless skyscrapers like a soaring eagle—graceful, beautiful and fearless. The crack of thunder rumbled in the distance as gloomy clouds began to weep for the city. In just a few minutes, Cindy's visor was drenched with raindrops as she approached Times Square. It was such a depressing sight to behold. What had once been a neon mecca full of tourists and vendors was now a desolate wasteland. The video billboards were shut off, only a dark grey background filled the frame, and the only people visible were mercenaries and soldiers battling for dominion of the legendary attraction. The situation for the U.S. forces was dire, and Cindy needed to act now if she was to have any hope of saving them.

She grappled onto the spike atop the 'Virgin' mega store and began circling around the antennae gaining momentum. She did several revolutions before reaching a blinding-fast speed, launching herself straight into the sky. She tucked her knees into her stomach and curled up into a tight ball as rain pattered all over her armor. She began rolling backwards as her body began to descend. Like a hawk diving onto its prey, Cindy reached terminal velocity, her body shaking from the incredible wind resistance.

She engaged the automatic grappling system, which oriented her body to the perfect swinging position. She made sure to keep her body as compact as possible while her arm shot out a hook towards the Times Square New Year's pillar. It latched onto the highest billboard and began guiding Cindy towards the biggest cluster of 1st Continental soldiers, who had no idea she was even in the area. The human wrecking ball crashed through the platoon like a cannonball on a French battlefield.

Piles of mercenaries flew into the air as Cindy's rolling body clanged into their hardened body armor. She swung through the army like a pendulum in a grandfather clock, rising up to the billboard at the end of her arc. When she reached the blanked out advertisement, Cindy released the hook and cocked her legs into her chest. As her feet made contact with an empty marketing board, Cindy sprang off of the wall and launched herself back into the fray with arms fully stretched in front of her. She flew through the air like a dart, heading straight towards another unsuspecting mercenary. Cindy's hands locked onto his shoulder pads, and while rolling over his head, she used all of her upper body strength to flip his body over and throw him across the street into another platoon.

The mercs fell down like bowling pins. But then, Cindy felt the rumble of tanks rolling down 6th Ave. The roaring monsters shook the buildings and pavement around her like a miniature earthquake. The rain began to pour even harder, dripping down her visor with waterfall-like streams. The radar began to ping with dozens of hits coming from mercenaries and vehicles encroaching on Cindy's position. At the same time, green blips on her radar signified that the U.S. forces had retreated east towards the river. Cindy had bought them enough time to regroup, but she still needed to fend off this massive army.

The mercenaries formed up in a crossfire pincer position locking their sights on Cindy. Realizing that armed soldiers had her surrounded on both sides, Cindy somersaulted out of the way of the oncoming bullet hailstorm. She used everything in her gymnastic arsenal—flips, pikes, rolls and cartwheels—to avoid getting tagged. Her graceful maneuvers allowed Cindy to trick the enemy into shooting their own comrades, causing the mercs to yell, "Friendly fire!" She kept luring more bullets to the other platoons of mercenaries, forcing the thugs to either risk shooting their comrades or cease firing altogether. One by one, friendly fire would bring down the squads, but this wouldn't last forever. The tanks had arrived; their mounted machine gun turrets whirred as they unloaded a molten volley of armor-piercing rounds towards Cindy's direction.

She drew out her forearm rail guns and fired two shots at the machine gun protruding from the top of the tank. KAH! KAH! The rail guns slapped the air with incredible force as the slugs flew towards the tank turret. The assisted targeting allowed the slugs to land at their destination with incredible precision and disabled the tank turret with ease. Cindy was startled by how loud the rail guns were, having never fired them before, but she was thankful to have them. But the tank still had one massive, rotating ace up its sleeve. Cindy listened to the sound of a mechanical turret whirring to life. Her eyes gaped as she prepared for the oncoming blast.

A percentage number appeared at the top of her HUD and increased in numerical value. Cindy didn't know what it meant until it reached one hundred percent. "Enemy locked on," the suit said. A series of yellow squares calculating the trajectory of the turret's shell folded out like dominos. Cindy found herself caught in the middle of one of these squares. As she tried to dodge the impending shell, the turret would follow her, which made the yellow square track all of Cindy's movements. A timer counted down signaling when the tank was going to fire. With the clock ticking, Cindy was forced to try something so ludicrous, she thought it could never work. With no other options available, she leapt straight into the air as the yellow boxes recalculated and locked onto her. An explosive flame burst from the muzzle of the tank as a shell of depleted death came charging towards Cindy.

She could see the over-sized bullet approaching her as if it was in slow motion; in reality, mere milliseconds were passing by, but in her mind, everything was caught in a time warp. She twisted her body at the last second, just narrowly avoiding the tank shell. While still spinning in the air, Cindy kicked the hulking bullet with such power that it changed trajectory. The shell turned an unexpected direction, barreling straight into another tank and ruptured its resilient armor. The tank exploded in a hailstorm of hot metal and fire, taking it out of the fight before it could even enter.

When Cindy landed on the ground, she knew she had mere seconds before another shell was headed her way. As the rain filled the streets with deep puddles, Cindy activated her wrist blade and cut deep into the asphalt floor. She dragged the blade across the surface of the street creating an odd, circular shape as she dodged fire from the hundreds of enemies surrounding her. Once she had completed the crooked cut, Cindy switched her hands to claws and wedged her razor sharp fingers under the carved asphalt.

Out of sheer desperation, she attempted to lift the gargantuan rock she had sliced from the street. The synthetic muscle fibers shot out from within her body and boosted her strength. The ground began to crack around her feet as Cindy continued to lift this massive chunk of black rock off its place of origin. The water main below burst open, blocking Cindy's vision with a geyser of torrential water. The water jet beat against her armor like rain on a glass window during a hurricane. She lifted the enormous earth over her head as the synthetic muscles strained to sustain the weight.

She placed one heel back and reeled her hands just behind her head. With one giant heave and a pained grunt, Cindy hurled the rock to the tank's barrel. A loud crash was heard as the chunk of asphalt landed on top of the barrel, bending the groaning metal into complete uselessness. At the same time, Cindy's artificial muscle fibers detached from her real muscles, shrinking her back down to her normal size. What was once a huge cluster of mercenaries was now dwindling down to pockets of resistance. The tanks became burning, useless husks, and the mercenaries fled in terror, surrendering their position to Cindy... or so she thought.

As she looked over the weeping horizon, the ground shook as a bipedal tank stomped its way through the city blocks. Escorting the mech were a fresh batch of infantry and two rail gun tanks rumbling down the streets. Freelance soldiers began to pour in from every avenue like cockroaches spilling out of kitchen walls. Cindy was outmatched and outgunned, but she had one more trick up her sleeve.

She placed her left hand on her right thigh and let it sit idle for a moment. Her fingers wriggled with anticipation as the item she wanted began to take form. She wrapped her digits around the grip of the weapon as the rain continued to hammer her body. Bullets began flying through the air, pinging and panging off of Cindy's armor. The smooth quicksilver would nick and scratch with each impact, but it held firm against the projectiles. Enemies continued to draw closer, unloading volleys of bullets upon her with each step forward. This was only an appetizer for the main course; the real threat was the mech and tanks getting ready to fire at her simultaneously.

A synchronized bombardment from three different vehicles would obliterate Cindy in an instant, but she had to hold fast in order to lure the army just a little bit closer. Finally, the HUD began to arrange boxes in a cone in front of her, flashing like police lights in the distance. After a few moments, the flashing turned into a solid color as the SIRCA locked onto all of the targets in Cindy's line of sight. She cocked her leg back and tightened her arm, lowering her body into an attack stance. The countdown for the tanks to fire commenced as Cindy stared down her opponents head on.

Water dripped from her chin as the all-encompassing rain refused to relent, but her focus was unshakeable. In her stoic stance, Cindy seemed at complete peace. The countdown timer hit zero and a bright flash consumed the theater district, but there was no rumble of thunder to follow. Instead, the world froze as the mercenaries stared at Cindy like statues in a museum. For a brief moment in time, everything was at silent peace.

The melody of rain colored the atmosphere with a mellow tune. Yet as time resumed to its normal pace, so did the destruction that followed. The legs on the bipedal mech exploded with incredible destructive force, shattering the glass of buildings nearby. The humanoid giant moaned as it tipped over its sliced knees and fell on top of the rail tank in front of it. The second tank couldn't even move an inch before detonating in a massive explosion that sent shockwaves throughout the troops nearby. A murderous cascade of blood began to explode from the torsos of all the mercenaries in the area as the poor saps split in half.

Horrified screams cascaded throughout the block as bodies became dismembered and limbs plopped down onto the street. The only one who remained standing was Cindy, alone in the middle of the rain-soaked street. In her hand was an undulating, ice-colored blade, its energy crackling in her hand. The rain drops sizzled and turned into steam upon touching the blade. She twirled her blade around, leaving a blue contrail in its wake, and then crouched into a Katana fighting stance with the blade's handle near her helmet and the sword pointing straight out.

A desperate soldier, who thought he stood a chance against the Silver Ninja, aimed his wavering gun at her steel frame. Without allowing him a moment to think about squeezing the trigger, Cindy gave her sword a hefty swing in his direction. The blade shot out like a whip towards the soldier and sliced off the end of his gun barrel. He screamed in terror as he ran away from the battleground, leaving Cindy standing in the center, surrounded by all the destruction.

Cindy released a deep breath from her chest as everything began to settle down. The rain continued to dance on the street, like fairies in an urban forest, as smoke billowed from the fresh wreckage of scrap metal. As the energy blade retracted into her suit, Cindy had a gut feeling that it wasn't over. Through the black smoke covering the charcoal skies, Cindy could hear a strange whistling sound, similar to a jet flying through the air. The suit began to flash warning signs as a red, circular disc appeared around Cindy's feet. The whistling drew nearer and louder. This was no jet. A barrage of artillery shells was incoming.

Cindy jumped out of the radius of the red disc just before the ground detonated with a bone-shattering explosion, rocks and debris shot twenty feet into the air. The shockwave knocked her off her feet, while snipers, perched on rooftops, began to take aim and fired potshots at Cindy's armor. More artillery shells began to bombard the iconic landmark. Like maneuvering through a deadly floor exercise, Cindy channeled her gymnastics training to avoid each shell. But even with the suit's incredible capacity to make Cindy superhuman, she was still susceptible to the one thing technology could never change: exhaustion.

The intensity of the explosions and gunfire continued to increase exponentially. Cindy's HUD began to flicker and scroll as her suit started to absorb the damage. Her health display changed to a sickening yellow. The suit was trying to make her avoid every single thing that was coming in her direction, but that was impossible, even for a superhero. There was too much data coming in at once, distracting Cindy and making her unable to recognize the greatest threats.

One moment of static, one brief delay in Cindy's evasive maneuvers, one millisecond of error, brought with it a barrage of punishment. When the static cleared, Cindy found herself staring at the business end of a rocket-propelled grenade. The explosion launched her backward into the foundation of a building. She crashed through the cement and brought down a chunk of wall that collapsed on top of her. Her vision blurred and distorted as high-pitched ringing oscillated in her ear. Her head was pounding, like a migraine, and her dizziness was overwhelming. Although the suit managed to resist the detonation from the RPG, the health display showed that her helmet was bordering on a dangerous red. She kept hoping that the health display in her augmented reality HUD would not turn completely red. She knew that if it did, the suit would begin to rupture, leaving her vulnerable to gunfire. The scent of smoke seeped into her helmet as bullets peppered her body like hail on a windshield.

The soldiers swarmed on her like ants to a picnic table. They climbed over the debris and helped each other up in a disturbing display of teamwork. In mere moments, Cindy found herself staring down dozens of rifle barrels, each holding quivering bullets in their blackened chambers. Cindy flinched in terror as the muzzle flashes from the weapons lit up her eyes. She drew out her wrist-mounted energy dagger and jabbed at the necks and stomachs of any soldiers that drew too close. Gushes of blood spilled over her visor, blinding her view, making her even more desperate to fend off what she couldn't see.

Her best efforts seemed to be in vain, as more and more troops continued to pile on top of her like a quarterback with a football. The integrity of her armor was beginning to fail and the tide of battle was shifting in their favor. As the blade continued to take lives, the power was beginning to fade; her eyes and weapon were dimming and flickering in intensity. The damage to her suit was becoming severe and at any moment, her metallic skin would be breached. She needed time to repair, but the enemy was relentless in trying to kill her.

Just before the suit was about to tear, a dark red splatter shot out from the head of one of the mercenaries. The troops looked around in panic as another shot pierced through the helmet of another mercenary. One by one, each of the soldiers dropped dead, giving Cindy enough time to recuperate and commence repairs on her suit. The snipers who had been harassing Cindy from a distance fell silent, and the pack dogs that had mauled her with their rifles were no more. Cindy looked up towards the sky and saw a friendly hand reaching out to her.

Malcolm pulled Cindy out of the building debris and wiped the red dust from her suit.

"Sorry, I'm late, ma'am. Putting the C4 on that bridge wasn't easy," he said.

"I don't care. You showed up just in time in my eyes."

Malcolm saw just piles upon piles of bodies strewn about the street. The rain washed the blood down into the subway tunnels, while tanks burned like torches in the distance.

Malcolm let out a long whistle and said, "Looks like you were busier than a cucumber in a woman's prison."

Cindy stared at him with a blank expression. "That's disgusting. What possessed you to say that?"

"Sorry," he said with a tinge of embarrassment.

"Did you find our boys on the way here? They retreated to the river when I— well... cleaned house."

Malcolm pointed his thumb over his shoulder toward the river and said, "There's a big ass spider thing shooting at 'em right now."

"What? Why are we sitting here?"

"I'm waitin' on you!" Malcolm said.

****

Meanwhile, at 1st Continental in the lonely offices towering above the Manhattan skyline, the quiet weeping of a broken man haunted the empty corridors. Inside the unlit office, Jonas held a picture of Cindy in his hands as years of love dripped from his eyes. Splashes of salty water fell upon Cindy's smile as Jonas mourned for his wife, even after all these months. The photo shook in his trembling hands as he rubbed his thumb over Cindy's cheek. While wallowing in despair, the door to his office opened without warning. Jonas slammed the photo on the desk and wiped his eyes so the visitor wouldn't notice. The red outline of a woman stood by the door, hidden in murky shadow.

"Jonas?" the woman spoke.

"Yes?"

"What are you doing?" she asked.

"I was taking a nap."

"Raymond wants to see you."

"Okay, I'll be right there."

Before the red-clad woman closed the door, she asked Jonas, "Are you all right?"

He waved her off and said, "Yeah, I'm fine, I'll be right there."

Jonas stuffed the photo of Cindy in his wallet and walked out of his office, wiping one final tear from his twitching eye.

****

Back in Midtown, a strained voice screamed, "Spread out!" as gunfire rained from every direction.

Hydraulic pumps hissed and whirred as eight metal legs stomped through the avenue. The M1 Abrams, considered the U.S. military's most powerful and indestructible tank, fired its shells at the gigantic monstrosity. The shells flew through the air and detonated in a plume of flame upon its insectoid frame. When the smoke cleared, the mech was still standing with nary a scratch.

The U.S. soldier yelled to his squadmates, "Adams, get that laser designator up! Yee, give me the horn!"

The radioman rushed over to the captain, handing him the radio in a feverish panic. The captain barked into the radio, "Big Apple, this is X-Ray. We need an airstrike on my laser! Danger close, over!"

A barely intelligible voice crackled over the radio, "Wilco, bombers are hustling to your position. ETA one minute."

"The flyboys are coming. Get down!" the captain shouted.

Right on time, the whoosh of jet engines began to approach the city block. The laser designator beamed its coordinates to the jets flying overhead. As the soldiers grabbed onto their helmets, the bombers dropped their payload over the spider. The bombs exploded upon impact with the mechanical behemoth, causing a huge shockwave that shattered windows and pushed the pooling rain out like an exploding water balloon.

The arachnid didn't even flinch and responded with a hidden anti-air missile system lurking upon its back. The missile battery fired at the jets flying overhead, shooting them down in a heart-wrenching fireball. "I'm hit! I'm hit! Going—" one pilot relayed over his radio just before his jet crashed into a building. The pilots inside the tarantula focused their attention on the soldiers and revealed a strange weapon from underneath the nose of the cockpit. The soldiers tried to fire at the weapon, but they didn't have any armaments that could pack enough punch to even leave a scratch. The strange gun began to glow as it charged up. The humming accelerated to a high pitch as the weapon prepared to fire.

A bright flash appeared at the tip of the weapon like a glowing star. It spewed out an indigo particle beam that tore through the city street in a wide arc. When the laser abated, its intended destruction seemed nonexistent. It appeared to have missed the soldiers completely without causing any damage besides scarring the street. It wasn't until a few moments later that a lava-like radiance began to bloom from the cracks. It grew more luminous with every passing second until the ground began to shake with the force of an earthquake. **BOOM!** A pillar of flame shot out from the street creating a hellish tower of fire twenty stories high. The troops fled from the destructive firestorm, almost tripping over one another, while trying to avoid the breadth of white-hot flames.

The tarantula drew out its twin rail guns and locked on to the soldiers through the wall of fire. But before the rail guns could finish them off, Cindy leapt atop the torso of the tarantula and detached one of the armor panels with her energy blade. Once the wiring and guts were revealed, Cindy jabbed her weapon through the body and ran across its armored abdomen, dragging the blade behind her. The spider split open with an earth-shattering shockwave as Cindy jumped off its head and landed in front of the U.S. soldiers. With the machine sounding its death knell behind her, the U.S. soldiers crept out of their hiding spots, almost too afraid to even stick their heads out. She put away her blade and stood up to greet the soldiers who approached her with caution. The rain began to subside, as the ominous dark clouds parted ways, revealing the brilliant light of the sun above.

The sergeant looked confused and asked his superior officer, "Are we supposed to shoot her, sir?"

The captain squinted his one eye and gave Cindy a wary look. "I don't think that will be necessary, Sergeant."

"Are you guys all right?" Cindy asked with genuine concern.

"Ma'am, thanks for taking out that walker before it blew us all to hell. It looks like my boys are all right," the captain responded.

"Can you ask your boys to stop staring, sir? It's making me a little uncomfortable."

The captain looked back towards his subordinates with an annoyed grimace; his squad quickly looked away, scratching the back of their necks in an attempt to look less obvious.

"General Ord asked us to find survivors from the 101st Battalion. Did you see any out there?" the captain asked.

"Sorry, I only found this guy." Cindy turned around and pointed towards Malcolm, who was climbing over the spider wreckage. "Malcolm, let's go!"

"Settle down. I'm coming. Not all of us can leap tall buildings in a single bound," Malcolm said.

The captain looked despondent and said to Cindy, "Then, we lost them all."

"I'm sorry, I didn't find anyone else," she said.

Malcolm interjected, "What happened to all your tanks? I'm pretty sure you guys had more than this."

"That damn monster over there blew up the entire regiment. Everyone was wiped out."

Cindy jumped into the conversation uninvited. "I'm sorry to interrupt, but who are you guys?"

"We're Green Berets, ma'am, 22nd Battalion," the captain said with pride. He pointed to himself and began to introduce everyone. "Captain James Colt. Under my command are Demolitions Sergeant Adams, Communications Sergeant First Class Yee, Medical Sergeant Jennings, and Weapons Sergeant Goose."

Malcolm stepped forward and shook the hand of the captain. He introduced himself and mingled with his cousins from another military branch. Cindy stood back and observed the group, feeling just a little out of place amongst the military boys.

She looked at each of their grungy faces. There were smiles to be had as they talked shop, but the dirt smeared on their faces told tales of loss and sadness.

Sergeant Adams seemed to be the youngest of the group, the classic high school varsity quarterback who joined the Army in search of glory and a higher purpose in life. Standing next to him was Sergeant Yee, who appeared to be of Korean descent. At first glance, he seemed to be the quiet, but deadly type. But when engaged in conversation, the killer mystique immediately disappears. He's just another regular guy like his buddies, no more threatening than a sober, college frat guy.

Next, she looked at Sergeant Jennings, who was of African-American descent. He was wrapping bandages around Goose's bleeding muscular arm. His quiet demeanor gave off an aura of intelligence, but his lack of emotion reminded Cindy of the classic doctor mannerisms—no sense of humor. Finally she observed the big lunk known as "Goose." He was a huge muscle-bound Latino that, despite being wounded, still carried a laid back attitude. If there was a stereotype for the typical jokester, Goose would probably fit the bill; he also seemed to be the squad's pack mule since he was the one carrying all the heavy gear.

Cindy turned her attention back towards Malcolm and looked at Captain Colt, the leader of the group. Out of the entire squad, Colt was the oldest. A heavy five o'clock shadow formed around his jaw with a scowl created from going through hell and back. His weary, piercing blue eyes told of a soldier that had lost many friends and wanted to go home. The only thing keeping him going through this torment was the love for his country and the men that gave their lives to protect it.

"Silver!" Malcolm yelled, "Why are you just standing there, girl?"

"I didn't want to break up the party," she said with levity.

"Silver, ma'am, is that a codename?" the captain asked with curiosity.

"Yes, sir."

"It's a pleasure to meet you," he said with a sincere smile. Colt looked back to his squad and said, "We should probably head back to base and get reinforcements."

"What? No, we need you guys." Malcolm said with an astonished look.

"Mr. Douglas, our tanks and bombs have done nothing against their weapons. We're out of our league here. I'm not sending my boys on any more suicide missions."

Malcolm immediately replied, "Captain, with all due respect—"

"I don't want to hear it! What are we supposed to do against giant robots? Our bullets are useless,"

"You don't need to fight the robots," Cindy interjected. "You just need to create a distraction in the 1st Continental building. I already paved the way for everyone."

"That's right!" Malcolm said while pointing towards the captain. "The plan is to rescue the hostages and blow the building to smithereens. Cut the head—right off the snake."

Captain Colt growled as he looked to his subordinates for an opinion.

"We've got plenty of explosives to blow the building to kingdom come," said Adams.

"Plenty of band-aids for everybody," Jennings said.

"I got bullets!" Goose yelled, only to be caught by uncomfortable stares from everyone. "Well, we need ammo," he said like a petulant child.

Yee looked towards the captain and asked, "Are we going to radio an evac, sir?"

The captain's face became grim. The duties of a man in his position weighed heavily upon his weary shoulders. Cindy noticed that his expression seemed almost angry and she understood where that anger was coming from. He wasn't just responsible for his own life, but the lives of men who have become his family. The captain looked around the ruined city block, debating his decision. Cindy could tell that the captain knew he didn't have a choice. Yes, he was responsible to make sure these men made it home to their families, but there wouldn't be a home to go to if they left now.

The captain placed his hands on his hips and said, "No, don't call evac." He turned towards his squad and said in a rallying cry, "We can't let these two hog all the kills, can we?"

The squad yelled in unison, "HOOAH!"

As the squad began marching to Raymond's headquarters, Goose asked Cindy, "So is that suit a new military prototype? Where can I get one of those?"

Cindy looked at him and replied, "Are you interested in wearing a metal thong? Because that's kind of what it feels like."

"It goes that deep?" Goose asked with naïve surprise.

Yee laughed and said, "You would like that, wouldn't you, Goose?"

"Hey! I don't roll like that!" he replied.

Adams asked Cindy, "Are you a robot or a human?"

"Don't worry. I'm not a terminator," she said.

"She's in better shape than you, Goose," Jenkins joked.

Goose shook his head and said, "Ahh, I can still take her."

Captain Colt chuckled and replied, "Goose, you ran behind a taxi while she blew up a tank with her bare hands. If I were a betting man, I'd put my money on the superhero here."

Cindy's helmet masked the huge smile that was crawling across her lips.

"Whatever," Goose said, defeated.

It was amazing how much faster the walk from Times Square to 53rd street was without any vehicles or annoying pedestrians blocking the way. Unfortunately, the path was littered with thousands of bodies. 1st Continental mercenaries and U.S. soldiers were sprawled all over the city street. Blood pools had become the new asphalt in this urban battle zone. There were going to be many sad trumpets after this day was done. Then, like a lair for all of hell's minions, the 1st Continental Skyscraper came into view.

Standing amongst the other injured buildings, 1st Continental stood in pristine form, unscathed by the ravages of war. So far, it had proven untouchable. The sun glimmered upon its glass windows as if the building sat atop a futuristic city paradise.

It covered the bombed-out skyline below with its looming shadow. Anxiety walked behind Cindy like a shadow, whispering in her ear what happened the last time she entered the building. She tried to block out the memory of the Ruby Ninja, but her image forced itself into Cindy's memories like a regret that never leaves.

Upon approaching the building, Captain Colt tapped the top his helmet with his palm. The squad ducked down acknowledging his silent command except, for the clueless Cindy who was standing out in the open, confused. Malcolm grabbed Cindy's hand and pulled her into cover behind the overturned cars.

The captain asked, "Any of you guys have a sharpshooter rifle?"

"I got this," Malcolm replied.

Malcolm pulled out a black carbine with a suppressor attached to the muzzle. He looked into his scope and took deep, controlled breaths. The first guard walked into his crosshairs, Malcolm placed the pad of his index finger on the trigger while keeping the guard in the center of his sight. With a very soft application of pressure, the gun clicked and sent the bullet careening out of the chamber towards its target. The snap of the gun firing echoed throughout the building corridor, alerting the guards, but the victim was already dead before he even knew what hit him.

"I thought your gun was silenced?" Cindy asked.

Malcolm replied, "It is. Don't distract me."

Goose whispered to Cindy, "The silencer just makes it harder to hear from longer range. But because city is empty, the sound bounces off the buildings and makes an echo."

"Huh... interesting. Thanks," she replied.

Three more consecutive shots cracked through the air like a person clapping their hands. Within seconds, the guards outside the building were neutralized, clearing the way for the team to infiltrate the 1st Continental building. The front doors to the main entrance and the garage were now accessible, but no one was fooling themselves into thinking that getting into the building was going to be that easy.

Malcolm turned to Cindy and asked, "Can you calibrate your suit to tune into our radio frequencies?"

"I have... no idea, lift it up so I can scan it."

Malcolm raised the radio up to her eyes as a little white box surrounded it. Cindy gave Malcolm a thumbs up and turned towards the squad who were already holding their radios up.

"Test, test, can you hear me through the radio?" Malcolm asked.

"Loud and clear," she said.

"Okay, here's the game plan." Malcolm turned to the squad and addressed the unit. "Captain Colt, you and your men will come with me to assault the garage. We'll search and rescue the hostages, then place C4 all over the structural weak points and bring this sucker down. Cindy, you'll be responsible for taking out Raymond Levreux and his cronies. We're gonna be goin' loud, so I'm pretty sure his army is going to come rushing to the garage. When his troops come downstairs, you sneak in and finish the job, got that?"

"Umm… 10-4!" she said with enthusiasm.

"Okay we're not cops, you can say 'wilco' if you want," Malcolm said with a grin.

"Never mind," she said annoyed.

Before parting ways, Malcolm told Cindy, "Listen, the explosives are going to be timed. Once the first explosive goes off, you're going to have seven minutes to get out of the building. Got it?"

"Roger that," she said.

"See, you're learning. Good luck out there."

"You too."

Cindy fired the grappling hook to the rooftop of the building, ascending slowly. With Cindy on her way up, the rest of the group moved into the lower parking garage ready to traverse the death gauntlet. They crouched low to the ground, spreading out between each vehicle parked inside. They would peer over trunks and peek through windows to see if any mercenaries were in close proximity.

The squad did an excellent job staying stealthy, but even though their lack of footsteps made them specters in the wind, they couldn't account for the invisible infrared sensors that were scattered around the garage perimeter. The alarm tripped and filled the cavernous facility with flashing red lights. The deafening klaxon alarm alerted the mercenaries, forcing the Green Berets into premature combat. Gunfire rattled the garage with booming echoes as the team took cover behind various cement pillars.

Captain Colt signaled the squad with various hand gestures to split up and flank the mercenaries. Malcolm and Adams went with the captain, while Yee, Jenkins, and Goose approached from the opposite end. The mercenaries poured through the doors as if the Green Berets had cracked open a loaded spider egg. Cars didn't make good cover—they weren't designed to stop bullets—but the soldiers could use the cars to mask their movements within the parking garage. The mercenaries were clustered together in the center of the garage, firing in every direction, riddling numerous cars with flesh-piercing bullets.

Malcolm signaled to the squad to throw grenades into the center area. The sound of two pins clinging on the floor panicked the mercenaries as gunmetal orbs flew through the air. The mercenaries made a grave mistake and prevented any escape from the front or the back. The grenades were cooked to perfection, detonating the moment they were near the enemy troops. Two explosions in rapid succession rocked the garage with apocalyptic force. Dust fell from the ceiling, as lights flickered and swayed feeling the side effects of an explosive blast.

The mercenaries' bodies were blown into the ceiling, flying over dozens of cars before landing on the cold, paved floor. The concussive blast obliterated a huge portion of them, but there were more reinforcements coming from the upper levels of the building. Hordes of troops stormed into the garage, surrounding the squad by taking the perimeter. They fired blindly into where they last saw the Green Berets, but the squad had already changed position. Colt saw a lone, panicked mercenary ripe for the picking. Colt drew his rifle and quietly inched up behind him, ready to pull the trigger. Without warning the mercenary turned around and prepared to unload his ammunition into the unsuspecting captain.

A revolting splat burst from the mercenary's throat, his gun fired wildly in all directions. A serrated knife protruded from his neck as if he were a medieval heretic impaled upon a spike. When the body fell down, Goose was revealed holding the knife and gave a thumbs up to Colt. Colt's relieved expression turned to a sour grimace, as he suddenly fired a shot past Goose. A sick pop rung in Goose's ears, as the grunt sneaking up behind him fell backwards. As the soldiers regrouped, Jenkins began laying suppressive fire against enemies who were approaching from the stairwell. During the mayhem of gunfire, Malcolm snuck up behind a soldier standing near an elevator and snapped his neck. Adams threw a remote-controlled satchel charge towards the stairwell and detonated it immediately. The entranceway to the stairs collapsed into itself as a rain of dust and debris filled the doorway.

With a momentary reprieve from the onslaught of well-trained mercenaries, the Green Berets rushed over to a control panel near a padlocked chain-link gate. Jenkins pressed one of the buttons on the panel, which brought up a massive service elevator behind the secluded entryway.

"What the hell is this?" Yee said.

"Let's find out. Cut the locks," Colt commanded.

Adams pulled out a giant wire-cutter and popped the locks off the gate. They gathered into the service elevator platform and descended into the belly of the beast.

Malcolm said to the squad, "Keep your eyes peeled. Who knows what we'll find down there."

The elevator whirred loudly as the buzzing of industrial construction surrounded the mechanical pit. When the fluorescent lights flashed into view, a massive underground complex revealed itself. The underground tunnel was filled with exotic machinery that looked as though it was capable of producing weapons of war. The squad stared in awe, realizing that the tunnel spanned for miles. They theorized that an exit existed on the other side of the empty void.

"I bet you this tunnel goes all the way to Roosevelt Island," Adams said.

"That would explain why they came from the Queensboro Bridge," Jenkins replied.

Sparks flew as the automated assembly line built a variety of equipment. Various sheets of metal were being fused together to create more ordinance for the enemy. Hover vehicles, jetpacks, armor plating... the entire 1st Continental arsenal was being manufactured in this secret complex. Malcolm observed that the steel sheets used for most of the manufacturing read: "Raymond Galvanizing." Dozens of trucks sat parked in the tunnel, each with the distinctive yellow New Jersey commercial license plates.

After exiting the elevator, the squad walked down the assembly aisle, amazed that no one knew what Raymond was plotting beneath the city. Well-placed vents hung from the ceiling of the tunnel, directing all the manufacturing gases and smoke out of the factory and into discreet locations around Manhattan. Walking deeper into the passageway, the squad spotted a glass cell holding dozens of prisoners.

"Mack, is that you?" a voice cried out from within the cell.

Malcolm turned to the cell with a relieved smile across his face. "Kendra!"

"Holy… this is where they took all the kidnapped politicians," the captain said.

"They're trying to brainwash people into joining the Forefather's party," Kendra said.

"Can't say I've heard of it," Malcolm replied.

A man stepped forward from the crowd. "No one has—it doesn't exist. Raymond's trying to create a new political party to 'reboot' the government."

Malcolm raised his eyebrows and asked, "And you are…?"

"Jonas Ames, I…" His words faltered as if reconsidering drawing attention to himself. "I designed the weapons Raymond's been using."

Goose charged forward and yelled, "We should blow his head off right now!"

"Get in line, Sergeant," the captain looked over to Jonas with a menacing glare. "I'm pulling rank for this one."

Malcolm raised his hands and yelled, "Whoa, now hold up! This man is Silver's husband. You boys need to calm down; no one is going to lay a finger on him."

"Malcolm, are you serious?" Yee shouted in protest.

"I can revive him so you can beat on him again and again. Just don't kill him," Jenkins said.

"No one's beating anyone. Adams, put some C3 on this door and get these people out of here," Malcolm commanded.

"Stand back," the captain said to the prisoners. He took one look at Jonas and said, "Except you."

Adams armed the C3 onto the door. He yelled to the prisoners, "Get back!" The squad turned away from the door as their plastic key unlocked the entry with a small explosion. The prison door swung open, swaying back and forth like a boxer wobbling on his knees. One by one, the elected and future officials walked out of the prison. Jonas however, was stopped in his tracks by Sgt. Adams. The angry soldier pushed Jonas back into the cell as the Green Berets followed closely behind.

"Where do you think you're going?" Adams asked.

The soldiers began to shove Jonas around the cell. His meek body bounced around like a pinball between the hardened veterans, with no training to defend himself. Despite his impending doom, Jonas seemed apathetic to the abuse that was about to befall him.

"Captain, tell your men to stand down!" Malcolm demanded.

Colt's voice was uncaring. "Why should I?"

Malcolm reminded the captain of the forces he was dealing with and whispered to him, "You saw what Silver did to that tank and Raymond's army. Picture that, one woman against an army... and she won." The captain looked at Malcolm with a stark expression of fear glowing from his eyes. "What do you think she's going to do to you and your men if even one hair is missing from her husband's head?"

The captain stared at Malcolm long and hard. He knew Malcolm was right, but the words to pull back his team didn't want to leave his lips. He growled as he turned his cold-blue eyes towards the squad and yelled, "Boys, leave him alone. We'll evacuate him with the others. But if he gets hit by a bullet from one of the weapons he designed, well... treason is treason."

Goose pushed Jonas' head and said, "You're lucky your wife's such a good lady. She must be a moron to consider staying with your sorry ass."

Jonas' apathetic facial expression suddenly brimmed with murderous rage. He looked at Goose with a crazed psychosis undulating in his eyes. He eyed up the giant Latino and stood next to Goose's feet. The sergeant towered over him by a foot's distance, and his muscles were probably as big as Jonas' head. Goose bumped his chest into Jonas nose and looked down at him with an intimidating glare. Jonas stared at Goose for a few moments before unleashing a physics-defying haymaker into the goliath's chin. He had decked him so hard that the titan was laid out flat on his back. Jonas was the one that needed to be stopped from killing someone.

"You want to talk about my wife? She's dead! You piece of sh—" Jonas thrashed about like a starving lion in a cage as Malcolm held back his arms.

Jonas yelled, "Let me go!"

Malcolm struggled to hold back the mourning widower. "Whoa, whoa, easy now. Easy, Jonas." When Jonas managed to settle down, enough to let Malcolm speak, the highly trained soldier whispered to him, "Your wife is still alive. Cindy saved the squad this morning."

Jonas froze in place as his body fell limp. The sting of fluid grazing the bottom of his eyes weakened him as he turned his head to the side. "What?" Jonas whispered.

Malcolm continued to whisper, "She's OK. She survived the fall. She's here lookin' for you."

Every breath Jonas took forced more tears to rise to the surface, but they refused to journey down his tired cheeks.

His withered voice asked Malcolm, "Where is she?"

"She's upstairs fighting for everyone."

"Can you help me get to her?"

Malcolm replied, "Those dudes over there are going to fill this place with so much C4 that they'll feel it in China."

Jonas pulled his arms out of Malcolm's grasp and said, "I'm going up to see her."

Malcolm looked befuddled and rhetorically asked Jonas, "Did you not hear what I just said?"

Jonas replied, "I heard you, but Raymond's not the only one up there."

Malcolm turned towards the captain and asked him, "Would you be willing to take your men up to rescue this man's wife?"

The captain pointed to Malcolm and said to him in a fit of anger, "You let him deck one of my boys and expect me to help him get to his wife? This man built the very weapons that killed my brothers, people I cared about. We owe a lot to Silver, but I can't promise we wouldn't kill Jonas ourselves. We're getting out of here with the hostages. You have fifteen minutes before Adams sets off the explosives."

"Let's go, Jonas. We're not gonna have much time." Malcolm turned to his sister and told her, "Kendra, you'll be safe with these guys. I'll see you after this is all done."

Kendra waved goodbye. "Be careful, Mack."

The captain turned his back, preventing his conscience from goading him into changing his mind. He supervised the placement of the explosives while Jonas and Malcolm ascended in the elevator.

During the lift's return to the main floor, Malcolm asked Jonas, "Why did you help Raymond do all of this?"

"I thought he was producing arms for U.S. military contracts."

"Is that the truth?"

Jonas looked away, staring at the cement wall scrolling in front of his eyes. "There were signs that he was going to cause problems, but... I didn't care."

Malcolm crossed his arms and looked at Jonas with disproval. "So why'd he put you down in the hole?"

"After he let my designs loose, I realized that Cindy would have been ashamed of me if I didn't do something to stop him. I tried to sabotage the equipment, but his guards caught me. He was still hoping to brainwash me despite what I had done," Jonas said.

"Well, she's up there now. I don't think anyone will be able to stop her," Malcolm said.

Jonas replied, "That's what I'm afraid of."

****

Outside of the 1st Continental building, Cindy's grappling line began to slow down as she approached the fiftieth floor. Throwing stealth out the window, Cindy braced her feet up against the glass and pushed off the surface. With the growing momentum, Cindy kicked through the window and rolled onto the familiar blue carpet. It was chilling to be back in this sterile, loathsome place. She felt trapped in a drywall prison of corporate machinations.

Walking down the unguarded hallway, Cindy noticed that the research lab was abandoned in its entirety. None of the scientists were present and most of the damage she had caused had been repaired. It was almost as if nothing had even happened on this floor. At the end of the corridor, two wooden doors stood before her like statues. Cindy pulled open the heavy wooden gateway and entered a massive room constructed almost entirely of marble. Six pillars lined the room in a row, standing across from each other like stoic sentinels. The creamy marble floor was so clean—that Cindy saw her own reflection within the surface. Hanging from the minty, dark-green walls were dozens of oil paintings featuring historical pictures of America's Founding Fathers: George Washington, Benjamin Franklin, Thomas Jefferson, John Adams, and finally… Samuel Adams.

Then Cindy saw —her— standing in front of the final doors leading to the executive offices. The woman clad in blood-red armor that had thrown her out of the fiftieth floor window all those months before was the final obstacle in Cindy's path. The woman's arms were crossed, defiantly daring Cindy to cross the threshold. Cindy gently pushed the doors closed behind her. She wanted no interruptions or distractions for the inevitable rematch. She could feel the grip of fear, begging her to turn around, but Raymond and his cronies were just beyond that door. They needed to be stopped, no matter how difficult the journey.

Ruby began walking towards Cindy with a cocky swagger to her hips. She shifted her weight over to one foot and placed a hand on her hip. She looked at Cindy with contempt, as if looking at an inferior version of herself.

The ninja leaned her head to the side and said, "You again?"

Cindy replied, "Let me pass or I'll do to you what you did to me."

"There are no windows here," the woman said.

"I'll make one."

The woman chuckled. "How'd that work out for you last time?"

Cindy leaned forward and yelled at the woman, "Who the hell are you anyway?"

"I'm the upgrade to your old suit, Ruby," she said.

"Umm, rubies aren't metals." Cindy said, stating the obvious.

Ruby let out an obnoxious sigh. "No duh! I told you it was an upgrade."

"Just get out of the way," Cindy pleaded. "I don't want to fight."

Ruby shook her head. "I can't do that. If you want to get in there, you need to go through me."

Cindy sighed and cracked her knuckles to hide her fear. Ruby had taught Cindy a lesson in humility, proving to the wannabe heroine that she wasn't invincible. A super suit was not a panacea for death and Cindy would do well to remember that. Cindy raised her hands to her helmet and settled into a combat stance. She stared directly into Ruby's fearless, glowing eyes.

A grinning monster crawled out of the abyss of their combined fear as a reaper of unease descended upon the chamber. Cindy's intuition told her not to fight Ruby, but there was too much at stake for her to turn back now. She wanted to listen to her gut and not be sucked into another battle, but there was no choice. Then... like a massive tsunami tidal wave, Ruby came bolting towards Cindy at full speed.

It was time to change history. Cindy charged forward to reluctantly embrace the possibility of death. The rush of adrenaline filled Cindy's veins, as the dangerous ninja closed in on her like two trains on a collision course. Cindy's senses heightened as her body braced for impact. She surrendered her body to muscle memory and forced her training to guide her actions. Cindy balled her hand into a fist and fired a mighty strike that traveled from her elbow to her fist.

All the kinetic energy Cindy released quickly dissipated into an unsatisfying whiff. Cindy stumbled over as her hand punched air. Ruby had jumped over her head like an Olympic pole vaulter. As Ruby flew down from the ceiling, she stretched her leg to kick Cindy squarely between the shoulder blades. But Cindy was ready this time… she rolled forward just in time to avoid Ruby's jump kick. Her opponent stuck a perfect landing, as Cindy recovered from her roll and turned towards her foe.

Ruby was already bounding for Cindy like a shark swimming to its meal. She threw a jaw-breaking punch towards Cindy's helmet. Cindy deflected her attack by sliding her palm on Ruby's forearm. Sparks slid across Ruby's arm as her strike missed and flew off in the wrong direction. Ruby growled at Cindy's newfound ability to deflect her attacks. Blinded by anger, Ruby retaliated by raising her leg like a chopping axe and attempted to cave Cindy's head in. Cindy rolled out of the way, her body twisting as Ruby's heel flew past her head, and slammed into the marble floor—cracking it like an egg.

Cindy looked down at the shattered tile, her heart pounding at the thought of being caught beneath that foot. She turned to Ruby and whirled around with a roundhouse kick. Ruby avoided the kick by bending so far backwards, she almost touched the floor. Ruby stood back up and back-flipped herself away from danger. She stood across the room and stared at Cindy with unspoken respect.

"You're not the same Silver; you sucked the last time we fought. You're someone else, aren't you?" Ruby said.

"Oh, no, I'm the same woman. I'm just not sleepy this time," Cindy said.

"Eff me," Ruby said, while placing her hands on her hips. "You're not going to make this easy, are you?"

Cindy beckoned Ruby with her fingers. "Let's go."

Although Cindy put on a good show of confidence deep down, she was petrified of slipping up against her nemesis. Cindy looked at Ruby and saw no signs of exhaustion. She wondered how long this fight would last and questioned if she would have the endurance to see this to the end. Ruby rose to Cindy's challenge and stampeded forward. Cindy had to think fast, she looked over to the marble walls and calculated a most unusual strategy.

She leapt past Ruby and landed on an adjacent marble pillar. Ruby looked up at Cindy, confused as to what the hell she was doing. Cindy jumped off the marble pillar and flew over Ruby's head to a nearby wall. Ruby raised her fists, ready to defend herself, as Cindy launched from the wall to Ruby's feet. Ruby took a few cautious steps back, hoping to avoid a potential dive-bomb. To her great surprise, Cindy landed on her hands and curled her body into a compact headstand like a coiled spring waiting to snap. With her feet pointed in Ruby's direction, Cindy cocked her legs like a revolver and boom! Cindy's feet collided onto Ruby's helmet like a ballista through a tower wall. Ruby's head jolted back onto her shoulders, almost as if her neck had been snapped. Ruby stumbled backward as her red glimmering body fell into the cold, unforgiving floor.

Cindy rolled forward and jumped to her feet, fixating her eyes on Ruby in case she was unfazed. To her surprise, Ruby was still on the floor clutching her head, writhing back and forth in the aftermath of the blow. The suit may have been nigh indestructible at full power, but it didn't prevent the user from feeling the effects of physics. The time was now for Cindy to finish off her vulnerable enemy. She dashed towards Ruby at full speed. The red ninja leapt to her feet suddenly, and kicked Cindy in the stomach, knocking the wind out of her. With the heroine reeling from the blow, Ruby delivered a flurry of strikes into Cindy's defenseless body. On the final punch, Ruby pulled her fist back and blasted Cindy with her strength. Cindy flew back, but managed to land on her feet. She clutched her chest and looked up to see that Ruby had ducked behind the marble pillars, trying to regain her breath. Cindy noticed a drastic difference in Ruby's body language. She was acting cautiously, and the break she took to regain her breath gave Cindy hope that the Ruby Ninja could be beaten.

Cindy shook off the beating she took and ran up to Ruby while throwing a right jab. Cindy gasped as her arm was caught by the crimson warrior. Ruby flipped Cindy onto the stone floor, causing an enormous dust cloud to rise from crater. Cindy hopped back up to her feet, but was immediately knocked back down by Ruby's merciless heel. Cindy felt as though a nail had been jabbed into her spine as sharp pains traveled throughout her entire body. Clouds of debris filled the room with smoke as particles of dust began to stick and dull Ruby and Silver's armor. As the pain began to subside to a much more tolerable level, Cindy grew concerned that her armor was beginning to weaken, or worse, that Ruby was much stronger than she had anticipated.

The razor-sharp pain still cut through Cindy's spine, she gritted her teeth and slowly rose to her feet. But Ruby was waiting for her, she grabbed Cindy by the shoulder and inner thigh. With a strong heave, Ruby chucked Cindy into a pillar. Huge chunks of marble rained down onto the floor as Cindy's HUD alerted her to the weakening status of her armor. Cindy looked at her hands and body, taking notice of the dents and scratches appearing on the surface of her quicksilver skin. The familiar pulsating aches of forming bruises began to spread across her body, despite being unable to see them.

While Cindy lay on the floor in a crawl position, Ruby leapt into the air with her knees almost touching her underarms, ready to split Cindy's spine in two. Cindy rolled onto her back, tucked her knees beneath her chest, and fired her legs into the Ruby Ninja, she flew back as if a cannonball were blasted into her stomach. "Ughn!" the woman cried as she flew through the air, appearing like a blur of red paint. Ruby crashed into the wall, knocking down the paintings of revolutionary heroes. Plumes of dust buried the Ruby Ninja in a cloudy veil. When the opaque fog cleared, Ruby was on the floor, gasping for breath.

When Cindy saw that the she had finally injured the ruby demon, her resolve to win shot to the surface. Her body filled with a rejuvenating burst of hope, but she couldn't ignore the stinging aches emanating from her swelling skin. Cindy slowly rose to her feet and placed her hand on her hip. Her abdominals flexed and unflexed as she tried to breathe. She tried to take a step forward, but winced at the feeling of sharp knives jabbing her stomach. Ruby watched Cindy, as she tried to consume as much oxygen as possible. Both women stared at each other, refusing to admit admiration for the other. Their once-brilliant suits of armor were now fully coated in a thin layer of dust like battle scars on a veteran.

Ruby wasn't ready to surrender and it didn't seem she would ever entertain the thought. She punched her fist into the floor and rose to her feet—battle ready. In her weakened state, Ruby flew towards Cindy like a red tornado of lethal roundhouse kicks. Cindy rolled under Ruby's kicks and then launched herself into the air with an elegant butterfly kick. Ruby saw the attack and somersaulted beneath the butterfly kick; neither ninja made contact with the other. When Cindy dropped back down to the ground, Ruby attempted to sweep Cindy's feet, hoping to knock her down. Cindy reacted immediately and hopped into the air just barely avoiding Ruby's kick. The two ninjas continued to fight like reverse images of the other for several minutes. They would leap, roll, and strike, never managing to make contact with the other. It was almost as if their thoughts were perfectly synchronized.

Cindy finally broke the looping cycle by exploiting a weakness in Ruby's offense. As if the world had slowed to a crawl, Cindy ducked her head as Ruby's leg swept over Cindy's helmet like a helicopter rotor blade. Cindy rolled forward towards Ruby and then launched herself into the air. Ruby looked up at the flying silver heroine and took a sudden barrage of kicks that were drilled into her chest. The relentless assault blasted Ruby through one of the marble pillars, exploding the motionless beam like a demolished building. It seemed as though Ruby was done for, but to Cindy's surprise, the red ninja kicked a large chunk of falling debris towards Cindy like a battering ram to a doorway.

The gaseous cloud pulled away from the chunk of marble like tentacles detaching from their fishy dinner. The marble mass crashed into Cindy like a spear stabbing her stomach, pushing her straight into the wall behind her. The remaining paintings of America's Fore Fathers fell off the broken walls. Cindy wheezed for air. It was so hard to breathe that both women considered taking off their helmets, but the air in the room was too polluted to breathe easy. Cindy knew she had to put an end to this exhausting battle, but her body was failing and Raymond still needed to be dealt with.

Cindy whipped her arm to the side and summoned the energy blade from her suit. She twirled the blade around as she entered into a combat stance. Ruby also called upon her own energy blade and prepared to meet Cindy in battle. The two women walked towards the center of the mutilated chamber. What was once a display of wealth and American history was now a ruined memorial. The walls were covered in veins of cracked stone and the surrounding pillars were shattered to oblivion. The floor was now a crater of conflict. Its only purpose now was to house the destruction caused by these two warriors. The blades hummed and crackled with controlled raw energy, eager to slice the other.

Cindy held onto her blade with an elegant one-handed stance, whereas Ruby used a classic samurai two-handed stance. Although Cindy was comfortable with the one-handed technique, she switched over to two-handed to increase the power of her strikes. Curiously, Ruby changed her stance to one-handed. It seemed as though Ruby was determined to beat Cindy in her own unique way, consciously refusing to use the same style as Cindy. Cindy readied herself in a defensive stance, as Ruby prepared to throw everything she had into this final assault.

Ruby rushed towards Cindy like a berserk barbarian with blade held high above her head. She dropped her arm forward in a chopping motion, attempting to cleave Cindy's helmet in two. Cindy raised her blade and blocked the strike, causing a loud, electrical crash, to sound from the two blades hitting each other. Her arms jolted back as they absorbed the shock from Ruby's mighty blow. Cindy pushed Ruby away from her and responded with her own series of strikes. Ruby was as skilled with a weapon as she was with her hands and gracefully deflected Cindy's attacks. Flashes of white light blinded the room as the blades clashed into one another, both ninja's held their ground in the center of the arena. Cindy's arms burned with exhaustion at every deflection of Ruby's attacks and fatigue began taking its toll on her. With this brief moment of weakness exposed, Ruby busted through Cindy's defenses and managed to knock her off balance. Ruby raised her leg and clobbered Cindy with a dizzying axe kick.

Cindy flattened backwards onto the marble floor as Ruby held her energy blade over Cindy's eyes. Cindy's fear instinctively rolled her out of harm's way just as Ruby sank her blade deep into the mangled surface. Cindy jumped to her feet and shook her head to brush off the dizziness, but the room continued to spin. Cindy regained her composure and switched back to a one-handed technique, tearing into Ruby with vicious, yet elegant moves. It was as if Cindy were dancing with a blade in hand, her feet glided across the surface with the poise of a practiced martial artist. Ruby didn't know what to do. Cindy's swings were so strong that the blade was extending further and further with each collision between the swords.

Ruby's hands and arms began to shake, as Cindy's battering brought her closer to utter exhaustion. Ruby's grip was loosening on the hilt, which motivated Cindy to hit harder and harder. She channeled all her rage to break Ruby's grip on the weapon. Out of desperation, Ruby rammed Cindy with her shoulder and nearly got herself sliced by Cindy's blade. Ruby attacked with a vengeful wrath, but like a tortoise hiding in a shell, Cindy defended against her assault, waiting for the Ruby Ninja to tire herself out.

At long last, the moment had finally arrived. Ruby's attacks were beginning to falter. Her swings were lacking energy and precision. Cindy had Ruby right where she wanted her. She could see Ruby's knees buckling under her own weight. Ruby's final swing made her look as though she were going to pass out. It was empty of all emotion, skill, and power. As Ruby stumbled forward, Cindy kicked the hilt out of the exhausted ninja's hands. Even unarmed, Ruby still tried to fight Cindy, but her punches were like smacks from a pillow. Cindy let Ruby throw one last feeble punch, before stepping beside her. She leapt into the air in a full three hundred and sixty degree motion. The momentum and force generated from the speed of her spin allowed Cindy to unleash a devastating finishing blow.

She extended her arm outward and slashed Ruby across the back with a very prominent diagonal slice. The once unbreakable suit split open, revealing Ruby's pale milky skin. Blood gushed out from her wound and poured down her back like a sponge being squeezed of water. Ruby let out a blood-curdling scream as the anguish from the burning wound crippled the Ruby Ninja. Cindy stared at her scorched, bleeding flesh, and remained cautious in case Ruby still had a fight in her.

The visage of a powerful, unbeatable demon crumbled before Cindy's eyes. Ruby's body seized on the floor as spasms crumpled her form with unimaginable pain. Knowing that she had destroyed her nemesis, Cindy sheathed her blade and walked towards her writhing foe. Vengeance was in Cindy's eyes, as she watched the pathetic Ruby tried to crawl towards the hilt of her sword. Cindy walked in front of her defeated rival and stepped on her hand, the masked woman screamed as the sound of crushing gravel popped beneath her palm. Cindy knelt down over Ruby and rolled her onto her back. Ruby grunted from the stinging pain and was then lifted up by the throat. Cindy held her aloft, giving Ruby just enough oxygen to keep her alive and breathing.

Cindy for a brief second had a flashback to when she dispatched the muggers. She felt the venomous power of controlling someone's life poisoning her conscience. She enjoyed every second of tormenting her killer and allowed herself to indulge in the cruel, unusual punishment. Cindy pressed Ruby up against the wall as bits of stone fell into Ruby's bleeding wound. Ruby uttered a tortured, "Aahh…"

Cindy leaned in and said to her vanquished foe, "I am going to enjoy this."

Ruby responded with a defiant, "I'm not afrai—auugh!" Cindy slammed Ruby's bleeding back into the wall again, exacerbating her pain, leaving terrible blood streaks across its surface.

Cindy was either going to break that defiance out of her or kill her trying. She threw Ruby down onto the floor, making sure her back took the brunt of the trauma. Ruby's agonized screams were chilling to the bone, but Cindy's apathy had already turned her into a merciless monster, unmoved by Ruby's cries for salvation. The damage from Cindy's cut began to spread throughout the crimson suit. Portions of the woman's red armor began to melt off, revealing more pale skin covered in welts and bruises.

Cindy gripped Ruby's neck once more and drew out her wrist blade. The dagger-like beam of energy roared like a fresh-lit blowtorch.

Cindy leaned in, almost touching Ruby's helmet and asked, "Do you have any last words?"

"My sister will come after you," Ruby said, as she surrendered to her inevitable death.

Cindy replied, "Good. I can clean out the rest of your gene pool when she shows."

Cindy drew the blade closer to Ruby's helmet. She could feel Ruby's throat compress as her defeated foe coughed out her last bits of air. There was neither remorse from Cindy, nor any chance of leniency for her fallen enemy. Cindy was driven by pure hatred, anger and trauma. The diseased well of emotions that swirled inside of her, corroded her conscience like a pool of acid. Cindy held the tip of the blade over Ruby's forehead. Smoke began to emanate from Ruby's skull like an ant under a magnifying glass. Cindy prepared to plunge the knife straight through her enemy's helmet and into the floor behind her. But she was going to savor every last second before doing so. Cindy could feel Ruby's fear squirming beneath her fingers, her defeated opponent whimpered at the thought of her impending doom; as the heat from the weapon began to singe her skin beneath the mask. Cindy began to push the blade in—

"Cindy, stop!" a voice cried out, freezing Cindy in place.

Cindy held the blade over Ruby's head and looked over her shoulder.

"Jonas?" she said through an aching heart. "No, please don't stop me now. I have to end this." She turned her attention back to Ruby who was trapped between

Cindy's vice grip, her wrist dagger ready to finish the job.

"You don't want to do this," Malcolm yelled, as he stood next to Jonas.

"Cindy?" Ruby uttered with a raspy voice.

"Don't talk to me! I don't want to hear one more wo—"

The blood-red metal from Ruby's helmet began to melt away into human white skin. The ninja revealed her familiar plump lips, the voluminous blonde hair, and those unmistakable blue ey—

"What…" Cindy whispered as her expression contorted with guilt, gazing upon her foe's face. She held back the tears as her voice began to crack and her stomach churned.

"…Jadie?" A small teardrop crawled to the edge of her eye.

Cindy removed her helmet, allowing her long brown hair to fall in front of her glassy eyes. Her cheekbones moistened as drops of regret showered her sister's weary forehead. The pungent taste of salt lingered on her lips. Her voice was trapped behind a sore throat that was clenching shut.

"Cindy, I'm so sorry, I didn't know it was you."

Cindy's body trembled with the guilt infesting her body, "You… you almost killed me, Jadie. Wh—I—" her emotions were jumping from one end to the other changing from sorrow to fury in a confusing loop.

A putrid concoction of emotions rushed into Cindy's mind as the thought of Jadie being her killer tore her innards like flesh-eating maggots. She loved her sister so much, but her festering anger burned with the intensity of a volcano. Cindy slammed her fist into the floor and bellowed a sorrowful wail, like a mother mourning the loss of her children.

She shook Jadie's head and yelled, "Why, why did you do this to me!" The cold tears ran down her skin like a river filled with corpses. The drops of water spilling from Cindy's eyes landed upon Jadie's chest, leaving clean streaks where the filth used to preside. Cindy broke down and cried, she cried and cried, purging out every feeling and emotion that had haunted her on this terrible journey. The guilt, the sadness, the anger, the love, the joy, all spilled in one salty capsule following another. As her tortured feelings poured from her body, a warm hand gripped Cindy's shoulder and pulled her away from Jadie. Her head instinctively turned towards the loving shoulder that was always there for her when she needed it most.

Her favorite cologne wafted into her nose as Jonas held Cindy like a family member reunited after twenty years. He turned his head away as a parade of tears marched down his own eyes. He was so filled with joy that his body was shaking just from holding his still-breathing wife.

He whispered into her ear, "I kept telling myself that time heals all things, that I would eventually learn to cope with the fact that you were gone. It wasn't true. I wasn't strong enough to live without you."

Cindy looked up at him with jewels in her beautiful hazel eyes and wrapped her arms around his neck. She said to her weeping husband, "I've missed you so much."

They wept into each other's shoulders, holding the other like a reunited lost soul, wanting to speak but not having the words to say anything. Their tears mixed with each other, forming into a unified essence that had lost itself in a valley of darkness. He rubbed his fingers through her hair and kissed Cindy on her lips, almost as if he were afraid to lose her again. She wanted to stay in his loving embrace so much, but Cindy knew she had to finish what she started. She gave Jonas a gentle push and pulled herself away from her longing husband.

Cindy looked at Jadie who said to her, "Oh, are we paying attention to me now? I'm only dying and bleeding before your very eyes."

Cindy held back a chuckle, afraid to laugh at her sister's situation. She pointed to herself with both hands. "I'm sorry, I am a horrible mess right now."

"You're sorry? How do you think I feel? I'm the one that—"

"Don't even say it, it's not your fault."

Jadie said, "You know, I probably would have let you through the door if I had known it was you." Jadie smiled, hoping to lighten the mood by antagonizing her angst-ridden sister.

"What do you mean 'probably'? Why are you even here?" Cindy asked.

"I asked her to test the suit," Jonas said.

Cindy looked confused and asked him, "Why her?"

Jonas replied, "After Michael confessed to me that he was using you as a test subject, he convinced me that Jadie would be the perfect match for the next suit revision."

"Wait," Cindy shook her head as pieces of the puzzle fell into place, "was Michael working for you the whole time?"

"Yes, since the day we all got fired."

Malcolm stepped in and said, "Sounds to me like someone's trying to hide something."

Cindy turned to her injured sister and asked, "Jadie, why were you guarding the door?"

"They told me they were going to torture Jonas and the hostages if I let anyone through. I wanted to stop them, but my suit shut down even if I thought about tripping them in the hallway."

Jonas added on to that by saying, "They made us install a fail-safe into her armor. That way she couldn't use the suit to attack 1st Continental employees. I thought it was a standard safety precaution. I had no idea it was to keep Jadie in check." Jonas paused for a moment as he looked at Cindy's silver body. "I guess he didn't install the fail-safe in your suit."

"Yeah, there's a lot of janitors and data entry specialists in Raymond's army right now," Jadie said.

"What?" Cindy said with a confused expression.

334

Jadie replied, "They had to be employees, remember? Mercenary isn't a job title."

Cindy grabbed onto her sister's hand and helped her up to her feet. With Jadie somewhat able to stand on her own power, Cindy turned to the group and said, "I have to put an end to this."

Jonas grabbed onto Cindy's hand and begged her not to go.

"Please, Cindy, I can't."

Malcolm slung Jadie's arm across his shoulders and escorted her to the hallway, ignoring the dispute behind him.

"Jonas, this was my fault, I allowed this to happen."

"Forget all of this. We'll leave to—"

The building began to tremor with the magnitude of an earthquake. Suddenly the floor gave way, dragging Malcolm and Jadie down through the crumbling vortex. Cindy grabbed onto Jonas' hand and pulled him out of the hole before it could take him away. She looked down into the lower floor and saw Malcolm and Jadie lying atop the broken desks below.

"Jesus! Thanks sweetie," Jonas said to Cindy.

"Are you two all right?" Cindy yelled down.

Malcolm replied, "We're fine, but I think you've got 7 minutes starting now." He helped Jadie to her feet as she winced in pain. Malcolm looked up towards the couple and said, "Make it count, Cindy."

Cindy looked to her husband and said, "You shouldn't be here. Leave the building with them."

Jonas ignored her plea and said, "If I die, I die with you. I turned my back on you twice and I almost lost you. I won't do it again."

Cindy was touched by his heartfelt words. She smiled and grazed her loving fingers across his cheek. She turned to the massive doors before her and pushed into the executive office, ready to confront the man behind the madness.

CHAPTER 9

FATHER OF THE REBELLION

The oak doors opened as if revealing the gateway to heaven. The brilliant light faded away to reveal the executive conference room. A slender, tall table encircled a hologram projector showing troop reports, maps and force projections. Coincidentally, the holographic display showed a ninety percent casualty rate in Times Square. The glass windows at the end of the room were completely washed out. The sun continued to pierce through the grey stormy clouds retreating to the Atlantic Ocean. A man with a sharp haircut, expensive suit and five o'clock shadow—Raymond—was holding a gun to Michael's neck.

"You told me you installed the fail safe into Silver's suit."

Michael panted with tears rolling from his eyes. "I'm not helping you anymore!"

"Raymond, let him go!" Cindy demanded.

"Cindy," Raymond said with a sly smile. "It's a pleasure to finally meet you."

"I wish I could say the same," she replied.

Off to the side of the conference room, a group of executives were heading up to the rooftop access. They fearfully looked at Cindy, but continued on with their escape plan. Black smoke began to rise behind the glass panes of the office, blotting out the light of the sun. The building was mere seconds away from imploding into itself.

"Let Michael go," Jonas demanded.

"You don't sound convinced, Jonas. Are you sure you want me to release him?" Raymond looked Cindy in the eyes and asked, "Did you know that Michael has been working for me since the first day you got that suit? Tell her, Michael."

Raymond pulled Michael's hair back, revealing the glistening sweat glazing the programmer's neck. Michael said, "I'm sorry Cindy, Jonas, I'm really sorry."

Cindy nodded her head in disappointment, but didn't feel justified in yelling at him. After all, Michael hasn't been the only one keeping secrets.

Raymond smiled and told Cindy, "Michael was the one that set up the initial connection for us to chat."

Cindy replied, "I already figured out that you were Samuel Adams."

"I knew you were a smart woman, I respect that immensely. Jonas, you take good care of her. Don't let that one go."

Michael pleaded, "Don't listen to him. He tricked Cindy into coming here so that Jadie could kill her. He couldn't control—"

Raymond jammed his weapon into Michael's neck, "That's enough out of you." He looked back at Cindy with sadness in his eyes. "Yes, I did try to have you killed. You were the only one left who could stop my plans. I had to remove you from the equation."

"Is it worth all of this, Raymond? Don't you feel guilt?" Cindy replied in anger.

"What was I supposed to do? You went rogue and ruined everything I was trying to accomplish. Had you just completed the assassinations, I could have taken the governor out of the picture."

Jonas looked at Cindy revolted by what he had just heard. "You're the one that..."

Raymond pulled Michael out of the chair and began walking with him towards the rooftop exit.

"Oh, that's right!" Raymond said with a smile. "He doesn't know, does he, Cindy? He doesn't know about all the killing you've been doing for me."

Jonas' reaction was so heartbroken, it seemed as though the perfect visage of his idol was ruined. He said to his guilty wife, "I can't believe you did that, Cindy. It's like I don't even know you anymore."

Cindy extended her fingers as if pushing down on an invisible table. "I wasn't well, Jonas. The suit made me do things and I'm not proud of it. I feel horrible for everything that happened and I'm going to have to live with that."

"But you did, and more than once. Yet somehow, Alvaro survived that encounter at the hospital." Raymond shook his head, reflecting on past disappointments. "That's when everything started falling apart."

Cindy suddenly felt a weight lift from her shoulders. "He survived?"

"Survived? He's damn near immortal," Raymond said frustrated. "I tried to have him killed by a sharpshooter at the fundraiser event, but he survived. After you refused to finish him, I sent in the hit squad. A lucky bullet hit him despite your meddling and he managed to survive that too. I should probably stop trying to kill him."

"Ya think?" Cindy replied.

Jonas asked Raymond, "Why did you use Cindy if you already had a hit squad?"

"You heard about the mess at the hospital. I needed a scalpel, not a sledgehammer. I didn't want innocent people to get hurt, and those boys only knew how to make a mess."

Cindy replied, "I should have never agreed to help you. People didn't need to die for your revolution."

Raymond replied with an arrogant tone, "Do you think the Egyptians and Libyan's would have succeeded in their revolution if they didn't spill any blood? Did you forget how America won its independence? If you want to change your government, you need to fight for it. I wish you could understand that."

The building began to rumble again. Various plants and lamps tipped over. Raymond opened the emergency exit door and pulled Michael up the stairs with him. Cindy and Jonas followed right on his heels as the frightened CEO continued to point the gun at his hostage. Upon reaching the roof, the muffled sound of an idle helicopter shook the walls with each rotation of the rotor. When Raymond opened the door, the deafening sound of the chopper engines filled the stairwell.

Raymond stood by the stairs leading up to the helipad and said to Cindy,

"Take Michael. He's no longer of any use to me."

Raymond pushed him towards Cindy and Jonas. But before letting Michael go, he aimed his gun at Jonas and fired a round at the defenseless designer. Cindy stepped in front of Jonas, deflecting the bullet with her chiseled back.

Cindy grabbed onto Jonas and asked him, "Are you all right?"

Jonas looked at Cindy shaken, but unharmed. When Cindy turned around, Raymond was already inside the cockpit of the black helicopter and Michael was lying on the floor, terrified to the bone. The plating on the choppers hull was full of rivets that kept its armor in place. The orange tinted cockpit glass glinted in the distant sun. Wide black wings for mounting missiles and rockets stared menacingly at the small heroine. With Raymond secure inside the armored transport, the torque of the engine increased, picking up the seemingly immovable fuselage into the air.

It seemed as though this was going to be the end. Raymond would get away, but at least the headquarters of 1st Continental would be destroyed soon. Cindy watched the helicopter lift off expecting it to fly away, instead, the helicopter hovered around the rooftop like a buzzard circling a carcass.

The loud speaker on the chopper bellowed, "Cindy, I know you won't let this go if I allow you to live. I'm sorry, but you must go down with the building."

Cindy pushed her husband aside and yelled, "Jonas, grab Michael and get to cover! I'll keep him distracted."

Cindy reactivated her helmet and raced towards the chopper. Jonas grabbed

Michael and pulled him towards the cement rooftop entrance. The helicopter opened its weapon-bay doors, causing Cindy's targeting system to lock onto more than 8 different weapons. EMP-charged mini guns and missiles hung below the fuselage, ready to make mincemeat of Cindy's plated body.

The first volley of machine gun fire came like a torrential downpour, as electrically charged bullets followed Cindy around the helipad. Cindy ducked behind the air conditioning units as the energized slugs pierced through the ventilation ducts. The helicopter pitched forward as the rotors wailed with an omnipresent fury. The air filled with the smell of burning wire and gunpowder as the chopper pummeled the rooftop with its munitions. The stream of bullets came towards Cindy like a buzz saw cutting into a tree. She cart wheeled out of the way and narrowly avoided getting blown in the torso by the bullet onslaught. When she landed back on her feet, the helicopter roared over her and circled around like a dragon going for another fire-breathing pass.

Suddenly, a massive explosion followed by a series of smaller ones detonated from the bottom of the building.

The vibrations knocked Cindy off balance as Jonas yelled to his wife, "Cindy, the building's coming down!"

Cindy screamed out over her comm link, "Malcolm, Malcolm, you need to get out right now!"

The building cried like a dying whale as the metal struts gave way. There was no answer from Malcolm and the skyscraper was shaking out of control. Her suit notified her that communications were jammed. It was then she realized, she was standing next to a jamming antennae running under an isolated power supply. The building began to plummet downward at an incredible speed, with smoke rising from the edges of the doomed tower. Jonas and Michael were flung out of the safety of the stairwell and slid off to the side of the building. The helicopter followed them down as Jonas barely managed to grab onto the side of the ledge with Michael clinging onto his other arm.

"Cindeeeeeeeeey!" Jonas screamed.

Cindy's eyes went wide with horror as she saw Jonas' fingers slipping off the ledge—one digit at a time. She ran towards Jonas and Michael while the helicopter blocked her way by continuously firing at her lithe frame. The bullets pinged and bounced off the floor like fire crackers during the fourth of July. Despite Cindy's incredible speed and dexterity, one of the stray bullets managed to graze her shoulder. A spurt of blood popped out of her retreating armor, causing her to clutch her shoulder. The charge of the bullets managed to shut down a portion of Cindy's suit, but thankfully it was only localized to a small section and did not spread elsewhere. The building lurched to its side, turning the rooftop into a giant slope. Cindy dove along the angle of the building and slid down the leaning roof like a baseball player sliding hands first to home plate. Sparks burst from under her armor like a tire rim dragging on the street.

She screamed, "No!" just as she witnessed Jonas' hand release from the edge of the building.

The two men screamed as they fell into the dust cloud, but Cindy was close behind. She tucked her body into a controlled dive and grabbed the pair mid-flight.

"Gotcha! Hang on and hold your breath!" she shouted, as the two men clung to her body for dear life. Cindy's grappling hook fired from her arm and pulled the trio into the billowing marshmallow cloud of crumbling infrastructure. The suffocating nebula enveloped their bodies in a thick layer of poisonous dust. They swung through the grey and yellow fog as particles of debris flew past them and ticked on Cindy's armor like sand on a tin roof. It was impossible to see anything. It was as if the city had been consumed by a massive sandstorm.

"You need to hold onto me as tight as you can," she said through her ventilated helmet. "Whatever you do, don't let go!"

Cindy continued to swing into the blinding void in front of her, the sound of the helicopter muted as they flew through the air at dizzying speeds. The line snapped tight pulling them deeper into cloudy wreckage. Various buildings continued to appear from the fog as Cindy deftly avoided crashing into each one using the suit's guidance system. Jonas and Michael wanted to scream, but kept silent for fear of inhaling toxic building materials.

Swinging through the ethereal cloud, the chopper screeched behind her like an owl chasing its dinner. It fired charged bolts of energy at Cindy. With Jonas and

344

Michael in tow, she was unable to fight back. Cindy weaved between the buildings and under sky bridges, hoping to lose the black menace behind her. But the pilot possessed incredible skill and flew over obstacles to keep close to Cindy. She needed to drop off her precious cargo in order to battle the chopper, but that was going to be virtually impossible. Cindy could feel their bodies begin to convulse in her arms, they were struggling to hold their breath for much longer. "Just hold on guys!"

Then, as if a holy light came down from heaven above, the poison clouds stepped aside and revealed the sunny skyline once again. Jonas and Michael gasped for breath, relieved that they could breathe again. Unfortunately, that relief was short-lived when Jonas looked back behind Cindy.

"He's getting closer!"

Although she tried her best to dodge the tunnel of bullets, her luck had finally run out. A streak of slugs popped into Cindy's lower back causing her to almost drop her cargo, her body shook from the sudden onslaught of excruciating pain. "Unngh!" she cried, while trying to block out the nerves telling her she was gravely wounded. Not only did she feel like she was going into shock, but she also felt a strange tremor from Michael's body. When she glanced at Michael, she noticed that he was in great agony. His eyes and mouth were wide open, as if someone had stabbed him in the stomach and caught him by surprise.

"Are you guys all right?" Jonas yelled.

"I can't feel my legs!" Michael screamed.

Cindy remained silent as the blood dripped down her back like running water, taking her strength down with it. She wasn't going to be able to keep this pace with a helicopter hot on her heels. Her breathing was becoming labored while the helicopter drew closer and closer. Time was running out. The helicopter was now so close, that its machine guns were not going to miss their shots. The barrels began to spool up, ready to fire at any second. Suddenly, a crimson angel fell from the sky. Jadie landed on the windshield of the cockpit, blocking its line of sight. The helicopter pitched like a wild bronco, giving Cindy a narrow window of opportunity to set Jonas and Michael down in a tight alleyway.

Cindy set her passengers down and stumbled over to a nearby wall. Jonas knelt down next to his injured friend, watching the tears stream from Michael's eyes.

"You're gonna be all right, buddy."

Beneath his river of tears Michael said, "I can't feel my legs. Am I paralyzed?"

"You're just in shock. You'll be fine."

Cindy clutched onto her lower back and groaned in agony. Her vision was fading in and out and she felt very cold. She placed her hand on her back and tried to apply pressure to stop the bleeding. Life spilled over her metal encapsulated fingers as she tried to ignore the sting from every breath. Jonas ran over to soothe her, but she raised her hand and kept him at a distance.

346

She uttered a feeble, "I'll be fine."

Cindy stood up and looked towards the sky, her head pivoted on a swivel as she searched for the helicopter. It wasn't until she heard the sound of engines increasing and decreasing in torque that she spotted Jadie hanging onto the out of control vehicle. Malcolm, who was perched on a nearby rooftop, tried to take a shot at the pilot, but the helicopter was spinning erratically. Jadie tried to draw her energy blade but the suit warned her that it would shut down if she attacked Raymond or the pilot. Jadie's inability to attack Raymond, gave him the perfect opportunity to rid himself of the pest. Raymond pressed a button inside the cockpit, creating an EMP burst which exploded on Jadie's armor like a fork stuck into a power outlet. Jadie fell from the windshield like an insect killed by bug spray, her flailing body gave no signs of life. The pilot steadied the chopper, giving Malcolm the perfect window of opportunity to take the shot. Malcolm steadied his hand and held his breath while placing his sights on the pilot. **BAM!** The bullet pierced the cockpit glass with a sharp crack; the pilot fell forward and surrendered control of the helicopter. *Should've gotten yourself some bulletproof glass,* Malcolm thought to himself.

Raymond pulled the pilot off the controls and yawed the helicopter away from Malcolm before he could take another shot into the cockpit. Once Raymond had full control of the vehicle, he circled back around towards Malcolm and fired a salvo of missiles. Malcolm fled from his rooftop perch as the building erupted in a fountain of destruction. Jadie, meanwhile, still hadn't regained consciousness and was falling from the sky. Jadie continued to plummet down to the waiting streets below, unconscious and unaware of her pending doom. Right before she could smack the ground, Cindy flew towards her sister and caught her in mid-flight. Cindy looked into Jadie's closed eyes and prayed that she was okay. She swung back to the alleyway and set her down near Jonas and Michael.

With Jadie now safe, Cindy turned towards the alleyway entrance and lifted her arm. But before she could shoot her hook, Jonas ran up to her and said, "Cindy, you're bleeding to death. You can't go back out there."

She lowered her arm and replied, "I promise I'll be back, Jonas."

Jonas grabbed her wrist and yelled, "No! I don't want you to go." He looked away trying to hide the tears in his eyes. "Please, I don't want you to die..."

Cindy deactivated her helmet and gently removed Jonas' hand from her wrist. She leaned in with her eyes closed and gave him a very deep, warm, loving kiss. She hugged him tightly, rubbing her hands up and down his back before whispering in his ear, "I have to go."

"Take me."

"I can't." She looked at him with the adoring eyes she had before acquiring the suit. The loving wife had come back after months of being suppressed, albeit with a few more scars. "I promise, I'll come back to you no matter what."

Jonas' held onto Cindy's cheek and wiped the drips of blood forming on her lip. He looked into her tired eyes and said through a wavering voice, "I can't live without you okay? I just can't."

"I love you."

Cindy slowly stepped backwards, fixated on the eyes of her loving husband. Her helmet formed over her head, masking a brave woman behind artificial eyes. She turned towards the streets and deployed her grappling hook. Cindy flew out of sight as she chased Raymond's transport helicopter through the winding New York City corridor. Jonas covered his face with his hands and prayed for her safe return. Cindy's dying body craved rest and sleep, but she powered forward beyond what her body was willing to do. The oxygen in her system was starting to thin out. Dried blood crystallized on the silver skin of her armor, but she still pushed on.

Cindy could see the black silhouette of a raven helicopter flying through the city tunnel, hunting for its prey. Cindy attached her grapple line to the belly of the beast and pulled herself to the bottom of the fuselage. Cindy clung to the underside of the chopper and held on for dear life as Raymond attempted to shake her off. Cindy drew out her energy blade and prepared to lunge her weapon into the armored hull. But Raymond had anticipated this and activated the EMP burst shield. The electrifying shock caused Cindy to lose her grip and fall onto a nearby rooftop.

Raymond's cockpit blared with warning alarms. He had engaged the EMP too early, it didn't have enough charge to disable Cindy's suit completely. The computer warned Raymond that the EMP generator was shutting down, nullifying a good portion of its combat capabilities. The electrical charge that enveloped all the munitions was now disabled, but Cindy's armor was weakened enough that Raymond wouldn't need it anyway. He pitched the chopper forward and saw Cindy rolling on the gravel after the crash landing. With his target caught out in the open, Raymond pulled the trigger and unloaded a devastating payload of armor-piercing bullets. Cindy's body erupted with numerous blood splats on her shoulders, legs, neck and stomach. Her wounds became swollen until blood spilled out of them like an overflowing dam. Her silver suit became stained with the hardened remains of her own essence. The silver sheen had long gone, replaced with a thin crust of dust, dirt, and the life of a woman trying to redeem herself.

Raymond released an angry grunt, frustrated that despite hurting Cindy, he still couldn't kill her due to bad aim. It was difficult for Raymond to maintain control of the aircraft and fire accurately at the same time. However, the few bullets that did manage to injure Cindy brought her closer to the brink of death. Her HUD was scrambling before her eyes, informing her that a suit reboot would happen in sixty seconds, but she didn't care about that right now, she was too busy fighting to stay alive. The helicopter hovered above the vulnerable heroine; Raymond had fired the cannons for so long that the barrels had turned to a bright red orange. Smoke emanated from the end of the barrel, preventing him from firing any more rounds until it cooled down.

350

Like shackles coming off of her wrists, Cindy pulled her hemorrhaging body away from danger and stumbled into the water tower nearby. As the suit began to reboot itself, Cindy activated her forearm's cannon and used every ounce of strength she had left, to run across the rooftop while firing at the helicopter. Just holding her arm up to aim caused her intense torment, but she kept pushing herself harder. She fired her guns but was unable to land any hits on the chopper. The guidance system was malfunctioning and her arms were too weakened to sustain an accurate shot. Cindy panted in exhaustion as the enormous blood loss began to take its toll on her body. Every time she closed her eyes it became harder to open them again. Her vision just couldn't seem to regain focus; everything remained covered in a murky haze with a black vignette surrounding her peripheral vision. It was so blurry, like looking through a foggy camera lens

Knowing that he had the upper hand, Raymond prepared to let loose the final volley that would destroy the persistent heroine. He had run out of ammunition for his turret, but he had plenty of missiles and rockets to finish the job. Raymond locked onto Cindy and readied a heat-seeking missile to finish her off. Her exposed skin and crumbling armor made her vulnerable to any manmade pistol or rifle. A direct missile hit would obliterate her from existence. Cindy's wavering body stood defiant against the bat-like aircraft, a plume of flame burst from behind the missile and twirled towards her in a controlled, straight line. Before the missile could get close enough, Cindy drew her energy blade and raised it over her head with two hands. Using every last ounce of strength she had left, Cindy swung the blade with such force, that it extended far across the sky. The beam of power cut through the missile and cockpit of the chopper, slicing Raymond in two. The helicopter shook violently as multiple eruptions ripped across the hull like a series of timed explosions.

The helicopter spiraled into the streets below like a bird with a broken wing. It exploded in a furious fireball, sending metal shards outward like an exploding landmine. Cindy gasped for air as her life continued to spill from her wounds and veins. She gathered her remaining stamina and did everything she could to go back and keep her promise, no matter what. While swinging through the city, her speed began to deteriorate, her lungs couldn't process air, and she was blacking out as if sleeping behind the wheel. Her blood seeped into the streets below as her body grew colder. In the distance, she could see Jonas, Michael, Jadie, and Malcolm surrounded by U.S. soldiers and a medevac chopper. Cindy came in fast and hard, brutally crashing into one of the cars nearby. The sickening crunch made it seem as though Cindy had broken every bone in her body. Her suit was in such a weakened state that it appeared like ribbons draped over her battered figure.

Cindy struggled to sit up against the concaved vehicle and looked down at the broken asphalt. She drifted in and out of consciousness as her head wobbled back and forth. Her labored breathing and dimming eyesight brought her closer to the point of no return; her damaged helmet retreated into her skin just before her eyes rolled into the back of her head. Jonas rushed to the side of his unconscious wife and tried to revive her, but she was not responding, her pulse was faint and she had stopped breathing.

"No, Cindy, you promised me!" Jonas yelled as he began CPR on his dying wife.

She remained unresponsive to his actions, but Jonas continued to repeat the routine over and over. He breathed into her lungs and repeated chest compressions to bring his wife back. Nothing was happening —and her pulse was gone. Her body shook with each press, but she remained lifeless. It was during Jonas' attempts that the suit activated emergency medical procedures. The suit said aloud in a mechanical female voice, "Please stand back." A high pitched whirr surrounded Cindy's body followed by a loud electrical jolt. Her chest jumped forward as the suit defibrillator and cloning system kicked into gear.

Her eyes continued to remain shut, but the suit was now switched into full repair mode. Again the suit repeated, "Please stand back." The suit gave Cindy another jolt of electricity. After another failed response from Cindy; the suit diverted a larger portion of power to the cloning system. The bullet wounds began to heal while her body regenerated lost blood at an accelerated pace. By this point, Malcolm and his sister had surrounded the couple, anxious to see if she would pull through. Once more the suit said, "Please stand back." The high pitched beep charged up and gave Cindy the strongest burst of electricity it could administer without killing her.

Cindy's eyes burst open as her chest expanded to inhale deep, life-rejuvenating air. Malcolm, his sister Kendra, and Jonas all surrounded her. They cheered jubilantly and clapped their hands as Cindy returned to the living world. Jonas tightly hugged his courageous wife and breathed a deep sigh of relief. He was overjoyed to have his wife back and helped Cindy get up onto her feet. Malcolm draped a blanket over Cindy's head, hiding her identity from the personnel conducting the evacuation. Her legs shook with each step as if she were a patient in physical therapy. Jonas took Cindy's hand and walked his wife over to the medevac helicopter. On her way to the aircraft, Cindy could see Jadie being hoisted into a separate chopper via stretcher. Jadie lifted her head—her helmet still intact— and looked over to Cindy. She raised her thumb in the air and rested her disguised head back down onto the stretcher. Cindy waved at her sister, relieved to see that she had survived after all. However, the wail of a man screaming nearby quickly snatched Cindy's attention away.

Looking in the direction of the screams, she saw Michael being placed into a wheelchair. His cries were not those of mind-numbing pain, but rather of a man who might never walk again. She shook her head as Jonas helped Cindy into the helicopter.

"Cindy," Malcolm called out.

She turned towards him with the blanket obscuring most of her face. .

354

"Thank you for everything you've done. I owe you a debt that could never be repaid," he said.

"We wouldn't be here if it wasn't for you," Kendra added.

Cindy smiled and looked past the siblings to see Captain Colt and his men approaching. He stood near the chopper with a big smile on his face, though he seemed slightly disappointed in not being able to see Cindy's identity.

"You're the bravest woman I've ever met. You really pulled all of our asses out of the fire and I'm grateful for the sacrifices you've made." The captain turned towards his troops and yelled, "Squad! Atten-tion!"

The Green Berets and Malcolm suddenly stood upright and clicked their boot heels together. They turned towards Cindy and saluted her as the helicopter took off. The weary warriors continued to salute her even as the helicopter rose hundreds of feet in the air. To them, Cindy was a hero that deserved their utmost respect. As the helicopter began flying towards the hospital, Cindy gazed upon the ruined city landscape. She could see the wreckage of Raymond's flaming helicopter below. Swarms of Army Corps engineers surrounded the wreckage like bugs crawling atop a rotting log. She had to turn away as they pulled out the mangled corpses of Raymond Levreux and the rest of his staff.

Cindy covered her eyes, blinding herself to the destruction, and tried to relax. Jonas gave her a gentle squeeze and peered his head beneath the blanket, kissing his beautiful exhausted wife. She smiled and placed her head on his shoulder while

355

covering her face with the blanket. She closed her eyes as the helicopter flew off into the warm, peaceful sunset.

One week later…

"Happy birth-day to yoooooouuuu." Jonas blew out the candles as light applause filled the dining room with joy. "Oh this looks delicious," Cindy said, as she swiped a goop of vanilla cream and smeared it all over Jonas' cheek while giggling. He glanced at his wife with an evil glare as frosting dripped from his cheek. "Oh, I'll get you back. Just wait until you go to bed tonight."

Cindy smiled and shoo'ed him away from the cake. She looked over to wheelchair-bound Michael and uttered a guilt-laced sigh. She was careful to hide her reaction from Jonas, knowing he would ask her what was wrong. For the sake of Michael's pride, Cindy put on her best social mask and asked everyone, "Who wants cake?" She distributed each slice to all present: Jadie, Michael and Jonas.

Jonas asked Cindy, "Aren't you going to have some?"

Cindy shook her head and said, "No thanks, maybe later."

"You sure?"

Michael took a bite from his morsel of pie and said, "I think she's probably going to stay away from junk food for a while."

Cindy scowled at Michael, while Jadie said aloud with a mouth full,

"Oh my God."

"What's wrong?" Cindy asked.

"This cake is way too good. You did not make this," Jadie said.

Cindy feigned insult and kicked a bakery-branded plastic bag out of sight. "Yes, I did!"

Jonas grabbed his wife and pressed his cheek up against hers while saying, "If my wife says she baked it, then I believe her."

Cindy stuck her tongue out at Jadie. Jadie reacted by reciprocating the gesture. But what Cindy didn't realize was that Jonas was transferring all of the frosting on his cheek to Cindy's. Jonas said, "I'll be right back," and walked over to the bedroom. Michael saw the smudge on Cindy's cheek and tried to speak up, but Jadie silently hushed him.

Jonas returned with laptop in hand. He walked past his wife and said, "Are you just going to leave that on?" Cindy, confused by what he said, pulled out a mirror and inspected her reflection. The embedded frosting smeared on her cheek looked like carnival pancake makeup. "Jadie!" she yelled, before wiping away the frosty deliciousness.

"Are you going to do it now?" Michael asked Jonas.

Jonas looked at Michael and said, "Yeah…" he turned to the sisters and beckoned them with his fingers. "Cindy, Jadie, come over here."

The sisters approached with hesitation as Jonas booted up the SIRCA control panel. He looked over to the duo and said, "You ready to take those things off?""

"No," Jadie said with arms crossed.

Cindy slapped her sister on the wrist and said, "Yes."

"Oh, come on, Cindy. Could you imagine what a difference we would make working together? Having the suits would beat anything I did in the Coast Guard. We could travel the world and stop people from getting killed. It'll be great."

She replied to Jadie in a stern tone, "Don't be naïve. You know it's not that simple."

Cindy couldn't deny that her sister had a point. But the burden of having the suit was too much for her to bear. It was then that Michael wheeled in and confessed Raymond's secrets to the group.

"I think you should keep the suit," he said. Everyone looked towards Michael, who carried a grim expression. "Raymond had a partner that helped organize this whole thing. He wanted me to complete the programming on project Sapphire. But I refused to help him any further."

"Why did you help him in the first place?" Cindy said with clear irritation.

"Raymond was going to hurt Jadie and he didn't want Jonas finding out about it since he needed him. I was trying to keep her safe for you," Michael said.

"Aww, that's so sweet." Jadie gave Michael a big hug. He chuckled at the surprise embrace and enjoyed the aroma of her strawberry-scented perfume.

"I see," Cindy said, but her narrowed eyes hinted of her skepticism.

Jonas asked Michael, "What the hell is project Sapphire?"

"I don't know," Michael said while shaking his head. "I only wrote a tiny bit of code for it."

Jadie yelled with excitement, "All the more reason why we should keep the suits Cindy. Just sayin'."

Cindy snapped at her sister and shouted, "No, Jadie." She pointed at her delusional sibling and said through gritted teeth, "You didn't have the suit as long as I did. I did horrible things that I'm never going to forget. Do you want to have that kind of guilt weighing on you for the rest of your life?"

The room fell silent. Jadie's gaping mouth closed as Cindy's menacing eyes stayed locked on her sister. Jonas walked up to Cindy and placed a manila envelope in her hand. He secretly hoped the distraction would calm his wife back down.

Cindy looked confused as she glanced towards the envelope and asked him, "What is this?"

"It came in the mail today," Jonas said. "I have no clue what it is."

It appeared to be an ordinary manila envelope with no special markings. Cindy tore open the envelope and pulled out a miniscule, black stick.

"It's a thumb drive," she said.

Jonas reached out his hand and said, "Let me see."

He took the small USB thumb drive from Cindy's hand and plugged it into the laptop computer. A folder popped up containing a video file with a date under

FATHER OF THE REBELLION

the name description. Everyone gathered around as Jonas played the file. They became mortified by what played next on the clip. There was surveillance footage of Cindy and Jonas going in and out of their home, day and night. There was even footage of Cindy bringing in Jonas' cake from the bakery. Jadie would have normally taken the opportunity to rip on Cindy, but she was too creeped out to say anything.

"Who sent this?" Cindy asked.

At the end of the video, the seal of the Central Intelligence Agency appeared emblazoned on the center of the screen. The video cut to black and read…

It's not over…

Cindy.

THE END